JD KIRK
A ROCK
AND A
HARD PLACE

 CANELO CRIME

First published in the United Kingdom in 2025 by

Canelo Crime, an imprint of
Canelo Digital Publishing Limited,
20 Vauxhall Bridge Road,
London SW1V 2SA
United Kingdom

A Penguin Random House Company
The authorised representative in the EEA is Dorling Kindersley Verlag GmbH. Arnulfstr. 124, 80636
Munich, Germany

Printed and bound in Great Britain by Clays Ltd, Elcograf S.p.A.

Look for more great books at
www.canelo.co | www.dk.com

Chapter 1

She could stick Art Garfunkel up her arse.

Reginald had been by Elsie's side for over fifty years now, man and boy. They'd been through thick and thin together, more than their fair share of ups and downs, and a few ins and outs along the way. Although, not nearly enough of the latter for Reg's liking.

If you'd asked him yesterday—hell, if you'd asked him five minutes ago—he'd have sworn they knew everything there was to know about one another.

He'd have been wrong.

Because that was before his wife had dropped the bombshell that she believed—no, that she was *labouring under the misapprehension*—that Art Garfunkel was the talented one out of legendary 1960s folk duo, Simon and Garfunkel.

And Reg wasn't having it. Everyone knew that Paul Simon was better. *Of course* Paul Simon was better! That was a hill he'd die on, if it came to it.

In fact, 'You Can Call Me Al' was very possibly Reg's favourite song of all time, even if, admittedly, he didn't have the first clue what it was actually about.

Why anyone would choose to address the multi-Grammy Award-winning singer-songwriter, Paul Simon, by any name other than his own—much less perform potentially dangerous bodyguard duties in order to do so—remained an enigma.

Still, there was no denying that the song was an all-time classic.

Reg knew all of them, of course. 'You Can Call Me Al'. '50 Ways to Leave Your Lover'. That maudlin one about hobos. All the hits.

Granted, he'd felt somewhat misled by '50 Ways to Leave Your Lover', given that the song featured only five unique methods with which to end a relationship, none of which proved particularly helpful or informative.

Especially the bits where he told Roy not to be coy, and suggested that Gus simply 'get on the bus'. In what world was that practical, actionable advice?

Still, what had Art Garfunkel ever done? Ridden on a great man's coattails, that was what. Reg doubted Elsie could name even one of the bastard's songs, let alone *nearly three*.

He was prepared to bet that she only liked him for the funny name. Aye, that would be it. That was the way her mind worked. This was Engelbert Humperdink all over again.

And, to a lesser extent, Tanita Tikaram.

He'd told her as much a few minutes ago when they'd been walking down the hill from the car park. And, of course, she'd been giving him the cold shoulder ever since.

It was times like these, of which there were plenty, that he wondered if the last five decades had been a mistake. Particularly since they hadn't been intimate for four of those, except for that one night after Auntie Jeanie's wedding in the autumn of 1992.

And, the less said about that, the better.

As they plodded in stony silence down the uneven hillside towards the darkness gaping at the bottom, Reginald wondered what advice Paul Simon might offer a man in his position.

If past evidence was anything to go by, it'd be something along the lines of, *push her in a hedge, Reg.*

And, tempting an idea as that was, he didn't think it would help matters in the slightest.

They continued down the slope in silence, only the *whoosh* of the occasional early morning vehicle passing on the road above breaking the monotony of their thudding footsteps. It was barely after six, but the sun was already up and hard at work, after its day off yesterday.

That was the thing with summers in the Highlands, you never knew what you were going to get. Rain, snow, hail, a rare glimpse of sunshine. Rain again. It was a lottery, all right, and even more so up here on the far north coast.

But Reg and Elsie enjoyed their wee morning walks. Although, 'enjoyed' was maybe over-egging the pudding a bit. It had become tradition, anyway. They'd done it for years.

Of course, ever since the bloody North Coast 500 nonsense had started, and the tourists had descended in their droves, it had been increasingly difficult to find somewhere quiet for a stroll.

Doing their favourite walk—the one they both genuinely took pleasure from—was now almost impossible without shuffling through throngs of Americans, Europeans and camera-wielding Chinamen.

Was that allowed these days? Could you still call them that? He could never keep track.

He knew you couldn't say 'Chinkies' when referring to Chinese restaurants nowadays, but that had never bothered him. He didn't touch the stuff. It always struck him as too mysterious and unpredictable a cuisine. When it came to food, he was quite happy in his comfort zone, thank you very much. Give him a culinary rut over an octopus on a stick, or whatever muck it was they served up.

The English visitors to the area were the worst, of course. And it was fine, he could say that, since he himself was English. Originally, anyway. It was one of the things Elsie had liked about him when they'd first met at that Butlin's caravan park in Ayr. It had made him, she'd said at the time, seem *exotic*.

That had been in the 1970s. They'd been together ever since, Reg ditching the faraway foreign climes of Stoke-on-Trent for a bedsit in Arbroath within a fortnight of the holiday's end.

And here they were now, all those years later, tramping in moody silence from the car park to the start of their favourite walk—a necessarily early-morning ramble into Smoo Cave to enjoy a breakfast of hard-boiled eggs and Müller Corners, with tea and coffee from their separate Thermos flasks.

The atmosphere between them was starting to get to him. Elsie could hold a stony silence for hours. Days, if it came to it. Reg was always the one to crack first.

And today was no exception.

'Here, Elsie,' he remarked. With a grin, he pointed to the simple wooden platform ahead that crossed the small stream running through the network of caves. 'It's a bridge over troubled water!'

As jokes went, it wasn't up there with the greats. Had there been a global leaderboard of humorous remarks, this one wouldn't have troubled the top twenty in any way. It didn't even make much sense, since the stream was barely more than a trickling brook.

Still, it did its job. Elsie tutted and rolled her eyes, but it was good-natured enough that Reg knew the argument had been safely sidelined.

He was pleased about that. He was more than happy to let the whole silly business lie.

Even if she was wrong.

The wooden bridge creaked under their feet as they crossed, the sound echoing off the limestone walls that rose around them. They still weren't saying anything, but it was a comfortable quiet now—a time for peaceful reflection, rather than the cold, hostile silence of a few minutes earlier. It was punctuated by the persistent drip-drip of water from the cave's entrance and the distant rumble of the waterfall within.

Smoo Cave had been a favourite haunt for the better part of two decades, long before the tourists discovered it. Back then, the path down had been treacherous—just a dirt track really, worn smooth by sheep and the occasional adventurous local. Now there were proper steps, safety railings and informational plaques that Reg pointedly ignored every time they passed.

'Watch your step there,' he said automatically as Elsie navigated a particularly slick portion of the walkway. She ignored him, as she always did. She'd never slipped once. Reg, on the other hand, had taken three tumbles in the past year alone. None of them serious, but his coccyx hadn't thanked him for any of them.

The cave mouth yawned before them, a great dark maw in the limestone cliff face. The morning sun, now fully risen, cast long shadows across the entrance, creating shapes that always reminded Reg of long rows of jagged teeth. Not that he'd ever mention that to Elsie. She'd just tut and say he was being dramatic again.

No imagination, that woman.

Their footsteps changed tone as they moved from the wooden walkway onto the cave's limestone floor. The temperature dropped several degrees, and Reg pulled his fleece tighter around his shoulders, hunching into it.

The first chamber of Smoo Cave was massive—the largest sea cave entrance in Britain, according to one of those plaques Reg never read. The couple's usual spot was just beyond the tourist viewing platform, in a little alcove they'd discovered years ago. It was perfect for their breakfast routine: just the right height for sitting, with a natural shelf for their flasks to rest on.

Elsie was already pulling out their picnic supplies as Reg fumbled with his torch. The beam cut through the gloom, illuminating the countless ridges and folds in the cave walls. Water trickled down in thin sheets, catching the light like liquid glass.

'Strawberry or banana cornflake?' Elsie asked, holding up two Müller Corners.

'I think we both know the answer to that,' Reg replied, and Elsie handed him the latter, while he unpacked their eggs from their little Tupperware nest.

The distant waterfall provided a constant background soundtrack, its rumble echoing through the connected chambers. It was louder today than usual—the recent rains must have swollen the burns feeding into it. The sound masked the drips and drops of the cave's constant weeping, and the rustling of their own movements, creating a whole new type of silence that was really nothing of the sort.

Reg cracked open his egg and nodded, satisfied, when the shell broke into two near-precise halves. He'd perfected the art of egg-boiling over the years, timing it to exactly six minutes and thirty seconds. Any longer and the yolk went chalky; any less and Elsie complained about it being too runny.

She'd cook them for longer, given the chance. Elsie liked her eggs like she liked her steaks—completely ruined.

They listened to the distant thunder of the waterfall as they ate, neither saying a word but not feeling the need to, either. The argument about Art Garfunkel seemed distant now, silly even. Reg knew he was still in the right, of course, but what a ridiculous thing to argue about.

Art Garfunkel.

What the hell was she thinking?

It was only after they'd finished their yoghurts that Elsie suggested they explore a bit further in. This was unusual—they typically stuck to their alcove, leaving the deeper chambers to the guided tours that would start arriving in a few hours.

'Why for?' Reg asked, screwing the lid back on his Thermos flask, and wiping traces of egg off the front of his fleece with the swipe of a hand.

'Do I need a reason?' Elsie asked. She was not a tall woman by any definition, and she was currently swamped by the waterproof jacket she wore zipped up to the neck.

She had a way about her, though, that meant she usually got what she wanted. Not just with her long-suffering husband, but with other people, too. Friends. Colleagues on the committee. Strangers, even.

Reg wasn't sure how she did it, exactly. If he had to guess, he'd say it was the look in her eyes, and the way she held her face. It was an expression that told the person on the receiving end that whatever they were planning to say or do would turn out to be far more trouble than it was worth.

'We haven't gone further in for years,' she said, offering the explanation that Reg had been too scared to push for. 'I want to see how much a mess of the place those bloody tourists have made.'

Reg knew better than to argue. The subject of 'those bloody tourists' was one very close to Elsie's heart, and not one you wanted to get yourself mixed up in.

'Right you are, Else,' he said, shoving the breakfast debris into his backpack and following her along the path.

The beam of their torch caught the calcite formations as they moved deeper into the cave system. Water droplets sparkled like diamonds in the light, and their footsteps echoed off the too-close walls. The path here was less maintained, the limestone slick and treacherous under their feet.

The roar of falling water grew louder as they approached the second chamber. Here, the cave split into two passages—one leading to the waterfall, the other diving deeper into the hillside.

There was no sign of any damage, as far as Reg could see. It was rare for them to trek this far into the caves, but he didn't think it had changed all that much since last time, if at all.

Elsie seemed to believe otherwise, though. She sucked in air, shook her head, and tutted as she led them off down the right-hand branch of the worn track, away from the roar of the waterfall.

Reg wanted to protest—they were venturing into new territory, and he wasn't sure what dangers might lie ahead—but something in Elsie's expression stopped him. Besides, the morning was still young. The tour groups wouldn't arrive until after nine.

That was good in that they'd have peace for a while. But, if anything happened to them, nobody would find them for hours.

The passage narrowed as they proceeded, the ceiling dropping so low in places that Reg had to stoop. Their torch beam seemed to grow weaker, as if the darkness itself was pushing back against the light. Water droplets kept finding their way down the back of Reg's neck, and he pulled his collar up higher.

The air changed as they moved deeper—grew thicker somehow, with an unfamiliar metallic tang that caught in the back of Reg's throat. Elsie must have noticed it too, because she slowed her pace, her hand reaching back to grip Reg's arm.

'I, um, I think this is far enough, Else,' he ventured, and she didn't voice any objections.

They stopped, old boots scuffing on the uneven stone floor. Reg's torch beam swept across the walls, catching glimpses of ancient marine fossils embedded in the limestone.

He remembered reading somewhere that this whole area had once been under some sort of ancient ocean or sea. The thought made him uncomfortable—all that weight of water and time pressing down on them, compacting them like lumps of coal.

'Here, hang on,' Elsie said. Her voice was a whisper, made louder and more shrill by the narrow passageway around them. 'What's that?'

Reg directed the torch, following Elsie's outstretched finger. A weak oval of orange light skimmed across the damp, rough surface until it settled on something strange. Something alien. Something that didn't belong here.

A squiggle of blood red.

'Is that what I think it is?' Elsie asked.

It took all of Reg's willpower not to pounce on the remark, and point out that, contrary to what his wife might think, he wasn't a mind reader.

That would only lead to more arguments, though. So, instead, he bit his tongue and followed her gaze until he saw what had caught her eye.

'Good grief,' he muttered.

Elsie shuffled on and Reg followed, dumbly. A few moments ago, he'd been worried about them falling or getting lost, or about part of the north coast shoreline collapsing in on them and smushing them to death.

Now, though, curiosity had gotten its hooks into him, and he was letting it drag him along.

The passage widened suddenly into a small chamber Reg didn't think he'd ever been in before. The thin torchlight revealed walls gleaming with mineral deposits, and a floor that dropped away sharply on one side into what looked like a natural pit.

Reg's knees cracked like gunshots as he crouched to examine this unexpected shock of red.

Before he could study the discovery, though, he was interrupted by the desperate, throaty screaming of his wife.

And the echoes of it reverberated through the suffocating darkness around them.

Chapter 2

As rolls and square sausage went, this one wasn't half bad. OK, it wasn't going to win any awards or anything, but it hit the spot—soft, floury roll, a thick slice of flattened sausage meat cooked until just starting to char around the edges, and enough butter and brown sauce to make each bite glide effortlessly down the gullet.

Jack Logan further helped the last bit on its way with a swig of piping hot tea, then dusted the flour from his hands, slid the plate into the centre of the table, and offered his compliments to the chef.

'No bother, Jack. But for God's sake, if Moira asks, tell her you paid for it.'

Logan finished wiping his hands, thumbed a smear of brown sauce from the side of his mouth, then wiped it on a scrunched-up paper napkin.

'I did pay for it,' he replied.

Across the table, Ben Forde, former Detective Inspector turned cafe owner, stacked Logan's plate on top of his own.

'Too bloody right you did. I'm no' made of money,' he replied. 'Just make sure you tell her, or she'll think I gave it to you for free.'

Ben glanced around at the spotless tables and empty chairs.

'And God knows, we can't afford to be doing that. You could have at least brought Shona with you. She's always good for a big breakfast.'

'She's on a call,' Logan said. 'Up north. Body found in a cave.'

'Oh.'

Both men ruminated on this for a few moments.

'Tourist, or…?'

'Don't know,' Logan said.

Ben nodded. 'Probably a tourist. Potholing, or something.'

'Aye. Probably.'

'Aye. That'll be it.' Ben nodded again, with a little more certainty this time. There was something in his eyes, though, that Logan couldn't fail to notice. Something that bordered on the wistful.

The cafe looked onto the back of the Burnett Road Police Station where, until recently, both men had been stationed. It had been over three months since Ben had stepped down from the force. Despite the building's proximity, he hadn't been back.

And nor, for that matter, had Logan.

'How's retirement treating you?' Jack asked, taking pains to steer the conversation away from dead bodies in dark caves. 'I'd ask if you're keeping busy, but, well…'

He mimicked Ben's glance around the cafe's interior from a few moments before. It wasn't a big place—there was room for maybe a dozen punters at once—but filling it seemed to be proving problematic.

'It picks up at the weekends,' Ben said.

'It's Saturday.'

The older man's grey eyebrows rose a little higher up his forehead, creasing the skin above into a series of parallel folds.

'It is? Bollocks. Well, Sundays are our big day,' he replied, rising from his seat with plates in hand. 'Anyway, I should be asking you the same question.'

Logan ejected a snort of air through his nose. It was a fair point.

'I'm not retired. I'm on leave,' he said, although there wasn't a lot of conviction behind it.

One of Ben's eyebrows settled down, while the other remained lofty and raised.

'So, you're planning on going back to work, then?'

Logan answered as truthfully as he could. As truthfully as he dared. 'Not sure yet.'

And he wasn't. He hadn't so much as taken a sabbatical as had one forced upon him. But the cloud he'd left under had now evaporated. He was free to return to work at any time. He'd been asked to, in fact, on more than one occasion.

And yet, he hadn't taken the bosses up on their offer. He'd stalled. Asked for more time.

He'd have to decide eventually, of course—he owed them all an answer—but for now, he was in no real rush to return. Not yet. Not quite.

Not after how he'd lied to his team. Not after how he'd treated them. Not now that everyone would see him for what he was.

Oh, sure, they'd all acted like nothing had changed when he'd last met up with them. The old team. They'd laughed and joked like they always had. To an onlooker—hell, to the rest of the team—it would all have seemed perfectly normal.

But he'd been able to detect something hidden in the music of their laughter. A change to the old melody. The odd bum note.

He'd left that last gathering with them, here in the cafe, wondering if things could ever be the same. If they could ever really trust him again. He'd been too afraid to go back to work and find out.

He was afraid of a lot of things lately.

The bell above the door *tringed*, pulling him from the edge of the pit of introspection he had been in danger of tumbling into.

Ben's face lit up at the prospect of another customer, fell slightly at the sight of his partner, Moira Corson, then rallied again before she had a chance to notice.

'God. You here again?' Moira asked, fixing Logan with a withering look. 'You not found anything better to do with your time yet?'

'Jack just stopped in for a wee bite to eat,' Ben told her, accompanying it with a little nod of his head that bordered on deferential.

The exact nature of Ben and Moira's relationship was a matter of a great debate. They ran the cafe together, despite it being named after Ben's late wife Alice, but there was some element of romantic entanglement, too. Just how romantic, and precisely how entangled, remained something of a mystery, and that suited everyone just fine.

Ben and Moira weren't interested in sharing any of the details, and Logan sure as hell didn't want to imagine them.

'That was a cracking square sausage roll you made me there, Benjamin,' Logan announced, before Moira had even closed the door behind her. He caught Ben's stern look as it came racing towards him, and blocked it with a smirk. 'Oh, print me off a receipt, will you?' Logan vaguely waved a hand as large as the plates Ben carried. 'You know, for tax purposes.'

The older man's shoulders slackened, as the panic that had bunched the muscles into knots eased away. 'Aye. Will do, Jack. You did pay for it, after all.'

'Oh aye, that right? Paid for it, did he?'

Moira shrugged her way free of her heavy tweed coat, arms flailing like she was wrestling the thing into submission. Behind her, the door closed with a *clack*.

'And what about *that*?'

A long, bony finger stabbed down at the space below Jack's table, where a small dog of uncertain pedigree was licking a plate that had, until recently, contained a number of sausages.

A number that Ben would take to his grave, if he had to.

'Did he pay for whatever that was, while he was at it?'

'Ach, them sausages were out of date yesterday,' the former detective inspector replied. He shrugged in a way that he hoped came across as relaxed. Casual even.

It didn't.

'It'd have been a crime to waste them,' he continued. 'They'd only have gone in the bin.'

The dog, Taggart, lamenting the now-empty plate, lay down next to it with his head resting on his paws, and stared at the spot where the sausages had been, hoping they might come back.

If Moira had anything to say about it, it'd be a cold day in Hell before they did.

She folded her coat sharply over her arm, then went marching through to the kitchen. Ben's thin smile was equal parts apology and cry for help. He leaned in a little closer to his old boss, and dropped his voice to a whisper.

'You don't actually need a receipt, do you?' he asked. 'It's just, I've no idea how to work the till beyond opening the drawer. And even that takes a bit of poking around.'

'You're fine,' Logan told him. He placed the flat of his hands on the table and rose into a standing position, growing taller and larger until he blocked out most of the light from the window behind him. 'I'd best get off. That daytime telly's no' going to watch itself.'

'Eh, not so fast there, Jack,' Ben said. His eyes had been drawn to the door, just as a figure approached it, gaze fixed on Logan's towering frame through the glass. 'I think there's someone here to see you.'

D-DING.

The bell above the door chimed. Logan turned to see a dark-skinned woman in a spotless white shirt staring coolly back at him.

Detective Superintendent Mitchell didn't bother to smile. Then again, she rarely did. 'Jack,' she said, gesturing to a table. 'If you've got a few minutes, I'd like a little word.'

Chapter 3

This was it. It was happening. There was no escaping it now.

Detective Constable Tyler Neish had been dreading this moment. He always dreaded this moment. He'd felt it coming for the past half hour or so, ever since that sharp swing right across the bridge just south of Achandunie.

That had caused the first twitch of his stomach. The first prickle of heat on his face. The first faltering step towards what had built, quite rapidly, into the inevitable reality of the here and the now.

Everything below Tyler's ribcage tightened. One hand clamped over his mouth, while the other tugged frantically on the sleeve of the car's driver, the recently appointed Detective Constable Dave Davidson, whose driving style was at least partially to blame for Tyler's current predicament.

'Oh! Shit! Don't you dare!' Dave cried, slamming on the brakes and swerving his compact Peugeot 208 with such force and suddenness that, had Tyler actually vomited at that moment, the contents of his stomach would have painted the entirety of the vehicle's interior from front to back.

Brake blocks bit. Tyres screamed. Tyler had the door open before the car had come to a full stop, his stomach contents painting the grassy verge like a chunky slug trail full of Coco Pops.

With a final rumble, the car Dave lovingly referred to as 'The Dave-mobile' stopped. Tyler fumbled for the catch of his seat belt, unshackled himself from the seat, then staggered into cover behind a bush before another bout of retching doubled him over.

Behind the wheel, Dave Davidson clicked on his hazard lights, tapped his fingers on the steering wheel, and waited.

It took a moment for the smell to come wafting in through the open door. Nostrils flaring, Dave unhooked the Magic Tree air freshener from around the rear-view mirror, and wafted it at the encroaching odour, like he was fending off a vampire with a bulb of garlic.

Outside, Tyler made a sound like he was attempting to turn himself inside out. Which, in a manner of speaking, he was.

'You all right, mate?' Dave asked.

A van went whooshing past, horn blaring, on the narrow road. The wind in its wake rocked the compact car, and headed off the worst of the smell.

Tyler's thin, croaky reply came sandwiched between two deep, rumbling *hwaurps*.

'Not really.'

Dave checked his watch. Rehung the air freshener. Tapped out a tune on the steering wheel.

'Take your time,' he said.

A hand raised into view from behind the bush, a thumb extended.

'Feel better for getting it up?' Dave asked.

The thumb was turned downwards. The quiet was rent asunder once more by the squawking of DC Neish's insides, and the faint *paff* of damp grass being made even more so.

Behind the bush, Tyler stood, bent nearly double. His hands gripped his thighs. A string of drool hung from his bottom lip, stretching almost all the way down to the ground. There was a pressure behind his eyes, as if something filled with fluid had ruptured behind them.

The pressure went away as soon as he straightened up, though, so he reckoned it was probably fine.

'Jesus Christ,' he muttered to nobody in particular. Then, taking out the packet of tissues he'd brought for just such an occasion, he wiped his mouth, dried his eyes, and returned, shrunken and vomit-spattered, to the car.

'You all right?' Dave asked once Tyler had clambered back into the passenger seat.

Tyler closed the door without a word. Quite forcefully, too.

'You don't look great,' Dave remarked. He pointed to his face. 'Quite pale.'

'That right, is it?' Tyler asked, arms folded, staring dead ahead through the bug-crusted window. 'Bit pale, am I?'

'Deffo,' Dave confirmed. 'What brought that on, d'you think?'

Tyler swung his head to look at him, both eyebrows raised, like the question had been some sort of damning personal attack.

'What do you mean?' he snapped. 'Your bloody driving!'

A smirk tugged at the corner of Dave's mouth, but the rest of his face remained a picture of practised innocence.

'What do you mean, my driving? What's wrong with my driving?'

'You know you're meant to slow down for corners, aye?' Tyler shot back. 'Or, you know, just in general sometimes. Like, it's not just zero or seventy. Those aren't the only speeds. "Dead stop" or "warp factor nine." Those aren't your only two options.'

Dave nodded slowly, ponderously, like this was all news to him and he was having a hard time digesting it. Although, not as hard a time as his companion'd had digesting those Coco Pops.

'Oh, and generally speaking, see when you're driving a four-wheeled vehicle? All four wheels should stay on the ground at all times,' Tyler added. 'You shouldn't go up onto two every time you hang a sharp bend.'

'Right. OK,' Dave said. He blew out his cheeks, promising nothing. 'I'll take that on board.'

'And that can fuck off and all,' Tyler snapped, tearing the dangling Magic Tree from the rear-view mirror and tossing it out his open window in one fluid movement.

Dave stared back at him, completely impassive besides the persistent threat of that smirk.

'That was Forest Fresh,' he said.

'I don't care what it was. It was horrible,' Tyler said. 'I swear to God, if Satan wore deodorant, it'd be Magic Trees. He'd just rub Magic Trees onto himself. All over.'

'That's quite an erotic image you've painted there,' Dave remarked, after just a moment's pause.

Tyler, despite the all-consuming hatred he'd had for his colleague just a few seconds before, couldn't fight back a smile at that.

'You're a sick man,' he said.

'That's a bit pot-kettle,' Dave said. He nodded to the open window. 'Given...'

'Aye, don't remind me,' Tyler said. He pulled on his seatbelt. 'How long until we get there?'

Dave tapped his phone in its cradle on the dashboard, waking the screen and the satnav app.

'About an hour and a half.'

'Right. And what if you drive like a normal person?'

The very thought of this made Dave suck air in through his teeth.

'About two hours.'

Hunched in the passenger seat, Tyler groaned. This had already felt like an epic journey, and they were less than a third of the way into it. He wished he'd been able to hang off an hour or two to drive up the road with Sinead, but orders were orders.

So the new boss kept telling him, anyway, and he'd been on the wrong side of the bastard too often to risk another ear-bashing. Or worse, the official written warning he'd been threatened with twice already. He couldn't afford that on his record, not with the twins at home, and his debt plan still in place.

'Fine. Just go,' Tyler said. He gripped the door handle and the edge of his seat, and fixed his gaze on a spot somewhere beyond the horizon. 'But one more handbrake turn, and I swear to God, I'm not going to hold it in.'

The smirk that had been needling away at Dave for the past few minutes blossomed into a full-blown grin as he adjusted the hand controls of his Peugeot.

'Don't you worry, mate,' he said, thumbing the accelerator. 'I'll have us there in no time.'

With a roar from the engine, and a cry of fright from DC Neish, the Davemobile's back tyres machine-gunned a spray of gravel into the air behind them, then screamed off, headed north, along the narrow Highland road.

Chapter 4

There was something about the way Detective Superintendent Mitchell stirred her tea that felt like a slap in the face. It was the slow, deliberate, methodical circling of the spoon, and the way it faintly *tinked* against the inside of the cup with no discernible rhythm or pattern.

The eye contact only added to it. She held Logan's gaze, making him wait in silence until she had stirred it all *just so*.

Jack wouldn't have minded nearly so much if she'd put sugar in the bloody thing, but all she was doing was mixing in the three minuscule drops of milk she'd added to the steaming hot brew.

When she was satisfied that the process was complete, she took out the spoon, tapped it once against the inside of the cup, just above sea level, then placed it down in the saucer.

Only then, did she commence her lecture.

'You're looking tired, Jack.'

'Nice of you to say so,' Logan countered.

'You ask me, all this time off isn't suiting you.'

Logan took a slurp of tea from his recently refilled mug. 'Aye, well. We'll agree to disagree.'

'Oh?' Mitchell arched an eyebrow. 'You think you're doing well, do you?'

Jack felt the sting of that one. 'Well enough.'

'Right. And what does Shona think?'

Logan hesitated, realised he'd done so, recognised the twinkle in Mitchell's eye, then tried to cover it all up with a second mouthful of tea.

He and the pathologist, Shona Maguire, had been an item for a few years now, and living together for nearly as long. They even had makeshift children together—the idiot canine son currently staring at an empty plate beneath the table, and a rebellious teenage daughter they were fostering, who may or may not be a murderous psychopath. The jury was still out on that one, but Logan had a pretty good idea which direction it was leaning.

Shona had been fully supportive of him taking time off following his last case, and everything it had dredged up from his past. She'd practically been the one to suggest it, in fact, following a particularly fraught nightmare that had woken him up screaming.

He'd claimed not to remember what the dream had been about, even though it had been imprinting itself on his brain every night for weeks.

A deep, dark hole in the ground. A maniac with a grudge and a gun.

And the thick, pungent stench of death.

The investigation into his actions had all been concluded by that point, and he was free to return to work. He'd been dreading it, and so when Shona had suggested he extend his leave of absence for a little while longer, he'd pretended to consider it, then begrudgingly jumped on the chance.

He had noticed, though, in recent weeks, a growing… not irritation, exactly, but some blood relative of it, at the fact he was still lounging around the house all day, doing nothing of any significance.

He'd tried to make himself useful by always having dinner ready, and keeping the house clean. But cooking wasn't really his strong point, he never seemed to arrange the cushions or load the dishwasher correctly, and he suspected it was only a matter of time before she caved his head in with a badly stacked frying pan.

'Aye, she's fine with it,' Logan replied, after far too long a pause.

Mitchell hadn't yet touched her tea, and the way she locked her fingers together suggested she had no immediate plans to.

'She's worried about you, Jack. She thinks you're slumping into depression.'

Logan snorted, scoffing at the very idea. 'Depression? She said that?'

'Not in so many words,' Mitchell admitted. She tilted her head, her gaze remaining fixed on the man across the table. 'But the concern was there.'

It was not unheard of for a pathologist and a detective superintendent to talk to one another about professional matters, but it was rare enough to be noteworthy. Had Mitchell contacted Shona specifically to ask about him?

Or was it the other way around?

'I'll talk to her tonight. I'm fine. She's got nothing to worry about.'

'You could talk to her this afternoon,' Mitchell suggested. 'Durness. Smoo Cave. Up on the North Coast 500 route. There's been a body found.'

Logan felt something stirring in his gut. He nodded to confirm that he'd heard about it already, but otherwise didn't respond.

'You could head up there. Chip in with the investigation. They're still short-handed. They could use the help.'

'Here we go.' Jack's chair creaked as he shifted his weight on it. 'Wondered when we'd get to the point. This you asking me to go up there and lead the case, is it?'

'Lead? No. DCI McCulloch's leading. He's a good man. Dependable.'

This took the wind from Logan's sails a little, but he did his best not to show it.

'Right. Good. McCulloch?' He rifled through the filing system in his head, then had a poke around in some of the dustier boxes at the back. 'Doesn't ring a bell. Do I know him?'

'Evan McCulloch. He's been CID down in the Borders for... well, forever.'

'And, what? He fancied a change, did he?' Logan asked. There was a note of outrage to it that surprised even him.

'No, the higher-ups requested him. With you and DI Forde both gone'—she didn't so much as glance in Ben's direction, even when mention of his name made him look up from where he was pretending not to listen in—'we needed someone to step in, and Evan has always been—'

'Dependable,' Logan said, finishing the sentence for her.

Mitchell nodded. At last, she picked up her teacup, but only brought it up to chin height before blowing gently on it and setting it back down.

'We're still short a DI. And I have a feeling that this case is going to be problematic.'

'Oh aye? How so?' Logan asked. His chair grumbled a complaint again, this time as he leaned forward.

Across the table, Mitchell waved two fingers, deflecting the question.

'This is what I'm suggesting, Jack. You join this investigation in an advisory capacity. A consultant, an extra pair of hands, call it what you like. McCulloch leads, but you're there to lend your experience and expertise. You'd be an advisor.'

The detective superintendent gave him a few moments to process that, before following up with the sucker-punch.

'And I know the team would enjoy having you back. They've missed you. DC Neish especially, but the others, too.'

Logan ran a hand down his face. There was none of the usual rasping of rough skin on stubble. He had time to shave these days. He had time to do a lot of things.

Too much time, some might argue.

'Do I have a choice in this?'

The only change to Mitchell's expression was a slow, deliberate blink.

Beneath the table, Taggart came to the conclusion that the sausages were never coming back, and huffed out a heavy sigh of resignation.

'Of course you do. That's exactly why I'm here. To offer you a choice,' the Detective Superintendent said. 'McCulloch wants to relocate. Here. To the MIT. Full-time.'

'He wants my job?' Logan asked, and the outrage was back again.

'He wants the job that you appear not to,' Mitchell countered. 'That's how the higher-ups are looking at it, anyway. And, like I said, they like him. They think he's dependable.'

'And? What do you think?'

'I think he does what he's told.'

Logan laughed at that—a gruff chuckle way at the back of his throat. 'That must be nice for you.'

'It's certainly a refreshing change,' Mitchell confirmed, granite-faced. 'I also think he's predictable, thinks inside the box too much, and—how can I put this?—is somewhat lacking in bedside manner.'

Logan's eyes widened, just a fraction. 'What are you saying? He's got worse people skills than I do?'

'Jesus Christ,' remarked Ben, who had been wiping the same square foot of countertop for the past five minutes. 'What is he, Frankenstein's monster?'

He raised both hands in surrender, then got back to wiping up the invisible spill.

'No' that I'm listening. Don't you mind me.'

'Like I say, I think the team would be delighted to see you. Let's put it that way,' Mitchell said, all her attention still laser-focused on the giant sitting across from her. 'But you asked if you had a choice, and I told you that you did. And I meant that.'

For the first time since sitting down, Mitchell shifted her body weight towards the centre of the table. Her diction slowed, like she was spelling out something important.

'But that choice is racing towards you at high speed, Jack, and while I've been content to put myself in its path these past few months, I'm not sure how much longer I can continue to do so. The higher-ups are going to make a decision soon, whether you're around for it or not. If you aren't, then that doesn't leave them with a lot of options.'

Her stare was intense, like she was trying to drill her words directly into his brain through his eye sockets.

'If you have even the faintest thought about going back, about leading the team again, then show face, Jack. Show willing. Remind them upstairs who you are, and what you can do. Or else...'

Mitchell took a sip of her tea at last. She rolled it around inside her mouth, coating her teeth with it, before swallowing and setting the cup back down.

'Or else there might not be anything for you to go back to.'

Logan opened his mouth to reply, but too many contradictory responses tripped over themselves in their rush to get out, so he closed it again.

He had always assumed that he *would* go back. Eventually. Someday. But it had been a far-off thought. Something to address at some unspecified time somewhere down the line.

Maybe he should just step back, let this McCulloch character take the job, if that was what he wanted. There'd be a decent pension pot to fall back on in a few years' time. It wasn't like early retirement was a new thing in the police. Very few stuck around in the job beyond their mid-fifties, and since Logan was firmly headed in that decade's direction, it wasn't out of the question.

Maybe it was time to let someone else take the reins. Although, the thought of stepping aside for a 'dependable' box-ticker who had the approval of the high heid yins stuck in the throat a bit.

What harm would one last outing do? One final hurrah? He wouldn't even have to bear the brunt of the responsibility of being

SIO. He'd be advising. Consulting. Chipping in with a few words of wisdom here and there.

Could he handle that, though? Could he really be the monkey to some by-the-book organ grinder?

He was still debating this when Mitchell derailed his train of thought. She had hoisted her briefcase into her lap, and was rifling through a stack of paperwork inside it.

'Before you make your decision, there's something I want to show you,' she announced, then she pulled an A4-sized piece of glossy card from the bag. 'The victim.'

Logan's eyes followed the page as she placed it on the table between them. The cafe's fluorescent strip lights reflected off the surface of the photograph, and the face of the man pictured in it.

The DCI's gaze crept up to meet his senior officer's. 'Is that...?'

Across the table, Mitchell nodded, just once. 'It is.'

'And he's...?'

'Apparently so,' the detective superintendent confirmed.

Jack returned his attention to the image, and mumbled, 'Bloody hell.' He touched the edge of the photograph, as if to make sure it was real, and not some figment of his imagination.

The face was older, craggier, the decades drawn deeply across its skin, but Logan had recognised it right away.

And no wonder. It had spent the latter half of the 1980s pinned to his bedroom wall, after all.

'And here I thought that bastard would live forever.'

Chapter 5

The car park just along from Smoo Cave was a kaleidoscope of flashing blue lights and yellow high-vis vests. Uniforms criss-crossed the uneven, puddle-dotted ground, doing nothing of note beyond trying to look busy.

The drive north had taken Logan just shy of an eternity, thanks to the steady stream of trundling caravans and campers that had brought traffic to a near-standstill every time they'd approached the slightest bend in the road.

The wider, two-lane sections had tested Jack's patience to the limit. The single-track stretches had made him wonder if he'd crashed the car without realising, and wound up stuck on some B-road through the outer suburbs of Hell.

Whoever had come up with the idea of promoting this winding, narrow, woefully underfunded route to a worldwide audience as some must-do travel destination deserved, in Logan's opinion, to have all their fingernails pulled out one by one.

Or, since he really wanted the bastards to suffer, they should be made to drive the bloody thing every day through August.

He'd been blocked at the cordon tape at the entrance to the car park, but a flash of his warrant card had seen him waved through. Showing the card had felt... odd. He'd hesitated, like he was embarrassed by the whole thing. Like he was a kid, playing pretend, but just a little too old to not feel self-conscious about it.

Now, pulled into one of the few unmarked spaces, he sat with the engine off, hands still gripping the wheel, Taggart regarding him quizzically from the backseat. The dog, having sensed he was going to be let out soon, had sat up, tongue lolling excitedly, as soon as the engine rumbled to a stop.

He'd remained that way for a few minutes, shooting meaningful glances at the rear passenger side window, and occasionally stamping a foot on the upholstery to remind the driver he was there.

Up front, Jack's hands remained fastened to the wheel.

The car park was an improvised one, tucked just off the main road on a flat expanse of grass that had already been churned up by the wheels of a dozen vehicles. The actual car park for Smoo Cave lay ahead, and Logan could see a few figures in white paper suits shuffling their way across it, searching for evidence.

It was possible that Geoff Palmer, head of the Scene of Crime team, was amongst their number, but more likely that he was standing on the sidelines somewhere, dishing out orders and trying to make himself seem important.

Christ. Palmer. It had been months since Jack'd had the displeasure of the man's company. He hadn't seen him since the 'coffee date' Logan had reluctantly agreed to go on during his last case. If it was a just and fair world, he'd never have to see the man again.

But it wasn't either of those, of course. It never had been.

In the backseat, Taggart let out an impatient whine. The steering wheel creaked in Logan's grip.

'Aye. Give us a minute,' he muttered.

Shona's car was parked just ahead of him, next to an RAF Mountain Rescue van. She'd have been up here for hours by now, carrying out her preliminary checks on the body, and making all the necessary declarations.

He'd texted her to let her know he was coming. He wondered if she'd told the others. Wondered what they'd said.

Jack's eyes wandered through the makeshift parking area, picking out the unmarked cars between the police vehicles.

He recognised DS Hamza Khaled's Volvo, and Constable—no, *Detective* Constable—Dave Davidson's much smaller Peugeot 208. There was also a big black BMW XM, polished to such a shine that it seemed to draw in the afternoon sunshine and shoot it back out as waves of pure onyx light.

It was a ridiculously expensive motor, parked at an angle, without thought for the two other vehicles it was blocking. As Logan had never seen it before, he could only assume it either belonged to, or had been provided for, DCI Evan McCulloch.

If the higher-ups had agreed to pay for an XM, then Mitchell hadn't been exaggerating. The bastard really must be their golden child.

Jack drew in a long, slow breath. He could do this. He just had to get out of the car, that was all. Get up, get out, pull on the coat, and act like he owned the place. The usual routine that had served him well for years.

And yet, his hands still gripped the wheel, and the windows were fogging over more with each breath he took.

From the backseat, Taggart gave another whine. This one wasn't impatience, though, it was excitement. He danced on the spot when a shadow fell over the driver's side window, and knuckles rapped on the glass.

Logan looked up into the shadowed face of a Uniformed officer, silhouetted against the sky. The window between them slid down at the touch of a button. Where Logan's hand had been, the leather shone with sweat.

'You all right there, sir?' the Uniform asked. He was a constable. Male. Early twenties, if that. He still had some bum fluff and the odd fiery-looking plook. Take a deep breath, Logan reckoned, and he'd be able to smell the lingering aroma of the canteen at Tulliallan Training College.

He didn't say 'sir' in a deferential, addressing-a-senior-officer sort of way. There was a sarcasm to it. It was the sort of 'sir' he might use when talking to a jakey acting up outside Tesco, or in order to deliberately wind up a mouthy van driver who'd been pulled over for a tyre check. It was a 'sir' that had been weaponised, with Logan locked firmly in its sights.

'Sorry, what?' Jack asked, then he gave a shake of his head, pulling himself together. 'I mean, aye. I'm fine.'

'Are you meant to be here, sir?'

The tone of this 'sir', was slightly different. It seemed to answer the question before it with a resounding 'No, you bloody well are not.'

The constable continued before Logan had a chance to reply.

'You can't be here, sir, if you're not meant to be. There's been an incident. I can't say what, but it's major. No public allowed. There's been a body found. I can't say any more than that. Someone famous, seemingly.'

'Aye, well—'

'Murdered, maybe. Or could be an accident. I don't know, they haven't told me, so I can't say,' the constable continued. He faltered, just for a second, then pressed on. 'Not that I could say, anyway. I'm sure you understand. You'll need to move along, sir.'

'Listen, son—'

'I'm not your son, *sir*.' This 'sir' had barbs on it. It was a slap in the face, or a blow to the back of the head with an old-style truncheon. 'Please don't patronise me. I'm a police officer, and if you don't have any business here, then you're going to have to...'

His voice became quieter, then slower, then finally silent, his expression turning increasingly quizzical as something on the other side of the car finally caught his attention.

Logan followed his gaze to find a sergeant frantically drawing his thumb across his throat, gesturing for the constable to do himself a favour and shut the fuck up. The sergeant, clocking Jack's head turn, hurriedly arranged his own expression into something warm and welcoming.

'Detective Chief Inspector,' he said, raising his voice to be heard through the glass, and stressing every syllable of those three words for the benefit of the younger officer. 'Long time no see!'

Chapter 6

Logan trudged along the roadside verge, boots squelching in the damp grass. The sun had been shining for most of the day, but the previous week had seen some pretty heavy rain, and it would take more than a few hours of clear skies to dry the place out.

It was hot, though. Far too hot for the long, heavy coat he was wearing. And yet, he hadn't been able to bring himself to leave it in the car. It was the closest he had to a uniform of his own. Or a suit of armour.

From somewhere a few dozen yards back, he heard a sharp wailing, like an animal in pain. His heart leaped into his throat, thinking Taggart had been injured, but then he realised it wasn't an animal that was responsible for the noise at all.

A blonde-haired woman in her forties was in the process of collapsing over by a stretch of cordon tape. It was quite a prolonged collapse, with a lot of howling and theatrical arm movements.

Two constables were either holding her back or holding her up, it was hard to say. She clawed at the air between them, like she could stretch through the gap and elongate her body so she could reach the path leading down to the cave.

Logan watched her as he walked, noting how performative her grief appeared to be. Either she was the most distraught person who had ever lived, or it was an act. If it was the latter, then she was hamming it up to a level that would've seen her kicked out of children's pantomimes for being far too over the top.

Either way, he made a note of her face, and left her as someone else's problem for now.

A few Uniforms shot him looks of suspicion or surprise when he plodded past them on the way down the hill towards the gaping black maw of Smoo Cave. Just inside the entrance, he could see Shona and Geoff Palmer engaged in what looked to be quite a heated debate.

It was impossible to make out what was being said over the clanking and rattling of a petrol generator standing nearby. Presumably, it was powering lights set up inside the cave to allow Shona and Palmer's team to do their jobs.

From the way Shona was peeling off her rubber gloves, stretching them until they came free with a *snap*, it was clear that she wasn't happy. Geoff's body language was harder to read, partly because he was cocooned inside an ill-fitting paper suit, but mostly because Logan was actively trying to avoid looking at him.

It was Palmer, however, who saw him first.

'Oh-ho! Who's this? Is this an apparition I see-eth beforth me?' the SOCO cried, deliberately mangling the words in what he no doubt considered to be 'a funny way', even if no other bugger would.

Palmer, more than anyone else Jack had ever met, had a belief in his own comedic talents that in no way correlated with reality. He had been doing stand-up for the past couple of years, reciting tired, borderline-racist jokes to an ever-dwindling audience of punters who ranged from the disinterested to the actively hostile.

Despite his repeated and, by necessity, public failures to raise more than the occasional sarcastic titter, he remained undeterred, convinced that his unique brand of comedy stylings would someday be recognised for the works of genius that they were.

Logan disagreed. He'd popped into one of Palmer's early gigs. It had been a load of old shite—a fact that had pleased the DCI immensely.

Palmer practically danced towards Jack as he plodded the final few paces down the hillside. The Scene of Crime man's face was its usual red circle, hemmed in by the elasticated trim of his paper hood.

He had grown a moustache since Logan had last seen him—a thin, Clark Gable thing that was notably narrower on one side, like he'd overshot the mark when shaping it. It made him look even seedier than he had before—something which Logan would previously have considered an impossibility.

'He's back from the dead! The wanderer returns! He is risen once more!' Palmer babbled, stressing the exclamation marks at the end of each remark.

He all but elbowed Shona out of the way in his hurry to intercept the approaching detective, and was completely oblivious to the double two-finger salute she waggled in the direction of his back.

'Geoff,' Logan intoned, just loudly enough to be heard above the din of the generator's motor. He looked down into the upturned face of the man now standing before him. 'You're still here, then.'

'Oh aye, there's no getting rid of me!' Palmer replied, and the way he said it implied this was somehow a good thing. 'Look at you, though. Back in action! Back in the saddle! Back on the job!'

Logan gave a non-committal tilt of his head that, to anyone paying attention, would have conveyed that things weren't quite that simple.

Palmer, however, was not paying attention.

'Aye, the police job, I mean,' he continued. 'Not... Not, you know, *on the job*. Like a prostitute. I'm not saying that. Although!' He gave Logan a playful slap on the upper arm. 'Strapping lad like you...!'

Jack considered a number of responses to this, before settling on an impassive, vaguely menacing silence.

Mercifully, Shona joined them before Palmer could say anything more on the subject. Or, on any other subject, for that matter.

'You made it, then,' she said. Her usual Irish accent was present, but it had lost some of the more musical elements, the lilt now sharper around the edges.

'Uh, aye,' Logan confirmed. He wanted to ask her what was wrong, what had so clearly upset her, but she didn't give him the chance.

'Where's Taggart? Did you bring him?'

Logan hoisted a thumb over his shoulder, indicating the route back up the slope. 'Left him with some glaikit young constable. He's giving him a walk.'

Shona nodded. This, at least, had satisfied her.

'Is, eh, is everything—?' Logan began, but the worms came bursting out before he'd finished turning the can opener.

'No, it's not. Your man in there. McCulloch.' Shona folded her arms across her chest, and drew them tight, like a knot. 'You know I don't like to speak badly of people, present company excluded.'

'Ha!' Palmer ejected, pointing at Jack in the mistaken belief that he had been the target of that remark.

'But, God Almighty, the man's an arsehole,' Shona continued. 'He wants to know the time of death! Can you believe that?'

Logan rocked his weight from one foot to the other, choosing his next few words carefully.

'Right. Aye. Well, I mean, that's... I suppose he would want to know that. That's pretty standard. Isn't it?'

The knot of Shona's arms tightened still further. A foot, still wrapped in a bright blue shoe protector, tapped the ground.

'No, but he wants to *know* know. Like, definitive, no backsies time of death.' She continued to stare up at Logan, then tutted when he didn't seem to be getting it. 'Like, not an estimate. I don't mind giving him that. That's fair enough. But, he wants to *know* know.'

Logan's eyebrows arched as the significance of what she was telling him finally filtered through.

'What, definitively? Before you get him back to the lab?'

'Exactly! Before I've cracked him open and done any proper poking around! Can you believe that? I'm supposed to just magic a time of death out of thin air!'

Beside her, Palmer shook his head and folded his arms, mirroring her body language in a show of support that was as performative as it was unconvincing.

'Like I said earlier, Shona, when you were crying on my shoulder about it, it's disgraceful.'

'I wasn't crying on your shoulder.'

'Metaphorically, I mean,' Palmer countered. 'When you were metaphorically crying on my shoulder.'

'Wait,' Logan interjected. 'Your metaphorical shoulder or your literal shoulder?'

The question caught Palmer off guard. From the corner of his eye, Jack saw the subtle changes to the lines of Shona's face. A softening.

'Eh, my...' Palmer's lips moved silently, like he was working out the answer to a difficult puzzle. 'My metaphorical shoulder.'

'Wait, no, hang on now, Geoff,' Shona said, getting in on the fun. 'How can you have a metaphorical shoulder?'

'Where would you keep it?' Logan asked.

'Would it be growing out of your back, or something?' Shona pressed.

Palmer glanced between them both, blinking. 'What?'

'I was *metaphorically* crying on your *literal* shoulder,' Shona told him.

Palmer, to both Jack and Shona's immense amusement, glanced down at his left shoulder, like he might see some evidence of this. Some metaphorical tear stains, or hypothetical snot.

'Right. Aye,' he said, uncertainly. 'That's, eh…' The frown he'd been wearing for the past several seconds deepened. It was like watching some old computer run out of processing power. 'What were we talking about again? Oh! That's right. That arsehole McCulloch asking the impossible.'

'Yes! Exactly!' Shona agreed, then she shrugged. 'I mean, not the *impossible*, I suppose. Last night between seven and nine, allowing for the temperature differential in the cave, but *still*. It's unreasonable to make demands like that is my point! I might get him back on the slab, cut him open, and find out I'm off by an hour or so.'

'A whole hour?' Logan asked, trying very hard not to sound like he was teasing her.

Shona unfolded her arms, and poked him square in the chest with a finger.

'I know! It's not on, is it?'

She sniffed, ran a hand over her tied-back hair, smoothing it down, then pulled together the best smile she could manage, given how her blood was still boiling.

'Still, you're here now, you can tell him to *F-off* and be on his way.'

'Amen, sister!' Palmer said. He held out a hand for a high-five, but even he could tell one wasn't likely to be forthcoming, so he lowered it again almost immediately.

For the second time in as many minutes, Logan shuffled uneasily on the spot.

'Aye, well, about that—'

'It'll be like the old days. Us three. The Three Musketeers,' Palmer continued, beaming away inside his hood. 'The Three Amigos! The Three… What's another one? Blind Mice?' He winced. 'That's probably not very fitting, is it? We're not blind.'

'Or mice,' Shona added.

'Yes. Exactly. Or mice. We'll stick to the first two,' Palmer said, then he put his hands on his hips, jerked his head in the direction of the cave, and lowered his voice like he was sharing a secret. 'What do you make of it all, then?'

'I don't know yet,' Logan said. 'All I heard so far was that—'

Palmer held both hands up in front of him, like he was envisioning a headline or a sign on a marquee. 'Rock Star Meets Rocky End!' He waggled his eyebrows so they popped in and out of view beneath the elasticated seam of his hood. 'Hm? Rocky Times for Rock Legend.'

Logan had never had much patience when it came to Geoff Palmer, and the Scene of Crime man was really starting to try what little he possessed.

'What the hell's he doing?' he asked, directing the question at Shona.

It was Geoff himself who answered. 'I'm brainstorming. For a funny bit. Rock star. Rocky end. I'm just, you know, honing the material.'

'Right. I see.' Logan sighed. He'd hoped that all the time he'd spent away from Palmer would make the man seem less objectionable. If anything, it'd had the opposite effect. Absence had not made the heart grow fonder. 'Can you hone silently, do you think? Or, even better, hone elsewhere?'

'Stooges.'

Logan sighed. 'What?'

'Three Stooges. That's another one,' Palmer said.

A voice rose from within the cave before Logan could reply. It was one of those voices that had any and all traces of an accent stripped out of it. It had been whittled down, hollowed out, until all that remained was the received pronunciation.

It was a voice that Logan instinctively disliked.

'Aha! At last.'

Logan, Palmer and Shona turned to look as a man almost as tall as Jack, but one-third the width, picked his way across the uneven ground. He was so thin he had jaggy edges, and as he came clattering out of the cave, he brought to mind the stop-motion skeletons from Jason and the Argonauts.

He wore a dark grey fleece, black waterproof trousers and a pair of hiking boots whose colour sat somewhere on the spectrum between the other two. Given his silvering hair and pale skin, the only colour about him was the yellow toggles on the ends of his laces, and the blue rubber gloves he was in the process of peeling off.

'Right. There he is. Tell him,' Palmer whispered from a corner of his mouth, sidling in close to Logan. Far too close, for Jack's liking. 'Tell him you're here, you're in charge now, and he can piss off.'

Before Logan could do anything of the sort, the bag of bones rattled to a stop in front of him. If the new arrival had noticed Shona and

Geoff, he certainly wasn't showing it. Instead, his gaze was fixed firmly on Jack—a laser targeting system, aimed right between his eyes.

He was older than Logan. Mid-fifties, at a guess, but his sallow cheeks and the dark hollows of his eye sockets added a handful of extra years.

'You're the assistant,' he said. It wasn't a question.

'I'm Detective Chief Inspector Jack Loga—'

'Yes, yes. I know.' McCulloch waved a hand, like he was batting the introduction away before it had a chance to land on him. 'But you have been sent here to assist, correct? Ergo, you are the assistant.'

On his periphery, Logan saw both Shona and Palmer turning to look at him, eyes widening. Before Jack could muster up any sort of response, though, the other man was back in full swing.

'Marvellous! I'm DCI McCulloch. M-C-C-U-double-L-O-C-H.'

He drew the letters in the air with a finger as he spoke them, reversed for Logan's benefit. When the man gripped him by the shoulder, Jack would've sworn he could feel cold radiating from his touch, even through the coat.

'Come, my boy. You and I have much to discuss.'

Logan could feel the heat of Shona and Geoff's stares on him now. Watching him. Waiting to see what he was going to say.

And he *should* say something to this bastard. He should shut him down, put him in his place.

And yet, nothing was coming to mind, and he found himself turning to follow as McCulloch went striding up the hill towards the road.

'Uh… The scene,' Logan eventually managed. He tilted his head back in the direction of the cave. 'I want to take a look.'

That wasn't true. Not exactly. The last time he'd been in a cave hadn't ended well. The nightmares were a testament to that. Being this close to one now, this close to the darkness, was making the skin on the back of his neck shift around like it was alive.

'I should take a look,' he said, though he couldn't say who it was aimed at.

McCulloch stopped.

McCulloch turned.

'I'm afraid that won't be possible.'

Some part of Logan wanted to laugh with relief. The other parts had questions. 'What? Why?'

McCulloch's sigh was a short but heavy thing. Logan was surprised he had the lung capacity for it.

'Not that I should have to explain myself to you, of all people, but do the words "crime scene integrity" mean anything? We can't have just any Tom, Dick or Harry trampling around down there, can we?'

Quietly, only just loud enough for Logan to hear him over the rumbling of the generator, Palmer whispered, 'God. Right. Here we go,' and took a shuffled step back, as if getting ready to flee some explosion or oncoming storm.

There was no great eruption of anger, though. Logan's response was more splutter than bang.

'I'm aware of that, aye. I just think it would be useful if—'

'*Mr* Logan,' the DCI said, stressing the prefix. 'You've been informed that I am SIO on this investigation, yes?'

Logan, much as it pained him, nodded.

'And that you, therefore, are *not* the SIO on this investigation. Correct?' McCulloch continued. 'You are aware of this? This is not news to you?'

There was a spark, then, somewhere deep down. Something flared, spluttering and struggling for life. Fingers twitched. A jaw clenched.

And then, it all died away again.

'Yes. I'm aware,' Logan confirmed.

'Marvellous.'

McCulloch turned and started off up the hill again, bones creaking under their thin blanket of sinew.

'Then come!' he barked, not looking back. 'There is much to be done!'

Chapter 7

'Boss?'

McCulloch snapped to a halt directly in the path of DC Tyler Neish, stopping so suddenly the heels of his hiking boots practically clacked together.

'Detective Constable, how many times must we have this conversation?' McCulloch asked. He sounded weary, like the DC was testing his patience.

Logan didn't like it. Aye, Tyler could be a tiring bastard to be around, but he'd never spoken to him like that. Had he?

'Oh, no, sir, I was—' Tyler began, before being silenced.

'You will address me as "sir", as per regulation, nothing else. Not "mate", or "pal", or "boss". Just "sir", plain and simple. Nothing else. Are we clear?'

'Completely, sir,' Tyler said. He added a salute that, to Logan's eyes, was at least 90 per cent sarcasm, but which McCulloch seemed to approve of nonetheless. 'But, I wasn't actually talking to you, sir. I was talking to him.'

He looked past the gangly knot of a man and met Logan's eye. A nod passed between them. Respectful, professional, affectionate. Everything.

'Good to see you back, boss.'

Logan started to speak, but a sudden hoarseness in his throat forced him to abandon the attempt. By the time he'd cleared it, McCulloch had already jumped back in.

'No, he's not the boss. I'm the boss.'

Tyler's brow creased in an exaggerated show of confusion. 'I thought you said you weren't the boss, sir?'

'No! I said nothing of the sort. DCI Logan is here to assist, that is all,' McCulloch stressed. He prodded himself in the chest with a thumb. 'I am very much the boss here.'

'Oh. OK.' Tyler blinked a few times, like he was lining all this information up in his head. 'Right you are then, boss.'

It was at that point that Logan had to bite his lip and turn away.

When he'd first met DC Neish, Logan had thought the boy to be something of an idiot. That opinion had not changed very much in the weeks that followed.

Or in the months and years after that.

Eventually, though, he'd seen something else in the young detective constable. He was smarter than he seemed. Which, granted, hardly counted as an achievement.

Now, though, watching on from the outside, he wondered if the whole thing had always been an act. There was no way he didn't know what he was doing with McCulloch. The whole conversation was a masterclass in piss-taking, and the DCI seemed completely oblivious to it.

As Logan tuned out McCulloch's follow-up tantrum, he took stock of the area around them.

The sun had moved west, casting long shadows across the makeshift checkpoint they'd set up in the empty car park. Crime scene tape fluttered between temporary barriers on either side, creating a maze of yellow and blue that Uniforms were directing the occasional tourist through, sending them on diversions down towards the beach, or back to the village, or anywhere but here.

From this elevation, Logan could see clearly to the North Sea, a steel-grey expanse that melted into the horizon. Closer in, waves hammered against the limestone cliffs, sending up plumes of spray that caught the late afternoon light.

There were no vehicles in the car park itself, though Logan didn't know if they'd been cleared away, or if the cordon had gone up before anyone had arrived. Given how many people visited the area these days, he suspected the latter was unlikely.

A team of SOCOs were just finishing up their sweep, photographing tyre tracks in the churned earth before taking casts. They worked methodically, saying nothing, in stark contrast to their team leader, who Logan could hear puffing and panting and wittering shite as he dragged himself up the hill, trying to keep pace with the much fitter Shona.

Further west, flanked by wire fences and dry stane dykes, the single-track road wound away towards Durness, now closed to all but police traffic. A smattering of local residents were being interviewed near the road barriers, probably the last of many who'd been turned away today.

Logan's attention was drawn to a figure crouched by the roadside—DS Hamza Khaled, examining something in the grass with his usual intense focus. Some things, at least, hadn't changed.

Hamza waved over one of the SOCOs, pointed down at whatever he'd seen, then took a step back while the woman in the paper suit moved in to investigate.

It was only then that the detective sergeant glanced in Logan's direction, did a double take, then hurried over, a smile spreading across the previous gloom of his face like a break in the clouds.

'All right, sir?' Hamza called when he was halfway across the car park.

There was something of a foghorn-like quality to Hamza's Aberdonian accent, and the greeting was loud enough to cut through both McCulloch's reprimands and Tyler's wide-eyed protestations of innocence.

'Hamza,' Logan said, tipping his head in the DS's direction.

'You're back,' Hamza declared, his smile broadening as he grasped for Logan's hand and shook it.

'Uh, aye,' Logan confirmed.

'In an assistant capacity,' McCulloch was quick to add. 'I am, and will remain, senior investigating officer. DCI Logan is here to help. As best he can. Now, where's—'

McCulloch pointed to Tyler and snapped his fingers a few times, like the DC should be able to read his mind.

Unsurprisingly, he couldn't, which only seemed to annoy the DCI even further.

'God, come on. You know. Wheelchair.'

Tyler frowned. This one didn't look put on for McCulloch's benefit. There was nothing sarcastic about it.

'Detective Constable Davidson, you mean?'

'Yes! God. Yes. Finally. Him. David. Detective Constable *David Davidson*,' McCulloch said, stressing the name like it was a slippery thing he struggled to hold onto. 'Where is he?'

'He's in his car, sir,' Hamza said, angling his body so he was slightly between Tyler and the DCI. 'You told him to wait there.'

'In the car?' Logan said, turning his gaze from Hamza to the other DCI. 'You told Dave to wait in the car?'

'Yes. Of course. I mean, it's hardly the right terrain for him, is it?' McCulloch said, gesturing around them at the damp grass and potholed tarmac. 'It's one thing putting on shoe protectors to avoid contaminating the scene, but we can't very well wrap his wheels in blue plastic, can we? It was best all round for him to hang fire in his car.'

Logan felt it again then—that sputtering flame deep down inside somewhere. The heat of it rose up the back of his throat, like bile.

'Tyler.'

'Yes, boss?'

'Go get him.'

Tyler didn't so much as glance in McCulloch's direction. He nodded, just the once, and turned to go.

'Will do, boss.'

'You will do nothing of the sort, Detective Constable,' McCulloch barked. 'Stay right where you are.'

Logan felt the eyes on him. *All* the eyes. Watching him again, waiting for him to react. Hamza. Tyler. Geoff Palmer and Shona now, too, who'd crested the top of the hill and stood at the start of the path leading down to the cave.

A few SOCOs. A couple of Uniforms. They were all watching him. Pressuring him. Expecting him to unleash something that he wasn't convinced he still had in him.

McCulloch was staring at him, too, his beady, hawkish eyes daring Jack to argue or defy him.

There was a time that Logan would have eaten the bastard alive for that look. There was a time that he'd have crushed him with a word, or a raised eyebrow, or, if it came to it, between the fingers of one hand.

Aye. There was a time.

'I just think that Dave's still learning the ropes,' he said. 'This could be good experience for him.'

'Yes. Well.' McCulloch smiled. McCulloch patted Jack on his chest, just below his right shoulder. McCulloch won. 'Thank you for your insight. I'm already a step ahead on the matter of Mr Davidson's training.' He continued to smile at Logan, but raised his voice. 'DC Neish?'

Tyler didn't reply right away. He was too stunned by what he'd just witnessed. Too numb.

McCulloch cleared his throat. 'Must I repeat myself? It seems so. Very well. *Detective Constable Neish?*'

The way his name snapped in the air brought Tyler out of his stupor.

'Uh, aye, boss? Sir, I mean. Yes, sir?'

McCulloch's smile widened. Another tiny victory.

'Go and join DC Davidson in his car,' the DCI instructed. 'I have a very special job lined up for the two of you.'

Chapter 8

Durness Village Hall was just a stone's throw from Smoo Cave, albeit one you'd have to put a fair amount of welly behind. It was quicker to walk there than to take the car, and yet McCulloch had insisted on hiking back to his BMW and driving it across.

When you had a car that flash, you might as well make the most of it, Logan reasoned.

He had opted to make the short trip on foot. Even after swinging by to relieve the young constable of dog-walking duties, he and Hamza were halfway to the hall before McCulloch had so much as started his engine.

Shona had headed down the road to prep for the arrival of the body. She'd said her goodbyes, then Logan had escorted her to her car, where she'd asked him twice if he was feeling all right, and he'd assured her that he was.

Tyler, much to his frustration and dismay, had been sent back down the road with Dave Davidson, so the recently appointed detective constable could experience his first post-mortem.

'Live,' McCulloch had said, with an unmistakable note of glee, 'and in glorious Technicolor!'

The thought of making the return trip so soon after getting here had prompted some top-drawer moaning from DC Neish, but he'd caved quite quickly, and gone trudging off to Dave's Peugeot, scrounging up a couple of carrier bags along the way. Better safe than sorry, after all.

'You all right, sir?'

Hamza's question reached Logan through the faint fog of the stupor he'd been in as they crossed the road and plodded up the driveway towards the village hall. There was no police station in the village—the closest being a half-hour drive away along another iffy road—and so the hall was being commandeered as a makeshift Incident Room until they figured out what was going on.

Early rumblings had suggested an accident—a drunken fall off a slippery ledge, and a skull-shattering impact on the rocky floor of the cave below. It had been Shona who had pointed out that, yes, this theory could be correct, assuming the deceased had then climbed back up to the ledge in order to fall off and strike his head a second time.

Two impacts, each one hard enough to be fatal. The fall theory was still possible—he could have hit his head twice on the way down—but Shona seemed doubtful, and that was good enough for Logan.

McCulloch was more dubious. He was still leaning towards it being an accident. Still, they'd know for sure in a few hours, once the post-mortem was underway.

'Sir?' Hamza said again, and Logan flashed him what he was reasonably confident was a smile.

'Sorry, aye. Miles away. I'm fine. I'm... good. You?'

'Uh, yeah,' Hamza said. 'Not bad, considering.'

Logan nodded, not yet saying anything. Hamza was a good, honest family man, but all that had been thrown into disarray a few months back when he'd walked in on his wife at the business end of a very passionate affair.

The last Logan had heard, they were starting divorce proceedings. Hamza had been staying with DI Forde for a while, but had moved into a rented one-bedroom flat in Inverness city centre after a few weeks.

Logan couldn't blame him. Ben would be easy enough to live with, but Moira? Other than maybe a nest of plague rats, he couldn't imagine anyone less appealing to share a house with.

Bob Hoon, maybe.

'That's... good,' Logan finally voiced. 'Everything, you know, settling down?'

'More or less,' Hamza confirmed. 'We're still talking custody arrangements and all that stuff, but we're getting there.'

'Good,' Logan said again. 'Glad to hear it.'

'And, eh, and you, sir? Are you OK?'

It was the second time Hamza had asked the question, but it had been implied in his eyes and the tone of his voice on the whole walk over.

'When I saw you, I thought *great!* I thought that was you back. In charge, I mean. But...'

He looked over his shoulder, back in the direction of the cave car park, like he could watch the memory of what had transpired there being replayed.

'DCI McCulloch's leading this one,' Logan said. 'Mitchell asked me to come along and—'

'Help out as best you can,' Hamza finished, echoing McCulloch's remark from earlier.

Down at Logan's feet, Taggart trotted along, tongue lolling, ears and tail pricked up. The immediate landscape was made up of little more than heather and bracken, and the dog looked keen to set about it.

'Aye,' Jack said, not meeting Hamza's eye. 'Something like that.'

They reached the village hall car park without another word. DC Sinead Bell's car was parked near the hall, along with half a dozen other vehicles of various shapes, sizes and states of disrepair.

Chief amongst them all was an ancient box van that someone, in what was presumably a moment of madness, had painted a shade of pink that made both detectives think of open wounds in long-dead flesh.

Above a set of fold-down iron steps, a front door—the sort that really belonged on a terraced house from the 1960s—had been installed in the side of the cargo box. It was complete with a brass knocker and a doorbell, and emblazoned with the number sixty-three in faded gold paint.

'What in the name of the wee man is that thing?' Hamza wondered.

It was some sort of amateurish campervan conversion, Logan reckoned, but he chose not to dwell on it. He'd encountered quite enough of those bloody vehicles that morning to last him a lifetime.

He had driven past the village hall on the way in and assumed it was some sort of council leisure centre. It had that feel about it—a municipal building so generic it could have been stamped out of a template and bolted together at the roadside.

Still, whoever ran the place had clearly made an effort. There was a nice wee garden next to it, and some ornamental bits and bobs to brighten the place up. Up close, it felt far more welcoming than it had from the roadside. Possibly a calculated ploy, Logan guessed, to keep the tourists away. A local hall, for local people.

What wasn't so welcoming was the big yellow sticker on the glass door declaring that dogs weren't allowed on the premises, with the usual caveat tacked on at the bottom that this rule didn't apply to service animals.

Logan ignored it completely, pulled the door open, and gestured for Hamza to lead the way inside.

Behind them, down at the bottom of the driveway, a shiny black BMW XM turned off the main road. It was too far away to see properly, with the afternoon sun reflecting off the windscreen, but Logan would've sworn he saw McCulloch's beady eyes locking onto him as the Beamer picked up speed.

'Eh, did you see the notice, sir?' Hamza asked, drawing Logan's attention to the yellow sticker on the door. 'About the dog?'

'Aye, I saw it,' Logan confirmed. 'But don't worry, it's fine.'

He tucked a foot behind Taggart's rear end and gently guided the pup inside.

'I've done some tests with him, and I'm fairly sure he cannae read.'

Chapter 9

The inside of the hall was just as by-the-numbers as the outside—glossy grey walls adorned with notices for upcoming events that ranged from car boot sales to flu vaccinations.

The carpet tiles could have been lifted from any school or council office building Logan had ever set foot in. In fact, he was fairly certain they would be a match for the ones back in his office in Burnett Road, assuming McCulloch hadn't swapped them out for oak flooring and a big Persian rug.

The thought of McCulloch sitting at his desk, in his office, lording it up, sparked up another little burst of flame deep in Logan's gut. The sound of raised voices from a double doorway, dead ahead, stamped it out again before it had a chance to spread.

'It's a disgrace, is what it is! It's a bloody disgrace!' The voice was female. Older. Shrill with indignation. 'This is our community. Ours, not yours. We've a right to know.'

The voice that replied was also female, but quieter, and instantly familiar to both detectives. And, judging by the wagging of his tail, to Taggart.

'I understand that, Mrs Kellerman,' said DC Sinead Bell. 'And I appreciate your frustration—'

'Oh, *do you?*' the older woman cried. 'Oh, you appreciate our frustration, you say? Oh, how very *considerate* of you!'

Out in the hallway, glances were swapped, decisions were made, and both men picked up the pace. They reached the double doors in a few big steps—two in Logan's case, three and a bit for Hamza—and each pulled one wide.

A small hall was revealed, maybe forty feet by a little under sixty, with varnished wooden flooring, stacks of chairs along one wall and a small fold-out stage down at the front, directly ahead of them.

Sinead's head snapped up at the squeaking of the hinges, and the look of concern on her face gave way first to surprise, and then relief.

'Sir,' she said. She nodded at him, but the word sounded questioning. Sceptical, even, like she couldn't trust what her eyes were seeing.

'Detective Constable,' Logan replied, and Taggart gave an excited *yip* to ensure he got noticed, too.

'Can't you read? No dogs allowed on the premises!'

It was the same woman who'd been ranting at Sinead a moment ago. She stood facing the stage a few feet away, surrounded by a seated semicircle of what was, presumably, some of her fellow locals.

She was in her seventies, Logan would guess, nudging up towards the upper end. It was ironic that she had an issue with dogs, because there was something of the terrier about her—small, wiry, and with an air that made you worried for the backs of your ankles.

She wore cream-coloured slacks with sturdy hiking boots and a cardigan that could only have been knitted freestyle, because nobody in their right mind would create a pattern like that. It was a muddy brown with what was either badly done straight lines, or deliberately wavy ones running through it in shades of lime green and turquoise.

Just looking at the bloody thing brought a throbbing pain behind Logan's eyes, and the shrillness of her voice only compounded it.

'Are you listening, young man? No dogs allowed in here! Get it out before it fouls the floor!'

She pointed to the door, raising the hand so suddenly that Taggart almost backflipped in his rush to spot what he assumed had been a ball or a stick thrown for his benefit. He stood facing the other way, tongue out and tail wagging, trying to see where the imagined object had landed.

'He's a service dog,' Logan said.

A grey-haired man sitting in the closest seat uncrossed his legs, then crossed them the other way. Her husband, Logan guessed, given his own questionable choice of knitwear—blood-red jumper with a yellow zigzag pattern stretching across his ample belly.

'A service dog? That thing? Come on! Do you expect us to believe that?'

'He's my emotional support animal,' Logan replied, and for a moment, he was back. He was the old Jack again. 'See, I have anger issues. When I hear people talking unkindly to my colleagues, like

46

Detective Constable Bell here, I get gripped with this all-consuming rage. Believe me, it's not something I'm proud of, and the dog here, well, he keeps me from exploding.'

He looked across the gathered faces. Most of them, with the exception of a bored-looking teenager and a man so old he looked like he had been carved out of driftwood, had their heads turned to look at him.

'So, believe me, it's in all our best interests if he stays,' the DCI concluded. He smiled at the standing woman, showing too many teeth. 'Detective Chief Inspector—'

'Evan McCulloch,' came a voice from behind him. A hand clapped Logan on the shoulder again, and the wiry apparition that was DCI McCulloch slipped in front of him. 'Thank you for that, Jack. I'll take it from here.'

McCulloch clapped his hands together and rubbed them. They were so bony and devoid of meat that they barely made a sound beyond a rough, sandpaper-like rasping.

'Ladies and gentlemen, it's my pleasure to meet you all, even if I am not entirely sure why you are gathered here.'

'They, uh, they just turned up, demanding to know what was going on,' Sinead told him.

McCulloch didn't respond. He just stood there, half-smiling at the audience, still rubbing his hands together.

Logan saw Sinead flinch, before she added a spluttered, 'sir,' that kicked DCI McCulloch back into life.

'Aha! I see. Well, I assume you informed them that, unfortunately, we are unable to divulge any information at this time.'

Sinead shot a quick, questioning glance at Logan, then returned her attention to McCulloch. 'I did, sir, yes. I explained that.'

'Well, then, perhaps there was a miscommunication somewhere,' McCulloch suggested. He drew himself up to his full height, and stretched his mouth into something that could generously be described as a smile. 'I'm afraid that you people can't be here. I, that is we, that is Police Scotland, have been granted sole use of this facility for the purposes of carrying out our investigation into the unfortunate business that transpired here between the hours of yesterday evening and this morning.'

'Unfortunate business?' a man in the second row piped up, his face set in a scowl of disapproval. He was in his fifties, with long shaggy hair that was streaked with shades of grey. 'He was my cousin. He was family.'

The man in the awful jumper rolled his eyes. 'Oh, God, Dougie, so you keep telling everyone. We've all got famous cousins, I'm sure, if we dig deep enough. I once met Stevie Wonder. You don't hear me crowing about it.'

The woman beside him, despite nodding along in agreement, looked down at him, frowning. 'What are you talking about, Reg? When did you meet Stevie Wonder?'

'A while back.'

'When, though?'

'Forget it, Elsie,' Reg snapped. 'It was before we were together.'

'Before we...? How old was he at the time? Eight?' Elsie asked. Her nostrils flared, like she'd smelled a load of old shite. 'If you've met Stevie Wonder, I've met Art Garfunkel.'

Reg threw his hands in the air. 'Christ! Not him again!' he ejected, then he folded his arms and fell into a deep, resentful silence.

Directly behind them, a man with weathered skin and tumbling blond curls sniggered like a schoolboy, earning himself a look of pure, unfiltered disdain from Elsie.

'And you can shut up, as well,' she warned, then she sat down heavily and joined her husband in adopting the defensive cross-armed position.

DCI McCulloch seemed a bit wrong-footed by all this. He cleared his throat a couple of times and stumbled over his next few words as he tried to regain some sort of authority. It was, far and away, Logan's favourite moment of the day so far, with the possible exception of that roll and square sausage earlier.

'Right. Yes. Anyway,' McCulloch said. 'As I was explaining, we have full use of the building. So, if you could all kindly vacate, we'll try not to outstay our welcome.'

Judging by the faces of some of the audience, that ship had already well and truly sailed.

The gathering wasn't a big one, barely hitting double figures, though there were chairs set out for three times that many. There were spaces between groups and individuals, suggesting that, while they might be neighbours, they weren't a particularly close-knit community. At least, the people in this room weren't.

While McCulloch continued to stress the importance of cooperation at times such as these, Logan scanned the crowd, getting the measure of them.

He already had a pretty good idea about Reg and Elsie, the old couple at the front, and it was safe to say he didn't consider himself a fan. The guy sat behind them—the sniggerer—had a look of a surfer about him, and if his weather-beaten skin hadn't already given it away, his combat trousers and multi-pocketed vest would have heavily suggested a man who spent a lot of time outdoors.

Logan would put him around his mid-thirties, although exposure to the elements could have aged him up a few years.

Three seats away on his left, a fifty-something woman with a good foot or so of blonde hair piled up on her head fiddled with an unlit cigarette, twiddling it between her fingers like she was teasing herself with it. She wore a silky blue sash that was wrapped across a chest that either defied gravity, or was held up by industrial scaffolding.

She, more than anyone else in the room, looked bored out of her mind. Even the younger lad sat up the back between what was presumably his parents seemed to be paying more attention.

He was sixteen or seventeen, tall and thin, like he was a runner or a swimmer. He had his mother's red hair, left shaggy at the back and on top, but shaved in at the sides. Squint your eyes, and it looked like part of his head was on fire.

It looked like it felt that way on the inside, too. He was squinting a little, massaging a spot just above his right ear, like he was in the early stages of a migraine.

The man beside him—his father, Logan guessed—was of a similar height, but heavier build. He sat with his hands gripping his knees, eyes darting from McCulloch to the backs of the heads of those seated in the rows in front of him.

He lingered, Logan noted, on the man who had claimed to be the cousin of the deceased.

Was there a family resemblance? Logan couldn't be sure. He tried to think back to that poster on his wall, and to all the hundreds of pictures he must have seen of the dead man in the years since then, in magazines, on TV, under scandalous headlines on the front pages of tabloid newspapers.

He thought maybe there was some similarity, although that might have just been the long hair.

The wood carving of an old man sat hunched in a chair that was separated still further from the rest of the group. He wore a flat cap, waxed jacket, and leaned on a walking stick with both hands, as if even sitting up wasn't possible without support.

His bottom jaw trembled, and his lips moved like he was constantly muttering something too quietly for anyone else to hear. From the way he stared blankly ahead, he either had extremely poor vision, or was off in a world of his own somewhere.

Either way, if this did turn out to be a murder investigation, Logan felt confident that they could rule him out as a suspect. The only way he was getting down that hill to the cave entrance was if he tripped at the top and rolled the rest of the way.

Nobody in the room was paying him the slightest bit of attention, although Taggart, who had now turned back around to face the audience, seemed to be developing a worrying interest in his stick.

'So, much as I appreciate your interest in this matter, and look forward to your full cooperation in our efforts to get to the bottom of it,' McCulloch announced, and Logan realised he was wrapping up, 'I invite you all now to leave, return home, go about your business, whatever that may be, and should we be in need of any of you, then one of my officers will be in touch.'

The dead man's cousin, Dougie, was the only one to get up. He rose to his feet like he was suddenly in a rush to leave, then headed for the door without a word.

He had a suggestion of a limp, Logan noted. Left leg. It wasn't obvious, but it was definitely there. Although, when he saw the DCI watching him, he made a concerted effort to disguise the unevenness of his gait.

The rest of the audience hadn't yet moved. There was some shuffling in seats, and some grumbled complaints. McCulloch took the edge off at least some of the muttered concerns when he raised a finger, cranked up his smile, and announced, 'And please, don't be concerned. I can assure you that the dog will *not* be staying.'

Chapter 10

'Ha! No, don't worry. I just told them that to put their minds at ease. Of course the dog can stay!' McCulloch said.

He slapped Jack on the upper arm, then waved around at the building in general, bony fingers fluttering like they were dancing through the air.

'Just pop it in a cupboard, or tie it in a corner somewhere out of the way.'

A shadow crept downwards across Logan's face, like a cold front on a weather map.

'Pop him in…?'

'A cupboard. There's bound to be one. If not, like I say, tie him in a corner in one of the other rooms.'

'He'll be fine in here,' Logan insisted.

'In here?' McCulloch's eyebrows arched so high they almost shot right off the top of his head. He gestured around to where Hamza and Sinead were dragging in tables from the hall's kitchen area. 'In our Incident Room? Don't you think that's a little inappropriate?'

Logan waited for the low, grinding sound of table legs on wooden floorboards to stop, then shook his head.

'Why would it be inappropriate? He's a dug. He's hardly going to run out and blab to the press.'

Shite. The press. The thought had only just occurred to him, but the media was going to be all over this. Celebrity deaths were always big news. Celebrity murders? That was the stuff of front pages.

'Speaking of those parasitic bastards…' Logan began, but McCulloch wasn't so ready to change the subject.

'What if it gets under our feet?'

'What?'

'The dog.'

'Oh.' Logan gave a shake of his head. 'He won't.'

'And how do you know this?'

'Because I'll tell him not to.'

Both men looked down at Taggart, who sat on the floor between them, looking up, one ear raised, his tongue hanging out the side of his mouth like it was trying to make its escape. He was blissfully unaware that his fate was being decided.

Then again, he was generally unaware of most things that didn't involve food, belly rubs or chasing fast-moving objects.

McCulloch exhaled through his long, hooked nose. The thick grey hairs that poked out of both nostrils vibrated like the reeds of some medieval musical instrument.

'Fine. But the moment it becomes an inconvenience, it's out. Is that clear?'

The sound of tables being dragged around had stopped now. Logan could sense Sinead and Hamza standing by the door, frozen, mid-step.

McCulloch's tone had managed to be both commanding and condescending at the same time. As far as he was concerned, this wasn't a conversation between equals. Not even close.

Sinead couldn't remember ever hearing anyone talk to DCI Logan like that. Not even Bob Hoon. Even when Hoon was in full-on rant mode, calling Jack every name under the sun, there had still been respect in there somewhere. Not much, granted, but it had been there if you looked hard enough.

Besides, Hoon and Logan went back years. McCulloch was fresh on the scene.

Surely, Jack wasn't going to stand for it?

'Is. That. Clear?' McCulloch asked again. Each word was a prod to the chest. A tug on an ear. A rapping of a ruler on bare knuckles.

Sinead held her breath, but Hamza took her by the arm and led her out into the hallway. Not to shield her from the explosion, but from the lack of one.

'Aye. Fine,' Logan agreed.

He turned, planning to go help Sinead and Hamza bring in more tables, but that icy hand was back on his shoulder again, stopping him before he could take a step.

'One more thing, Jack. And, forgive me, it's quite a sensitive subject,' McCulloch said.

He chewed on a thin, dry lip for a moment, trying to work out the best way of phrasing what he wanted to say.

Eventually, though, he just shrugged and came out with it.

'I think it would be best for the team if, while you're here assisting, you address me as "sir".'

None of the possible reactions that leaped immediately to Logan's mind felt appropriate. Some of them were far too strong. Others, not nearly strong enough.

So, he just stood there in silence and hoped that the look on his face provided a suitably coherent response.

'I just think, with both of us here, there's a real danger that they'll forget who the SIO is. Who's in charge, I mean,' McCulloch said. He folded his hands crisply behind his lower back, his pigeon chest puffing up. 'Given the significance of this investigation, I feel it would be unfair to... confuse things. Them. The situation. I just think it would be helpful for them if you were to address me as "sir", while you're here assisting.'

Clearly, the look on Jack's face hadn't been enough to get his point across. The more strongly worded responses that had first sprung to mind were now even more so, and it was all he could do to swallow them back and instead just splutter out a, 'Sir?' of disbelief.

McCulloch brightened immediately. He slapped Logan on the upper arm again, not once, but twice.

'Marvellous! That's the spirit, Jack!'

'What? No, that's not—'

But McCulloch was no longer listening. He marched off, taking his phone from his pocket, not glancing back.

'Now, I'm going to go find myself an office, and call Detective Superintendent Mitchell with an update,' he said, his voice echoing around the mostly empty hall. 'If you could find your way to the kitchen and the tea-making facilities, that would be very much appreciated!'

–

Once again, Logan could feel the eyes on him as he sloshed water into the kettle and slammed it down into its base. The light on the handle turned an appropriately alarming shade of red when he forcefully flicked the switch.

'You all right, sir?' Sinead ventured.

Logan didn't look at her. Instead, he just gripped the edge of the countertop and kept his gaze locked on the kettle.

'Everyone keeps asking me that. Aye. I'm fine,' he said.

Hamza walked one way across the hall's large kitchen, looking for something. When he caught a snippet of the ongoing conversation, he turned, put his hands on his hips, blew out his cheeks, raised a finger, mumbled something about checking next door, and then went hurrying out.

It was, Logan thought, just about the most awkward five seconds of his life.

'It's just...' Sinead stole a glance at the open door. 'DCI McCulloch is—'

'He's right,' Logan said, cutting her short. 'I'm not in charge. I'm here to assist, that's all. I'm not running the show, he is.'

'No, I know, but...' The detective constable looked him up and down, just quickly, like she was checking it was still him. 'The way he was talking to you, sir.'

'I'm fine, Sinead,' Logan stressed. Behind him, the kettle started to roll towards the boil.

'Yes, sir, but—'

'Just don't, all right?' The words snapped out of him, a whip crack in the air between them. 'Let it go. McCulloch's in charge. That's the end of it.'

Something flitted across Sinead's face, then was gone. Hurt, maybe. Disappointment.

Pity, even.

'Right you are, sir.'

She caught the end of the kitchen's last remaining table and started to drag it towards the door. Logan moved to help her, but a shake of a head, and a curt, 'I've got it', stopped him dead.

Taggart went trotting out after her, tail wagging, leaving Logan with only his regret and the rumbling of the kettle for company.

—

DCI McCulloch was a slurper. He eyed Logan over the rim of his mug as he noisily sucked up a mouthful of steaming hot tea, swirled the stuff around in his mouth for a few seconds, then swallowed it down.

The smacking of his lips and the appreciative, 'Aaah,' felt, to Jack, like the twisting of a knife.

'That's not a bad cup of tea that, Jack,' McCulloch declared. He raised his mug, as if offering up a toast. 'You've a real knack for it.'

Logan took a gulp from his own mug, if only to stop himself saying anything. It tasted thin and watery. Sour, even, like the taste had been tainted by his emotional state.

The hall, mostly down to Sinead and Hamza, had been transformed into, if not an actual Incident Room, then a close approximation of one.

Four tables had been arranged in the shape of a cross in the centre of the room, with a square gap left where the narrow ends didn't quite meet. A chair had been placed at each makeshift desk, and while the tables were a little too high, they would do the job.

The hall had two big rolling whiteboards tucked away in a big cupboard just off the main hallway. They were covered in scribbled training instructions for some sort of fitness class. The writing had been on there for so long that it took a bucket of hot water and a lot of elbow grease to wipe it away.

Logan had offered to help, but Sinead and Hamza had assured him they had it under control.

Instead, he'd gone around and closed the blinds over the windows, preventing anyone outside peeking in. He wasn't sure about the locals, but he knew for a fact that, as soon as the journalists started to turn up, an uncovered window would be considered fair game.

Throughout this, McCulloch sat on his seat on the fold-out stage, like an old king in a storybook watching over his loyal subjects.

It was only when the last blind was drawn that McCulloch got up from his seat, marched to the closest of the two whiteboards, and snatched up one of the marker pens.

His height meant his shoulders were level with the uppermost part of the whiteboard's frame, and his arms jerked and swooped as he wrote across the top in heavy block capitals, reciting the name aloud as he did.

'John-ny Free-stone,' he said, dragging out the syllables so he finished speaking and writing at the same time. He stabbed a full stop at the end of the name, clicked the lid back on the pen, then turned to address all three detectives and the largely disinterested dog.

'Our *victim*, and I use that term loosely until we have more inform-ation to go on. Not his real name, of course, that's—'

A knock on the hall door forced him to cut the sentence short. He sighed impatiently, and shot Logan a look that said he should go and see who was there.

The door opened before anyone could move, and the head of DC Tyler Neish appeared warily through the gap. His eyes were ringed with red, and his cheeks had just the faintest suggestion of green to them.

'Detective Constable Neish?' McCulloch ran his tongue across his teeth, then tutted loudly. 'I assume you are some sort of apparition, given that I gave you an order to return to Inverness?'

'Eh, aye, boss. I mean, sir. I mean, no, sir, I'm not a… ghost, or that. There was, eh, there was an accident.'

Sinead was the first to react, sitting upright in her seat, one hand flying to her mouth. 'Oh, God. What happened? Are you all right? Is Dave all right?'

Tyler scratched at the back of his head and tried, without much success, to smile. 'Eh, aye. No. It, uh, it wasn't that sort of accident. Dave's fine, he's just a bit…' The detective constable swallowed. 'Vomity. Quite a lot vomity, actually. He's mostly vomity, in fact.'

McCulloch's eyebrows bumped heads, as he tried to figure out what this meant.

'What are you saying? He's ill?'

'Dave? No. Well, aye. Not originally, though.'

'He threw up,' Logan explained. He could speak fluent Tyler by this point, and though he didn't want to imagine the events that must have transpired in Dave's car, he was having a hard time not doing so. 'He threw up in the car. On Dave.'

Tyler nodded and mustered a grateful look. 'That's right, boss. All over Dave. All over the car. And then, well, the smell was pretty bad, so Dave then—'

'Yes, yes, thank you, Detective Constable,' McCulloch said, holding up a hand for silence. 'I'm sure we can picture the rest.'

Tyler groaned. 'I wouldn't recommend it, sir. But, it was decided by Dave, um, by Detective Constable Davidson, I mean, that I should get out of the car and walk back, and I was in agreement.'

'Yes. I bet you were,' McCulloch said. 'Well, I'm sure we can find alternative transport for you.'

The hint of green in Tyler's face became a full-blown tinge. His mouth opened wide, either in shock, or because he was about to throw up again.

'We could use him here,' Logan said, coming to the younger officer's aid.

It was McCulloch's turn to look surprised. 'Here? Whatever for?'

The tone was incredulous, as if Logan had just said something so patently ridiculous it was worthy only of ridicule.

'To help with the investigation,' Logan said, standing his ground. 'DC Neish is a good officer. I've a feeling we're going to need him on this.'

McCulloch looked Tyler up and down. As the only part of the DC that was currently visible was his head, this didn't take long.

'Well, God help us, if that's the case,' he muttered. He considered Logan for a few long, uncomfortable moments. 'You do seem to like your waifs and strays, Jack,' he finally declared, then he granted permission with the swooping of a hand. 'Very well, Detective Constable Neish, you can stay. But, like the dog, you will be DCI Logan's responsibility. And, also like the dog, I don't want you getting under anyone's feet.'

'No bother, sir. Cheers for that,' Tyler said, brightening a little. He looked down at himself, hidden behind the hall's swing door. 'But, eh, I think it might be in everyone's best interests if I go get cleaned up a bit first.'

Chapter 11

At the peak of his career, back in the late Eighties, Johnny Freestone had been one of the biggest stars on the planet. He had sold out Wembley Stadium, entertained millions with his world tours, gone multi-platinum with his second album, and even made an appearance on *Sesame Street*, where he'd taught Oscar the Grouch how to turn his trash can into a drum kit, and openly flirted with Elmo.

He had dated supermodels, performed at presidential inaugurations, graced the covers of magazines and newspapers across the globe, and been blamed by Pope John Paul the Second for the ongoing downfall of Western society.

He'd had a string of top ten singles both in the UK and abroad, topping the Billboard charts in the US, though never quite hitting the number one spot in the UK. His fourth single, 'Slippery Love', had come closest. It had peaked at number two, and stayed there for seven weeks, blocked from the top spot by Yazz and the Plastic Population's 'The Only Way Is Up', and 'Nothing's Gonna Change My Love for You', by Glenn Medeiros.

A year later, Freestone allegedly headbutted Medeiros in the toilets at the 1989 MTV Music Awards, and had been charged with aggravated assault. Things had spiralled for him after that, and he'd spent the next few years going in and out of various expensive rehab clinics.

None of this came as news to Logan. He had been eight years old when Freestone burst onto the scene with his explosion of blond hair, his leather jacket, and sticking-plastered fingers that flew across the frets of his ever-changing roster of elaborate guitars, pulling sounds from them that had never been heard before. Certainly not around the east end of Glasgow, anyway.

He wore cowboy boots and top hats, had earrings in not just one but *both* ears, and seemed possessed by the unshakeable conviction that he wasn't just better than the people around him, but was of an entirely different higher species.

He'd told Michael Aspel to stick his big red book up his arse when presented with it on a never-aired episode of *This is Your Life*. He'd thrown dog shit at Rick Astley, repeatedly spat on the cast of *Neighbours* during an episode of Saturday morning kids' show, *Going Live*, and—in what would later turn out to be an acutely accurate accusation—had called Jimmy Savile a kiddie-fiddler on *Top of the Pops*.

The then nine-year-old Jack Logan had loved him—no, been obsessed with him—not just for all this, but because he'd done it all while being unashamedly and unapologetically Scottish.

But, while Logan was well-versed in the life and career of Johnny Freestone, the same could not be said for his colleagues.

'What do you mean you've never heard of him?' Jack demanded, rounding on Tyler and Sinead like he was about to give them both a dose of the Glenn Medeiros treatment.

The husband and wife team exchanged sideways glances, as if each egging the other to be the first to reply.

It was Tyler who finally broke.

'Just… *that*, boss. We've never heard of him.'

'Johnny Freestone?' Logan stared at them both in turn. '*Johnny Freestone.*'

'It doesn't matter how many times you say it, boss,' Tyler replied. 'We don't know who he is.'

'"Slippery Love"! "Lord of the Morning After"! "Freestone Rollin'"!'

'Oh!' Sinead perked up at that. 'The Rolling Stones, you mean? Was he in that?'

Logan recoiled like he'd been slapped. 'The Rolling… No! They bloody wish.' He stuck out a thumb and began counting off some of Freestone's better-known hits on his fingers. '"How Can I Miss You If You Won't Leave?" "Can't Cage the Wild". "Thunder and Rain"? No? None of these ringing a bell?'

'You're just saying words at us, boss. It's not helping,' Tyler protested.

'"Take Me to the Edge Then Push Me Over"?' Logan all but gasped.

'Is that another song, sir?' Sinead asked. 'Or a cry for help?'

'Jesus!' Logan threw his arms into the air in frustration, then turned and shot a pleading look to DS Khaled. 'Hamza! Come on! You've heard of him.'

Hamza, who was half-sitting on one of the tables, nodded. 'Oh aye, sir. I've heard of him. He was into big rock ballad-type stuff, wasn't he?'

'Yes! Thank you!'

'He did that song from the Robin Hood film, didn't he? Number one for ages.'

Logan practically choked on his response. 'What? No! That was what's his face?'

'Bryan Adams,' Sinead ventured.

'Oh, I've heard of him!' Tyler chimed in. 'Did he not do "Summer of '69"? Good song that.'

Sinead and Hamza both mumbled their agreement, before Logan shouted them down. 'No, it isn't. It's a shite song. "Love is a Loaded Gun". Now *that* is a good song.'

'Never heard of it,' Tyler said, taking his life in his hands.

Beside him, Sinead had taken out her phone and was studying the screen. 'Says it came out in 1988.'

'Ah. That'll be it, then, boss. I wasn't born until 1999.'

This seemed to Logan like it couldn't possibly be correct. In his head, the 1980s were about ten years ago. Fifteen at a push. Which would make Tyler around five years old.

When his mental arithmetic finally caught up, Logan felt older than he ever had in his life.

'That's not the point,' he said, weakly. 'You've heard of Bryan Adams. You've heard of The Beatles.' A thought worried him. 'You have heard of The Beatles?'

'Course I've heard of The Beatles, boss. Everyone's heard of The Beatles. But that's because The Beatles were famous. Johnny... Firestorm, or whatever, couldn't have been.'

'Freestone! And aye, he was!'

It was the sharp, sudden clearing of McCulloch's throat that curtailed the argument before it could go any further.

'I think we get the point,' he intoned from his seat on the stage, casting his gaze across the others like a headteacher with an unruly class. 'Perhaps we can steer ourselves back on topic?'

Logan wanted to keep arguing, to keep going until Tyler and the others admitted that, yes, Johnny Freestone had been a legend, actually, and they were wrong.

But, on this occasion, he was prepared to be the bigger man. He chewed up and swallowed down his outrage, then tipped his head in McCulloch's direction.

'Aye. Sorry.'

McCulloch waited, an eyebrow arched, his whole body poised, *just so*, while he waited for Jack to say more.

He wanted to hear 'sir', coming out of Logan's mouth. Jack couldn't do it, though. He wouldn't. He might not be quite himself right now, but he wasn't *that*, either.

He added a curt, 'DCI McCulloch', as a sort of compromise, then turned back to the board, where Sinead had begun to write and stick the information they'd pulled together.

'Right. So, as I was saying,' she said, shooting warning looks to both Logan and Tyler, 'Mr Freestone's real name is Jonathan Cairns. He was born in Inverness in 1963, brought up here in Durness until he moved away in 1981 to pursue his music career.'

She flipped over a page of the printout she'd pulled together from various online sources, and skimmed through the highlights.

'Married four times. First wife died of cancer in 1991, other three lasted from a few weeks to a few years before filing for divorce. Two live in the US, one in Australia. No kids.'

'Bet one of the wives did it,' Tyler said. 'Tenner on it.'

He looked around to see if anyone was taking the wager, but nobody did.

'Does he live here now?' Hamza asked, before wincing at his choice of words. 'I mean, not *now*, obviously, but until recently? Did he move back?'

'Not according to Wikipedia.' Sinead flipped back a page. 'He's got a house in Malibu, a flat in London and a place just outside Edinburgh.'

'Bloody hell. He must've been minted,' Tyler remarked. 'I mean, have you seen the prices in Edinburgh?'

'He would've been minted, aye,' Logan crowed, seizing on the remark like it was some admission of defeat by the younger detective. 'Because he was a global superstar.'

'What was he doing here, then?' Hamza asked, doing his best to keep the conversation on track. 'Just visiting home, or…?'

'There was some talk on Reddit of him coming here to work on a new album or launch a comeback tour, but I couldn't find anything concrete about it anywhere,' said Sinead.

'That fella, with the limp,' Logan began. 'He said he was his cousin. We should talk to him. He might be able to fill us in.'

'Makes sense,' Hamza agreed. 'Do you want me to go talk to him, or should we bring him in? We can set up an interview room through next door.'

Up on the stage, McCulloch cleared his throat again. This one was louder, and even more protracted than the last time. It barked and echoed around the hall, continuing until long after everyone else had fallen silent.

'I'm sure I don't need to remind you, Detective Sergeant, that Mr Logan is not the lead officer on this investigation, and therefore has no authority to decide on our next course of action,' the DCI said. 'I do agree that Mr Freestone's cousin should be spoken to in due course, but until such times as we hear from pathology'—he tapped his watch and glowered at Logan, like the lack of report from Shona Maguire was somehow his fault—'I think it's best that we hold off.

'Instead, I believe our first port of call should be the couple who found the body this morning. Getting their insight will help us build a more coherent picture of events, don't you think?'

It was a rhetorical question, and nobody bothered to answer. McCulloch's mind had already been made up, and there'd be no dissuading him.

And, besides, much as they all hated to admit it, it was a sensible approach.

'I'll get on that then, sir,' Hamza said, but McCulloch stopped him with a raised hand, and a sharp, 'At-at-at!'

The DCI ran a finger and thumb down either side of his mouth, like he was wiping away crumbs. He tapped a skeletal finger on his chin a few times, then nodded, his decision made.

'It would be good if DCI Logan could make himself useful on this one,' McCulloch declared. 'And, while he's at it, he can take that drooling, glaikit-looking creature of his along with him.'

His eyes sparkled with amusement as he turned to DC Neish. A smile tugged at the corner of McCulloch's chapped lips.

'And, ah, what the heck? Maybe best to bring the dog along, too.'

Chapter 12

The front door of the village hall closed with a *bang*, as Logan and Tyler left the building.

'You're not going to grass me up if I call McCulloch an arsehole, are you, boss?'

Logan shook his head as Tyler fell into step beside him. 'I'll think less of you if you don't.'

'That's good. Because he is. He's an arsehole of the highest order,' Tyler said, though he kept his voice low and glanced back at the hall in case the windows were open. 'He's a whole new previously undiscovered species of arsehole, in fact. David Attenborough could do a documentary on him, just called, "Check Out this Arsehole".'

'Aye,' Logan agreed, but Tyler wasn't done yet.

'It'd just be footage of him going about his business, and Attenborough'd be whispering, "Look at him. Look at this absolute arsehole."'

Logan felt the programme was unlikely to earn the same sort of attention or accolades as some of Attenborough's other works—it was no *Blue Planet*—but Tyler was on a roll, and clearly needed to get things off his chest, so he didn't bother to say as much.

Instead, he unclipped Taggart from the lead, and let the dog trot off to sniff around the hall's tidy little garden.

'Anyway. Cheers for sticking up for me in there, boss. No way I could've faced going back down the road yet.' Tyler shot another look back at the hall, though didn't bother to lower his voice this time. 'Think he just wants rid of me, anyway. I don't think he likes me.'

Logan's reply was a shrug and a grunt. It was patently clear that, no, McCulloch didn't like the detective constable, but Jack didn't think Tyler really needed to hear that right now. Projectile vomiting all over the inside of Dave Davidson's car had probably dented his ego enough for one day.

'And it was good to see you standing up to him,' Tyler added. There was a wariness to the words, like he was feeling his way across a landscape dotted with mines. 'Being a bit more like your old self, I mean.'

Logan offered no response. They walked on in silence, but Tyler's inability to keep his mouth shut for more than a few seconds at a time soon put paid to that.

'So, you were a fan of Johnny Freestone, boss?' he ventured.

'Back in the day, aye,' Logan confirmed.

'That's crazy.'

Jack squinted at him. 'Why's that crazy?'

'Just, you know, *you*. Being a *fan* of something. Actually liking something. Properly being into something, I mean.' He blew out his cheeks. 'I can't get my head around it.'

'What do you mean? I like stuff,' Logan protested. 'I like plenty of stuff.'

'Do you?' Tyler's surprise was evident both in his voice and on his face. 'I thought tolerating stuff was about as far as you got.' He mimed a three-tier scale, raising his hand higher each time. 'Despise, indifferent, tolerate. I thought that was the three levels you had.'

Logan's boot scuffed on the pockmarked road surface as he stopped and looked at the younger detective. He opened his mouth to object, but then thought better of it.

'I mean, you're not far off, I suppose. I was only eight—it's no' like I've still got my posters of him up on the wall, or anything—but Freestone was something special. Larger than life. A proper living legend, you know?'

'Wait! Back up!' Tyler spluttered. 'You had posters? *You* had posters? Of another human being? *You?*'

'Like I said, I was eight,' Logan shot back. He slipped a finger in between his neck and the collar of his shirt, and tugged on it, like he was suddenly feeling a rush of heat. 'And they were only wee, out of a magazine.'

'Bloody hell. I'm seeing you in a whole new light here, boss,' Tyler declared, and the big beamer of a smile on his face said he was very much enjoying that fact. 'Did you have the long hair and leather jacket, and that?'

'No,' Logan was quick to reply. His eyes narrowed. 'And if you don't know who he was, how'd you know what he looked like?'

'He was an Eighties rock star, boss. What else was he going to be wearing? A pair of flares and a cardigan?'

Logan picked up the pace as if he could separate himself from this conversation by outrunning it. Tyler's grin only widened as he trotted to keep up.

'Were you more of a double denim guy, boss?'

'Shut up!'

They reached the end of the car park, where it narrowed into the driveway that connected at the bottom with the single-track road. Police vehicles were still knotted together at the top of the cave path. Cars and caravans slowed and indicated at the approach to it, only to be flagged down and sent on their way by a Uniformed constable who, even from this distance, seemed sick fed up of it.

'Sorry, boss,' Tyler said, wiping the smile from his face as best he could. 'Did you ever go see him live, or anything?'

Logan sighed, hesitant to give the detective constable any more ammunition.

'Aye. Once,' he begrudgingly admitted. 'Years later, though. He was doing a gig in Glasgow. King Tut's. Not a big place. Far cry from his days filling Wembley. Couple of hundred people there.'

He gazed off into the distance, as if the past was playing out there, and he might be able to catch a glimpse of it, just beyond the horizon.

'Must've been about… what?' Logan ran the numbers. '2007? Thereabouts. He was older, of course. Hair was shorter. He ended up in rehab a few weeks later, I think. He was certainly pissed and on something that night, anyway. He was overweight, breathless. Could barely make it through half of his songs, and the ones he could were off-key.'

'Oof. Must have been disappointing.'

'What? No. It was one of the best nights of my life.'

Logan blinked, coming out of a trance. He shoved his hands deep in his coat pockets, and glanced at Tyler's pocket where he knew his notepad would be.

'This couple, then. What's the address?'

'Oh. Aye. One sec. Sinead wrote it down for us.'

Tyler took the pad from his pocket, licked a finger, then swiped hurriedly through the pages. Somewhere near the middle of the book, he stopped and rapped a knuckle on the paper.

'Here we go. Elsie and Reginald Kellerman.' Tyler frowned, flipped a page, then turned back. 'It just says their address is "Number sixty-three". Doesn't give a street. Maybe she forgot to write it down.' He ran a hand down his face, groaning. 'God, does that mean we have to go back in?'

'Number sixty-three?'

Logan about-turned so he was facing back in the direction of the village hall. Between them and the building's front door, parked just off on the left, was the converted box van he'd seen earlier, with the fold-out steps and the door in the side. The faded golden numbers on the side glinted in the sunshine.

He raised a hand and pointed, like an accuser at a trial.

'Found them!'

Chapter 13

The box van's steps were in the folded-up position, which suggested that nobody was home. Logan knocked anyway—not quite his usual hammering polis knock that urged whoever was inside to get their arse to the door, sharpish—but something a few notches down from it.

It was a knock that asked for attention, not demanded it. It was a knock that asked politely to be let in, and didn't threaten to kick the door down if it wasn't.

Tyler noticed, but said nothing.

There was a sound from inside. Several of them, in fact, in quite short succession. The first was a thump, like something had been dropped. It was followed by a creak, then some whispering, too quiet for the detectives to be able to hear, even through the relatively thin walls of the van.

The couple was inside, all right. They were just trying very hard to make it seem like they weren't.

Logan thought he caught a few words of the whispered conversation. 'Idiot', jumped out at him. 'What were you thinking?' 'Shouldn't have done it.' Everything else was too low to pick up.

Tyler, a step further back, heard none of these details, and since it didn't appear that Jack was going to do so, he stepped forward, raised a clenched fist, and thumped four times on the door.

'Mr and Mrs Kellerman? It's the police. We'd like a word,' he said in what, if he'd been forced to describe it, he would have called his "big boy voice".

It was a decent attempt, too, Logan had to admit. Deep, commanding, authoritative—or, in other words, nothing like the detective constable's normal voice at all.

'Where the hell did that come from?' Logan asked.

Tyler winked at him. 'Learned from the best, boss,' he said. He smirked, then looked ahead at the door as the sound of footsteps approached from the other side. 'DCI McCulloch, I mean. He's been giving me lessons.'

Logan snorted at the very thought of McCulloch willingly imparting any advice to anyone, let alone Tyler. Besides, the bastard had probably never knocked on a door in his life. He most likely just turned into a bat and slipped in through the letterbox.

The door opened, just a crack, just a creak. Reginald and Elsie Kellerman, the old couple who'd been causing most of the trouble in the hall, peered down at the detectives, their faces hooded by shadow.

A security chain was fastened across the gap of the door. Given the height of the van, and the fact the steps were still raised, the chain seemed like overkill. If anyone wanted to burst in on them, they'd have several seconds of awkward clambering ahead of them.

'We've spoken to the police already,' Elsie said. She still wore the same migraine-inducing knitted cardigan she'd had on back in the hall. She'd added to the look now with a tweed flat cap and a pair of brown leather driving gloves.

The cardie, however, remained the star of the show.

'She's right. We told them everything.'

Her husband was taller. Standing behind her, even from this low angle, he rose a full head above her, hanging over her like the spectre of death.

'We've got nothing more to say,' Elsie insisted.

She began to close the door. Despite the vague, not-quite-there stupor he was in, Logan instinctively placed a hand on the wood, stopping her from shutting them out.

'We appreciate that. But we have a few more questions. You can either give us five minutes of your time and let us in, or you can come with us down to the station in Inverness for a lengthier chat with a solicitor present.' He shrugged to make clear he had no real preference which one they opted for. 'Your choice.'

A look passed between the couple, although it had to go through the top of Elsie's head to get there.

She huffed out a sigh and tutted to make it clear how *bloody ridiculous* this was, then said, 'Fine! But the dog stays out there!'

Logan removed his hand from the door, letting her close it. There was a rattling of metal as the chain was undone, then the door sprung wide, revealing only Reginald.

'Back up. Both of you,' he instructed. When the detectives didn't immediately comply, he rolled his eyes and gripped his forehead like they were giving him a blinding headache. 'Unless you want your kneecaps shattered, you'll back up.'

'Is that a threat, sir?' Tyler asked, before Logan nudged him back a pace.

Reg stamped a foot. There was a loud, jangling clank as the metal steps fell into position just a few inches from where Logan had retreated to.

Up in the van, Reg raised an index finger and pointed to them both in turn. 'Five minutes. That's what you said,' he reminded them, then he shuffled aside to let them in.

Logan looped Taggart's lead around the step, then clipped him to it. The dog cocked his head expectantly, then got stuck into the handful of treats Jack produced from his pocket.

With Taggart occupied, Logan led the way inside, and the whole van seemed to tilt on its axles as the steps took his weight. It was a full-height door, but the same couldn't be said for the ceiling of the room beyond it.

And it *was* a room. Stepping into the van was like entering the living room of a house from the late Seventies. Wallpaper patterned with flocked brown leaves and flowers covered the van's walls. A carpet riddled with the same greens and blues of the zigzags in Elsie's cardigan was spread over the floor.

A two-seater couch filled much of the space. It was an ancient, tired-looking thing, with a base colour that had probably once been milky white, but which had long ago curdled into cream.

Most of it was covered with an autumnal pattern of leaves and root vegetables in shades of orange and brown. A swirl of dark wood on the front of each arm set the whole thing off.

A low coffee table—also dark wood, with two lace doilies for coasters and another larger one sitting like a spider's web in the middle—squatted in front of the couch. It was angled to one side so as to leave a clear path to a narrow door up the back. Presumably a bedroom or bathroom.

There were no photographs on the walls, or on the mantle above the small gas heater that was currently switched off. Instead, they were decorated with cheap paintings in scratchy plastic frames, of horses, and landscapes, and landscapes filled with horses.

There were no windows inside the box compartment, besides the three small ones at the top of the door, which were covered by a roll-down blind. The only light came from what, at first glance, looked to be an old ornate gas lamp on a nest of tables in the corner. Upon closer inspection, though, you could see the electrical cable running out of the back of it.

Probably just as well. Now that Reg had closed the door behind the detectives, the whole place felt worryingly airtight. And, though it felt a little chilly in the van, Logan was relieved the gas fire wasn't on.

It wasn't just the temperature that was cold, though. The atmosphere was bordering on the Baltic.

'Nice place,' Logan said, trying to warm things up a bit. 'Nice wee caravan this.'

'It's not a *caravan*,' Elsie all but spat at him. 'It's a mobile home.'

'Gypsies live in caravans!' Reg added, matching his wife's outrage and then raising her a decibel or two. 'Do we look like bloody gypsies to you?'

And that was the end of that. There were no offers of tea, no chit-chat or small talk. Rather than helping to thaw the atmosphere, Logan had only chilled it further.

Reg and Elsie both sat on the couch—the only seats available—and crossed their legs in unison. It was a united front, although they were jammed up close to the sofa's arms, as far apart as they could possibly be on the small two-seater. It made the gap between them seem more like a gulf.

The couple's faces were matching masks of impatience. Their feet tapped in near-perfect synchronisation.

'Well?' Elsie demanded. 'What do you want to ask us?'

'Is it about Declan?'

Logan frowned. 'Sorry, Declan...?'

'Declan Sinclair. The young lad with the red hair at the meeting. We saw him talking to Jonathan yesterday, didn't we, Reg?'

'We did,' Reg confirmed. 'Chatting away they were. Outside the shop. We mentioned it to the police. Seemed a bit odd, if you ask us.'

'No. It, eh, it wasn't about that,' Tyler said. 'But thanks, we'll look into it.'

'Well? What was it, then?' Elsie demanded.

Tyler looked to Logan, expecting the DCI to take the lead. Instead, Jack just raised his eyebrows and tilted his head. Which was no mean feat, given that he was having to duck to avoid stoating if off the ceiling.

'Eh, aye. OK,' Tyler said. He cleared his throat and looked at his notebook, like he might find a list of questions there. When he didn't, he went for the catch-all approach. 'Can you tell us what happened?'

'What, all of it?' Elsie cried.

'If you could.'

'Oh, for God's...' She shook her head, shot her husband a look that suggested this was somehow all his fault, then folded her arms. 'We went for a walk to the cave. It's our favourite route. We have to head out early, of course, before the bloody tourists arrive and spoil it. They're everywhere that lot. Like locusts. Ruining everything. Blocking the roads, littering everywhere, doing their *dirty business* on the verges. Some of these laybys are all beer cans, crisp bags and shitty nappies. Disgusting is what it is. Vermin, the bloody lot of them. Absolute vermin.'

'Right. Aye,' Tyler said. He clung to the one aspect of the conversation he was interested in. 'And by early, that was around...?'

'Six thirty. That's when we set off. We were at the cave around seven. We had our breakfast—'

'Hard-boiled egg and a yoghurt,' Reg interjected, which drew the ire of his wife.

'Do you think they care? Do you think that matters?' she snapped. 'Why don't you tell him how long you boiled it for, while you're at it?'

'Six minutes and—'

'Oh, for goodness' sake! I didn't mean actually tell them!' She turned to Tyler. 'I'm sorry about him. He's a bloody idiot sometimes.'

'It's fine,' Tyler assured her. He offered Reg a supportive smile, but it fizzled out against a wall of cool hostility. 'So you had breakfast at seven?'

'No, we had breakfast at seven fifteen,' Elsie barked back at him. 'That's what I was saying before he started going on about his eggs. We had breakfast at seven fifteen, packed up by seven thirty, and then we... explored the cave a little.'

It was Logan who picked up on the hesitation. Who saw the slight dipping of Reginald's eyebrows, and the glance he shot in his wife's direction.

'Explored?' Logan said, cutting in before Tyler could continue. 'I thought you said it was a regular haunt?'

There was, just for a moment, a flash of something on Reg's face. A widening of his eyes. A downturn of his mouth. All tiny movements, but Logan had been watching for them.

'It is,' Elsie insisted. 'But today we decided to venture a little further than normal.'

'Right.' Logan stooped a little further so he could angle his head in the opposite direction, saving his neck from freezing in that one position. 'Why?'

'I'm sorry?'

'Why did you decide to do something different today?'

Reg glanced at Elsie. His gaze lingered there, just for a moment, and Logan got the impression he was waiting for the answer to that question, too.

'Just, I don't know, for a change. Because I fancied it.'

'Because *you* fancied it?' Logan said, seizing on the word. 'So, it was your idea to go further?'

Elsie shifted on the sofa, compressing the cushion beneath her. 'Well, I mean—'

'It was a joint decision,' Reg said. 'We both thought it would make a nice change to go take a look at the waterfall. It's been years since we saw it.'

He reached across and patted his wife on the knee. She didn't react to it, or even seem to notice. Both the gesture, and the words that had come tumbling out of Reg's mouth, felt false, but Logan just nodded and shuffled back again, letting Tyler carry on.

'So, you went for a walk into the cave, and that's when you found the body?'

'Yes. Exactly,' Elsie said. 'He was lying down in a sort of, I don't know, pit? Hole? We assumed he'd fallen. We couldn't get down to him, so after shouting a few times, Reg returned to the surface to call for help.'

'No signal in the cave,' Reg added. 'The rock blocks the—'

'I'm sure they know how it works,' Elsie said.

'So, you found the body around seven thirty, and then you called the police?'

'No,' the couple both said in unison.

Tyler's gaze shifted between them. 'To which one?'

'Yes to the time, no to the police,' Elsie clarified.

'We called Dougie,' Reg added.

Tyler once again consulted his notebook, despite knowing full well he wouldn't find anything helpful there.

'Um, Dougie?'

'Dougie Cairns,' Reg said, with an emphasis that suggested this explained everything. When it became clear that it didn't, he sighed. 'John's cousin?'

Tyler blinked. 'John?'

'The dead man!' Elsie cried. 'What other John would we be talking about, man?'

'Why call him?' Logan asked. 'Why not nine-nine-nine?'

'Do you have any idea how long it takes police to get out here?' Elsie asked. 'A long time. Now, maybe that would've been different because a... a... *pop star* was involved, but we had things to do. We weren't hanging around to find out.'

'Dougie's his cousin,' Reg reiterated.

'So John's his problem, not ours,' Elsie added. 'We called him, and he came down to meet us. And, well...'

She stopped talking and bit down hard on her lip, like she was too afraid to let herself keep talking.

'And what?' Tyler urged.

'Nothing.'

Logan adjusted his head in the opposite direction again, and rubbed the back of his neck. 'Mrs Kellerman, if you have information that could be of use...'

'He just... I don't know. I'm probably wrong,' Elsie said. 'Though, I don't think I am.'

'About what?' Logan pressed.

Elsie shot her husband a look. Logan thought, for just a moment, he saw Reg give a near imperceptible shake of his head. His wife pressed on, regardless.

'Dougie,' she said, interlocking her fingers and squeezing her hands together. 'When we told him what we'd found, about John. Well, I could be wrong, like I said.'

She took a breath, then leaned in closer, like she didn't want to risk anyone outside the van hearing her.

'But he didn't strike me as being the least bit surprised.'

Chapter 14

Detective Constable Dave Davidson had never been in the mortuary before. Not the proper bit, through the back, where the action happened.

He was not relishing the prospect.

The doors to the mortuary's front office were awkward and heavy for a man in a wheelchair. The automatic closing system fought against him, constantly trying to shove him backwards, like he wasn't welcome here. Like he didn't belong.

It took three attempts and a muttered, 'Right, ya bastards,' before he was able to overcome the obstacle and enter the office-cum-laboratory on the other side. The doors swung heavily closed behind him with a thump, and he took a moment to twist in his chair and fire a two-finger victory salute at them.

Shona Maguire was not in the office. The lights were on, and an active computer monitor suggested she couldn't be far away.

Dave wasn't quite sure what to do. All of this was new to him. He'd enjoyed a perfectly pleasant career as a Uniformed officer—losing the use of his legs not included—and had never had any great interest in becoming a detective.

But he'd been stuck behind a desk for too long, and while he enjoyed not having to go out in the rain, or to deal with drunken arseholes on a Saturday night, he was starting to wonder if filling in forms and tagging evidence was all he had to give.

He didn't think so. He was sure there was more.

Well, not sure. Hopeful, perhaps.

And then Detective Superintendent Mitchell had pulled him aside one day and offered him the chance to find out.

He'd said yes, assuming he'd be working under DCI Logan. Had he known that DCI McCulloch would be in charge—a man who seemed to consider him both an inconvenience and a liability—he'd have stuck where he was.

Where he was *now* was out of his depth. And treading water wasn't easy for a man in a wheelchair.

Dave was just contemplating whether he should call someone when he heard the rasping of a saw. Back, forth, back, forth—a ragged blade cutting into something he didn't really want to think about.

The sound affected him on some deep, primal level. Most of him either tightened, constricted, or puckered up as the saw's jagged teeth tore through something that managed to sound both liquid and solid at the same time.

'Hello!' he called, putting some real welly into it to try and drown out the sound coming from through the back. 'It's, eh, it's Dave! It's Dave Davidson!'

The sawing continued.

'Shit,' Dave muttered.

He tried shouting again, even louder this time, but with the same lack of result.

Turning in his chair, he considered the doors that he'd recently wrestled his way through. Exiting, he thought, would be even more problematic than entering had been.

And besides, he was here for a reason. He was here to do a job.

With one big push, he rolled himself over to the inner doors. The sound of sawing became even louder. Here, though, between the rasps, he could pick out the faint *tss-tss-tss* of music playing quietly through a speaker.

He knocked—thumped, really—on one of the swing doors with enough force to nudge it inwards an inch or two.

'Hello! It's Dave!' he called again, really belting it out this time.

The sawing stopped. He heard the clank of metal on metal as the tool was set down.

Dave wheeled back from the doors just in time for one to swing open, revealing something from the final act of a horror movie. Shona Maguire stood in full protective gear—plastic apron, rubber gloves, shoe protectors and a transparent visor pulled down over her face.

Or, mostly transparent, anyway. Flecks of blood dotted it. Similar dark red smears covered the apron and the fingers of the gloves. Despite all this gore, Shona beamed brightly at him from behind the mask.

'David! Hello! They said you were coming!'

'Eh, aye,' Dave said. His eyes darted to the cold, cavernous room behind her. 'Sorry I'm a bit late. I had to go home and get cleaned up.'

Shona winced. 'I heard. Jack texted me. Tyler?'

'Very much Tyler,' Dave confirmed.

'How's the car?'

'Smelly. And damp. But mostly smelly.'

He took a deep breath, then looked past her again. He didn't want to look—he didn't want to know what was going on in there in any more detail than he had to—but the mortuary was a siren, drawing him in.

'I'm, eh, I'm supposed to come in and… see what's what,' he said.

Shona nodded. 'So I hear. And that's, you know, it's fine, obviously.' She smiled at him again. It was smaller this time, thinner, yet somehow more sincere. 'You don't have to, though. It's not for everyone. There's no need.'

Dave shifted in his chair. He was a big man, well-built. He'd never been scared of much even before the accident. Now, though, after what he'd been through—after what he'd lost—he was fearless.

Or, so he'd thought.

'No, I better,' he said, though he wasn't happy about it. 'McCulloch insisted.'

'I bet he did,' Shona said. 'I get the impression he likes to dish out the dirty work and keep his own hands clean. I won't tell him, though. We can say you came in.'

It was tempting, Dave had to admit. He could go sit in the wee coffee shop out front, have a cup of tea and sausage roll, and wait for the pathologist to ping him with the results.

But, he was here for a reason.

He was here to do a job.

And, despite what his pulse rate was telling him, Dave Davidson was afraid of nothing.

'It's grand,' he told her. He raised both hands, fingers spread. 'Glove me up, and let's do this!'

Chapter 15

'Right, then, boss. What should we do?'

Tyler looked deliberately from the village hall on his left to the driveway leading away from it on the right. The sun was inching towards the horizon, painting the sky over the North Sea in fiery shades of orange and red.

When Logan didn't answer the question, Tyler offered some more encouragement.

'They did give us Dougie's address. We could just swing by and talk to him.'

Logan had followed the DC's gaze along the driveway, and seemed to have got himself lost somewhere beyond the blazing horizon. He gave himself a shake.

'It's not up to me. It's McCulloch's investigation. It's his decision.'

'Aw, come on, boss!' Tyler cried, then he lowered his voice to just above a whisper, worried they might be overheard. 'Better to ask for forgiveness than permission. You said that to me before. I think. More or less that, anyway. I might be paraphrasing. But that was the gist of it.'

He gestured to the front door of the hall. 'We go in there, and McCulloch'll just have some pointless shite for me to do. He only let me come and do the interview with them two because they'd already been spoken to. He was just getting me out of his way. But I can be useful, boss. I can do stuff!'

'I know you can,' Logan told him. His eyes drifted back down the hill, to the houses that now stood silhouetted against the flaming sky.

It would be easy to just head down there and talk to Freestone's cousin. Jack knew all the questions to ask, all the signs to look for, and all the weak spots to press his thumbs into. That stuff was ingrained. Automatic.

It wasn't far away, either. Elsie and Reg had given them directions. A five-minute saunter, if that. A few hundred yards. They could be there in no time.

It would all be so easy.

So why was his heart beating faster at the thought of it? And why was his shirt sticking to his back?

'It's not my decision,' he said. The words were muttered. Mumbled.

'It can be, though! OK, McCulloch's the SIO, but you're the *boss*, boss. You're still a DCI. You can decide.'

'I can't.'

'You can, boss! You totally can.'

Logan gritted his teeth. 'It's not that simple.'

'Aye, it is!' Tyler insisted. 'It's easy, you just have to—'

'*People died, Tyler!*'

The words tolled—the solemn clanging of a funeral bell that rang in the silence that followed.

Tyler stared, for once, saying nothing. Logan's breath caught. His chest tightened. The fire on the horizon blurred into a streak of glowing orange.

'All right? I made a decision, and people died!' The words choked him. Stuck in his throat. 'They died because I was distracted. Because I wasn't quick enough, wasn't smart enough. Because I'd let it all get too personal.'

DC Neish shook his head, slowly at first, but quickly picking up pace.

'Aye, but… No, boss. That's not fair. You couldn't have known. No one could. It wasn't your fault.'

Logan wasn't listening. He was back out there somewhere, trapped between the fire and the sky.

He'd thought about them every night since that day.

The armed unit.

The bomb.

The screaming.

God, the screaming.

'No?' Logan turned from the flames on the horizon. 'Then whose fault was it?'

The look he gave Tyler was pleading. Begging. Hoping the detective constable had an answer that would satisfy him. That would make the pain and the guilt all go away.

But Tyler had nothing to offer. And so, he just stood there, mute, as Logan marched over to the entrance of the village hall. Jack took a second or so to compose himself, then he hauled open the door, and surrendered to the gathering gloom inside.

–

Dave had no idea why Shona was looking at him like that. She was visibly concerned, leaning over him, waving a leaflet about genital herpes.

The breeze was nice. It felt cooling against the skelping hot heat of his cheeks.

He closed his eyes, letting the air cascade over him. In the darkness, broken fragments of memory squirmed around, slotting themselves back together to gradually reveal one awful, embarrassing whole.

In his defence, he hadn't been in a very good place to begin with, having recently spent almost three hours driving along windy roads with half a litre of vomit sloshing around in the passenger footwell, and the other half soaking through his clothes.

As baselines went, it wasn't a great starting point.

Had it not been for that, the smell in the operating theatre might not have bothered him too much. As it was, though, his gag reflex had been on a hair trigger since Tyler had opened fire just outside Durness, and the odours there in that room—sour, meaty, so thick they were almost viscous—had seemed all the more pungent.

The operating table had been a bit too high for him to see the body properly. Part of him had been relieved by this, given that getting an eyeful of a freshly cut-open corpse wasn't high on his list of priorities.

But, when Shona had tried to draw his attention to something, he'd stupidly gripped the edge of the table and hoisted himself up into a near standing position... where he'd stared straight into the open cavity of Johnny Freestone's chest, and the glossy, red and purple organs contained within.

Dave remembered the sharp, sudden shock of it, and the rush of prickly heat that had raced up his neck like thousands of tiny spiders wearing high heels.

He remembered the saliva that filled his mouth, and the taste of bile that followed.

And then...

And then...?

'You fainted,' Shona said, as if reading his mind. 'Landed in your chair, thankfully, so I wheeled you back out here.'

Dave's eyes snapped open. He felt heat racing up his face again, but this time, it was the hot sting of shame.

They were back in the outer office, safely away from the dead man beyond the swing doors.

'Don't worry, it's fine,' Shona told him. 'It's normal. Happens all the time.'

'Fainted?' Dave shook his head. 'I don't... That doesn't... I don't think...'

He groaned then, and ran a hand down his face. The rubber of the gloves surprised him, sticking to his sweaty forehead and almost tearing off his eyebrows on the way down.

'Well, that's embarrassing,' he eventually conceded.

'Ah, away with you,' Shona said. 'Sure, that's nothing. First PM I ever went to, I threw up, *then* fainted. And then wet myself, if I'm honest. Only lightly, mind, but still. Happens to the best of us.'

She smiled, stopped waving the STD leaflet, and backed up.

'And, you know, I'm just relieved you didn't die. I'd have had a hell of a job explaining that one.' Shona nodded to the door that led out into the hospital. 'Want to go get a coffee, or something?'

Dave did want to go get a coffee. He very much did. He'd love nothing more than to leave that place, with its smell, and all its wet, knobbly internal organs.

But now, more than ever, he had to prove that McCulloch was wrong, that the doors trying to keep him out were wrong, that even he, himself, was wrong.

He had to prove he belonged here.

'No. I'm fine. I can... I can go back in,' he said.

Shona laughed. It wasn't cruel, more like she assumed the detective constable was making a joke, and she was joining in with it.

'Ha! Yeah. Good one.' Her laughter died away into silence. 'Oh! You're serious? Right. OK. Well, no. I'm not sure that's a great idea.'

Dave sat up straighter in his seat, ignoring the throbbing headache that tried to push him right back down again.

'No, I should go in. I should do it. I, eh, I need to.'

Shona's smile faltered. She glanced over at the doors, and when she turned back to the detective constable, he could see she'd already made her mind up.

'Sorry, David. It's better if you don't. But here, if you want to make yourself useful...' Shona strode over to the printer and pulled a couple of sheets of paper from the tray, each one dense with graphs and text. 'You can give Sinead a call for me and fill her in on what we've got so far.'

Dave reluctantly accepted the pages the pathologist thrust towards him, and skimmed through them.

'I mean, I'd love to, but I don't have a clue what any of it means,' he told her.

'What?' Shona took the pages back, flicked from one to the other, then shook her head. 'No. Wrong thing. Christ, even I don't know what half of this stuff is.'

She looked around the cluttered office, eventually finding what she was looking for under a big bag of Monster Munch that she was saving for later.

Flicking the paper out from below the crisps like a magician with a tablecloth, she presented it to Dave. A list of bullet points filled the page. It was the one at the top that caught the detective constable's eye, though.

'Right. God. OK. So, it was definitely—?'

'Oh, yes!' Shona declared, before he could finish. She put on a thick New York accent, mimicking Max, the butler from the old TV crime show, *Hart to Hart*. 'It was *moider*!'

Chapter 16

DCI McCulloch had a face like a bulldog licking piss off a nettle. Or, no—maybe not a bulldog. Something skinnier. A whippet. A greyhound. Whatever the breed, he appeared increasingly unhappy as Sinead rattled through the list of details Dave Davidson had called her with.

There was now no doubt about it—Johnny Freestone hadn't accidentally fallen and hit his head. He'd suffered two blows to the skull from the same blunt instrument. Something heavy, though Shona hadn't yet been able to figure out what.

According to the notes Dave had falteringly relayed, the first impact had struck Freestone just above the left temple, fracturing the temporal bone and likely causing immediate disorientation or unconsciousness.

The second, delivered with even greater force, had landed on the occipital region at the back of his skull, shattering the bone and creating a deep depression fracture.

The pattern of damage suggested that the first blow had been enough to incapacitate him, leaving him vulnerable to the fatal second strike.

Extensive subdural haemorrhaging had followed, flooding the cavity around the brain, causing rapid swelling and catastrophic intracranial pressure.

Even if Freestone had survived the initial attack, according to Shona—via the medium of Dave Davidson—the resulting brain herniation would have killed him within minutes.

There was no sign of defensive wounds—no bruised arms, no fractured fingers or bloodied knuckles—suggesting that the victim had been taken by surprise and knocked unconscious by the first hit.

Or, that he had trusted whoever had stood over him with the murder weapon in hand.

Logan and the others listened as Sinead continued to relay the message Dave had passed on. It was too early for detailed toxicology reports, but an initial blood test showed high levels of alcohol in the dead man's system. There was alcohol in his stomach, too, still waiting to be processed when he died.

'That matches with what I noted at the scene,' McCulloch said.

'And what was that?' Logan asked, before reminding the SIO, 'I didn't get a look.'

'The smell of booze,' McCulloch explained. 'He was reeking of the stuff.'

'Right. OK.'

As Sinead continued to list off the less interesting findings, Logan wandered over to the white board where photos of the scene had been arranged.

Johnny Freestone didn't look much like a rock legend in the pictures. He didn't look like much of anything. There was still some length to his hair, though nothing like there used to be. It was matted across his face, held there by the sticky paste of his blood.

There was nothing outlandish or noteworthy about the way he was dressed. No leather or ripped denim, just a sensible waterproof jacket, a pair of dark trousers with a lot of pockets, and some sturdy-looking walking shoes.

Had Logan not already known who he was looking at, he'd never have recognised the man as one of the biggest music stars of the twentieth century.

Well, of one specific decade in the latter half of the twentieth century, anyway.

Back in the day, Johnny Freestone had held almost god-like status in the eyes of the young Jack Logan.

Now, though, he was just a man. And a very much dead one, at that.

Sinead had just gone on to talk about some signs of cirrhosis in Freestone's liver when Logan cut her off.

'When were these taken?' he asked, studying the photos.

'When do you think they were taken?' McCulloch replied, and there was a note of amusement in his voice, like he was talking to a child. 'This morning. At the scene. That's why the body's there.'

'I can see that, Evan, I'm no' blind,' Logan replied, the words rushing out before he had a chance to second-guess them. 'I meant when specifically? Before or after Palmer's team had been in?'

McCulloch's tongue flitted across his dry, cracked lips, back and forth, side to side. He wouldn't have liked his first name being invoked like that, and was probably considering his response.

'Before, sir,' Hamza said, jumping in before the DCI had finished formulating his reply. 'Palmer's team took the pictures before touching anything.'

Logan nodded. That was the usual order of things, but he'd wanted to be sure.

He thanked Hamza, then turned back to contemplate the pictures. They were from a variety of angles, and while most of them showed the body, a few focused on other bits of potential evidence, marked by numbered tents.

A disposable vape.

A shiny guitar plectrum.

A few dots of blood.

A footprint.

'And that's it?' Logan asked the room at large. 'That's everything they found?'

Over on his throne, McCulloch sniffed. 'Well, I highly doubt they're holding anything back from us.'

'Where's the booze?' Sinead wondered.

Logan turned to her, pointed, and made a clicking sound at the side of his mouth. 'Exactly what I was thinking. You said he was stinking of it. It was in his blood, but in his stomach, too, meaning he'd recently knocked it back, so...' He gestured to the photos, arms wide. 'Where is it?'

'Precisely,' McCulloch said, as if he'd been the one to bring it up. 'I'm assuming Scene of Crime went through the cave and surrounding area?'

It wasn't clear who the question was aimed at, so Hamza volunteered a reply. 'Yes, sir. Full sweep. Nothing in the early report about alcohol containers, but I can double-check.'

'Aye, do that,' Logan said, on autopilot. He realised what he'd done, and looked around at McCulloch. 'I mean, assuming that's all right with you?'

McCulloch didn't look best pleased, but he couldn't exactly say no, so he just nodded curtly, interlocked his fingers, and tried to regain control of the situation.

'So, we have an intoxicated man, but no sign of the intoxicants.' The DCI flinched, just a little, like he wasn't quite sure if this was a real word. He pressed on all the same. 'And we have no idea about the murder weapon, either. Not a great start for us, eh?'

It sounded like an accusation. Like the team hadn't been doing its job. Like they'd personally failed him in some way.

Maybe that was what drove Logan's deductive leap—the sheer, pig-headed refusal to let the man be right. He had no idea if his theory was right. It was a guess. A shot in the dark.

Literally.

'A torch,' he said.

Sinead let out a breath. Tyler full-on gasped.

'A torch! Yes, boss!' he ejected. 'It'd have been dark down there. Pitch black. How could anyone see enough to do him in? They couldn't!'

'Not without a torch,' Sinead concluded.

'A big, heavy bastard,' Logan said, clutching some intangible version of a big police-style flashlight, imagining the weight of it. 'Load of batteries, metal case, easy to swing.'

'A big torch!' Tyler cried, his excitement propelling him out of his chair and onto his feet. 'I bet that's it, boss. I bet that's what it was.'

DCI McCulloch *harrumphed* the room into silence. 'It's a theory,' he said. 'But let's not put our eggs in the one basket, shall we? Sinead, run it by pathology, see if it's a possibility before we all start high-fiving and...' He stumbled over the rest of the sentence. '...slapping each other's arses.'

All eyes turned to look at him. While the others were content to let it lie, Tyler couldn't help himself.

'Slapping each other's arses, sir?'

McCulloch twitched, though it was hard to tell if it was through irritation or embarrassment. 'In a locker room, flicking towels kind of way, I meant,' he clarified. 'Nothing... mucky.'

Sinead wrinkled her nose. 'Sounds a bit mucky, sir.'

Hamza nodded in agreement. 'Not sure it'd be entirely appropriate.'

'Have we even got towels?' Tyler wondered. 'Were we meant to bring our own, or...?'

Logan stood with his back to them, facing the board, shoulders shaking as he fought to keep his laughter in check.

For the first time in months, he almost felt normal. This almost felt right.

And he realised then just how much he'd missed it.

'Right! Enough!' McCulloch barked. If he'd hoped for it to come out as an authoritative boom, he was disappointed. It was thin and reedy, and seeped into the fabric of the hall like rising damp. 'Enough speculation. What do we actually know? What did the Kellermans have to say for themselves?'

The question was aimed at Logan, but he deferred to Tyler, giving the DC his chance to shine. Tyler recounted all the key parts of the interview, from finding the body, to calling Dougie, and the ten minutes of finger-pointing the couple had gone on to do after mentioning the victim's cousin.

'They think he did it?' McCulloch asked. 'That would be nice and neat. Be good to get it wrapped up quickly.'

Better to get it wrapped up right, Logan thought, though he didn't say as much.

'They stopped short of actually blaming him,' Tyler said. 'But they were definitely hinting at it. They said he didn't seem surprised when they called him, and suggested that they weren't on the best of terms.'

'He wasn't surprised that his cousin was dead?' McCulloch rubbed at his chin, as if stroking a beard he'd never quite had the courage to grow. 'That's interesting.'

'I, eh, I thought maybe me and DCI Logan should go and talk to him,' Tyler suggested. 'You know, since we heard all this stuff first-hand, and that.'

McCulloch sighed. 'You mean you thought "DCI Logan and *I* should go and talk to him."'

Tyler frowned. 'Eh, no. I mean, obviously you can if you want, sir, it's your call. I thought *I* should go with him. But, if you want to—'

'Give me strength,' McCulloch muttered. He waved a hand, dismissing the detectives. 'Yes, fine. Talk to him. See what he has to say.'

DC Neish stopped just short of punching the air in celebration. 'Nice one,' he said, flashing a smile in Logan's direction. 'Decision made. You all right with that, boss?'

Logan rolled his tongue around inside his mouth for a moment, then shrugged. 'Aye. Works for me,' he said, reaching for his coat. 'One thing, though. The couple. The Kellermans.'

'What about them?' McCulloch asked.

'I think we should poke around there. They seemed... I don't know. Off. They were whispering about something while we were outside. Something about how they shouldn't have done it.'

'Were they? I didn't hear that, boss,' Tyler said. He held up his hands in a show of surrender. 'Not that I'm doubting you.'

'Could be nothing,' Logan conceded. He met Sinead's eye, and she nodded back at him. Message received and understood.

'Leave it with me, sir.'

'Yes, well, hopefully it's the cousin, and nothing more complicated than that,' McCulloch said. 'Detective Sergeant Khaled, go with them. Let's pile on the pressure.'

'I was going to go back to the scene, sir,' Hamza said. 'Thought it was worth checking in with Palmer in case he's got anything to report.'

'Yes, yes, you can do that on the way,' McCulloch said, dismissing the objection. 'Then, you can all go see Mr Cairns together.'

'Uh, sure, sir.' Hamza shrugged. 'If you really think it needs three of us...'

'Why not? The more the merrier.' McCulloch checked his watch, and tapped a fingernail against the glass. 'If we can get a confession out of him soon, we can all be tucked up back home in our beds by midnight.'

Chapter 17

The generators were still chugging away when Logan, Hamza and Tyler arrived down at the bottom of the slope by the entrance to Smoo Cave. Earlier, the inside of the cave had been a deep, dark hole in the world. A tear in the very fabric of reality.

Now, though, with the sun having gone down, and the spotlights shining inside the cave, things had flipped around. Now, the rest of the world was the dark place, and the cave the only source of light.

Despite this, Logan's legs grew heavier with every step. The soles of his shoes seemed to stick to the ground, and the closer they got to the cave entrance, the more effort was needed to peel them free.

The last time he'd entered a cave, just a few months back, it had been through a narrow passageway that had squeezed in on him, pressing down. The memory of it, and of everything that had happened down there, still woke him in the wee small hours, and came flashing at him out of nowhere even when awake.

The entrance to Smoo Cave was much, much wider. This wasn't a narrow passage, it was a mouth, opening wide. It was the maw of some great and terrible beast, and the light in its throat was the burning of its insatiable hunger.

Logan didn't think of any of this consciously. He didn't imagine the monster, but he felt it in his chest and in his stomach. Sensed its evil presence.

Since the scene and surrounding area were still being searched, he'd left Taggart with Sinead, much to McCulloch's annoyance. Thankfully, the dog had been on his best behaviour, avoiding the need for any direct confrontation between Jack and the SIO.

Confrontation. It was something he'd never been worried about in the past. It had been his go-to response, a lot of the time. Now, though, the thought of it made him uneasy.

Confrontation was risky.

Confrontation meant people died.

One foot stuck fully to the ground, trying to hold him back, to keep him from following the other detectives into the belly of the beast. He slid. Tripped. Flailing, he stumbled through the gloom until hands caught him by either arm, holding him up.

'You all right, sir?' Hamza asked.

DC Neish was mostly silhouetted by the light in the cave ahead, but Logan could still make out the contours of his grin.

'Enjoy your trip, boss?'

Logan shrugged them off. 'Aye, very good,' he said. 'When did you hear that one? When you were eight?'

Tyler's smile remained undiminished. 'The old ones are the best.'

Another silhouette broke away from the mouth of the cave, like a tooth coming loose. It waved and picked its way towards them, gesturing for them to stay back.

Logan was only too happy to comply. There had never been a time, he thought, when he'd been more pleased to see Geoff Palmer.

'There they are! The lads! The lads, the lads, *howay the lads*!' Palmer announced, before air boxing each of the detectives, punctuating each punch with a *doof-doosh* like he was knocking them all out.

Logan, Hamza and Tyler just stood their ground, not reacting. Palmer laughed like they'd all shared a great joke, then put his hands on his hips and tried to play it cool.

Given that he was dressed like he was appearing as a sperm in a theatrical version of the human reproductive cycle, he fell some way off the mark.

'How can I help you, gents?' he asked.

Hamza looked to Logan, as if seeking permission. Jack was staring ahead into the cave, though, so the DS went ahead with his questioning.

Logan didn't hear him. Hamza's words stretched, thinned, faded—until there was nothing.

Only the generators remained. A low, menacing growl, vibrating from just inside the monster's mouth.

Logan's breath caught at the back of his throat.

In the distance, deep within the earth, the occasional voice rang out, then was suddenly silenced. Short. Sharp. Snatches of words.

Cries for help, maybe, though none of the other men seemed to be listening.

An elastic band pulled across Jack's chest. It tightened, like someone was behind him, twisting it, and twisting it, and twisting it until he could only take breaths in short, shallow sips.

And the hole in the earth growled, and burned, and waited for him.

It was in no rush. It would wait forever, if it had to. But at the same time, Jack got the feeling that it could come for him any time it wanted.

'What do you think, boss?'

Tyler's words reached him, though they sounded like they'd had to come a long way. Jack blinked. Breathed.

'What?' he muttered.

There was a pause. Logan got a sense of Tyler shooting Hamza a worried look, but that could've been imagined.

'I asked if you wanted a look,' Palmer told him, filling the silence that Tyler's hesitation had left. 'You said earlier you fancied a look at the scene, but that old bastard turned you down—which, I'll be honest, was humiliating to watch. But since he's not here, if you wanted to—'

'I'm fine,' Logan said.

He thought of the dark, and of the cold, and of millions of tonnes of rock, dirt and soil shifting and groaning above him.

'We've got the photos. It's good enough,' he insisted. He turned to Hamza. 'We good? You got what you need?'

He could see the detective sergeant's uncertainty. He could hear it, too, in his reply.

'Um, yeah. Got the update, sir. Good to go.'

'Right. Fine, then,' Logan said. He turned his back on the cave without giving it another look. 'Let's go pay this Dougie Cairns a visit.'

And before anyone could suggest otherwise, he clenched his fists, set his jaw, and marched as quickly as he could back up the hill.

Chapter 18

Dougie Cairns lived in a converted stone barn adjacent to a crumbling farmhouse that had mostly surrendered to the elements.

The walls of the conversion were thick stone, with a row of windows far wider than they were tall, all high up near the sloping slate roof.

Without a ladder or a pair of stilts, there was no way of looking inside. But a couple of cameras mounted up near the eaves would allow anyone inside to look out.

There was some wood cladding on one of the narrower walls, facing onto the driveway. A pair of oak double doors were set into it, with black handles, metal studs and a knocker shaped like a musical note.

From a distance, the place looked decidedly plush. Up close, though, the cracks were beginning to show. The wood was weathered and splitting, with damp patches where rain blowing in sideways from the North Sea had soaked in.

The grey mortar holding the walls together was crumbling away. Weeds sprouted from the gaps, stretching outwards and upwards, like they might someday spread to cocoon the place.

A light above the door burst into life as the detectives approached, bright and blinding in the evening gloom. A cloud of midges leaped into action as if they'd just been powered on. They swarmed to the light, flitting around it in frantic patterns of panic.

'Jesus, that's a bit full-on,' Tyler said, shielding his eyes. 'What's he trying to do, summon Batman?'

Logan hung back, letting Hamza take the lead. They'd barely spoken since the cave. Or maybe they had, but Jack hadn't heard them over the din of the voices damning him in his head.

There had been some brief conversation between the other two detectives about the vacant detective inspector role, he thought. Hamza had brought it up, but Tyler had been quick to change the subject.

93

If either one had asked Logan for his thoughts on the topic, he hadn't heard them.

'Right. Game faces,' Hamza said, directing the remark squarely at DC Neish.

Tyler nodded, looked down at his feet, and when he looked up, he was all business. Or, mostly business, which was about the best you could really hope for.

Before Hamza could knock on either of the double doors, one of them was pulled sharply inwards. A short, heavily built man emerged, head turned, spitting venomously back over his shoulder.

'And don't you even fucking think about calling the—'

He stopped when he collided with Hamza, ejected a strangled cry of fright, then whipped around to see who was blocking his path.

It may have been the intensity of the white light shining on the group, but all the colour seemed to drain from the man's face.

He was in his mid- to late fifties, with long, greasy black hair that was receding so badly it looked like a wig that was slipping backwards off his head. The end of his nose was a red bulb, pitted with open pores and blackheads. Below the nose sat a pair of cracked, bloated lips, like two slugs copulating on a bed of salt.

The light above him picked out the crags and crevasses of a face that carried the scars of teenage acne or terrible illness. He looked like someone had taken a cheese grater to a map of the moon.

His eyes were narrow, piggy little slits, although that could've been the fault of the thousand-watt lightbulb. Logan didn't think so, though. The shifty squint suited the man far too much for it to be an accidental one-off.

He wore a suit jacket with blue and pink checks through it, on top of a silky black shirt. Neither one fit. Neither one even came close. The arms of the suit were too long, while the shirt was stretched across the bulge of his belly.

His jewellery was a better fit. He had two gold necklaces—one thick chain, one thinner—and a ring on six or seven of his fingers. These were mostly also gold, but with a few precious stones thrown in for a bit of variety. Every carat shone in the beam of the spotlight.

He ran a hand back through his thinning hair, revealing a glimpse of a few bracelets and buckles on his wrist.

'You OK there, sir?' Hamza asked.

'What? Yeah. Course.'

He spoke with a London accent. Not from one of the more affluent parts. He sounded like someone who might have hung out with the Kray twins.

'There a problem? What's the problem?' he demanded, all bluff and bluster.

He ran a hand through his thinning hair again, then smoothed down the front of his shirt. If it was an attempt to impress, he'd have to work a hell of a lot harder.

'Who're you lot?' he asked, eyeing the three men in turn, before lingering on the towering figure standing silently at the back. 'You with the police, or something?'

'We are,' Hamza confirmed. 'In fact, we're not just *with* the police, we *are* the police.' He smiled politely, but with just a suggestion of menace tucked in behind it. 'And you are?'

The man in the terrible suit pulled the door closed behind him before replying.

'I'm Ray. Ray Simpson. I'm sure you've heard of me.'

He puffed up a little at that. So much so, that the buttons of his shirt almost became tiny projectiles.

The danger soon passed when Hamza confessed that no, actually, they hadn't heard of him.

'Fack's sake. Johnny's manager,' Ray explained, with a sigh that suggested he shouldn't have had to. 'Forget it. Don't matter. You found Old Bessie yet?'

'Old Bessie?' Tyler asked. He looked around at the others, then back to Ray. 'Who's that?'

'What? No one,' the manager replied. 'It ain't a who, is it? It's a what.'

Logan blinked. The name struck against something buried deep— some forgotten fragment of childhood.

Red. Sleek. A flash of light on polished wood. Fingers flying across the frets, striking out the soundtrack of his youth.

'His guitar,' the DCI murmured. 'That's what he called his guitar. Or, one of them, anyway.'

'His baby girl, yeah,' Ray confirmed. There was reverence in the way he said it. 'His special lady. 'Er indoors. With him from day one, that thing was. And now...' He held his hands out, as if presenting the empty space between them. 'No bugger knows where it's gone.'

He was looking up at Logan, but stabbed a finger at Tyler, instead, figuring this was the safer option.

'You want to find out who done Johnny in? You want to know who killed my boy?' The finger prodded Tyler in the chest. 'You find who took Old Bessie.'

Chapter 19

After Ray Simpson went on his way, Hamza rang the bell. It took just a few seconds for Dougie Cairns to haul the door open, face twisted up in anger, like he was ready for round two of whatever argument had been taking place just a moment before.

When he saw the three police officers standing on his doorstep, his initial surprise quickly gave way to a stony-faced resignation. He ushered them inside with minimal fuss, glanced out into the darkness, then closed the doors behind them.

Before them was a cavernous open-plan space that stretched almost the full length of the converted barn. The ceiling soared overhead, timber beams spanning the width like the ribs of some ancient wooden whale. Light fixtures dangled from chains, their dusty glass shades casting a yellowish glow that didn't quite reach the room's darker corners.

The kitchen dominated one end. It was a relic from the early 2000s with oak-effect cabinets and speckled granite countertops that had probably seemed luxurious when they were installed. The gold-toned handles had tarnished, and water damage had caused the laminate to bubble and peel around the sink. A large American-style fridge hummed aggressively, as if angry about the fact that its ice dispenser had been sealed up with masking tape.

The living area was furnished like someone had gone on a shopping spree at three different house clearances. A leather corner sofa that had seen better days slouched against one exposed brick wall, its tired cushions propped up by throws that didn't quite hide the worn patches. Beside it, an ornate side table that projected 'early Victorian era' sat uncomfortably beside a wonky bookcase that screamed '2009 Argos winter sale catalogue'.

A large flat-screen television took up a big chunk of one wall, though its mounting bracket sat slightly askew so the telly was lower at one end than the other.

The dining table was solid oak—a genuine antique that deserved better company than the mismatched chairs surrounding it. Each chair seemed to tell a different story: two leather executives rescued from an office clearout, what looked like a couple of refugee kitchen chairs from the 1970s and a carved wooden stool that might once have graced a Welsh dresser.

The overall effect was of a space that had been furnished in bursts of affluence, then left to gradually decay between cash injections. Even the artwork on the walls—a mix of cheap prints and what might have been valuable originals—hung at slightly different heights, like a gallery curated by someone who'd lost interest halfway through.

Logan's boots *thunked* on the exposed floorboards as he walked with Hamza and Tyler to the low-backed sofa and mismatched armchair.

Dougie Cairns followed behind them, and though he was still trying to hide it, that suggestion of a limp was undeniable.

'Um, tea? Coffee? Something stronger?' Dougie asked, running a hand back through the shambles of his long, grey-streaked hair. 'Take your pick.'

'I'll have a tea, cheers!' Tyler replied. 'Milk, two sugars.'

He sat on the sofa, underestimated how saggy the cushions were, and let out a little yelp of panic as his arse almost hit the floor.

Logan and Hamza both said they were fine, which prompted Tyler to reluctantly withdraw his request, so that he wasn't the only one holding things up.

Logan took the armchair, lowering himself into it slowly, his hands on the arms so they could take some of the weight. Fortunately, the cushions and springs were firm enough to support him. They weren't comfortable—not by a long shot—but they served their purpose.

There was a scrunched-up yellow tissue on the arm of the chair. It looked damp, the paper ruffled and torn, like someone had been crying and really got their money's worth out of that one tissue.

Logan automatically scanned the room, looking for more, but finding none.

Over at the couch, Hamza took more care than Tyler had as he sat beside him. He still sunk low into the seat, but without the same shock and panic that had befallen the detective constable.

Dougie, meanwhile, stood in the centre of a worn, threadbare rug, arms folded, his hands clutching his elbows like he was cradling a baby.

'So,' he began, clearly keen to get started. 'What is it you want?'

He directed the question at Logan, who answered with a question of his own. 'You're Douglas Cairns. That right?'

'Eh, aye. Dougie. But, aye.'

'DCI Jack Logan. DS Hamza Khaled. DC Tyler Neish,' Logan continued, nodding to his colleagues in turn.

It occurred to him then that he was doing the talking. He hadn't meant to do the talking, but had somehow auto-piloted his way into it.

He considered shutting up and letting Hamza take over, but his mouth was already in the process of overruling him.

'I'm sure you have some idea of why we're here, Mr Cairns.'

'Dougie's fine. And, aye. I mean, of course. Johnny.'

'You're his cousin?'

'Well, I was,' Dougie replied. 'I don't suppose I am now.'

It could have sounded cold and, while there was a chilliness to it, there was something else, too. Regret, maybe. Frustration.

'We spoke to Reg and Elsie Kellerman earlier,' Logan continued. 'They said they called you when they found Johnny's body.'

It wasn't a question, but Logan stopped anyway, so the other man could confirm the statement was correct.

Dougie sighed, just faintly, and smoothed down a wrinkle in the rug with the sweep of a foot. 'Aye, that's right. They called me, I went down to see, then I called the police.'

'You saw him?'

'From a distance, aye. It was pitch black down there, though, and he was on a lower ledge. I could see he was dead, though.'

He looked away, eyes darting to one of the little windows built high up on the wall. Emotion flickered across his face—quick, raw, and unreadable. It could have been regret. It could have been guilt. It could have been something darker.

Logan barely noticed this, though. He was too busy feeling... something. A shift. A stirring inside him. He gripped the arms of the chair.

His breathing changed. An electrical current skipped across his skin, pinging from pore to pore.

It was pitch black down there.

He thought of another dark cave.

Of a body, freshly dead.

Of a nightmare that would not leave him in peace.

'I'm sorry for your loss, Mr Cairns,' the DCI managed, then he nodded across to Hamza to carry on with the questioning.

The detective sergeant effortlessly picked up the ball and ran with it.

'Dougie. Can I call you Dougie?'

'Course, yeah.'

Hamza flashed a smile of thanks. 'When did you last see Johnny?'

There was a pause. Not long, but noticeable. 'Yesterday lunchtime.'

'So, around one o'clock?'

'Thereabouts, aye,' Dougie confirmed.

'And where was this?'

Dougie pointed to Tyler. 'That seat.'

DC Neish looked momentarily panicked, like he was sitting in the dead man's lap, but he was far too low down to jump up off the sofa, even if he'd wanted to.

'He came to see you?' Hamza asked.

'No. He was staying here. He turned up a few weeks back. I assumed it was a flying visit, given that he hadn't been back here in about ten years, and even that had only been for about twenty minutes, but then...' Dougie shrugged. 'He just didn't leave. He's been sleeping through in the studio.'

Hamza scribbled a note. 'A studio apartment?'

'What? Oh, no. Recording studio, sorry,' Dougie clarified. 'There's a spare bedroom. I told him he could stay there, but he wanted to crash in the studio. *Just him and his music,* he said. Which sounds pretentious when I say it, but when he said it...'

He drifted off for a moment, emotion—whatever it was—choking him.

'It sounded less cheesy,' Tyler guessed.

Dougie laughed. 'God, no. More cheesy, if anything. He always had this fake sincerity about him, and came out with shite like that all the time, thinking it made him sound wise, or spiritual, or whatever. It didn't. It just made him sound like a twat.'

'You don't sound like you were particularly close,' Hamza ventured. 'If you don't mind me saying.'

'We weren't. I mean, we were once, years ago,' Dougie said. 'Or so I thought, anyway. I toured with him for a bit when I was younger. Sixteen, seventeen. Said he'd show me the world.'

'And did he?' Logan asked, his curiosity dampening down the sense of panic that had flared up a few moments before.

Dougie met his eye. This time, it wasn't exactly an emotion Logan saw there. It was something rawer.

'Not parts of it I wanted to see.' He drew in a breath. It shook all the way down. 'My parents didn't want me to go. They were dead against it, but Johnny convinced me. He made it sound like an amazing opportunity, told me I'd be an idiot to pass it up. Told me he was my big cousin, he'd look after me.'

The laugh that scraped at the back of his throat was a hoarse, dry thing.

'Just more of his usual bullshit.'

'But you let him stay here with you?' Logan asked.

'I didn't let him. He stayed. What Johnny wants, he usually gets.' Dougie looked across the faces of the detectives. 'Do you know what happened yet? At the cave?'

'We're still working on that,' Logan said. 'Yesterday. Lunchtime. How did he seem? Was he, I don't know, worried about anything?'

'Worried? Johnny Freestone? Ha! That would have been a first.'

'He didn't mention having fallen out with anyone, or...?'

Dougie's posture stiffened, then slackened again, his shoulders slumping lower than they had been a moment before.

'So, he was murdered, then?'

'Like I say, we're still working on it,' Logan told him. 'Did he say anything?'

'No.'

'Can you think of anyone who might want to harm him?'

This time, the laugh that exploded out of Dougie felt real. Bitter and angry, but real.

'Oh, God, let me think. His ex-wives, his old bandmates, the women he shagged then ghosted, the *husbands* of the women he shagged then ghosted, his record label, his managers—past and present—half the people here in town, oh, and me, if that's what you're building up to.'

'Hang on, hang on,' Tyler said, writing frantically in his pad. He held a finger up and slowly lowered it as he finished the note. 'Aaaand done. Sorry, go on.'

'That's quite a list,' Hamza said.

'Aye, well, he was a singularly irritating human being,' Dougie concluded. He rubbed at his forehead and exhaled, like he was fighting off a migraine. 'But he was the only family I had left, and vice versa. And yesterday, I thought maybe that actually meant something.'

'How do you mean?' Hamza pressed. 'What happened yesterday?'

Dougie slipped his hands into the back pockets of his jeans and shrugged. 'It was probably nothing. His usual big talk. But yesterday, he came out of the studio at lunchtime, all excited. Told me he'd had "an epiphany". His words, not mine. Said he'd realised that all the money, and the fame, and the women, they didn't matter. That only one thing mattered.' He hesitated before saying the next word, like he was embarrassed by it. 'Family.'

Dougie looked over at a door by the far wall, past the kitchen. It was a heavy-looking, bugger of a thing, with a layer of foam sound insulation on the outside.

'I asked him if he was drunk, or high, but he said he wasn't. He said he was going to prove to me how important family was to him,' Dougie continued, faltering a little. 'I asked him what he meant, but he said he'd show me that night. He'd be back later, he said, and he'd show me then. Then, he gathered up a load of stuff and left.'

'Stuff?' Logan prompted.

'Uh, yeah. Just some portable recording equipment and a couple of bottles of Jack Daniels. Oh, and his guitar.'

'Old Bessie?' Tyler asked.

Dougie's eyebrows rose. 'Um, aye. Yeah. Old Bessie. He's been using her for the new stuff he's been recording.'

Logan's ears—or maybe the ears of the ten-year-old version of him—pricked up at that.

'New material?' he asked.

'Yeah. Very different to his usual stuff,' Dougie said. 'It's actually pretty good.'

It wasn't clear if the second part of that comment was directly connected to the first bit, but if it was intended as a slight on Johnny's earlier work, Dougie's expression gave nothing away.

'And that conversation, that was the last you saw of him?' Hamza asked. 'He didn't come back?'

'No. He didn't come back,' Dougie confirmed. 'And then, I got the call from Reg, and, do you know what? I wasn't even that shocked. Because that's what Johnny did—promised something, got you excited about it, then let you down. He did it for decades—I've *put up with it* for decades—so it didn't really come as a surprise when he did it to me all over again.'

Tyler piped up from his too-low seat. 'I mean, in his defence, he probably didn't set out to get murdered.'

'No,' Dougie admitted, though it sounded grudged, like he hated offering this concession. 'Even for him, that'd be a bit much.'

'When you went into the cave—when you saw the body—did you happen to see anything around it?' Hamza prompted.

Dougie seemed confused by the question. 'Like what?'

'Anything. Anything he might have brought down with him. Anything someone might have left behind...'

'Uh, no. No, I don't think so. I mean, Old Bessie wasn't there, if that's what you mean? No sign of the other equipment he took from me, either. Looks like I won't be getting that back, and that stuff's not cheap!'

'If you give us a list, we'll keep an eye out for it,' Hamza promised. 'Nothing else? No alcohol bottles, cans, nothing like that?'

Dougie shook his head. 'Not that I saw. He was supposed to be off it, but, well, that never really stuck. And, like I said, he took two bottles of Jack with him.'

Logan shuffled forward in his chair, and Hamza took the hint, conceding the floor.

'You mentioned all the people that would want to do Johnny harm,' the DCI said. 'Can you elaborate on that?'

Dougie blew out his cheeks and shrugged. 'I mean, a lot of it is self-explanatory. He was an arsehole to a lot of people. He cut his bandmates out of songwriting credits, so they lost out on shitloads in royalties. One of them, Carl Jepson, killed himself a few years back. Walked off the top of a multi-storey car park in Aberdeen. He was tens of thousands in debt and had just had his house repossessed.'

'Bloody hell,' Tyler murmured, still scribbling.

'His ex-wives hated him because, well, you would, wouldn't you? He used to enjoy the groupies. Teenagers, mostly, back in the day. Aye, eighteen and up, he wasn't like *that*. Preferred the slightly older married ones, actually. Got a kick out of that.'

Logan, to his surprise, found all this disappointing to hear. Yes, Johnny Freestone's whole appeal had been as a rock and roll bad boy, but what Dougie was describing wasn't so much *Rebel Without a Cause* as *Arsehole Without a Conscience*.

'He shafted one manager, had just fired another one—Ray, the prick who just left—and the people round here…?'

Dougie glanced at the door, then lowered his voice, like he was worried the locals might be listening in.

'Well, let's just say that at least a few of them did not want my cousin around.'

Chapter 20

'Well? Did we get him?'

McCulloch stood with his back to the whiteboards, hands tucked behind him, his back straight and shoulder blades almost touching. He looked like someone had shoved a stick up the arse of an already wound-too-tightly army sergeant major.

Logan snorted out a little half-laugh, like they were sharing a joke. Then he stopped, midway through pulling off his coat, when he realised his fellow DCI was not in on it.

'Wait. You were being serious?' he asked. He shot a questioning look at Hamza and Tyler, who both seemed equally as baffled. 'You actually thought we'd end up charging him?'

'Well, I had hoped that the three of you might conspire to impress me,' McCulloch shot back. 'But it looks like those hopes have been dashed. DC Bell!'

He snapped his fingers, drawing the attention of Sinead. She was ducked low at a laptop on one of the makeshift desks, like she'd been trying to hide from him.

'Sir?'

'It looks like we'll need to sort out accommodation. I, for one, won't be driving back down that road in the dark,' McCulloch declared. 'If the rest of you want to, fine, but I'll expect you back here by seven tomorrow morning, so you'll be leaving Inverness by four thirty, and I'm going to assume that none of you enjoys the thought of that.'

Logan met Sinead's eye. 'You sorted with the kids?'

'Yeah. They're fine,' Sinead told him. 'I mean, they're with Bob and Berta, so probably not *fine* fine, but safe enough. Harris'll be all right on his own.'

'He'd better be on his own!' said Tyler. 'I think him and Olivia are still a thing.'

Logan ran a hand down his face. He still couldn't quite explain how he and Shona were now the legal guardians of Olivia Maximuke. She was the teenage daughter of Bosco Maximuke, an old enemy of Logan's who was now languishing in jail.

She was also, Jack was fairly certain, a sociopath.

It had been a few months since he'd caught her in the garden shed with Sinead's younger brother, Harris. Shona's talk about the birds and the bees—complete with a condom and a banana as props—had ensured they didn't so much as talk to each other for several weeks afterwards through the sheer force of their embarrassment.

Lately, though, they'd been 'hanging out at the Victorian Market'. Jack didn't think this was a euphemism, but who knew with kids these days?

'Shona'll be at home with Olivia soon,' he said. 'She'll keep an eye out for any...' He sighed, reaching for an appropriate word. 'Shenanigans.'

'And I have no life whatsoever,' Hamza said, smiling just a touch too broadly. 'So, count me in for the sleepover.'

Despite all this being McCulloch's idea, he seemed annoyed by how many of the detectives had jumped on the suggestion.

'Well, we'll be lucky to find anywhere for all of us at this hour. It's not exactly a bustling metropolis, is it?'

'Not compared to all the other big cities dotted around up here, no,' Logan replied, and the wee dollop of sarcasm tasted sweet on his tongue.

McCulloch arched an eyebrow like he was going to say something, but whatever it was, he decided against it.

'It's fine, sir. Already sorted,' Sinead announced. 'I checked online and got us all booked in earlier.'

'On whose authority?' McCulloch asked, rounding on her.

Sinead blushed. She stammered out the start of an apology, before Logan butted in.

'Mine,' he said. 'I told her to do it.'

'You?' The word was sharp around the edges. '*You* told her to? Without consulting me?'

Logan shoved his hands in his trouser pockets. 'I just thought—'

'Do we need to have this conversation again, Jack?' McCulloch asked. 'You are here to assist. Me. That's all. The thinking? The decision making? That's down to me. Is that clear?'

A silence hummed through the room. There wasn't a whisper. Wasn't a breath.

Logan contemplated the question for several long, tortuous seconds.

'Apologies, Evan,' he finally said. 'Won't happen again.'

The tension in the room didn't pop so much as deflate like a sad, saggy balloon a few days after a birthday party. Only Sinead looked Logan in the eye as she mouthed a silent, 'Thank you', that he accepted with a nod.

'Good. Right. Hopefully that's now settled,' McCulloch said. 'Where are we staying? And if you tell me it's a campsite, you're fired.'

He didn't say it like it was a joke. He smiled, which suggested it might be, but there was no note of humour in his voice.

'Close. Glamping pods, actually, sir,' Sinead said. She clocked the look on his face and hurried to head off the immediate termination of her employment. 'But not you. I managed to get you a room in a local hotel. They've even thrown in breakfast.'

McCulloch smoothed down his fleece and nodded sharply, as if this was only fit and proper. 'Right. Well, glad to hear it. As it should be,' he said. 'The rest of you will just have to make the best of it, I'm afraid. Hopefully, we can get this wrapped up tomorrow.'

He reached for his jacket, which hung on the back of a chair. Logan, once again, couldn't help himself.

'What? Is that us?' he asked. 'Are we just packing it in for the night?'

'Yes. We are. We'll come back to it first thing,' McCulloch confirmed. 'Mr Freestone is unlikely to be any more dead by then.'

'But the interview. His cousin,' Logan continued. 'We should talk about it. Get it all written up.'

'Absolutely. And we will.' The DCI once again patted Logan on the shoulder. 'Seven tomorrow, sharp. We'll go through it all then.'

He jerked his head forward, bidding farewell to the rest of the team, then went striding out of the hall, letting the door swing closed behind him.

It wasn't until thirty seconds later, after the engine of McCulloch's BMW had rumbled awake outside, that anyone spoke.

'Is it just me,' Tyler began, 'or is he becoming even more of an arsehole every time he opens his mouth?'

Chapter 21

It took Logan a second longer than he'd have liked to recognise the man handing him the key. The guy was smiling, which may have explained the delay. Back at the meeting in the village hall, he hadn't looked happy in the slightest.

Not that the smile seemed all that genuine now, either. It was very much a *service industry* smile, plastered on for the benefit of the customer, but barely hiding the growing cracks beneath.

He was the father of the red-headed boy who'd been at the meeting. Logan remembered him now, and the way he'd stared at the back of Dougie Cairns's head.

What had that look meant? What had been behind it?

'So, you're number eleven. Up at the back. Hope that's OK,' he said, handing Jack the key.

Logan was the first to arrive at the site, the others having headed off in search of a shop, or a takeaway, to pick up some food.

'Aye. Fine,' he said, tucking the key and its enormous wooden keyring into his coat pocket. 'Sorry, didn't catch your name.'

'I didn't give it,' the other man replied, then his smile became something a little more natural. 'Charlie. Charlie Sinclair. I run the site. Me and the family. If you need anything, just come back here and ring the buzzer. I'll be right out with you.'

Logan looked around at what was essentially a shed, and not a particularly roomy one, at that. The walls were bare, untreated wood, and a chill rolled in through gaps around the roof and windows that spiders had done their best to try and block up.

He'd never been in a glamping pod before. He hoped they were better than this.

'Right. Good. Thanks. Will do.'

He started to turn towards the door, then stopped.

'You were at the meeting earlier, right?'

Logan wasn't sure why he'd asked the question. He hadn't been intending to when he'd made to leave, but it had found its way out, all the same.

'Eh, aye. We were just being nosy, really,' Charlie replied. 'You know, there's not a lot happens round here. So, when the police descend en masse... Well, curiosity got the better of us.'

'Aye. I can imagine,' Logan said. 'You know him?'

'Who, Johnny Freestone? Not really, no. Saw him a couple of times in passing. Nobody really bothered with him round here, though. We all tend to mind our own business.'

Logan couldn't quite make people minding their own business align with attending a public meeting called specifically for the purposes of gossiping, but he chose not to say as much.

'What about his cousin?' he asked. 'Dougie. You know him?'

This time, the response took a little longer to arrive on Charlie's lips.

'Course, yeah. He's a good guy. Terrible what happened to him. It's amazing, if you ask me, that he wanted anything more to do with Johnny after that.' He shrugged and closed over the key box, making a show of how keen he was to leave. 'But, he's a bigger man than me, clearly.'

'After what happened?' Logan asked. 'Why, what did happen?'

Panic flashed across Charlie's face, making it all the way to his eyes before he was able to wrestle it under control.

'Eh, nothing,' he said, then he realised how that sounded and shook his head. 'I mean, not nothing, obviously, but it's not really my place to say.'

'If you have information that could help us...' Logan said, leaving the rest of the sentence hanging.

'I don't. I mean, it's ancient history, I suppose. And it's not my story to tell. You'll have to ask Dougie yourself,' Charlie told him. He squeezed past, opening the door and letting in more of the cool evening air. 'Or, if you don't want to do that, I'm sure you can read all about it on Google.'

The pod, thankfully, was not a shed. It was a large circular hut, like a whisky barrel lying on its side, with a door and window at the front that looked out across the foamy white horses of the North Sea.

Or, at least, it would when the sun came back up. Right now, it faced only darkness, broken by the lights of the neighbouring rentals.

There were a dozen or so pods on the site, from what Logan had been able to see. Around half of them looked to be occupied, and Hamza, plus Tyler and Sinead, would add to that total when they arrived.

One of the closer neighbours was currently playing dance music too loudly for Logan's tastes. Although, when it came to dance music, any volume would fit that description.

As he unlocked the front door to his pod, he could hear the odd screech of laughter, and the shrill, piercing vibrato of a woman with an Essex accent coming from the same hut.

'I know, babes! I know, I know! What am I like? I'm crazy, I am!'

There was some snorting. More laughter. It was only when he heard the splashing that Logan realised the originators of what he was already thinking of as *that fucking racket* were lounging in a hot tub in front of their pod.

He checked his watch. It was just before ten. He'd give them until eleven, then put a stop to it.

Stepping inside, Logan was surprised by a rush of warmth that rushed to meet him at the door. A small log-burning stove stood at the far end of the pod, insulated from the wooden wall by a layer of polished grey slate.

Three logs sat in a basket beside the stove, with one already crackling away behind the smoky glass.

There wasn't a huge amount of space inside the pod, but it had been well organised, so it felt roomier than it was. The interior curved around him like the inside of a seashell, its wooden panels gleaming with a honey-coloured finish that caught the warm light from the stove.

A single bed was tucked against one wall, dressed in crisp white linens, with a thick duvet whose edges were trimmed in a subtle green and blue tartan that echoed the shades of the sea outside.

Opposite the bed, a deep wingback armchair in burgundy leather commanded the best view of both the stove and the window. A clever piece of engineering allowed a small oak table to swing out from the chair's arm, perfect for holding a cup of tea or a dinner plate without taking up permanent floor space.

The kitchenette was compact but thoughtfully equipped—a single induction hob sat beside a microwave, both mounted at just the right height for a person of normal size to cook without stooping. There'd be a bit of bending required for Logan, but he had no intention of using it, anyway, so it made no odds.

What he *was* going to use, though, was the kettle. It was one of those fancy digital ones that let you choose the exact temperature, though Logan would never use anything but the 'boiling' setting for his builder's tea.

Below the counter, a mini-fridge hummed quietly. Opening the door, he found two bottles of water and a small carton of milk lined up inside like new recruits at an inspection.

Everything in the pod had its place, with hooks for coats, shelves for books, and even a little nook beside the bed that was just the right size for his phone and wallet. The overall effect was like being in the cabin of a particularly well-designed boat—snug rather than cramped, cosy rather than confined, even for a man of his height.

Aye, Logan thought. *This'll do.*

He hung his overnight bag on one of the hooks, then his coat on its neighbour beside it.

The first problem he encountered was with the kettle. Or, more accurately, with the sink. It was a small, narrow hand basin, and far too shallow to allow the kettle to fit under the tap.

To his shame, he spent a good thirty seconds trying to get it to fit before realising he could just slosh water into a cup a few times, and fill the kettle that way.

He was glad Tyler hadn't been here to see that performance.

Kettle on, he went in search of the bathroom. He found it quickly—there weren't many places to hide a whole other room in the pod—and after some figuring out of the sliding door mechanism, he sidled inside.

It was a wet room, with a toilet at one end, and a shower at the other. Although, calling them 'ends' was over-egging the pudding a bit. Turn on the shower, and it would be impossible to stay dry while having a shite.

Still, two birds with one stone, he supposed.

After a quick pee, he squeezed himself back out and slid the door closed.

He made his tea, settled into the seat, and manoeuvred the little fold-out table into place across his lap.

It was then, moments before he took his first sip, that he remembered he'd left the dog in the car.

'Bollocks!'

The little table was easy to fold out, but a bugger to put away, especially while holding a hot cup of tea in one hand.

With a bit of experimentation and quite a lot of swearing, he finally got it moved aside, rose to his feet, and set the tea down on the tiny kitchen worktop.

Pulling on his coat, he opened the door and stepped out. The outside air was far less welcoming than the inside had been. It hadn't felt cold on the walk to the pod, but having been inside for a few minutes, he could feel a sharpness to the breeze blowing in off the water.

It clearly wasn't bothering whoever was making *that fucking racket*, though. They were still out there in the hot tub, still inflicting their terrible taste in music on everyone within a quarter-mile radius.

Half-ten. He'd give them until half-ten.

The car park was at the other end of the site, between the shed where Logan had been given the key and a detached bungalow with lights on in every window.

As Logan marched down the limestone path towards the car, a spotlight illuminated on the roof of the shed, drawing a hiss of surprise and forcing him to shield his eyes with a hand.

The light was a circle, and in the half-second that Logan had instinctively looked straight at it, he thought he'd caught a glimpse of a lens filling the space in the middle.

A security camera, then. Someone somewhere was quite possibly watching him.

It didn't swivel to follow him as he trudged around the side of the shed, headed for the car park. By the time he reached his car, the light had clicked off, plunging the area back into darkness.

Opening the rear passenger side door, Logan found Taggart sleeping on the backseat. The dog opened one eye, closed it, then sat bolt upright once his brain had made sense of what he'd seen.

He sprang for Jack, all paws and tongue, transitioning from *fast asleep* to *impossibly awake* in a couple of shakes of a tail.

'All right, all right. Aye. I see you,' Logan told him, tolerating the face-licking for a second by way of apology for leaving the dog behind. 'Down you get.'

He stepped aside and Taggart flung himself out of the car, plunged the three feet to the ground, and landed clumsily at Jack's feet.

After raising his head for a congratulatory pat, he sniffed around in a circle, then made a mad dash for the closest vertical object on which to relieve himself.

The closest vertical object turned out to be the back tyre of a silver Mercedes-Benz. It was an older model—2005, going by the plate—but it had been well cared for, and looked immaculate.

Well, apart from the lightly steaming dog piss.

'Right, you fit?' Jack asked, and Taggart trotted over to him.

They headed back across the car park together. This time, Logan didn't go around the side of the shed. Instead, he followed the route between it and the bungalow, sticking to the grass, letting Taggart have a good sniff around.

That was what he told himself, anyway.

As they walked, though, his eyes were drawn to the house, and the well-lit windows, and the people moving around inside.

He could see the red-haired woman from the village hall meeting standing in what was presumably the kitchen. She was facing the window, but stooped over. Washing her hands, maybe, or doing the dishes.

Logan watched her from the darkness. Her head was down, and she was saying nothing, but every so often she'd raise her eyes to the ceiling and sigh, like she was becoming increasingly frustrated by something.

A stubborn stain? He didn't think so. More likely, it was some-thing she was listening to that was bothering her, judging by her body language.

The next window along was frosted glass, and the only one without a light on. Bathroom. Had to be.

To the right of that was some kind of family room, by the looks of things. Jack couldn't see a TV, but where one might have been mounted on the wall was a shiny white electric guitar hanging straight down. Tall bookcases flanked it on each side, like they were standing guard.

A movement back at the kitchen drew Logan's eye. The woman who'd been at the sink had disappeared. There was someone else there now. Blonde hair, sullen features, eyes ringed with red.

He knew her.

Where from?

It was when she clutched at her head, her face screwing up in grief, that it clicked. She'd been the woman by the cordon tape back at the cave. The one having the meltdown.

Logan looked through the gloom in the direction of his pod. He could still hear the music, and the shrill laughter from his nearby neighbour. He should go back there, have that tea, wait for Tyler and the others to turn up with whatever food they'd been able to rustle up.

If it came to it, he had a Pot Noodle that Shona had packed for him. And, if he couldn't stomach that, she'd packed a couple of tins of dog food, too.

Aye, he should do that. He should go put his feet up.

He wasn't in charge of this case. He wasn't here to make decisions. Decisions were dangerous. Decisions could be fatal.

The dog snuffled around at his feet, nose to the ground.

Logan stood there, not moving. A statue staring into the darkness.

Behind him, the warm glow continued to spill out through the kitchen window.

He thought of the woman in there. The answers in there.

'Ah, fuck it,' he decided, and he turned towards the light.

Chapter 22

The back door of the bungalow led directly into the kitchen. Logan knew this because he'd taken a moment to size the place up before making his move.

He knocked, a quick rat-a-tat-tat that was almost apologetic. No point worrying them with his thumping polis knock. Not yet, at least.

There was some murmuring from the other side, some scuffing of feet on old lino. Then, the door was opened by the red-headed woman who'd been sighing over the sink.

'Yes?' she demanded. Then, when the light from the kitchen hit him and she realised who he was, she took half a step back, like she was preparing to run. 'Sorry. I didn't see you properly there.'

'No worries,' Logan said. 'I'm staying in one of the pods. But there's no milk in the fridge.'

Two or three different expressions all jostled for room on the woman's face. 'Isn't there? There should be. Charlie should have stocked you up.'

Logan shrugged and shook his head. 'Sorry. Do you have any there that I could have?'

She hesitated, then hoisted up a smile like a flag of surrender. 'Of course, yes. No bother. Just one sec.'

She vanished into the house without inviting him in. That wasn't ideal. Logan looked around to make sure nobody was watching, then grabbed Taggart and half-pushed, half-launched him into the kitchen.

'Taggart! No! Bad dog!' he said, following the animal inside.

Taggart, for his part, had absolutely no idea what was going on, so assumed it was all part of some game or other which he had yet to learn the rules to. As a result, he went tearing around the kitchen, bumping into the furniture in a fit of tail-wagging, tongue-lolling exuberance.

'Oh, God, and now there's a *dog!*' wailed the blonde woman, like Taggart's arrival was the worst possible thing that had ever happened to anyone.

'Sorry,' Logan said, making a show of grabbing for the fast-moving mutt. 'Taggart! Here!'

'Wait.' There was a scraping of chair legs as the blonde woman, who had been sitting with her head on the table when Logan entered, suddenly stood up. 'Are you with them? Are you with the police?'

'Um, aye. I am. Though, I'm off duty at the minute,' Logan said. Technically true.

She practically fell against him, grabbing onto his arm like it was the only thing preventing her from falling flat on her face.

'Oh, tell me you've found out who did it!' she cried. 'Tell me you found out who killed my Johnny!'

She was, Logan thought, like an actress in an early colour film, hamming up a performance that favoured volume over nuance. Any second now, she'd press the back of her hand to her forehead and faint clean away.

'Not yet. I'm sorry. But we're working on it,' Logan said.

Everything after the 'not yet', was drowned out by a squeal so high-pitched that even Taggart skidded to a stop to see what the fuck the noise was all about.

'You were in a relationship with Mr Freestone?' Logan asked, still supporting her.

'Yes!' she declared.

'Oh, my arse you were, Alanna!' the redhead shot back.

There was a similarity there, Logan noted. In the bone structure, and in the eyes. Sisters. He'd put money on it. The blonde was five or six years older, but trying desperately not to be. Both in their forties, but sitting at opposite ends of the seesaw.

'It was on and off, Coleen, you *know* that!'

Coleen, the younger sister, slammed the fridge door, muttered something below her breath, then returned with a small carton of milk that she presented to Logan.

'Here. Sorry about that. Charlie must've forgotten. Everyone's heads are all over the place today.'

'I get it,' Logan said. 'It must have been a big shock. For all of you, I mean.'

'Oh, it was! It *was!*' Alanna yelped. She fished in the pocket of her jeans and pulled out a handful of grubby, well-used tissues. Yellow, Logan noted, like the one on Dougie Cairns's armchair. 'I can't believe my Johnny's gone!'

The sentence sounded like air being squeezed from the neck of a balloon. It started high, then got higher, until it became too much for her throat to bear, or too quiet for his ears to hear. Either way, it petered off into a silence textured by her snuffles and snottery sobs.

By this point, Taggart had come to the conclusion that nobody was actually chasing him, so he trotted back over to the door and sniffed at the salty sea air. He shot a look at Logan to see if he'd taken the hint, then sat down on the doormat and waited.

'Well, if that's all you need...' Coleen began, looking pointedly at the dog.

'Wait, no! He can't go yet!' her sister cried. 'I want to know everything! I want to know what they've found. I *need* to know that someone is going to pay for what they did to my Johnny.'

'You don't know anyone did anything!' Coleen said. 'For all you know, he drank himself unconscious, slipped, and banged his head.'

'Did he?' Alanna gasped, and Logan would've sworn her eyes actually shimmered with hope as she looked up into his. 'Is that what happened?'

'We're still looking into it,' Logan said. It wasn't quite a lie, though it was certainly skirting around the edges of one. 'We're still trying to build up a picture of his last few days and hours.'

He ignored the glare from Coleen. It wasn't difficult, as she was doing her best to hide it herself. She was staring at him, but in short, stealthy snatches.

'I can help! I spoke to him!' Alanna said.

'Right. That's good to know,' Logan said. 'We can maybe chat at the hall tomorrow.'

'No! Why wait? We should do it now. Right now!'

'I'm sure the detective wants to get to his bed, Alanna,' her sister said. 'Tomorrow will be—'

'No! The sooner the better!' Alanna said, shutting her up. She tugged on Logan's arm, guiding him towards one of the seats set up at the kitchen table. 'Come on, sit. You can ask me anything.'

Logan looked out into the night. Some part of him was considering going out there, but a much bigger part was otherwise preoccupied.

It was counting to five.

'Ah, what the hell?' he said, pretending to have come to a difficult decision. He pulled out the chair. 'I'm game if you are.'

Chapter 23

Even by Alanna's own admission, her relationship with Johnny Free-stone was more off than on. They'd definitely had sex, though, she wanted to make that very clear. Which she did. Repeatedly.

From the way she described it, it had been a near magical experience for both of them, even the last time, a couple of weeks back, bent over the bins at the back of the village shop.

Especially that time, in fact.

'We could hear people inside,' she'd recounted, her face wistful, her voice a whisper. 'After he was done, he just walked away without a word. He was like that. Commanding. In charge.'

Her sister, Coleen, had mumbled, 'Jesus Christ', at that, and gone back to slamming dishes in and out of the kitchen sink.

And Alanna had returned to the nittier and grittier details of her and Freestone's relationship. Logan had listened, while an old grandfather clock in the corner had ticked loudly, like it was repeatedly tutting its disapproval.

It had mostly been sexual, she admitted. It had *only* been sexual, as far as Logan could tell, and though she romanticised it, not one word out of her mouth made it sound anything other than abusive.

'We did share other things, too,' Alanna insisted. 'Hopes for the future. Dreams. Regrets. He had a few of those. His ex-wives, mostly! Well, not the dead one. She was fine. He didn't mind her.'

'Did he share anything about any problems he'd been having lately? Any fallings out, or...?' Logan prompted.

'What, while he was shagging her over the bins?' asked Coleen from the sink.

Alanna shot a scathing look at the back of her head, then turned her attention back to the detective. 'No. He didn't mention anything like that.' She dabbed at her eyes with her sodden tissue and choked her way through the next few words. 'I wish he had! I wish he'd opened up to me.'

'Would've made a change from you opening up to him,' Coleen muttered, plunging her hands into the steaming hot water.

'How did it start?' Logan asked. 'Your relationship with Johnny, I mean.'

Alanna brightened at the question, and Logan got the impression she enjoyed telling this story.

'Well, we sort of vaguely knew each other from just living in the village, you know? His parents were still here for a while, before they died, so he'd come back, and I'd see him around. I spoke to him once or twice. Just in passing, though, nothing much. A wee "hello". The odd "How's it going?" You know, just casual. He was older, obviously. Fifteen years, almost to the month. Anyway, it was just that. Friendly enough, but just... Nothing like later.'

She moved her chair in closer to the table. Closer to Jack.

'So, anyway, fast forward. It's 2007. He's doing a gig in Glasgow—'

'Wait. At King Tut's?' Logan asked.

Alanna leaned back a little, looking him up and down. Coleen, too, shot a look back over her shoulder.

'How did you know that?' Alanna asked.

'I was there,' Logan told her. 'I went along to watch. Good gig.'

'Bloody hell! Hear that, Coleen? He was there, too! Small world! And yes, it was a good gig. It was a *great* gig. In more ways than one!' She tapped her hands on the table, raised her eyebrows, and smirked. 'You might have been at the gig, but did you wake up in his bed the next morning?'

Logan was forced to admit that no, as far as he could recall, he hadn't.

Alanna prodded a thumb into the middle of her chest. 'I did,' she said, in case that wasn't already clear enough. 'I woke up in his bed.'

The way she said it implied she was looking for some kind of acknowledgement of this. A 'congratulations' or a hearty pat on the back.

Instead, Logan just pressed on with his questioning.

'And that's when the relationship started?'

'Well, duh! Yes!' Alanna laughed, but there was a flicker of doubt there that she acknowledged. 'I mean, I was pretty pissed, so I don't actually remember much.'

'Who says romance is dead?' her sister asked, still busy with the dishes.

'We went to the bar after the gig, didn't we, Coleen? We went to the bar, and saw him there. You said we should leave him be, but I went over to talk to him. He didn't recognise me right away, but when I reminded him, he did, and we had a few drinks, then a few more, and...'

Her grief, which had been temporarily forgotten, was suddenly remembered. It emerged as a seal-like bark that brought with it a fresh cascade of snot and tears.

Neither Logan nor Coleen spoke while Alanna burned through this fresh wave of sorrow. Or maybe hysteria would be a better descriptor. Only Taggart let out a quizzical whine, and even he didn't seem all that interested. And this was an animal that had once stared at a single chip on a plate for over forty-five minutes straight.

'But, yeah, that's when it started,' Alanna wheezed, once the sobbing had subsided. She sniffed. 'I mean, I didn't see him or hear from him for about ten years after that, but that was when we first got together.'

'When did you, uh, reconnect?' Logan asked.

'Here. Back here. Not here in the house, obviously. My place. He was back home scattering his mum's ashes. I bumped into him and, well, let's just say this time he was the one waking up in my bed!'

'But he wasn't,' Coleen said. 'He didn't. He fucked off again as soon as he was done with you.'

Alanna didn't acknowledge the remark. In fact, Logan wasn't sure she'd even heard it. She was staring off into space, lost to thoughts of the past.

'We hung out a few times after that. Once on that trip, and then a few times since he came back. I... I got the impression he was lonely when he wasn't with me.' Her brow furrowed, just a line or two, just for a moment. 'Or even when he was with me, sometimes. Like, really lonely. Deep down. I think he would've liked to have kids. A boy and a girl. Maybe a couple of each.'

That did it. Coleen, who had been aggressively scrubbing a plate, now slammed it down on the drying rack and spun around, bubbles spiralling from her fingertips and dropping like bombs to the floor.

'Kids? And he told you this, did he? You and him actually had this conversation?'

Alanna sighed heavily and rolled her eyes, like a surly teenager who'd taken this telling-off a hundred times before.

'Well, no. I just said I *thought* he would've—'

'No. Exactly. No. He didn't say that. You imagined it, Alanna! Like you imagined this whole... fucking...' She waved her hands, fingers curled into claws, her frustration taking a physical toll. 'Weird fantasy!'

'Um, fantasy? Hello?' Alanna sat up straight, her face twisting into a sarcastic *as if* sort of sneer. 'We shagged six times. Six. Three of those in one night. Does that sound like a fantasy to you?'

'No, it sounds like he was using you!' Coleen cried. Her wet hands were still in front of her, fingers still gripping thin air, like she wanted to either shake some sense into her sister or throttle the life right out of her.

'How *dare* you!' Alanna demanded, rising to her feet. 'You're just jealous!'

'Jealous?! Ha! Of what? Of getting treated like shit by a fucking has-been?'

Alanna practically flew at her sister, but Coleen wasn't backing down. She lunged forward a pace, and they were suddenly face to face, nose to nose, eye to eye.

Taggart sat up. This was getting interesting.

'You always wished it had been you who'd ended up in bed with him that night!' Alanna screeched.

'Are you out of your mind? Can you hear yourself, Alanna?' Coleen scoffed. 'I told you he was a creepy bastard! I didn't even want to go and talk to him!'

'Because you knew you wouldn't have a chance with him!'

Coleen laughed, shook her head, and started to turn away.

'I'm not doing this,' she said, but then her sister caught her by the shoulder and spun her back around.

'Don't turn your back on me! And don't you dare call my Johnny a has-been!'

'He was never *your Johnny*, Alanna! And he was a has-been. And he's even more of one now! He's a *had-been*, past tense!'

The slap came out of nowhere. Even Logan, from his vantage point a few steps away, barely saw Alanna's arm move. He heard the crack, though, as her hand connected with Coleen's cheek. Saw the way the younger sister's head snapped to the right, and the wide-eyed look of shock when she turned back.

Logan was on his feet, hands raised to try and calm the situation before it got any further out of hand. More slapping would be bad enough, but there was a whole pile of kitchen knives drying within very easy reach. And, though any subsequent murder investigation would be a quick one to wrap up, he really didn't fancy being the catalyst.

Before he could intervene, though, someone beat him to it. The kitchen door opened, and the young lad with the shock of red hair, who Logan had seen back at the villagers' meeting, considered the scene in confusion.

'Mum?' he asked, his gaze shifting from Coleen to Alanna and back again. 'What the hell's going on?'

—

The sisters came to a ceasefire after Coleen's son, Declan, appeared on the scene. When her husband, Charlie, arrived a few moments later, Logan was politely encouraged to leave.

'Just one quick thing,' Logan said, as he got to his feet. 'Declan, was it? You were talking to Johnny yesterday. That right?'

Declan looked at his mum and dad, then nodded. 'Yeah. He's been showing me some guitar stuff. Dougie asked him to.'

'Right. Fair enough. Good to hear,' Jack said. 'What time was this?'

'Uh, about four. Half past, maybe.'

'I see. OK. And, sorry to ask, but where were you between seven and nine that evening?'

'Now, hold on a bloody minute!' Charlie objected.

'Sorry, I'll be asking more or less everyone sooner or later,' Logan said. 'It's got to be done.'

'He was here. All evening,' Charlie stated. 'He was running the site check, going door to door. You can watch the video yourself and talk to the guests. They'll tell you.'

'OK. That's great,' Logan said. 'Sorry again. Just have to check these things.' He turned back to Declan. 'How did he seem to you?'

Declan shuffled uneasily. 'Eh, bit drunk,' he said. He looked worried, like he was grassing Johnny up to a headteacher. 'But otherwise fine.'

'Didn't mention being worried about anything? No arguments with anyone? Nothing like that?'

'No. Nothing,' Declan said.

'Did you see where he went?' Logan asked. 'Once you'd finished talking to him?'

Declan shook his head. 'No. I just came back here. Didn't really see. Sorry.'

'It's fine. I appreciate the help,' Logan said.

He thanked them for their time, nudged Taggart in the direction of the door, then felt the wind and heard the *bang* as it was slammed shut behind him.

The argument between the sisters resumed then, but it was quieter, more contained and, he hoped, less likely to spiral into violence.

Johnny Freestone had done a real number on that lassie, Logan concluded, as he trudged away from the house, past the shed, and the all-seeing eye of the camera. Mind you, he'd be prepared to bet she wasn't the most stable of characters even before drunkenly hooking up with a faded rock star some fifteen years her senior.

'Over the bins,' Jack muttered, boots crunching on the limestone path. 'Jesus Christ.'

The dance music was still blasting out across the site. A few folks stood at the windows of the pods on either side of the path, looking out, making their disapproval apparent without going so far as to make any sort of actual fuss.

A laugh like a barrage of gunfire spat from the darkness over on the right. There was some splashing. A cheer. The music throbbed and pulsed and *doosh-doosh-dooshed*, building towards a frenzied, frenetic crescendo.

Logan's pod was a little further along the path, up on the left.

He went right, marching through the gloom, letting his ears lead the way.

A few moments later, he found the hot tub. Two people sat in it, across from one another. Logan had seen them both before, and one of them very recently.

The woman—the cackler—was the bored-looking fifty-something he'd seen in the audience at the village hall, fiddling with an unlit cigarette and paying almost no heed to what Reg and Elsie had been saying.

She was smoking now, the cigarette clutched between the tips of the middle and index fingers of her left hand, an overflowing ashtray on the edge of the hot tub revealing it wasn't her first of the night.

Her dyed blonde hair was still piled up on top of her head, but the steam from the water had played havoc with its structural integrity, so it now resembled an ice cream sundae that had been out in the sun for too long.

She wore a leopard print swimsuit that showed off an impressive cleavage of cellulite dimples and fake tan.

Directly across from her, sweating like he was being boiled alive, sat a semi-naked Ray Simpson, Johnny's manager.

Or, ex-manager, if Dougie was to be believed.

While his face bore the scars of old acne, his chest and shoulders were dotted with fresh stuff. Bumps, and plooks, and big red blemishes covered the parts of him that Logan could see above the bubbling waterline.

Earlier, his nose had been the reddest part of him, but the rest of him had now caught up. He looked like a freshly cooked lobster, though one that would be guaranteed to have you shitting through the eye of a needle if you ate it.

He smoked a fat cigar with a ringed finger hooked around it. There were bracelets and bangles on his wrists, as well as a few knotted circles of leather and cord. It was a fashion that Johnny Freestone and several other rock stars of his era had leaned into, but which looked ridiculous on the chunky wrist of a portly, balding slug like Ray Simpson.

'Whoa! Watch out! It's the rozzas!' Ray jeered when Jack appeared from the shadows. This earned another strafing of laughter from his lady friend that almost made Logan dive for cover.

Ray beckoned to him. A garish charm bracelet laden with little silver guitars, microphones, and dollar signs jangled as he gestured for Jack to get closer.

'Come in, mate! Join us! Plenty of room, even for a big lad like yourself.'

'Especially for a big lad like yourself!' the woman added, eyeing him hungrily.

'I'll pass, thanks,' Jack said. He pointed to a Bluetooth speaker that sat on the front porch of the pod, just a few feet from the hot tub. 'Would you mind turning that down?'

Ray followed Logan's finger, like he had no idea what the DCI was referring to.

'What, the music?' he asked, turning back.

'That's a generous way of describing it,' Jack said. 'It's almost eleven. Turn it down. All right?'

He had no intentions of sticking around any longer than necessary. The sight of the two of them stewing in their bubbling juices was already spoiling whatever dinner Tyler and the others might bring back.

When he turned to leave, though, Ray stopped him.

'Or what?'

Jack was fully aware that he wasn't himself right now. He agonised over decisions. He panicked at the thought of responsibility. A lot of things—far more than ever before—now terrified him.

This was not one such thing.

He turned without a word, snatched up the battery-operated speaker, and launched it into the darkness. It disappeared from sight long before the sound of it faded.

It grew quieter, more distant, and then stopped abruptly with a *crack* as it hit the ground.

Down at his feet, Taggart looked up at Logan as if to check whether he should be running to retrieve the thing, but made no move to do so.

'What the...?' Ray looked in the direction the speaker had gone, then back to Logan. 'What the hell? You can't do that! He can't do that!'

The woman looked the detective up and down, and took a long, slow draw on her cigarette. 'You ask me, this one can do whatever he likes.'

She raised her gaze until she met Jack's eye, then winked at him.

'Thanks for your cooperation,' Jack told them. 'Enjoy the rest of your night.'

He started to walk off, but stopped again.

'Oh, and the Mercedes in the car park. That yours?' he asked, firing the question at Ray.

'Yeah. So? What about it?'

'My dog pissed on it,' Logan said. He returned the woman's theatrical wink. 'No real reason for telling you. Just wanted you to know.'

And with that, he and Taggart turned and headed back to his pod, accompanied by a faint ripple of applause from the neighbours.

Chapter 24

The stag showed zero interest in getting out of the way. It stood in the middle of the road, chewing slowly and thoughtfully, as it considered the vehicle whose headlights shone on it like theatre spots.

It had been standing there when they'd approached, its eyes reflecting in the darkness before the rest of it appeared at the edges of the headlights' reach. Sinead had hit the brakes, causing Hamza to eject a panicky, 'Shit!' and Tyler to spill his Fanta.

That had been over a minute ago. Despite a few horn beeps and a slow creep forward on the clutch, the animal had demonstrated no desire whatsoever to move.

'What do we do?' Tyler asked, his voice low and urgent. He was sitting in the front passenger seat, one hand gripping the handle of the door and holding it shut, presumably, in case the stag walked around to his side of the car and tried the handle.

'Why are you whispering?' Sinead asked.

Tyler looked at her, then very deliberately side-eyed the stag. 'What do you mean? In case it hears us.'

'Why does it matter if it hears us?' asked Hamza from the back. 'It's not like it's going to understand what we're saying. We want it to hear us, if anything. In fact...'

He slid down his window, leaned his head out, and shouted, 'Oi! Piss off!' at the animal.

The stag stopped chewing and swallowed whatever had been in its mouth, but otherwise didn't shift an inch.

'You've fucking annoyed it now,' Tyler whispered. 'You can see from its face.'

Sinead blasted the horn again, making her husband jump in fright.

'Jesus!' he protested. 'Bit of warning!'

Sinead's window slid down at the touch of a button. 'Right. Shift!' she barked. She clapped her hands a couple of times, but the deer wasn't bothered in the slightest.

'Shut the window!' Tyler urged.

'It's not a wasp, Tyler. It's not going to fly in,' Sinead said, but the breeze blowing in from the north was cold, so she closed the window, anyway.

The stand-off was taking place about fifteen miles east of Durness, on a desolate stretch of single-track road, with nothing but brown scrub and heather on either side. They'd spotted a few other deer dotted around, munching away, but this was the first one they'd seen on the road.

And, it seemed, it was perfectly content to stay there.

'What about them weird whistle things you get?' Tyler asked. 'I saw them in a petrol station. They go under the car and make a whistling noise that scares these things away.'

Sinead turned her head to look at him. 'What about them?'

'Have you got one?'

Sinead continued to look at him, but he just stared back, apparently waiting for an answer. 'You know I don't have one, Tyler. And, if I did have one, clearly it wouldn't be working.'

Tyler tutted, like their lack of weird whistle thing was all Sinead's fault.

He took a moment to prepare himself, then slid his window down an inch or so, and raised his pursed lips as close to the gap as he could get them.

The whistle he let out was a thin, warbling sound, tuneless and shrill. It rose up through the octaves, then dropped back down again.

'What are you doing?' Hamza asked.

'What does it sound like I'm doing?' Tyler asked between two piercing notes.

'I don't know. Deflating?'

'I'm trying to do the whistle thing that scares them away.'

Sinead met Hamza's eye in the rear-view mirror, then pressed the button that closed Tyler's window. He stretched in his seat to follow the gap until it was all the way shut, his whistling growing louder, then fading away when he ran out of air.

'I don't think that was working,' Sinead told him. 'You'll need to get out and chase it away.'

'Fuck off!' Tyler ejected. 'That thing? Have you seen it? Have you seen the horns on it?'

'Antlers,' Hamza corrected from the back.

'It's a monster!' Tyler continued. 'If I go out there, I can tell you now *for a fact* it'll trample me and ram a horn up my arse.'

'Antler,' Hamza said again. 'It'll ram an antler up your arse.'

'Whatever it's called!' Tyler cried, twisting to face the detective sergeant. 'I don't want one being rammed up me.'

'It's not going to ram anything up you,' Sinead assured him.

'Look at it!' Tyler said again. 'Aye, it will! Up me, in me, through me. It'll be at me like I'm a voodoo doll.'

He pointed this time to the beast standing outside. Its head and antlers must have reached well over seven feet, and while some of the deer they'd passed a few minutes before looked slight and scraggly, this one had clearly eaten well. It must have weighed about four hundred pounds, and its densely packed muscles were like chiselled granite beneath its reddish-brown hide.

A faint mist had swirled in off the North Sea, and wisps of white floated around it, giving the animal an almost supernatural aura. This wasn't just a stag. This was some ancient and mystical Monarch of the Glens.

At least, that was how it looked to Tyler. To Sinead, it was just a deer being a pain in the arse.

'Just try and make yourself look bigger,' she suggested.

Tyler's eyebrows almost shot off the top of his head. 'Bigger? How am I meant to do that? Concentrate really hard and grow another six inches? If I could do that, do you not think I'd have done it years ago? *Make yourself look bigger!* I'm not a fucking pufferfish, Sinead. I can't blow my neck up like one of them African toads.'

Sinead bit her lip, but it wasn't enough for her to stop herself from laughing. Whether the trigger had been the image of Tyler with a vastly inflated throat, or his obvious distress, though, she wasn't quite sure.

'It's not funny!' he protested.

'It's pretty funny, mate,' Hamza chipped in.

'You do it, then! You go out!' Tyler yelped, flecks of foam flying from his mouth. 'In fact, you want me to look bigger? Come on out,

Ham, and I'll sit on your shoulders. You can come, too, Sinead. We'll make a human pyramid! See if that's enough to scare the— Oh. Wait. There he goes.'

They all watched as the stag decided it was bored of the car, and sauntered off to investigate the bracken on the left-hand side of the road.

'Aye, that's it. Sling yer hook, pal,' Tyler muttered, like he'd just personally sent the beast packing. 'Just you keep walking.'

Sinead eased off the clutch and crept forward slowly, keeping an eye on the animal in case it pulled a sharp about-turn.

As they passed it, Tyler wound down his window just a fraction.

'Twat!' he shouted. Then, when the stag turned its head to look at him, he hurriedly slid the window back up and shouted, 'Go, go, go!' like all their lives depended on it.

It was only when they were a few hundred yards down the road, with no sign of the stag giving chase, that Tyler exhaled again.

'That was close, eh?' he said. 'Thought he was going to come after us for that.'

'Again, they don't understand English,' Sinead pointed out, but the tilt of his head and the raising of his eyebrows suggested he wasn't so sure.

'Think the boss is going to be annoyed?' Hamza asked, after they'd trundled on in silence for a while longer.

'About the stag?'

'About the food,' Hamza said.

The inside of the car smelled like a chip shop fryer, interwoven by the sharper tang of vinegar and pickled onions.

All the food places in Durness had been shut, and after a bit of exploring and some searching on Google Maps, they'd finally found a takeaway open in a place called Tongue.

This had caused Tyler no end of amusement.

Unfortunately, Tongue was a fifty-minute drive in each direction, and while they'd all scoffed their own food while it was still piping hot, Logan's was now a sad, steam-sodden mound cocooned in a carrier bag on the parcel shelf.

'I can't imagine he'll be over the moon,' Tyler said. 'Though, I'm not sure he'll make that big a deal of it. He's, eh, he's struggling, I think.'

The other detectives just nodded in agreement. They'd all noticed it. Of course they had.

'He's probably just easing himself back in,' said Sinead. 'And his hands are probably tied, since McCulloch's technically the one in charge.'

Tyler looked out of the side window, watching the bracken rush by. It was more than that, he thought, though he didn't say as much. The boss wasn't holding back, he was being held back. Something—guilt, or fear, or whatever it was—was pushing him down, keeping him in check.

'I really hope he sorts it out,' Tyler muttered. 'For his sake, but ours, too. I can't be doing with McCulloch all the time. And God knows who we'll get as DI to replace Ben.'

A thought struck him. A terrible, awful, horrible thought.

'It'd better not be Heather Filson!'

Sinead laughed at that. 'No chance. You think she'd work under McCulloch? She'd knife him in the throat halfway through the first morning briefing.'

Tyler thought about this for a few moments, then shook his head. 'Nah. Still don't want her. Hope it's someone decent.'

Sitting in the back, Hamza quietly cleared his throat. 'I was thinking, well, half-thinking, that I might see about applying for it.'

He sounded unsure. Nervous, even. Like they might laugh at him for even suggesting it.

'You should!' Sinead said, meeting his eye again in the rear-view mirror. 'You'd be great. Wouldn't he, Tyler?'

Tyler blinked, his mouth hanging open ever so slightly. It took another prompting from Sinead before he blurted out his agreement.

'Eh, aye. Aye. That'd be… You should. You definitely should do.'

'I'm only half-thinking about it,' Hamza said. 'I probably won't.'

'Aye, fair enough. It's a big jump, and you probably wouldn't get it,' Tyler said, then a sharp look from his wife forced him to add an addendum. 'But still, you should definitely go for it, mate.'

He turned and offered Hamza the best smile he could muster. Even from the inside, where he was sitting, it almost felt convincing.

'You've got my vote, all the way.'

Logan had just sat down in the armchair and jostled the wee fold-out table into place when there was a knock at the door.

'Aw, for fu—' he muttered, before beginning the complicated process of stowing the table back into the arm of the chair.

He half-expected it to be Ray Simpson, wrapped in a towel, demanding an apology for either the Bluetooth speaker or the dog piss. Instead, when he opened the door, Declan stood there, a carton of semi-skimmed in one hand.

'You, eh, you forgot your milk,' he said. Even as he spoke, his gaze flitted to the cup of tea in Jack's hand, and the open carton sitting on the draining board.

'Oh. Thanks. I found some, though,' Logan told him. 'Turns out it was there in the fridge all the time.'

'Right. Oh. OK,' the lad said. He made no move to leave, though.

'Everything all right, son?'

'What? Yeah. Sorry. Yeah.' Declan looked past the DCI again. 'Is that your dog?'

Taggart lay sleeping on his side in front of the log burner, legs twitching occasionally as he ran around in his dreams.

'Aye. His name's Taggart. You know, after the detective on the telly?'

Declan just looked blankly back at him. Logan shrugged and took a slurp of his tea.

'Probably before your time, right enough.'

'Aye. Probably,' he said. 'Um, my dad wants your email address so he can send you the footage from last night. Of me. Here.'

'Oh. Right. Aye. That would be great,' Jack said. He handed the boy a business card. 'It's just procedure, that's all. You were seen talking to him, so we need to rule out—'

'I get it. I do,' Declan said. He pointed to a few of the neighbouring pods. 'I, um, I spoke to people in there and over there. They should still be around. And if you need phone numbers of the others who've already left—'

'I'm sure that'll be fine,' Logan told him. 'Thanks.'

The lad passed the milk carton from hand to hand, still showing no signs of wanting to leave. He was fairly tall—six foot, maybe—with a build that was just starting to fill out from what must have been some gangly early teenage years.

Logan would put him around seventeen or so, right in that awkward transition phase between leaving boyhood and becoming a man.

As he fiddled with the milk carton, his fingers tapped out a beat, like he was trying to send a message. It was more Mötley Crüe than Morse code, though, a fast, rhythmic tap-t-tap-tap that had a definite tune to it.

'Was that a guitar I saw back at the house?' Logan asked.

The tapping stopped.

'Yeah. Yeah. On the wall? Yeah. I play. A bit, I mean. You?'

Logan shook his head. 'Me? No. Not got a musical note in my body.'

'People say that, but everyone's got music in them,' Declan replied, then he winced, like he'd just heard that statement played back to him on tape. 'That sounded really cheesy. It, um, it sounded better when Johnny said it.'

His gaze flicked up to meet Jack's, then returned to the dog.

'Did you know him well?' Logan asked. 'Johnny?'

'Yeah. I mean, no. I mean, sort of. Dougie, you know Dougie? His cousin? He teaches me guitar, so I met Johnny a few times there. I'd heard stories about him being a bit horrible, but he was really nice, though. Really encouraging and stuff.' A smile played across Declan's face, tipping him all the way back into being a boy again. 'We played together. The three of us. Just like a jam session, you know? Nothing too major. But... it was cool. Really cool. He let me listen to some of his new stuff. Said I could even play on one of the tracks if I kept practising.'

His burst of excitement stuttered then and died away. It was like watching the element of an old light bulb slowly burn out.

'I, eh, I know a lot of people round here didn't like him, or whatever. And other people had problems with him, too, from what I read. But, he seemed all right. He was nice to me, anyway.'

Declan tore his eyes from the sleeping Taggart again, and forced himself to look up at the giant standing over him.

'Do you think you'll find who, you know? Who did it? Do you think you'll get them?'

'We're certainly going to do our best.'

Declan shifted his weight from foot to foot, then nodded, apparently satisfied by this answer.

He thought for a moment, then handed Jack the milk carton. 'In case you need extra. Or for the dog, or whatever,' he said.

Then, before Jack had a chance to thank him, he turned away, pulled up the hood of his hoodie, and went scurrying off into the night.

–

'Sorry, boss.'

It was twenty minutes since Declan Sinclair had handed Logan the milk carton and gone darting off. Jack had spent that time sitting in the armchair, sipping his tea and scribbling down some thoughts on the day's events.

Taggart lay snoring on the rug. The fire crackled and spat as it devoured the splintered log, filling the pod with a smoky warmth.

He had just been thinking that he could get used to this when the door went again, and he had to piss about with the folding table once more.

Tyler stood solemnly on the step, a carrier bag held deferentially in both hands like they were the ashes of some recently deceased loved one.

The bag was made of plastic so thin it bordered on transparent. Through it, Logan could see a paper-wrapped bundle that he assumed was the smoked sausage supper he'd requested.

The paper looked grey and sodden, though, as if it had been dropped in a puddle.

'We, eh, we got back as fast as we could,' Tyler told him. 'But the nearest takeaway we could find was nearly an hour away, we got harassed by a big monster stag on the way back, and, well...'

He held out the bag, and at least had the decency to look embarrassed about it.

'I think your chips are probably cold.'

Logan took the bag. He could feel the wetness from where the steam inside had cooled.

'Oh, you think?'

'You can probably give them a blast in the microwave,' Tyler suggested. 'The chips might be a bit mushy, though. And my smoked sausage tasted like soap, for some reason. But yours might not.'

Logan contemplated the congealing mass of grease and paper wrapped up in his hand, then tossed the whole thing straight in the bin.

'Aye. Probably for the best, boss,' Tyler said. He fished in his pockets. 'But, hang on, I did get these.'

He produced an assortment of chocolate bars and fanned them out, like a magician inviting their target to pick a card.

'I got a few, boss. Mars. Twix. Bounty.' He frowned at that last one. 'Bounty? Why'd I get a Bounty? Who eats a Bounty?'

Logan took the Twix and tucked it into his shirt pocket. It was better than nothing, and certainly better than a Pot Noodle.

'Right, well, I'll, eh, I'll shoot off, then, boss,' Tyler said. He looked back over his shoulder, but his feet remained planted on the spot.

'Something up, son?' Logan asked.

'What? No! Nah. Nothing, boss. All good. No problems. Everything's fine,' Tyler said, each denial only further weakening his case.

'Right. Fair enough,' Logan said, and he reached to close the door.

'Hamza's going to apply for the DI job!' Tyler blurted before the door could be swung shut. 'Ben's old job,' he added, in case Logan had forgotten the details.

The door creaked as Logan opened it further. 'Good for him.'

'Aye. Great. Good on him,' Tyler said. He chewed on his bottom lip. 'You think he'll get it?'

'Maybe. Not up to me,' Logan said. 'Not up to McCulloch, either. Though, I'm sure we'll both be asked for our thoughts.'

'No. Right. No, aye,' Tyler said. 'Makes sense, boss. He probably will. He could get it, I mean. He should. Shouldn't he?'

Logan sighed. 'What's the problem, Tyler?'

'Nothing, boss! No, nothing. It's just...' He scratched at the back of his head. 'Everything's changing. Ben. You. Dave joining the team—which is great, he's great, I'm happy about that—but if Ham moves up, then we need a new DS, and maybe that'll be someone else, or maybe it'll be me.'

Logan's eyebrows twitched at that notion. Over the years, he'd grown to be one of Tyler's biggest supporters, but the idea of *Detective Sergeant Neish* was proving difficult for his brain to process.

Even Tyler seemed to be having trouble with the idea.

'Or Sinead. Could be Sinead. Probably Sinead, actually, that's more likely. Whoever it is, though, it'll all be different.' He rocked back on his heels, like the force of the realisation had almost knocked him onto his arse. 'Ben's gone, you might not come back, Hamza and Sinead might both move up. I just... I don't know how I feel about it, boss. It just feels a bit like... I don't know.' He shuffled his feet. 'Like everyone's leaving me behind.'

'Nobody's leaving you behind, Tyler,' Logan said. 'Trust me, I know, because I've tried a few times, but you always bloody catch up.'

Tyler let out a dry little chuckle at that, but it was mostly for show and didn't hang around for long.

'Anyway, don't stress too much,' Logan continued. 'If McCulloch gets my old job, he'll fire you or ship you off elsewhere, so you won't have to worry about it.'

Tyler's mouth flopped open and closed, making him look like a fish on the deck of a trawler.

'I'm kidding,' Logan assured him. 'It's fine. You'll be fine. It'll all work out.'

Tyler rallied, straightening up and plastering on a smile. 'Aye. You're probably right, boss. I'm worrying about nothing,' he said, and though the words were coming out of his mouth, he wasn't doing much to sell them. 'I'm sure everything'll work out just fine.'

Chapter 25

To Logan's relief there was a cafe open early next morning, so he arrived at the station loaded up with enough bacon rolls for everyone, and every intention of eating them all himself.

Guilt got the better of him, though, and he ended up passing them around to the others before taking a seat. McCulloch turned his down, explaining in harrowing detail how he'd already had a 'hearty breakfast' of green tea and Alpen, with a spoonful of Greek yoghurt on the side.

For the first time since meeting the man, Logan actually felt sorry for him.

'Aye, well, all the more for me,' Jack said, taking the roll back.

McCulloch took the floor while the others ate, standing between the two whiteboards and waving his hands around like a conductor. He hadn't written a single word of the information up there on the boards, but he was holding the pen and using it to point with as if it had all been his work.

'Right. So, yesterday,' he said. 'Who wants to tell me about the interview with Douglas Cairns?'

The pen *eenie-meenie'd* between Logan, Tyler and Hamza, either hoping for a volunteer or hunting for a victim.

After a mouthful of tea, Hamza stepped into the line of fire.

'So, from talking to Dougie, it's fair to say there was no real love lost between him and his cousin. He wasn't making any effort to hide it, either,' the DS recounted. 'And, if what he says is true, he's not the only one. Johnny made a lot of enemies.'

'I also met a couple of fans last night,' Logan said, cutting in. 'Well, one superfan, in particular. Alanna… something. Didn't get the surname. She was bawling her eyes out at the cordon yesterday. Claims she and Johnny were in a relationship, but it didn't sound that way from how she described it.'

138

'What do you mean, boss? How did she describe it, like?' Tyler asked.

'I mean, I'm paraphrasing,' Logan replied. 'But, "He shagged me over the bins then walked away without a word", is about the size of it.'

'Jesus Christ,' Sinead mumbled.

'I didn't speak to her for long, but enough to know that she seemed like an absolute nutter,' Logan said. 'Someone should talk to her. Bring her in, maybe. I think she's probably got a lot more to tell us.'

'I could do that, boss,' Tyler suggested.

'Aye. She'll like you,' Logan said. 'Bring her in, we can make a room here for interviews.'

'You said you met a couple of fans, sir?' Sinead reminded him. 'Plural.'

'Aye. Other one was a young lad. Declan Sinclair. He was the one seen hanging around with Johnny the day he died.'

'You think he could be involved?' Hamza asked.

Logan shook his head. 'I got sent video footage showing him at the campsite, working around the time Johnny was killed. It's not easy to see it's him on the camera, but I spoke to the neighbours and they confirmed he'd come to the door to check up. Said the dad usually did it, but it was definitely the son on Friday night.'

The clearing of DCI McCulloch's throat was so loud it sounded painful.

'I'm sorry, did we forget again?' he asked. 'Did we lose track of who's running this investigation, I mean?'

The question hung in the air like a bad smell. Logan ran a hand down his face, clearly agitated.

He was going to say something. He was. The others were sure of it.

And he did. Just not the sort of thing they'd been hoping for.

'Sorry, Evan. My mistake.'

McCulloch arched an eyebrow. It was a reprimand, no two ways about it.

'Right. Good. Then, do you mind if we get back to Douglas Cairns, like I said?' he asked. 'Would that be too much trouble?'

'Sorry, sir,' Tyler mumbled.

'Forget it, Detective Constable, I expect it from you,' McCulloch said. The look he shot Logan bordered on the toxic. There would be words exchanged later, that much was clear. 'Detective Sergeant Khaled. You were saying?'

Hamza looked down at his notes, found his place, then continued. He filled McCulloch and Sinead in on everything that had been discussed the evening before. He told them about Johnny's revelation on the importance of family, about the list Dougie had rattled off of people who'd want to harm Johnny, and about the missing equipment the dead man had taken out of the house with him.

'There's the guitar, Old Bessie,' Hamza said, checking the notes he'd taken at the end of the conversation. 'Plus some recording equipment that belonged to Dougie. Quite expensive, by the sounds of it. He'd like it back.'

'I'm sure he would,' McCulloch said. 'Let's hope, for his sake, that he has adequate insurance.'

On McCulloch's instruction, Sinead set down her half-eaten bacon roll, took the pen from him, and jotted down all this information, including the names of the ex-wives and bandmates Dougie had provided.

By the time she returned to her roll, it was stone cold.

'There was no sign of that equipment anywhere, no?' Logan asked. 'Nothing at the scene.'

'You've seen the photographs, Jack, and—hopefully—have at least skimmed the report. You know the answer to that,' McCulloch told him. 'But, for the sake of clarity, no, nothing was found at the scene. No recording equipment, no guitar, nothing. Just a vape—Johnny's, we believe—and a dead pop star.'

'Rock star,' Logan corrected.

McCulloch made a big show of closing his eyes, drawing in a breath, and then opening them again. 'Sorry?'

'He wasn't a pop star. He was a rock star.'

'Is there a difference?'

'It's an entirely different type of music,' Logan explained.

The corners of McCulloch's mouth twitched. It wasn't a smile. Nor was it in any way like one. 'Is there a difference in terms of this investigation?'

Logan shrugged. 'Don't know yet. But always good to get the facts straight early on.'

Tyler glanced across the makeshift desks at Hamza and Sinead, his mouth pulling into a tight circle—a silent *ooooh* of anticipation.

Was this it?

Shots had been fired. Was this when Logan squashed the other DCI beneath a size fourteen boot?

'You're right, of course,' McCulloch told him. He held up the pen that Sinead had handed him back. 'Perhaps you could come and write that for us on the board, so I don't forget?'

'I'm sure you'll be fine,' Logan told him.

McCulloch continued to hold the pen out. 'Please. You're here to assist. I would like your assistance in this matter.'

There was no big face-off this time. No *cut-it-with-a-knife* tension. Instead, Logan got to his feet, took the pen, scrawled the words 'Rock star' under Johnny Freestone's name, then returned to his seat.

It was only when he picked up his tea that the others noticed how white his knuckles were.

'Thank you, Jack. Like you say, important we all know the facts, and where we stand, right from the start.'

McCulloch turned to Hamza. The smile and the nod of his head he gave made him look like some benevolent old king.

'Did you have more to add, Detective Sergeant? Did we find out anything else?' he asked. 'Was there more to be gleaned from Douglas Cairns, or is that all the three of you could rustle up?'

Hamza glanced at his notes, slightly flustered. There was more, he was sure of it, but the deliberate emasculation of DCI Logan had thrown him off his game a bit, and he couldn't quite read his own handwriting.

'Yellow tissue,' Jack announced.

McCulloch, who had been on the cusp of making some withering comment at Hamza's expense, let out a little sigh, like a teacher plagued by a disruptive pupil who didn't know when to quit.

'I'm sorry, Jack? Did you say something?'

'There was a yellow tissue. On the arm of Dougie Cairns's chair.'

'Fascinating. *Yellow,* you say? We'd better get that up on the board, quick-smart.'

Logan didn't rise to that. Somehow.

'Alanna whoever...'

'The bin lady?' Tyler asked.

'We can't call her *the bin lady,*' Sinead objected.

'You know what I mean,' her husband said.

'Aye. Her. She was using the same tissues. Same colour, anyway. I only saw one in Dougie's place, and he didn't strike me as being all that upset.'

'Quite the opposite,' Hamza agreed.

'So, what are you saying, boss? You think the bin lady was round there?'

'Can we please not call her *the bin lady*?' Sinead asked.

'All right, fine, sorry,' Tyler said. 'The bin *woman*. Better?'

'Not really, no!'

'I think she might've been,' Logan confirmed. 'If she was, I want to know why.' He heard his own voice rolling around the room, then turned to McCulloch. 'I mean, if it was up to me, I'd be looking into her, at least.'

McCulloch's expression gave nothing away, but the others could sense the anger bubbling away beneath the surface.

'I'm sure you would. Before we do that, though, perhaps you'd all take a look at the inbox. Jack, you'll have to squidge up next to someone else. I don't think you currently have access, but I'll grant permission for you to look on this occasion.'

Without a word, Tyler angled his laptop so Logan could see the screen, then clicked into the MIT mailbox. There were a few recent emails in there—preliminary reports from Pathology and Scene of Crime, along with another with the subject line 'Phone records'.

'While you three were out, Sinead and I arranged to get Mr Free-stone's phone records. Double-click the attachment, if you would.'

He raised a hand and mimed clicking twice on a mouse button, in case anyone was struggling to follow his instructions.

'As you can see,' he continued, as the files opened up. 'Mr Jonathan *Cairns* made and received a number of phone calls in the few days running up to his death. I spent some time yesterday evening on the phone myself, talking with our tech team, and with representatives of various phone networks.'

He interlocked his fingers over his belly—or over the concave spot where a belly should be, at least—and tapped his thumbs together. For such a minor gesture, there was something distinctly arrogant about it.

'As a result, I was able to identify many of the numbers our victim had been in contact with. Also of note, and which you won't see on those records, many of the people whose calls he declined to answer.'

'And?' Logan asked.

'Elsie Kellerman, who found the victim's body along with her husband yesterday morning. She called him the day before.'

'Oh?'

That was… interesting, Logan thought. Sort of.

'Eleven times,' McCulloch continued. 'And seven times the day before, and fifteen the day before that.'

'Bloody hell,' Sinead said. 'Did he answer?'

'Once. Only once. Five days ago—a day when she called fourteen times over the space of three hours. The call lasted for three minutes and seventeen seconds.'

'What was it about?' Tyler asked, then he grimaced. 'I mean, obviously, we don't know that, do we?' He glanced around. 'Or do we?'

McCulloch barely glanced at the detective constable. 'No. We don't. But I think another little chat with Mrs Kellerman could be enlightening.'

Logan sat back in his chair, fingernails rasping on the stubble of his chin as he tried to picture Elsie Kellerman as a killer. She had the temperament, he reckoned. Physically, she might not be the strongest, but with a heavy enough object…

'She said they explored further than normal,' he muttered.

McCulloch, who had started speaking again, stopped with another pointed sigh. 'I'm sorry, Jack? Did you have something to add?'

'Elsie Kellerman. When we spoke to her, she said they'd gone further than normal yesterday. In the cave. On their walk, or whatever.'

'She fancied a change, she said,' Tyler chimed in. 'That's right, boss! She said they went into a different part of the cave.'

'And that's where they found the body,' Logan concluded.

'Wait,' Sinead said, getting to her feet. She picked up the pen from where Logan had sat it, pulled off the lid, and wrote Elsie's name on one of the whiteboards. 'So, on the one day that she decides to go into a part of the cave they don't normally visit, she finds the body of the man she's phoned, like, a hundred times in a week?'

'That definitely sounds iffy,' Hamza said.

'Sounds more than iffy, mate. It sounds...' Tyler tapped his pen on his notebook, trying to find a suitable word. '*Really* iffy,' was the best he could come up with.

'Before we all get excited, there's something else,' McCulloch announced. His tongue flitted between his lips and he rocked on his heels, clearly pleased with himself. 'DS Khaled. There is another attachment on that email, correct?'

Hamza scrolled his screen and nodded. 'An audio file.'

'An *audio file!*' McCulloch echoed, widening his eyes and smirking like he'd just pulled off some dazzling feat of magic. 'Well, well. I wonder what that could be?'

He turned his back on them as if consulting the boards, though this was clearly for dramatic effect.

'Play it, if you would be so kind?'

Hamza keyed the volume all the way up on his laptop, then opened the audio attachment.

There was silence to begin with.

Not complete silence, though. Not all the way. It was textured, layered, like there was something lurking in it, waiting to pounce.

'So much for fucking family, eh?'

Dougie Cairns's voice crackled from the speaker. It was slurred. He was drunk. Angry, too.

'I should've fucking known. You're a fucking waste of space, Johnny. Always were. You think you're the big fucking *I Am*, but you're nothing. You're a pathetic, washed-up has-been who doesn't give two fucks about anyone but himself.'

There was a crack and a hiss. A can being opened. They heard the glugging as Dougie necked half of the contents in one go, then burped into the phone.

'And that new music? It's fucking shite. You really think this is going to turn things around for you? Make you relevant? There's no fucking chance, Johnny. None. In fact, know what? See your big career comeback you're planning? Forget it. It's fucking done. You'll see what I mean when I see you. You'll get what's been fucking coming to you all these years. It's about time you fucking paid for what you did to me.'

There was more glugging. Another burp. The clank of an empty can hitting the floor.

'And I don't mean chucking money at me this time. I mean properly paid. It's time you fucking suffered, cuz!'

Dougie raised his voice and brought the phone closer to his mouth, distorting the next few words. It was still possible to make them out, though. There was no denying what he said.

'It's time you paid the fucking price!'

There was some rustling and clattering, then the audio ended. This time, the silence was absolute, until Tyler finally broke it.

'Holy shit! What was that?'

'A voicemail, unopened, provided by the network,' McCulloch said.

He turned then, and the look on his face was somewhere between *nauseatingly smug* and *infuriatingly self-satisfied*.

'In case you couldn't follow, it was a call made to Johnny's phone by his cousin, Douglas Cairns. The man that you three spoke with yesterday afternoon. And though the most gripping revelation that came out of that visit appears to have been the discovery of a single yellow tissue, as you just heard, some of us were able to obtain some far more compelling evidence.'

Logan nodded. It was annoying, but there was no point in denying it. 'Good work, Evan. Are we going to bring him in?'

McCulloch checked his watch. 'Oh, I don't know, Jack...'

He crossed to the window. It was quite a distance away from the board, so the dramatic pause stretched on far too long, and became quite awkward for all involved.

When he was finally there, though, he pulled on the cord that opened the blinds. They rose halfway, then got stuck, and he had to fiddle about with a second cord to open them fully.

Outside, two Uniformed officers were escorting Dougie Cairns from a marked car to the entrance of the village hall.

McCulloch smirked. The reveal hadn't been quite as seamless as he'd hoped, but it would have to do. He threw in a raised eyebrow to try and compensate.

'*Are* we?'

Chapter 26

Moira Corson smiled.

This was a rare event, and worthy of note at the best of times. The fact it was happening now, though, while there were two screaming toddlers raising the roof of the cafe, was something of a miracle.

'Look at him,' she said, savouring the misery of the man currently wrestling with the crying children, like his suffering was a fine wine. 'Absolutely clueless. Them two bairns are running rings around him. He looks about one dirty nappy away from a complete mental break-down.'

Ben Forde glanced up from where he was attempting to draw a design on top of a cappuccino. He'd seen it done in other places, and it always seemed like a piece of piss. A wee swirl of the foam, a shake of cocoa powder, and job done.

For the life of him, though, he couldn't get it to resemble... well, anything. He'd set out to try and draw a flower, but had quickly realised that he'd set his sights too high. He'd tried turning it into a leaf, without much luck, and then just sort of freestyled it from there, hoping that it would at least look like a nice pattern.

But, looking at it now, it wasn't a nice pattern. Not by a long shot.

Still, it would have to do.

'Aye,' he said, picking up the tray with the coffee on it. 'He's got his hands full there, right enough. Mind you, if he does have a mental breakdown, we probably won't want to be around to see it.'

Ben sidled through the open hatch, and carefully carried the tray across to the cafe's one and only occupied table. The closer he got, the louder the crying became. It had been bad enough from across the room. Up close, though, it was ear-splitting.

'There we are,' he said, raising his voice to be heard above the din. He set the tray down and then, with shaky hands, picked up the cup by its saucer, and placed it on the table just beyond the reach of the squirming infants. 'Enjoy!'

'The fuck's this?'

Ben looked down into the scowling face of his one-time detective superintendent, Robert Hoon. The foul expression itself wasn't unusual. Nor was the week's worth of stubble, or the suggestion of mania that burned behind his eyes.

The dark circles under them were more prominent than usual, though. He was paler, too. He looked like a man who'd had less than three hours of sleep in the last twenty-four.

Which was precisely what he was.

'It's a cappuccino,' Ben said, tucking the tray under his arm.

'All right, one. I asked for a coffee, no' a fucking hipster's milkshake. And two'—he pointed at the design in the foam—'is that a cock and balls you've drawn on there?'

'What? No!' Ben looked down at the cup, then twisted himself around a bit to try and see it from Hoon's angle. 'I mean, I can see what you're saying, I'll give you, but it's a swan.'

'A swan? Aye, a well fucking endowed one taken from a low angle, maybe. That, *Benjamin*, is a cock and balls. No two ways about it.'

One of the twin toddlers he was holding slapped him on the forehead. Hoon took a breath, then went back to jiggling both children, one in each arm. There was a double buggy at the table beside him, but neither child showed any interest in being strapped into it.

'But whatever it is, why have I got it? I asked for a fucking coffee.'

'Aye. I know,' Ben said. 'Then I asked you what kind, and you said, and I quote, "Any fucking kind, do I look like I give a flying fuck?" and then you came and sat down. So, I made you a cappuccino.'

'I meant Nescafé Gold Blend or fucking...' He sighed. 'What's another one?'

'Kenco?' Ben suggested.

'Aye! Exactly. One of them. Fucking ALDI's own brand, if you want, I don't care. Just not this foamy liquid shite.'

'Right, fine. I'll get you another one.' Ben picked up the cup by the saucer, then nodded at the screeching twins. 'Tyler and Sinead got you on babysitting duty?'

A pudgy finger poked Hoon in the eye. A grasping hand tugged on the opposite ear.

'Still no' lost that fucking detective instinct, have you?' Hoon said. 'Nothing gets past you.'

There was a *tring* from above the door. Ben and Moira both turned to look at the same time. It was rare enough to have one customer in the cafe, let alone two.

Though she was still taking pleasure from Hoon's obvious misery, Moira's smile died away when she saw the man in the wheelchair rolling in through the door.

'Oh, great. Another one of your lot,' she said, shooting a look at Ben. 'Full price, remember? None of your nonsense.'

'Dave!' Ben cried, ignoring her. 'How's it going?'

Dave Davidson barely had time to respond with a, 'Not bad', when a cup was thrust out in front of him.

'You're a cappuccino man, aren't you?' Ben asked. 'Got one ready for you.'

Dave didn't have the heart to say that he wasn't, in fact, a cappuccino man, and instead just nodded for Ben to set it down on the nearest table, which he then wheeled himself over to.

'Cheers,' he said.

'It's not on the house!' Moira called over.

'Eh, no. Didn't think it was,' Dave said. He looked down at the froth, then up at Ben. 'That a cock and balls?'

'Fucking told you!' Hoon called from the next table over.

'It's a swan,' Ben insisted.

Dave turned the cup around a few times, trying to find an angle from which this statement might be true. He gave up after the third complete rotation, and tipped in some sugar. It immediately sunk through the foam, destroying the artwork forever.

It was then, Ben noticed, that a hush had fallen. Cal and Lauren, the twins that Hoon was holding, were no longer crying. Instead, they were both staring at Dave Davidson, eyes wide, like they were in some sort of hypnotic thrall.

'How the fuck did you do that?' Hoon whispered, wary of triggering another screaming fit.

'It's my big head,' Dave replied.

A look passed between Hoon and Ben. 'How d'you mean?' Ben asked.

'My big head. Babies love it,' Dave said.

He rapped his knuckles on his shaved scalp. Sure enough, now that Ben looked at it, the recently appointed detective constable's head was, indeed, massive.

'I reckon they think I'm, like, the uber baby, or something,' Dave continued. He seemed completely unfazed by the way the twins were staring at him, like it was the most normal thing in the world. 'And then, when I do this—'

He stuck out his tongue at the twins and waggled his eyebrows. They both giggled hysterically.

'They lose their minds.'

'Fuck me,' Hoon remarked. 'You need to stay with me all day.'

Dave shrugged. 'Aye, why not? Might as well. Not like I've got anything else to do.'

Ben pulled out a chair across from him and sat down. Moira scowled behind the counter, then went stomping off into the narrow kitchen at the back of the cafe, possibly to breathe fire into the oven.

'I thought you were all headed up north?' Ben said. 'Yesterday. You're not done already, are you?'

'Done? Nah. I mean, don't think so.' Dave shrugged. 'McCulloch sent me back down the road, and called last night to say it would probably be best if I just stayed down here.'

'McCulloch?' Hoon said, spitting the name out like it was smeared in something unpleasant. 'What, Evan McCulloch? Skinny bastard? Looks like a fucking paper Halloween skeleton, but with all the charisma sucked out and a load of liquid cat shit poured in in its place?'

'That's him, aye,' Dave confirmed.

'Fuck me!' Hoon cried, and it was probably just as well there were no other customers in the building. 'You know how many times that seeping bag of fucks tried to transfer up here?'

Ben and Dave both shook their heads.

'Aye, well, nor me. But it was a fucking lot. I had to keep putting the kibosh on it,' Hoon continued. The very thought of the man was contorting his face further and further, so that his sneer was threatening to turn the whole thing inside out. 'I actively fucking chose to keep *Snecky* here as DCI, rather than have to put up with that fucking... clattering Sally.'

Ben frowned. 'Clattering Sally?'

Hoon sighed. When he spoke, it was controlled, but impatient. 'I don't fucking know, Benjamin. This shite just comes out on its own sometimes, don't fucking ask me what it means. But *Snecky*! Imagine willingly saddling yourself with that glassy-eyed fuckrod. That's how bad Evan fucking McCulloch is.'

'Right. I see,' Ben said. He turned slowly to Dave and smiled supportively. 'How are you finding him, though?'

Dave just extended a finger and pointed to Hoon to indicate that the former detective superintendent had nailed it.

'And what? He's giving you grief, is he?' Ben asked.

Dave took a sip of his cappuccino, winced, and tipped in another sachet of sugar.

'The body was found in a cave, down a steep slope. No paving. McCulloch reckons that I'm probably, what will we say? Not best suited to the terrain.'

The twins had started to get grizzly again, so Dave wagged his eyebrows and crossed his eyes, sending them into another fit of the giggles.

'And, I don't know. He's probably right, I suppose.'

Ben sat straighter in his seat, a fingernail tap-tap-tapping on the Formica tabletop. 'And what about the witnesses?' he asked. 'They live in caves, too? The suspects, they all bloody mole-people, are they?'

Dave opened his mouth to reply, but Ben was just getting started.

'You know why I recommended you for detective, Dave?'

'Was it all the blood loss you'd suffered?' Dave asked. Enough time had passed since Ben's near-fatal injury for him to be able to joke about it, he reckoned.

'No. And it wasn't for your bloody agility or gymnastics ability, either.' Ben tapped at the side of his head. 'It was because of what's up here. Because I saw what you were capable of. Jack did, too. You shouldn't be down here drinking coffee, you should be up there, helping to solve this bloody thing!'

Dave shrugged. 'Aye, well, not up to me, unfortunately. Boss's orders, and all that.'

'Boss's orders? Boss's orders!' Ben ejected. He turned to Hoon, but pointed to the detective constable. 'This one, he's been working with us for three, maybe four years now. And do you know how many times he's called me "sir" in that time?'

'The fuck am I? Mystic Meg?' Hoon asked. 'How should I know?'

'None. Not once,' Ben said. 'And I know, because I counted. Or didn't count. Or... You know what I mean. You know how many times he called Jack "sir", or Mitchell "ma'am", or kowtowed to anyone? I'll give you a clue. Same again. None. Hee-haw. Bugger all. Not once!'

Dave raised the cappuccino cup halfway to his mouth, then thought better of it and reached for the sugar. 'Sorry, I didn't realise that bothered you,' he said.

'Bothered me? My backside, did it bother me! It was a breath of bloody fresh air. And it's another reason I put you forward, because I knew, deep down, you had a complete disregard for authority. You wouldn't just do as you were told, you'd *question* it.'

Ben rapped his knuckles on the table, making sure he had the detective constable's undivided attention.

'I put you forward, Dave, because I knew you'd be a pain in the arse. So, are you going to let that...' He pointed to Hoon.

'Haunted penguin's cock.'

The exact nature of the insult caught Ben off guard, but he didn't miss a beat. '...lay down the law without question?'

He stood up and tucked his tray crisply under his arm again.

'Or are you going to go up there and make yourself a right royal pain in his arse?'

Chapter 27

As soon as Dougie Cairns was in the building, DCI McCulloch announced that he would be the one to lead the interview, like he was claiming dibs. It wasn't that he was the best man for the job, but he was a glory-seeking bastard, who sniffed the possibility of an imminent arrest.

He ordered Hamza to accompany him, spent a few minutes quietly explaining how the interview was going to work, then went striding through to the manager's office that was now doubling as an interview room, clicking his fingers for the DS to follow.

'Good luck, Ham!' Tyler said, offering up two raised thumbs and a smile of encouragement. 'You've got this.'

The moment Hamza left the hall, Tyler spun his chair around to face Logan and Sinead.

'Christ. Imagine being stuck in a room with that horrible bastard.'

'Who? Cairns?' Sinead asked.

'What? No. He seems fine. I mean, for a potential murderer. I meant McCulloch. Having to sit next to him and, like, be on his team. Have the other guy think you're friends with him, or whatever.' Tyler shuddered at the thought. 'I don't think I'd be able to do it.'

'Aye, well, I don't think he's likely to ask you to,' Sinead pointed out.

'Good! I wouldn't do it if he did!' Tyler cried, then he buckled. 'I mean, I'd have to, obviously, but I wouldn't be happy about it.'

He looked across at Logan, who was sitting staring into space, his eyes narrowed.

'What's up, boss?' he asked. 'You look constipated, or something. You thinking you should be in there interviewing Dougie Cairns?'

'Hmm? Oh. No. No, let McCulloch do it. Keeps him out of our hair for a while.'

Sinead twisted her chair from side to side, looking from the door to the whiteboards and back again. 'You think he did it?'

'Too early to say,' Logan told her.

'I'm no expert—' Tyler began, but Logan leaned over and held a hand out, palm raised towards him.

'Can I just stop you there, Tyler? You're meant to be an expert,' the DCI reminded him. 'You're a detective in the polis. This? This whole thing? You're supposed to know what you're talking about.'

Tyler's mouth formed a few different shapes and stuttered a variety of sounds, then he nodded. 'Fair point, boss. Well, OK. *In my expert opinion*, then, that voicemail sounded well dodgy. I mean, he was basically threatening to do him in.'

'He didn't actually say he was going to hurt him,' Sinead said.

'No, but he *basically* did,' Tyler countered.

Logan got up out of his chair. Taggart, who had been sleeping under the table, raised his head in the hope that there might be a walk in his immediate future. When Jack stopped at the whiteboards, he let it sink back down again.

'That Alanna. The one I met last night.'

'The—'

'Don't say "bin lady"!' Sinead warned.

'I wasn't!' Tyler protested. 'I was going to say *the nutter*? What about her, boss?'

Logan considered the boards, then ran a hand up and down his face like the skin was itchy. He groaned, deep at the back of his throat. It was a pained sound.

'You two go talk to her, will you? Officially. Find out where she was the night of the murder. If you think she's hiding something, bring her in.' He turned to them, a warning finger raised. 'But, for God's sake, be careful. Anything seems off, anything doesn't feel right, you get out of there. All right?'

'I'm sure we can handle it, boss,' Tyler told him.

'That's not what I asked,' Logan barked back at him. 'I mean it, trust your gut on this. If it seems off, leave, then call in backup.'

'Will do, sir,' Sinead confirmed.

'Aye, we get it, don't worry. We'll be on red alert,' Tyler said. He smiled in what was presumably meant to be a reassuring way. 'But, seriously, boss. She's one woman. How dangerous can she really be?'

Logan pinned him in place with a cold and pointed look. 'Jesus Christ, son,' he muttered. 'You had to bloody go and jinx it.'

–

Logan almost chased down Sinead's car as it drove away from the village hall, headed down the hill in search of the address they'd pulled for Alanna Swain.

The situation was not the same. The circumstances were entirely different.

But the last time he'd sent officers to investigate an address, they hadn't come back. And those ones had been heavily armed.

'They'll be fine,' Jack said. He hoped that saying the words out loud would help him believe them.

It didn't.

Taggart sniffed around the car park, tail wagging away, head lowered. The Kellermans' box truck hadn't shifted from its parking bay. There was no sound from inside it, though, so it was possible the couple had gone out.

The office that McCulloch was using as an interview room was around the other side of the building, so Logan couldn't lug in on that conversation, either. Mind you, he'd only end up trying to chime in through the window—or climb in, maybe—so it was probably for the best.

Down at the bottom of the driveway, Sinead's car was still sitting with its indicator on, trying to pull onto the main road. A relentless convoy of traffic was making it difficult, though. It clogged up the narrow single-track artery, and horns were blaring in both directions as frustration bubbled over into rage.

Part of the problem was the cordon around the entrance to the Smoo Cave car park. The cordon didn't cover as large an area as yesterday, but visitors were still being turned away at the entrance, which was only adding to the congestion.

The small army of Uniforms that had been guarding the place yesterday had been shaved down to just two officers, who had their hands full trying to unclog the traffic jam.

Beyond the cave, in the distance, lay the shore, the rocky outcrops tortured by the relentless cruelties of the North Sea. Logan was watching the waves crashing in when another movement caught his eye.

A man, ducking low, creeping through the foliage near the far side of the cave car park. He was dressed in dark clothing, blending him with the scrubland around him. Had Logan not been looking almost directly at him, he'd never have known he was there.

Jack blinked and glanced away, just for a second. By the time his gaze swept back across the shoreline, the figure had moved. A subtle shift. A change in the way the shadows fell. Just enough to set his instincts humming.

He was headed for the cordon tape.

Headed for the cave.

'And just what the hell do you think you're up to?' Logan muttered.

The Uniforms were busy at the roadside. No chance they were going to turn around and spot the bastard, and shouting from here was a waste of time.

Logan's coat was back in the hall, his car keys in the pocket. Driving would be pointless, anyway. He'd be waiting at that junction all day.

He whistled, shrill and sharp, drawing the attention of Taggart, who was still sniffing around in front of the village hall.

'Right then, dug,' Jack announced, setting off at a stride. 'Walkies!'

Chapter 28

Dougie Cairns, for the moment, had opted out of having his solicitor present. This was just as well, given that his solicitor was based in Inverness, and would take hours to drive up the road.

He sat across the table, tightly wound, one hand wrapped around the opposite fist, kneading the knuckles as he listened to his voicemail message being played back to him, his eyes never moving from Hamza's laptop.

It had been DCI McCulloch's idea to hit him with the recording right at the start. And, though Hamza had felt it better to save it for later and let him incriminate himself first, McCulloch had been quick to dismiss the suggestion.

'After hearing that, he'll have nowhere to go,' the DCI had said before they'd entered the room. 'He'll have no choice but to own up to it.'

It was clearly making for uncomfortable listening, that much was obvious. Hamza could hear Dougie's breath shaking in and out as his voice on the recording hissed its final ominous threat.

The recording ended. Hamza closed over the lid of the laptop and slid it aside, while McCulloch steepled his fingers, tip to tip, in front of his chin.

'"It's about time you effing paid for what you did to me."' The DCI looked at Hamza, seated on his left. 'That's what he said. Right? You heard that?'

He didn't wait for the detective sergeant's reply before turning on Dougie.

'That was your voice on that recording, Douglas. Correct? It came from your number. That was you. Calling Johnny.'

Dougie swallowed. Nodded. 'Aye.'

'On the very day he died.'

'I didn't kill him!' Dougie replied, putting paid to McCulloch's immediate confession theory. 'I know it sounds bad, it does. I mean, it really does. But I didn't kill Johnny.'

Already, McCulloch was on the back foot. Hamza wasn't sure if he'd been serious about Dougie buckling as soon as he heard the recording, but the way he stumbled over his response said he must have been.

'Really? Is that...? Do you honestly expect us to believe that?'

'I didn't. I swear to God. I wouldn't. He's an arsehole—*was* an arsehole—but he's family.'

McCulloch's response was a series of incredulous huffs and sighs, none of which was particularly helpful.

'So, what did you mean?' Hamza asked, stepping into the breach. 'You said it was about time he paid for what he did to you. What did you mean by that?'

Dougie was still massaging his clenched fist. He looked down at it, realised how it might look, and laid both hands flat on the table instead.

'Like I said back at my place, we... didn't have a great relationship.' The words came slowly, hesitantly, like he was checking them over one by one before saying them out loud. 'We've had our ups and downs over the years. The ups were usually when Johnny needed something, and the downs were, well, every other time.'

'So, you hated him,' McCulloch said, jumping back in. He tapped the lid of Hamza's laptop. 'You made that very clear.'

'Yes. Aye. I suppose I did hate him,' Dougie admitted.

'I knew it.'

'But I loved him, too.' He grimaced, sitting back. 'Ach, I don't know. It's complicated. You know what families are like.'

Hamza knew exactly what families were like, though he couldn't vouch for McCulloch.

'What did you mean he was going to pay?' the DS asked. 'You said you didn't kill him, fine. But you can see how that sounds, can't you? Especially after everything else you said. It sounds like a threat.'

'It does. Aye. I know. And... and it was,' Dougie admitted. 'I was angry at him. I thought after he'd had his big "family is everything" moment earlier, that this was it. He was going to make up for everything. We were going to sort it all out.'

He looked to the window, but the blinds had been drawn to stop anyone looking in from outside.

'And then, when he didn't turn up...' Dougie's voice cracked. He rubbed at his forehead as if fending off a headache, but used the hand to hide his eyes from the other men. 'I'd been drinking. I shouldn't have been drinking. I'd had way too much. I fell asleep on the couch. Must've slept right through Declan coming for his lesson. Didn't hear him. When I woke up, Johnny wasn't there, and I kept drinking, and...'

The emotion of it overwhelmed him. He buried his face in his hands, shoulders shaking as he choked down deep, silent sobs.

McCulloch folded his arms, unimpressed. Hamza spotted a box of tissues on a cluttered shelf beside the table, and slid them across to Dougie.

'Thanks,' Cairns said, after blowing his nose and wiping his eyes. He took a breath, held it, then let the words tumble out with it. 'I was going to delete his new music.'

McCulloch arched an eyebrow. 'Sorry?'

'His new music. The stuff he's been working on while he's been here. It's on hard drives in my studio. I was going to wipe all of it. Destroy it all,' Dougie said, and he looked shamed by what he was saying. 'You asked how I was going to make him pay. That was it. That's what I was going to do.'

'And did you?' Hamza asked.

Dougie sagged, shrinking down into himself. His, 'No', was so quiet the detectives struggled to hear it in the otherwise silent room. 'I couldn't. I mean, I wanted to, but... He let Declan play guitar on one of the tracks, and he was so chuffed about that. I would have done it if it wasn't for that. I'd have gladly done it to Johnny, but it wasn't fair to take that away from Declan.'

'You were going to *delete some music*?' McCulloch asked. 'That was all?'

'All?' Dougie's forehead creased in disbelief. 'Music was his life. He's been working on this stuff up here for months. He's poured his heart and soul into it.'

'But you said it was awful,' McCulloch reminded him. 'On the voicemail, you said it was'—his bony fingers made the air quotes—'"shite". Didn't you?'

Dougie shifted around on the chair. It was a horrible hard plastic thing brought in from the hall, so Hamza couldn't blame him.

'I mean, aye. That's what I said. But I wanted to hurt him. It's...
decent. Nothing like his old stuff. It mostly leans more folky. A lot of
it's acoustic, and his voice has aged into—'

McCulloch held up a hand, silencing him.

'Irrelevant. So, you're saying that your big threat of making him pay
was going to be by deleting the music he has recorded here?'

'Yes. Aye. Exactly. I knew how much that would hurt him. He'd
have been devastated. It'd have destroyed him.'

'What did he do to you?'

Dougie's eyes widened slightly at the DCI's question, but he otherwise didn't react.

'Well?' McCulloch demanded. 'If, as you say, you were prepared to
devastate and destroy him, he must've done something pretty terrible
to deserve it. No?'

Dougie looked to Hamza, then back at McCulloch, as if searching
for something. When he didn't find it, he leaned back in the chair.

'You mean, you don't know?'

'Know what?' McCulloch replied.

'About the accident.'

McCulloch exhaled through his nose. '*What* accident?'

Dougie hoisted a leg up, one hand pulling it by the front of his jeans.
It gave a solid *thunk* when it landed on the table.

He pulled up the denim, revealing a shin of sleek carbon fibre.

'*That* accident.'

Chapter 29

Logan recognised the Uniforms working the cordon. It was the constable who had tried to send him packing at the car park yesterday, and the sergeant who had intervened. Both looked hopefully at him as he came striding towards them between stationary cars, like he might be there to take charge, or at least to provide some backup.

Instead, he tied Taggart's lead onto a railing, ordered the constable to 'Watch him', then continued on down the hill in the direction of the cave, apparently oblivious to the tooting horns of the irate drivers.

There was no sign of the figure that Logan had seen sneaking onto the scene on the path down, and he wasn't hanging around at the cave entrance, either.

That wasn't good.

Logan stopped halfway down the slope, peering into the deep pit of darkness that lay in wait beyond the cave's mouth.

A knot of pain throbbed between his eyes. Every intake of breath tightened a belt around his chest.

He should call the Uniforms down. Send them in. Stay out here in the light and wait for them to come back. Bide his time.

But he'd been biding his time for months.

His feet resisted, fighting him. He forced them to comply. One step, two, onwards, downwards, closer and closer to the yawning, howling dark.

He stopped again where the line of shadow cut across the ground. Right in the cave's jaws. Right between the bastard's teeth.

The horns were still blaring. The voices were still raised. But he couldn't hear any of it. All he could hear was months ago. The echoes of gunshots and screaming.

Jack closed his eyes, summoning the courage to enter. When he did, though, he was no longer standing there. He was in another cave, another time. Hunted. Scared.

Face to face with madness.

And death.

He could still back out. He could go get help.

He could leave. Run.

But he'd been running for months.

And he couldn't keep running forever.

One step. Two. He crossed the threshold.

The air tasted thicker. Sourer. It caught in his throat, choking him, trying to turn him around, drive him back.

He stood there, steeping in it, breathing it in. Even here, just a few paces into the darkness, he could feel the weight of the world pressing down on him. Thousands of tonnes of rock and soil compressing him, crushing him.

A stream ran into the cave. A bridge spanned it.

He aimed for it, threw himself at it, grabbed the railing and held on.

The water raced by beneath his feet, an artery connecting him to the world outside. For a moment, he considered jumping into it, wading out. Swimming, if it came to it.

What had he been thinking? Why had he done this? He wasn't ready. This was all too soon.

He sensed a killer lurking in the shadows. Heard a gunshot. Saw the flash.

Pain. Blood. Panic. Fear.

The weight. The darkness. Pushing down. Rushing in.

His hand slipped on the railing. The bridge spun beneath his feet, twisting, bucking, trying to throw him off.

He stumbled. Staggered. He was falling.

He *had* been falling.

For months now.

And then, up ahead, he saw a light. A real one, this time, sweeping across the walls. A torch. A tether, holding him up.

The intruder.

A man trespassing on a crime scene.

A criminal breaking the law.

An anchor to cling to.

'Right then, you bastard,' Logan wheezed, though he wasn't sure who the words were aimed at. He straightened himself up, straightened himself out. 'Let's be having you.'

—

'I think that's it,' Sinead announced, looking past her husband at a house on the left.

It was fairly unremarkable—the sort of place you wouldn't look at twice as you drove past. A detached, pebble-dashed box, similar to half the houses in the village, with a neatly kept garden out front and a driveway just wide enough for the five-year-old Ford Mondeo currently parked in it, nose out.

The curtains in the downstairs windows were drawn, but the upstairs ones were open, the glass catching the late morning light and reflecting the foaming crests of the North Sea.

'Looks normal enough,' Tyler murmured, though his tone suggested he wasn't entirely convinced.

Sinead didn't reply, just shifted in her seat, her eyes flicking past the house to the large shed that loomed behind it.

It was a proper shed, not some flimsy B&Q job for storing a lawn mower. Bigger than a garage, maybe twice the size, with a sloping roof and thick wooden walls that had weathered to a dull grey. The doors were shut, and very possibly locked, but there was a small side window, just high enough that nobody could glance inside without making an effort.

'Bit overkill for a shed, isn't it?' Tyler mused. 'What do you reckon? Storing a boat? Home gym? Meth lab?'

'Or, you know, just a shed,' Sinead said, though her gaze lingered a fraction too long.

They unclipped their belts, found their warrant cards in their pockets, then got out of the car and headed up the path. Tyler knocked, then stepped back behind his wife, electing her to do the talking.

'Think she's in?' he whispered, after thirty seconds of waiting.

Sinead looked over at the closest window. As far as she could tell, the curtains hadn't so much as twitched.

Tyler took another step back and checked the upstairs windows, but saw nobody lurking up there, peeking out above the sill.

'Try again,' he suggested. 'I'll go check out round the back.'

While Sinead rapped her knuckles on the door's narrow frosted glass pane, Tyler followed the uneven slab path to the driveway, where a second path led around to the shed and the back of the house.

As he passed the parked car, something caught his eye. Or, no, not *something*. Lots of things. The backseat was awash with discarded drinks cans, crisp bags, plastic sandwich wrappers and at least five little boxes that had once contained Maltesers, but which had since been repurposed as ashtrays.

The detritus covered the seats, the floor, the parcel shelf—the wrapper of a sausage roll and half a Curly Wurly even stuck out of the pocket on the back of the driver's seat.

Dotted amongst the litter was a star field of spilled crumbs, cigarette ash and a single orange Smartie sitting there like some far-off alien sun.

It had all started to spread to the front of the car, too. The passenger seat and footwell weren't *quite* as badly contaminated as the back, but the infection was taking hold. Plastic juice bottles, soiled food containers and a couple of local newspapers either sat on the seat or spilled over onto the floor.

The dashboard was a graveyard of Highland Council car park tickets, the print on all but the scattered top layer mostly faded, the paper yellowed by the sun.

The most recent ticket he could see was from a couple of weeks ago, for the Eden Court car park in Inverness. He very much doubted it was important, but took note of the details, anyway.

Sinead had moved away from the door and was now trying to find a gap in the living room curtains to see inside. Tyler left her to it and continued around the back.

The kitchen window was uncovered, but he couldn't see any signs of movement within. Then again, the lights were turned off, and the window lay directly in the shadow of the shed, so even if there had been someone standing in there, he'd have struggled to spot them.

He gave the door a knock, had a sneaky wee try of the handle, then danced from foot to foot, impatiently clicking his fingers and humming below his breath.

His gaze swept across the back garden. It didn't take long for it to settle on the shed.

The building dominated the narrow space, both with its size and its placement, slap bang in the centre of the garden. It couldn't be for anything big, like a boat, or a caravan, because it wasn't connected to the driveway, and unless either of those vehicles could be folded away, they weren't fitting through the door.

Nothing about the house suggested that anyone was home, so Tyler crossed to the only window he could see in the shed, and stretched up onto his tiptoes to look inside.

He wasn't tall enough.

'Bollocks,' he muttered, then he spied a large plant pot that he improvised into a stool.

It gave him the extra height he needed to reach the window, but the shed was too dark for him to see inside. He took out his phone and shone the torch, then fell off the shoogly plant pot when he saw a face staring straight back at him.

It was only when he was back down on the ground that he realised the face had been his own.

Climbing back up, he tried again. And, again, all he could see was himself. There was something draped across the window. A swatch of black fabric, stretched across the frame, blocking the light coming in from outside.

A photographic darkroom, maybe? Was that still a thing?

He dismounted the plant pot, returned it to where he'd found it, then considered the front door of the shed. There was no slide bolt or padlock, but there was a black metal door handle with a keyhole in it.

Holding onto the handle for support, Tyler squatted to peer through the keyhole. As soon as he lowered the handle, though, the door swung outwards, slammed into one of his knees, mid-bend, and bounced shut again.

Tyler landed heavily on the ground, knee throbbing, brain still rushing to compute what the hell had just happened.

He stood up quickly before anyone could see, trying to convey through body language that he had *totally* meant to do that, actually, but he didn't have the time or inclination to explain why, so don't bother asking.

After dusting himself down, he looked around to see if anyone was watching, then inched the door open a crack and shone his light inside.

His heart dropped into his stomach. His stomach tightened all the way down to his arse which, in turn, gave a squeak of fright.

'Oh,' he whispered. 'Oh, for fuck's sake.'

—

It helped to remind himself of the differences.

This cave was not like the last one. That one had been a tunnel down into the earth. An old mineshaft, littered with rusted memories of the past. This one was higher, wider, more open.

The silence in the other cave had been stifling, but noise filled this one and brought it to life. The trickle of the stream. The roar of a distant waterfall. The irregular drips and plinks of droplets falling on smooth stone.

They were not the same place.

This was not like the last time.

Nobody would die down here. Not today.

He kept his torch off, following the pale glow of the intruder's so as not to give himself away. He'd thought about shouting, but that might make the guy run, and the only route open to him would be deeper into the cave.

And Logan wasn't ready for that yet.

With the sun-warming stone creaking far overhead, Logan forced himself onward, following the light.

–

Tyler's torchlight pushed back the darkness, and picked out a thousand tiny faces staring back at him from inside the shed.

Well, one face, technically, but repeated a thousand times from different angles and with different expressions.

They lined the walls, in colour and black and white, smiling, and sneering, and laughing, and leering. Pretty much anything it was possible to do with a mouth, two eyes, and a nose, in fact, the faces were doing it.

Johnny Freestone. An army of him, carefully cut and carelessly torn out of newspapers and magazines, then pasted into a vast collage that covered the back wall, and at least part of the walls at either side.

His name had been spelled out in letters ranging from around six to ten inches high, each one also pulled from the pages of some publication or other. It looked like a ransom note, albeit one where the only apparent demand was for a recently deceased rock star from the mid- to late Eighties.

The letters were dotted among the photos, roughly at the same height, but spaced several inches apart so they spanned the whole wall. Tyler swept his torch beam across them, then let out a scream of fright when the light picked out a figure standing fully upright in the shadowy back corner of the shed.

All his major muscle groups contracted at the same time, and as his hand squeezed his phone, the torch blinked off, letting the darkness come rushing back in.

'Ohshitohshitohshitohshit!'

Tyler frantically poked and prodded at the screen. Where was the button? *Where was the button?!*

Finally, his finger found the icon and the light returned. He angled the beam back up at the figure, babbling out a 'Police! Don't move!' with as much gusto as he could rustle up.

The cardboard cut-out in the corner was only too willing to oblige.

Johnny Freestone. Life-sized. Well, two dimensions of him were life-sized, at least. He was undoubtedly a good bit thicker than that in real life.

He looked young, and the details were all quite blurry, suggesting this was an old photograph blown up far larger than its resolution allowed. Still, now that he had the light on it, there was no mistaking it as Freestone.

And, if there had been, the other strip of ransom note lettering spelling out his name would have soon cleared up any confusion.

Tyler edged the door open further, letting the weak, grey, outside light seep into the shed. He immediately wished that he hadn't.

The floor was covered in photographs, printouts, magazine pages. Johnny Freestone, Johnny Freestone, Johnny, Johnny, *Johnny*. Everywhere he looked, the bastard looked back. Smirking Johnny, scowling Johnny, sultry Johnny, sad. Headshots, longshots, two-shots with the other person torn out, or cut away, or scribbled over in jagged black streaks.

Logan had said Alanna had come across as a nutter. But *this*? This was unhinged.

Tyler had just concluded that he should get the hell out of there when something slammed into him from behind. He stumbled forward, phone flying from his hand, feet slipping on a page from a 1989 issue of *Smash Hits*.

Which, ironically, quite accurately described what happened next, when he reached the back of the shed, collided with the wall, and landed heavily on the floor.

He scrabbled and slipped on the scattered glossies, rolling over, turning himself around to face his attacker.

She stood there, framed in the doorway, fingers curved into claws, her anger palpable even in the shadow of her silhouette.

'Who are you?' screeched Alanna Swain. 'And just what the *fuck* do you think you're doing in my grotto?'

Chapter 30

Logan was deep in the darkness when he heard the cry. It was sharp, sudden, all-too-brief. The pale torchlight he'd been following snapped off, and the cave seemed to close in, shifting and tightening around him like a boa constrictor.

'Fuck,' he muttered, if only to prove to himself that he still existed. That he wasn't already dead.

He found his phone and activated the flashlight function, forcing the shadows back the way they'd come. Up ahead, the passageway narrowed and lowered, the rocky ceiling becoming just a couple of metres high.

He'd have to duck. The rock, scarred by centuries of trickling water and seismic shudders, would be right there, right above him, pushing down.

Waiting.

Some part of him stressed that it wasn't too late to turn around. Asking for help was never a bad idea, and ordering some other poor bastard to do the dirty work was an even better one.

But the cry had been of fright. Of pain.

And he'd already lost too many people to holes in the earth.

He shuffled on, pulse racing, heart quickening, breath held. The rocks on either side of the narrowing passageway were sharp and jagged. They dragged on him and clawed at him as he pushed on, pushed through.

'Help!'

The voice came from everywhere. Every direction, all at once. Like the last time. Exactly like the last time.

He'd had to sneak then, stay quiet to stay alive.

But that was then.

'Hello? Where are you?'

There was a moment of shocked silence, like the person shouting hadn't dared to hope for any sort of response.

'Shit! Aw, mate! Thank Christ!'

The accent was Australian. It still came from everywhere but more ahead than to the sides. Ahead and... down?

'I'm in a fuck-off big hole!' the voice said.

That cleared that up.

'Hang on, I'm coming. Keep talking,' Logan instructed. 'You had a torch, didn't you?'

There was another pause, a little less fleeting than the one before.

'Nah. I mean, yeah, but nah. It's fucked. Smashed to buggery.'

Logan's head scraped off the ceiling. He grimaced and ducked further, but this pushed out his shoulders, forcing him to twist so he was partly shuffling sideways through the tunnel.

After a few seconds of this, he reached what seemed to be some sort of junction. The path split into three tight, winding tunnels. Logan imagined veins of lava erupting up through them, then wished that he hadn't.

He shone his torch along each passage. The light reflected off cold, damp stone, then petered out into a wall of impenetrable black.

'Which way did you go?' he asked. His voice had been echoing until then, but now it sounded flat. Lifeless.

'Pretty fucking abruptly straight down,' the other man replied. Evidently, his injuries weren't enough to completely rob him of his sense of humour.

Jack, however, wasn't in the mood. 'I've got three passages,' he announced, shining his torch into them again. 'Which one?'

'That one! Whatever one that is! I can see your light.'

Logan stood at the opening to the tightest, narrowest artery of the three.

'Course it is,' he muttered, then he made himself as small as he could, and sidestepped, crouching, along the passage.

'Whoa, whoa, whoa!'

The shout came from just a few feet ahead of him, but several feet down. He stopped, the scuffing of his boots sending pebbles and gravel tumbling down into a deep pit that opened up directly ahead of him.

'Careful there, mate.' The torchlight swept down into the hole, forcing the blond-haired, bronze-skinned Australian currently standing in it to screw his eyes half-shut. 'Fat lot of good you're going to be if you're stuck down here with me.'

The hole was nine, maybe ten feet deep. The Australian trapped in it was maybe six. Jumping was no good, and there was nothing obvious down around the bottom of the hole for him to climb up or stand on.

'Think you might need to go get a rope, brother,' he declared.

Logan wasn't sure what he'd done to be upgraded from 'mate' to 'brother', and he wasn't sure either one would stick once he'd arrested the bastard for trespassing on a crime scene.

The legal stuff could wait, though. For now, he had to get him out.

'Or, maybe, do you have, like, a belt on, or something you could lower down to—?' the Australian began, only to fall silent when the long arm of the law—literally, in Logan's case—reached down and offered him a hand.

'Grab on,' the DCI instructed. 'I'll pull you up.'

'I don't know, brother,' the man in the hole said, as he reached up and took Logan's hand. 'I'm pretty heavy.'

Logan pulled. The angle wasn't great, thanks to the narrow walls and the sharp rocky edge of the hole, but with some muttering, gritting of teeth, and some light to moderate cursing, he hauled the other man up out of the pit, and deposited him unceremoniously on the ground beside him.

'No you're no',' Logan told him.

It would have been quite an impressive moment, had he not then stood up and cracked the top of his head on the roof of the tunnel.

The darkness surged. Colours sparked and danced in it, like comets, and stars, and distant supernovas. He staggered, one foot flailing above the drop, hanging there with only empty space below.

'Christ,' he hissed, several seconds too late, the impact having caused some temporary disconnect between his rattling brain and his mouth.

Then, the colours died off, leaving only darkness, which gave way again to the glow of his torch.

Logan looked around.

The Australian was nowhere to be seen.

He heard rustling back along the passageway. Footsteps rushing. Clothes brushing against stone.

'You ungrateful little bastard,' he hissed.

And, with all fear now replaced by indignation and rage, Logan lowered his head, angled his body, and sidestepped off in hot pursuit.

–

Johnny had been driving, Dougie explained. Drunk. Wasted. Not paying attention. More than that, in fact. He'd been showboating for the benefit of the two lassies in the backseat. And maybe just a little for his cousin riding shotgun up front.

He'd gone through three red lights before the inevitable T-boning happened. Dougie was looking at Johnny when it happened. He remembered the way the light spread across his face. How his shadow scurried up onto the inside of the roof, like it was trying to get clear before the impact.

And then…

Dougie didn't remember anything else from that day. Nothing much from the following weeks, either.

Looking back, his first solid memory—his dad helping him out of the wheelchair and into the newly adapted house—was from almost twelve months after the crash.

There was a hole where a year of his life should be.

And that wasn't the only thing he'd lost.

'I'm told they tried to save it,' he said, then he rapped his knuckles on the metal shin, and slid the jeans leg down to hide it again. 'Obviously, that didn't work out all that well.'

'I'm sorry,' Hamza said.

Dougie slid the leg back down onto the floor. His foot gave a *thunk* when it landed.

'Not your fault,' he said. 'He didn't have insurance. Didn't even have a licence, it turned out. He'd lost it six months earlier. Two-year ban.'

Dougie sucked in his cheeks and rolled his tongue around inside his mouth. His eyes darted away, the emotion still raw after all this time.

'I was nineteen,' he said, forcing himself to continue. 'Johnny told me he'd take care of me. Make sure I was looked after. "You'll never want for anything", he told me. "I'll sort it." He said that a lot. You know what he never said, though? Not once?'

'Sorry', McCulloch guessed.

Dougie tapped an index finger to his nose and pointed at the DCI with the other. 'Spot on. Not once. Not ever. Oh, sure, he chucked me some cash when it suited him. When he wanted to ease his conscience, or whatever. Every time he did, it felt less like compensation, and more like hush money.'

He glanced away like he was ashamed to have accepted the cash.

'But whatever they were, the payments got fewer and farther between, and even then, that money was never mine. Not really. I bought the house, built the studio, so he said that entitled him to come here and stay and record his album. Like it was his, not mine.'

'Is that why you did it, Dougie?' McCulloch asked. He was half-smiling, head tilted, voice soft. It was the closest to human he'd come since Hamza had met him, but even then, there was so much insincerity dripping off him it pooled in puddles at his feet. 'Is that why you killed him?'

Dougie shut his eyes and let out a heavy breath. 'No.'

McCulloch leaned forward suddenly, like a trap that had just been sprung.

'Then why did you kill him? For his money, is that it?'

'No.'

'You're the only family he's got left,' McCulloch pressed. 'What happens to his song rights? To his royalties?'

'I told you lot, I didn't kill him!' Dougie spat, eyes snapping open. 'Am I glad he's dead? No. Maybe. Yes. I don't know. Sort of. But mostly? Mostly no. Mostly, I'm fucking devastated. Mostly, I just want him to be here so I can shake him, and punch him, and hug him and ask him why?'

'Why what?' Hamza probed.

'Why *everything*!' Dougie's voice vibrated with emotion. 'Did he hate me? Was that it? I don't think so, but maybe. He sure as hell didn't love me, because he couldn't. He wasn't capable of loving anyone but himself.'

He sat back suddenly, like some self-preservation instinct had finally kicked in to stop himself saying anything more.

'So, you had motive. That's very clear,' McCulloch said, apparently ignoring most of Dougie's previous outburst. 'And from what you told DS Khaled and his colleagues, you were alone the night Johnny died. The night *he was murdered*, I mean.'

'I was asleep,' Dougie replied. His burst of anger had burned away now, and he mumbled his way through the words. 'I'd had a bit to drink.'

'You'd had. A bit. To Drink,' McCulloch repeated, reflecting the words back at him, slowing them down. He clasped his hands, thumbs tapping. 'And, as you so effectively pointed out earlier'—his gaze flitted to Dougie's artificial leg—'people can do some very silly things while under the influence.'

'He was down a hole when they found him!' Dougie protested. 'On a ledge. I couldn't climb down there.'

'He could've fallen down there,' McCulloch reasoned. 'In fact, we're pretty sure he did. But then, you know that, don't you? You hit him. You knocked him down onto that ledge.'

'No! I didn't kill him!' Dougie cried.

Hamza jumped in before McCulloch could reiterate again that he *definitely had*.

'Then who did?' he asked. 'You knew Johnny as well as anyone. Better than most. You need to think, Dougie. Did he say something? Was he afraid of anyone? Had he been threatened?'

'No. I don't know.'

'I want to believe you. I do. But you have to help us,' Hamza stressed. Pleaded, almost. He went for broke. 'Why was Elsie Kellerman phoning him all the time?'

'Elsie didn't kill him. There's no way,' Dougie said.

'Because you did?' McCulloch interjected.

'No! Jesus. No, just… She was furious at him, aye. But not just her. She was just, like, the spokeswoman.'

Hamza picked up his pen and flipped a page of his notebook. 'Spokeswoman? For who?'

'For everyone. The locals. They—*we*—are sick of what this place gets like in the summer. Most of us have either lived here forever, or moved to get some peace and quiet. But you've seen it out there. We get a thousand cars a day in each direction. It's chaos. It's destroying the place, and people have had enough. Elsie's the head of the village hall committee and the parish council, or whatever she calls it. She was just the one passing on the message.'

'What message?' Hamza asked.

Dougie looked pained at having to spell it all out, but did it anyway. 'They thought—a few of them, anyway—they reckoned that Johnny doing a new album here would only add to the problem. Like

Glenfinnan, with all the Harry Potter fans coming to see the steam train crossing that viaduct and trashing the place.'

Hamza was quietly grateful for the fact that Tyler wasn't here to announce the close call he'd once had with that very train.

'I'd hardly equate Johnny Freestone with the global phenomenon of the Harry Potter franchise,' McCulloch said, and he sounded just a touch outraged by the suggestion, like he was a close personal friend of the boy wizard. 'I doubt his making music up here would have much of an impact.'

'It doesn't need to have much of an impact,' Dougie told him. 'It's on a knife-edge up here as it is. It's at breaking point. Five per cent more people—God, three per cent—and we're screwed. Everything collapses. Even the hotels and restaurants are sick of it. They loved it to begin with, but now they're fed up. There's just too much demand.'

'We were able to get rooms last night no bother,' McCulloch said.

Hamza didn't bother to correct him. Technically, only one of them had been able to get a room. Still, it was a fair point.

'That's true. Can't be that busy,' he agreed.

'That's a choice. Like I said, we're all sick of it. The guys at the hotel, Charlie and his family at the pods, they're running half-full. Just blocked off half their rooms to force people to keep going and move on. Doesn't help, though, just shunts the problem somewhere else.'

He realised how all this was starting to sound, and shook his head. 'But they wouldn't kill him over it. They wouldn't.'

He looked from one detective to the other, like he was choosing his next few words carefully. McCulloch and Hamza both left him space to talk.

'Ray Simpson. That's who I'd look at.'

'His manager?' McCulloch asked.

'Ex-manager. Johnny fired him, and Ray wasn't happy about it. He came round to see me last night, telling me he was legally attached to whatever Johnny had been working on, insisting he had rights to his back catalogue, too.' Dougie's face screwed up in distaste. 'An absolute fucking vulture. He was asking about Declan, too. About signing him. Trying to get his hooks into the kid. Over my dead body, though.'

The Ray Simpson lead was definitely promising, but Hamza stuck a pin in it for the moment, and hoped McCulloch would have the sense to leave it embedded there.

'Actually, speaking of Declan,' the DS said, leaning forward a degree or two. He smiled, keeping his voice light. 'What can you tell me about his auntie, Alanna?'

Chapter 31

Tyler scrambled back to his feet, ready to defend himself if Alanna lunged again. Fortunately, she didn't get the chance. Sinead appeared behind her, grabbed a wrist, applied pressure, and forced her to the floor of the shed.

Alanna hissed and squealed all the way down, not taking her eyes off Tyler until the angle made it impossible for her to hold his gaze. Even then, she kept staring at his feet.

'Thanks,' he whispered, and Sinead winked up at him.

'Anytime.'

'Get off me! Get off! Don't touch anything. You'd better not have fucking touched anything!'

'Relax. Alanna, is it?' Sinead said, still pinning her to the floor. 'We're police officers. We're just here to talk to you.'

Alanna immediately stopped wriggling and fell totally, perfectly still. She went limp, in fact, practically melting into the plywood floor.

'Jesus. Did she die?' Tyler whispered. 'Did you kill her?'

'No! Course she didn't die,' Sinead shot back. 'She's fine.'

'I'm fine,' Alanna confirmed, though the words were slightly muffled by their proximity to the floor.

She sounded completely rational now, her voice devoid of all the anger that had been poisoning it just a moment before.

'My mistake. Thought you were a vandal.'

'If I let you up, are you going to stay calm?' Sinead asked.

Alanna confirmed that she would. She waited until Sinead had climbed all the way off her, then got to her feet with as much dignity as she could muster, brushed herself down, and then lunged straight for Tyler.

He started to scream, then stopped when she grabbed a hand and shook it, babbling out an apology that threatened to reduce her to tears.

'Sorry, I'm so sorry. It's my fault. I'm so stupid.' Her face screwed up. 'Stupid, stupid, stupid!'

'It's fine,' Tyler told her.

'It's *not* fine!' she sniped, then her smile returned, wider than before. More unhinged. 'I should've stopped to think, or to ask you, but oh no, I had to rush in. I had to just push a police officer right in the back!'

Her grip tightened. Her bottom lip shook. There was something in her eyes that made Tyler deeply uncomfortable.

'It's the stress. Everything's so raw. Losing Johnny. It's like a pain I've never felt. I wasn't thinking straight. I'm not sure I was even thinking at all. *Idiot*. But, I'm sorry. I really am.'

'Honestly, it's fine,' Tyler promised.

Technically, he shouldn't have set foot in the shed without permission or a warrant, and since the only thing hurt was his pride, he felt it best not to push it.

'Oh, you're so sweet!' Alanna told him. Her eyes searched his face, then up to the top of his head. 'Love your hair, by the way. It's really nice.'

Tyler was very aware of the fact that, though she'd stopped shaking it, she was still holding his hand.

'Um, thanks,' he said, pulling his arm back. He shot a quick sideways look to Sinead, who made no effort to hide her amusement.

'Is it gel you use, or wax, or...?'

The care and sculpting of Tyler's hair was a complex process that involved a range of products, three different types of comb and a degree of luck. It was also not something he had the inclination to discuss with a woman he had already concluded Logan was right about.

She was a proper nutter, no two ways about it.

'We'd like to ask you a few questions about Johnny Freestone,' he told her, cutting to the chase. If she was disappointed by the lack of hair care chat, she didn't let on.

'Well, good! I'm glad to hear it!' Alanna replied. She brightened and gestured at the legion of Freestones plastered across the wall. 'As I'm sure you can see, you've come to the right place!'

—

It was the flash of a camera that gave the Australian away. Logan had been sidling past a passageway running off towards a small chamber when the light had activated, blinking on in the darkness.

The 'fuck', that followed was barely even a whisper. Had he not been so close, he'd never have heard it.

He found the man waiting for him in a chamber, phone in his hand, a look on his face that was roughly halfway between a cheeky grin and a pained grimace.

'Ah, shit. Guess you found me.'

'Looks like it,' Logan said. He angled the beam of his torchlight directly into the other man's face. 'You legged it as soon as I dragged you out of that hole. You got something to hide?'

'Nah. I mean, yeah. I mean, I guessed I might be in the shit for sneaking around down here.'

'It's an active crime scene, so that's a pretty safe guess,' Logan replied.

'No, I know. I know it is. But, it's also my bread and butter.' The Australian held out a hand. 'Name's Fozzy. That's what folks call me, at least. I got me a tour business, see? Leading folks in and out of the cave. Showing them the sights. Taking them on the boat into the deeper sections, if they're up to it.'

'So?' Logan asked.

He was slightly breathless from tracking the bastard through the cave. Now that he'd found him, he could feel the fear creeping back in at the edges, too.

There was no time for that, though. He pushed it away, swallowed it down, and continued.

'Maybe this is your usual workplace, son, but right now?' Jack pointed to the floor. 'Right now, it's mine. I own this place until I say otherwise. I don't care about your business. It's not my concern. That clear?'

'Yeah. Yeah, I get it.'

'Good. And anyway, what kind of tour guide falls down a big hole in the ground?' Logan asked. 'Are you no' supposed to be aware of these things?'

'I was. I mean, I am,' Fozzy insisted. 'I just slipped is all. I wouldn't normally go that way, but I didn't want to mess up you guys' stuff. Compromise the evidence, or whatever.'

'That's very generous of you,' Logan told him. 'Now, it's lucky for you I'm in a charitable mood, or I'd be dragging your arse to a cell now for attempting to pervert the course of justice and obstructing a police officer.'

'Ah, come on, mate! I didn't do anything!' Fozzy protested.

'Aye you did,' Logan shot back. 'You got on my tits. And trust me, of all the places you don't want to find yourself, *on my tits* should be up near the top of the list. Now come on. Out. Shift your arse.'

Fozzy pocketed his phone and held his hands up. 'All right, all right! I wasn't going to stick around. I just wanted to see where it happened. Get a photo for the website and socials.'

'Don't even fucking think about it,' Logan snapped, but the first part of what the Australian had said filtered through, and he looked past him into the dark.

This was it. This was where the body had been found.

This was where Johnny Freestone had died.

Jack's boots scuffed on the stone as he took a step closer to where the floor dropped away. He got as close to the edge as he dared, then leaned over, bracing himself for a vertigo-inducing chasm below.

Instead, he saw an uneven rocky floor less than a dozen feet further down. Palmer's evidence marker tents were still there, though it wasn't immediately clear what they were drawing attention to. Blood spots, maybe. Footprints. Some other physical clues that had been collected, bagged up, and recorded.

There was no cartoonish chalk outline, of course, but a few discreet strips of tape marked the outer edges of where the body would have been.

'Hard to believe he's gone,' Fozzy said, stepping up beside him. His voice was lowered, but it echoed oddly off the ceiling and walls. 'Thought legends lived on forever.'

Logan side-eyed him. 'You were a fan?'

'God, yeah! My brother got me into him. Played me "Lord of the Morning After" one day, and I was hooked.'

'Great song,' Logan said.

'Fucking epic. That guitar solo? I mean, Christ Almighty. I'd never heard anything like it. And then "Thunder and Rain". I mean, come on!'

'Classic,' Logan agreed. '"Can't Cage the Wild".'

'Are you fucking kidding me?' Fozzy threw back his head, screwed up his face, and belted out the title line from the chorus. 'Can't caaaage the wi-ild! The guy was a musical genius!'

Between them, they rattled off a few more of Freestone's biggest hits.

'"Slippery Love",' Logan said.

'"Freestone Rollin'"!' Fozzy countered.

'"How Can I Miss You, If You Won't Leave"?' they both said at the same time, and the Australian laughed out loud.

'You know who that was about, don't you?' he asked.

'Madonna,' Logan said.

'Fucking Madonna!' Fozzy cackled. 'Queen Madge! Guy was an absolute legend. Oh! Shit! "Wings of Glory"!'

Logan nodded appreciatively. '"Dog on a Chain".'

'"Take Me to the Edge, Then Push Me Over"!' Fozzy said, then the smile fell from his face and both men looked down again at the ledge below. 'Doubt he ever expected anyone to take that literally,' the Australian added, more subdued than before. 'Damn shame. Poor bloke.'

He sniffed and rubbed at his nose with the back of his hand. Some clearing of the throat only added to the sense that he was struggling to keep his emotions in check.

'Lot of folks round here fucking hated him. Thought he was going to bring on the tourism apocalypse, or some shit. Get the whole place overrun.' He laughed at the ridiculousness of it. 'They didn't get it. The people who actually appreciated him—guys like me and you—we're not going to make some special trip to see the place he recorded his ninth fucking album, or whatever.'

Logan almost corrected him. It would be his tenth album.

The point he was making was still valid, though. At this stage in his career, Johnny Freestone's fanbase would be almost exclusively made up of middle-aged men. In fact, the Venn Diagram of Johnny Freestone fans and people who loved the Jeremy Clarkson era of *Top Gear* would be almost a complete circle, with just a sliver of space at either side.

A sliver in which Logan himself would reside, given that the sight of Jeremy Clarkson made him want to punch something.

Ideally, Jeremy Clarkson himself.

'Then why did you take a photo for your website?' Logan asked him. 'If you don't think people will be interested?'

Fozzy shrugged. 'I said they wouldn't be interested in seeing where he recorded his album,' he replied. 'I didn't say they wouldn't want to see where he died.'

It was all Logan could do not to sigh. The guy was right, of course. When it came to celebrity deaths, people could be right ghoulish bastards.

He held out a hand. Fozzy tutted. 'Seriously?'

Jack nodded. Waited. After a moment, Fozzy pressed his unlocked phone into the detective's hand. Logan went to the photos, deleted the one of the crime scene, then handed the phone back.

'If I see that anywhere—'

'You won't, you won't. I felt like a real shitbag taking it,' Fozzy said. He returned the phone to his pocket and turned his attention back to the ledge below. 'What was he doing down here, anyway?'

Logan was about to say that he didn't yet know when the Australian answered the question for him.

'Acoustics, probably. Bet that was it.'

'Sorry?' Jack turned to him, but his gaze darted around the cave. The photos hadn't made it clear, but this section was an almost perfect sphere. An auditorium beneath the earth.

Fozzy continued to speak, but Logan's mind was already racing ahead, slotting the pieces together.

'Acoustics. Recording equipment. He took his guitar.'

'What? Old Bessie?'

'He brought them here. He was recording.' Logan peered over the ledge again, like he might just have overlooked all Johnny's gear. 'So, someone took them. From here.'

'The killer, I betcha,' Fozzy said. 'Maybe that was the motive. Old Bessie's got to be worth a chunk of change, right?'

'Maybe,' Logan conceded, but he was already listing a few alternatives in his head. 'Probably, aye.'

'It's like they say, I guess,' the Australian remarked. 'The cave you're most afraid to enter is the one that holds the greatest treasures.'

Logan gave this some thought.

He could feel his heart racing. His pulse picking up the pace.

But it wasn't fear now. It was something else. It was the thing that had driven him on for years, through all his decisions and all his mistakes. The thing that defined him, and made him who he was.

The thrill of the hunt.

'Aye, maybe there's something in that, right enough,' he said, turning his back on the drop. He shone his torchlight ahead and motioned for Fozzy to lead the way. 'Now, shift. You might be on a career break, son, but some of us have got a job to do.'

Chapter 32

DCI McCulloch was not happy. It was entirely possible, of course, that he had never been happy. Right now, though, he was even less so than usual.

'What are you doing here?' he demanded, his arms folded. The points of his elbows stuck out like knife blades beneath his shirt. 'You weren't summoned.'

Dave Davidson tipped himself back in his chair a little, riding the balance point of the back wheels so he could look straight up at McCulloch without craning his neck.

'That's all right. I'm not a genie. I don't need to be summoned,' he said. 'I hadn't heard anything more, so I thought I should come up.'

McCulloch's eyebrows arched. His nostrils flared at the same time, like they'd all got together to coordinate the move beforehand.

'You thought you should come up? You're not here to think, Detective Constable. That's my job. You're here to follow orders.'

'I wasn't here at all,' Dave countered. 'I was twiddling my thumbs down in Inverness.'

'Where I'd sent you.'

'Where I was doing hee-haw,' Dave said. 'I reckoned I could be of more use up here.'

Sensing an explosion was imminent, Hamza jumped in. 'I think that makes sense,' he said. 'The more hands on deck, the better.'

McCulloch's jaw tightened. He had something to say. Probably quite a lot. But Hamza's interjection made him think twice about it.

Instead, he turned his ire on the other two detective constables in the room. Tyler stood slightly in front of Sinead, readying himself to take the brunt.

'And you two. Did I instruct you to go and start questioning the locals?'

'No, sir,' Tyler replied.

'*No, sir.* Did I order you to leave this room, in fact? Did I mention anything about you taking matters into your own hands?' He looked at them both, hawk-like eyes flitting between them. 'Hmm? Did I mention anything of the sort? Please, do tell me, because if so, I'll need to get myself checked out. A brain scan, perhaps. Because I have no memory of doing so.'

'No, sir,' Tyler said again.

'*No, sir.* No. Exactly. And yet, for a reason I'm sure you're both about to explain, you decided to do just that.'

He rocked back on his heels. Behind him, Dave scratched his chin with his middle finger, angling it in the DCI's direction. Tyler had seen this, and was having to bite down on his bottom lip to stop himself laughing.

'Something funny, Detective Constable Neish?' McCulloch asked.

Tyler shook his head. Dave immediately lowered his finger.

'No, sir.'

'*No, sir,*' McCulloch mimicked. 'I agree. There's nothing amusing about any of this.'

He took a step closer, peering down his long, narrow nose at the much shorter Tyler.

'So, I'm going to give you a chance to answer again before I pass you over to DS Khaled for disciplinary action. What possessed you to leave here and question a witness without my direct authority?'

'I told them to.'

'Oh, thank God,' Tyler wheezed. He sagged with relief, as all eyes turned to the man in the doorway with the wee dog at his feet.

'I told them to go and talk to Alanna Swain,' Logan said, striding into the room. He nodded to the man in the wheelchair. 'Dave. Good to see you, glad you're here.'

He strode past McCulloch, looked the whiteboards over for any new information, then turned to Hamza.

'What's the score with Dougie Cairns? He confess?'

'Eh, no,' Hamza replied. 'We—DCI McCulloch, I mean—sent him home for now.'

'Hang on, hang on. Let's cool our jets here.' McCulloch raised both hands, like he could hold back the conversation and compress it down into silence. 'What do you mean *you* told them to go and talk to her? Need I remind you yet again, Jack, that you are here to assist?'

'No,' Logan said.

'Good, then in that case, I'll ask again. What do—'

'I'm not.'

McCulloch blinked. 'I'm sorry?'

'I'm not here to assist, Evan. That's not what Mitchell said. She said I was here to *advise*.' Logan stepped in. Stepped up. Met McCulloch's stern look and matched it. Raised it. 'And I *advise* you never to let me hear you talking to any member of my team like that again.'

McCulloch opened his mouth to reply, but it snapped shut again, his teeth *clacking* together like they were refusing to let him say anything that might get them knocked out. He glanced at Hamza, then at Sinead, like he was looking for backup.

If he was, he was looking in all the wrong places.

'Tyler,' Jack called.

'Yes, boss?'

'Do I hear that kettle boiling?'

'Not yet, but you will in a minute, boss!'

'Good lad,' Logan said. 'Teas and coffees all round. And Sinead, I think I saw a cafe down the road. Reckon they do takeaway?'

'I'm sure they can be persuaded, sir.'

'Aye, well, if anyone can convince them.' Logan took his wallet from his pocket and held it out to her. He still hadn't taken his eyes off DCI McCulloch. 'Lunch is on me,' he said. 'Let's get some food inside us.'

He turned away from McCulloch and looked across the faces of the team. They stood staring. Smiling. Mesmerised.

The cave you're most afraid to enter holds the greatest treasures.

'And then, let's get our fingers out of our arses,' he proclaimed. 'And let's get to work.'

–

The rolls were decent. Sinead had taken it upon herself to add a few cakes and iced biscuits to the order. Logan had raised an eyebrow at that, but had said nothing as she handed him back a wallet that felt significantly lighter than when he'd given it to her.

'French Fancy, Evan?' Logan asked, indicating the last remaining cake. It sat on top of the bag, in a little paper case, yellow with a stripe of orange icing across the top.

DCI McCulloch considered the offer, then shook his head. His eyes remained fixed on the cake, though, and he didn't object when Logan slid it across the table towards him.

'In case you change your mind.'

Jack sprang to his feet and clapped his hands, officially marking the end of the lunchtime break.

'Right, bit of business before we get stuck in,' he declared. 'To be clear, DCI McCulloch is still SIO on this investigation. I'm here to offer advice and to help, but this is still his case.'

McCulloch paused, hand halfway to the French Fancy, and looked over to where Logan stood watching him from the whiteboards.

'With your permission, Evan, I'll take us through the recap so we're all on the same page.'

McCulloch looked confused by this, like he hadn't realised he had any choice in the matter. His gaze darted around to the other detectives, then he nodded.

'Please. That would be useful.'

'No bother,' Jack said, like he was doing the other DCI a favour. 'First of all, Tyler, Sinead, you spoke to Alanna Swain?'

Sinead confirmed that they had been to see her.

'Thoughts?'

'Off her trolley, boss,' Tyler said, before Sinead could offer a more diplomatic answer. 'Absolutely batshit. She's got a shrine to him. To Johnny Freedom.'

'Freestone,' Logan corrected.

'Shite, aye. Him. Whole wall and a bit of photos cut out of papers and magazines, and that. All pasted up. Cardboard cut-out, too. Nearly shat myself when I saw it.'

He didn't mention the shove in the back, but skirted around the edges of it.

'She absolutely lost her shit when she saw me looking at it,' he continued.

'She was keeping it a secret?' Logan asked.

'Well, I mean, you would, wouldn't you, boss?' Tyler reasoned. 'But, no. I'm not even sure it was that. The shed wasn't locked. I think she just thought I was going to mess it up, or something. She didn't seem embarrassed by it, or anything. It was like it was normal, just… important.'

'She insisted they were in a relationship,' Sinead said. 'Said they loved each other, that they were going to live together someday, just not yet. When the new album was done, and he'd finished touring it.'

Hamza stole a glance at McCulloch to see if the DCI was going to add anything, but he was chomping his way through the French Fancy.

'We heard the opposite,' the detective sergeant said. 'When we spoke to Dougie, he said Johnny had no interest in her. And he'd made that clear to her. She'd come to the door a couple of times, and Johnny had got Dougie to say he wasn't in.'

'Was this before or after the bin shagging?' Tyler asked.

Hamza shrugged. 'Not sure. But Johnny had told Dougie that the bin shagging was the one and only time they'd had sex.'

'Can we please stop calling it *the bin shagging*?' Sinead asked.

'What about *the bin fuc*—' Tyler began, before a look from his wife scared him into silence.

Hamza continued recounting what Dougie Cairns had told them.

'Last time she turned up, she'd followed Johnny to the house, so she knew he was there. She wouldn't leave. Jammed her foot in the door so Dougie couldn't shut it on her. Eventually, Johnny came out and told her to piss off. Told her she was mental, that he was going to call the police, and that on the one time they'd been together, she'd only been somewhere to—and I'm quoting here—"get his dick wet".'

Across the table, Sinead grimaced. 'Jesus.'

'Can't imagine she took too kindly to that,' Dave said.

'When was this?' Logan asked.

'Thursday, sir,' Hamza said. He looked pointedly around at the others. 'The day before Johnny died.'

There was a buzz in the room after that. Alanna clearly had a motive. The jilted lover with a shrine in her garden shed. Johnny's guitar would be a prize addition to her collection.

'We'll bring her in,' Logan said. 'Assuming you agree, Evan?'

DCI McCulloch scrunched up the paper of his French Fancy, swallowed, then nodded. 'Yes. Of course. Haul her in.'

'Before we do,' Logan said, turning back to Hamza. 'Did you ask Dougie about the tissue?'

That yellow tissue on the arm of Dougie Cairns's chair had been on his mind since he'd seen Alanna at her sister's house the previous night. She'd been there, at Dougie's, earlier that day.

Logan wanted to know why.

'Uh, no, sir,' Hamza said. He aimed a meaningful look in McCulloch's direction. '*We* didn't consider it relevant.'

The emphasis on 'we' meant it had been anything but a joint decision.

Logan stared back at the detective sergeant. On the surface, he looked calm. Impassive, even. Dip below it, though, and he was far from it.

Of course it was relevant. It was more than that. It was *important*.

And McCulloch, for whatever reason, had deliberately avoided asking about it. Did he really not think it was significant? Or was there something more at play here? Not a cover-up—he was far too by the book for that—but a power play, maybe. A demonstration of his authority.

Well, bollocks to that.

'Right, I'll talk to him once we've spoken to Alanna Swain. Hamza, you can come with me since you've already talked to him twice,' Logan said. 'Dave, I want you there, too. You can follow us down in the car. Be good to get you a bit of experience.'

Dave sat up straighter in his wheelchair. 'Oh. Cool. Right. Aye. Nice one.'

'So. Acoustics,' Logan announced, which earned only blank stares of confusion from the rest of the team. 'I think that's why Johnny was in the cave. The acoustics. We know he had his guitar and recording equipment. The acoustics down there are pretty unique. The cave he was in is far enough away from the waterfall that you can't really hear it. I think he was down there recording stuff for his album.'

It made sense, they all agreed. Or, at least as much sense as any other theory, and more than most.

Sinead wrote it up on the board, then took the stage and explained some of the other notes she'd added over the past few hours, as calls had come in and inquiries had paid off.

None of Johnny's ex-wives was in the country in the days leading up to his death. They had all been informed of his passing, and while none of them appeared to be particularly upset, they all sounded convincingly shocked.

Of his ex-bandmates, only Rodney Nisbet was both alive and within travelling distance of the murder scene. He lived in Inverness, on one of the housing estates out near Culloden. He ran a gardening firm that had recently branched out into rendering and roof work.

He had gone silent when informed of Johnny's death, before eventually muttering a quiet, 'Ah well. No great loss,' and ending the call.

Logan had Sinead give him the address. Sure enough, as he'd guessed from the description, it was right around the corner from Ben Forde's house. He rattled off a quick text to Ben asking if he knew the guy, then listened as Sinead wrapped up.

There was still no sign of the murder weapon. Beyond 'blunt heavy object' they remained at a loss. The search had gone through the cave, across the hillside, and even through the bins a mile or so in either direction, but had turned up nothing.

Divers were being brought in to search the water in the cave, but dredging and specialist camera equipment had already both drawn a blank, so hopes weren't high.

Sinead was just touching on the preliminary toxicology reports that confirmed Johnny had been drinking heavily the night he died, when Tyler's phone rang.

He checked the screen, frowned when he saw the unfamiliar number, and stepped away to the back of the hall to answer it.

'Hello?'

Sinead tried to continue, but her husband's voice made it difficult.

'What? No. How did you get this number?' Tyler demanded.

He turned and looked over his shoulder. Logan's heart sank when the detective constable whispered, 'It's the press, boss!'

'What was that?' McCulloch asked, sidling up to Logan.

'The press. The bastards must've cottoned on, at last. Amazed it's taken them so long.'

Tyler rubbed at his forehead. 'No, I don't want to give a quote. Who are you calling…? No, wait. Listen. Who are you calling from?'

He listened. Grimaced.

'It's the *Sun*, boss,' he whispered.

Logan went striding over, hand reaching for the mobile, a string of expletives already lining themselves up on his lips.

McCulloch got there first, swooping in and snatching the phone before Jack could get to it. He pivoted on a heel, the mobile already at his ear.

'This is DCI Evan McCulloch. To whom am I speaking?' he asked, his tone professional, but not unfriendly. 'Adam. Right. Well, this number is for a member of my team, Adam. I'm going to give you another number to reach me on, and I'll give you what information I can. If you call this number, or any other member of this team again, then you can forget about me sharing anything with you. Is that clear?'

Tyler looked up at Logan, who looked just as confused as the DC felt. Neither of them said anything, just watched and listened as McCulloch rattled off an 0800 number from memory.

'That will divert to me as and when I am available to talk, and have information to share,' the DCI said. 'If you wish to stay in my good books, you'll use it, and it alone. Do we understand each other, Adam?'

There was a garbled reply from the other end. McCulloch nodded, ended the call, then handed the phone back to Tyler.

Tyler reached for it slowly, like he suspected some sort of trap. McCulloch nodded, encouraging him to hurry up and take it.

'For my sins, I used to be a press liaison,' McCulloch said, once Tyler had accepted the mobile. 'I know how to deal with these people. I'll do my best to buy you all some time before they descend.'

He looked around at the others, who seemed just as surprised by all this as Logan and Tyler.

'I suggest you try to wrap this all up before then.'

There was some shuffling of feet and some scratching of heads. It was Logan who finally broke the silence.

'You heard the detective chief inspector. Let's move our arses,' he said, turning to face the others. 'I'll be damned if I'm letting the bloody tabloids crack this case before we do.'

Chapter 33

'You sure about this, boss?'

Logan reiterated for the second time that yes, he was sure.

Alanna Swain had come in willingly, and had gone visibly giddy when Tyler had met her at the door.

She'd insisted on bringing her brother-in-law, Charlie, along as her legal representative, despite the fact that he was not, and had never been, a solicitor. He *had* worked for a few months in an estate agent's, but he didn't seem surprised when informed that this didn't qualify him to be Alanna's legal counsel.

He'd seemed quite relieved by this news, in fact, but Alanna was insisting that the only way she'd agree to be interviewed was if he stayed.

They'd offered alternatives, including a duty solicitor from Inverness, but she'd stood her ground. It was Charlie, she said, or nothing.

Logan was content with 'or nothing'. If she wanted to refuse a solicitor, then that was on her. It was Sinead who had proposed an alternative solution, during a huddle with the rest of the team.

'Look, Alanna is clearly mentally—'

'Unhinged,' Tyler agreed.

'Vulnerable,' Sinead said.

'She does really seem to like Tyler, right enough,' Dave said.

'Here! What's that meant to mean?' Tyler had demanded, once his brain had finished processing the jibe.

'Under PACE rules, we could allow her an appropriate adult,' Sinead continued. 'For moral support, obviously, not legal advice.'

Logan had pursed his lips and *squinched* his mouth from side to side a few times, considering this, until eventually agreeing to it.

It was then that he'd dropped the bombshell. Tyler and Sinead were to handle the interview themselves. The thought of it had nearly knocked Tyler flat on his back.

'But, just us, boss? Shouldn't Hamza or someone be in, too?' he asked, a few shallow breaths away from hyperventilating. 'Or you could do it.'

Logan clamped a hand on Tyler's shoulder. The weight of it almost buckled the DC's knees.

'You've got this, son. And Sinead'll look after you. Won't you?'

Sinead smirked as she patted her husband on the back. 'Don't you worry your pretty little head about anything,' she told him. 'Just sit there and smile, and leave the rest to me.'

They quickly went over their line of questioning with Logan. Then, at his insistence, they ran it past McCulloch, too. He was speaking in quite clipped tones to someone from the Scottish *Daily Mail*, and only gave their notes a cursory glance before nodding and waving them away.

With that done, and a pep talk from Logan that largely amounted to, 'Get your arse in there,' Tyler and Sinead joined Alanna and Charlie in the makeshift interview room.

The day was knocking on, and the weather was taking a turn for the worse, a blanket of grey cloud having swept in to cover most of the sky. This was all the excuse Logan needed to pull on his big coat. He shoved his hands deep in his pockets, fished out a couple of dog treats, then tossed them to Taggart.

Then, with both the dog and the other DCI distracted, he jerked his head, summoning Hamza and Dave.

'Come on, then,' he instructed. 'Let's get to it.'

—

Number sixty-three—the mobile home of Reg and Elsie Kellerman—was still parked in the same spot outside the village hall when Logan, Hamza and Dave emerged.

They could hear the sound of a radio playing—BBC Radio 4, Jack thought—but there was no other sound from within.

It was only now that Logan realised the box van's tyres were a little on the flat side, like it hadn't moved in a while. He had Hamza call through for a status check on the vehicle as they plodded down the hill, and Dave headed for his car.

'They're going to email me the details,' Hamza said, once he'd ended the call. 'You think there's something dodgy about it?'

'Dunno,' Logan said. 'We'll soon find out.'

He looked out across the nose-to-tail traffic that still clogged up the road in both directions. A couple of other Uniforms had come to lend support, but their presence didn't seem to be making a lot of difference. It was still a scene of absolute chaos.

'No wonder the locals hate it,' Hamza remarked, falling into step beside the DCI. 'Imagine dealing with that all summer.'

'To be fair, we've no doubt made it worse,' Logan replied. 'But, aye. Must be a nightmare.'

They stepped aside to let Dave's car pass them. Spots of rain were blowing in from the north, and though he slowed to offer them a lift, Logan turned him down. The cave had been claustrophobic enough. He didn't think he could face being scrunched up with his ears around his knees in the passenger seat of Dave's Peugeot.

Besides, he knew for a fact that Tyler had been sick in there less than a day earlier. A walk in the fresh air, even with the rain coming on, was far preferable.

'It's, uh, it's good to have you back, sir,' Hamza said, when they resumed their walk down the village hall's driveway.

'Aye. Well. I'm not sure I am back,' Logan replied, not looking at him. 'We'll see.'

Hamza fell silent for a few moments, processing this information.

'DCI McCulloch mentioned that they're training up his replacement down in the Borders,' the DS said. 'I think he's keen to take over up here.'

'So I hear,' Logan told him. 'Like I say, we'll see.'

They reached the road, where Dave was trying to inch the nose of his car out into the motionless traffic. He rolled his eyes at them, promised to catch up, and then went back to staring down the driver of the closest campervan on the left.

'I was going to ask you for your opinion on something, sir,' Hamza ventured, as they turned onto the side road that led to Dougie's house. This one wasn't part of the North Coast 500 route, and so apparently held no interest for the ten-mile tailback of tourists on the main road.

'Oh aye?'

'Eh, aye. Aye. I was… It's about DI Forde's job. His old job, I mean. Not the cafe.'

'You're thinking of going for it,' Logan said. It wasn't a question. 'You should. I'd back you all the way.'

'Really? Wow. Thanks, sir,' Hamza said, and his next few steps had more of a spring in them. 'It's just… I worry about what might happen if I do get it.'

Logan turned his head to look at him, just as the rain spots upgraded themselves into a light drizzle. 'How d'you mean?'

'Well… Tyler and Sinead, really,' Hamza said. 'I don't want to mess them about. If I move up, the DS job becomes available. If one of them wants to go for it—'

'Then they probably won't get to work together,' Logan concluded.

'No. I mean, aye. That's the issue I'm having,' Hamza said.

He looked worried. Troubled, even. The thought of messing up the team was clearly weighing heavily on him.

Logan stopped. After a couple of paces, Hamza realised this, and he stopped, too.

'You're a good man, Hamza. Too bloody good, sometimes,' Logan said. 'Tyler and Sinead are both adults. I know it's hard to believe with Tyler sometimes. And I fully respect that you care about them. But, sometimes, when it comes right down to it, you've got to do what's best for you.'

He looked taken aback for a moment, like his own words had caught him by surprise.

'They're your friends. They're your colleagues. And, aye, as their DS, they're your responsibility,' Logan continued. 'But only up to a point. Do you know who else is your responsibility, Hamza?'

Hamza shook his head. 'Who?'

Logan prodded him lightly in the middle of the chest.

'Things change. Situations. People. Nothing stays the same forever,' Jack said. 'Now, you can fight against that all you like, but you're pissing into the wind. So, if you want to go for it, you go for it. I don't think anyone on this team would hold it against you.'

Hamza nodded. 'No, sir. Thanks. I'll, um, I'll keep thinking about it.'

'I wouldn't take too long,' Logan said. 'They'll no' leave it open forever.'

He looked up at the thick black clouds, and pulled his coat around him as the rain began to rattle off the ground at their feet.

'Right, enough with the touchy-feely shite. Let's get going before we drown out here,' he said, and they both set off to where Dougie Cairns's converted barn stood silently against the darkening sky.

Chapter 34

It wasn't that Alanna Swain was being difficult, exactly. There had been no problem in getting her talking. Keeping her on topic, though, was another matter entirely.

She really liked Tyler's hair. She was fascinated by it, in fact. When she wasn't asking questions about it, her eyes would drift up to admire it. On at least three different occasions, she'd started reaching out to touch it, before thinking better of it and pinning the wandering hand beneath its more sensible opposite number.

They'd read her her rights, explained who they were and what the interview was for, reminded Charlie that he was there only for moral support and not legal advice, and then cracked on with the interview.

She hadn't objected to any of it, and had actually seemed quite excited when they'd told her the conversation was being recorded.

'For posterity,' she'd said.

'Something like that, aye,' Tyler had replied.

That had been ten minutes ago. He hoped she'd got all the hair chat out of her system by now, but he wasn't pinning his hopes on it.

'Just to clarify, Alanna,' Sinead asked. 'You said that your relationship with Johnny began in 2007?'

'King Tut's in Glasgow,' Alanna confirmed. 'October the eleventh. I've still got the tickets. Coleen chucked hers away, but I kept mine.'

She shot a look over her shoulder at Charlie sitting in the corner. It was a sour, accusatory thing, like he was responsible for his wife's decision not to hang on to a concert ticket from almost eighteen years earlier.

'It's in my memory box,' she continued. 'With other important stuff.'

'Relating to your relationship with Johnny?' Sinead asked.

'Not just that. Other stuff. Things I've done. Places I've been,' Alanna said, and there was something slightly defensive about it. 'I wasn't *just* Johnny's partner. I'm my own person, too.'

Over in the corner, Charlie muttered a 'Jesus Christ', and shook his head. 'You're not his partner. You were never his partner!'

'Mr Sinclair, please,' Tyler said, shutting him down. 'You're not allowed to interject.'

'She's bloody delusional!'

'If you're going to keep interrupting, I'm going to have to ask you to leave,' Tyler told him.

Charlie looked quite happy about that idea. For a moment, it looked like he was going to get up and walk out. But then he thought better of it and sat back, crossing his arms and sighing.

Throughout her brother-in-law's outburst, Alanna had remained perfectly still, like a small animal freezing in place until danger had passed.

'If you could just give me a yes or no answer please, Alanna. That night in Glasgow. Was that when your relationship began?' Sinead pressed.

'Yes. Officially, anyway. We'd seen each other around before then, but that was when we first got together.'

'Right. It's just that Johnny told his cousin that wasn't the case. He said he'd only been intimate with you on one occasion, and that was quite recent.'

Alanna had become momentarily distracted by Tyler's hair. When she realised the detectives were waiting for a response, she asked them to repeat the question.

'That's not true,' she said, once Sinead had obliged. 'Ask Coleen. She knows. She knows about Glasgow. Doesn't she, Charlie? She knows that Johnny and me made love that night.'

There was something salacious about the way she said the words 'made love'. She looked at Tyler as she said it, like she was trying to conjure up an image in his head.

Sinead and Tyler both looked over at the man sitting huffily in the corner. He scowled back at them.

'What, I can talk now, can I?' He grunted and shrugged. 'Far as Coleen told me, that's true, aye. Alanna and him disappeared together.'

'I took pictures of myself in his bed the next morning,' Alanna added, like this was a perfectly normal thing to do.

'With him?'

'No,' she admitted. 'He'd gone out to get us breakfast. He brought back a Gregg's. Two sausage rolls and a bottle of Pepsi Max. Aye, all for me, not to share. He wasn't tight, or anything.'

'Do you have those photos?' Tyler asked.

It was, he realised, probably a daft question, given the whole wall of pictures he'd stumbled upon earlier. Sure enough, Alanna confirmed that they were there in the collage.

'Middle left, about halfway up,' she said, closing her eyes for a moment as she recalled their placement. 'I took a few, but there's just the one there.'

'So, it's just a picture of you in a bed by yourself?' Sinead asked. 'It doesn't really prove much.'

'I laid out some of his clothes next to me,' Alanna countered. Again, she said this as if it was a perfectly rational thing to do. 'You can definitely see it's his bed. And Coleen'll back me up, too. Won't she, Charlie?'

Charlie just sat in silence, arms folded, slowly puffing out his cheeks and letting them deflate again. He was sick of his sister-in-law's shite, that much was obvious.

'When was the last time you spoke to Johnny, Alanna?' Sinead asked. She smiled, keeping her voice light and conversational.

It didn't work, though. Across the table, Alanna's face fell.

'Why are you asking?' she demanded. Her eyes were suddenly suspicious, her movements furtive. Tyler's hair was completely forgotten. 'What does that matter?'

'You spoke to him on Thursday, didn't you?' Sinead continued.

The question made Alanna visibly uncomfortable. She shuffled around in her chair, before finally confirming with a nod.

'Could you answer out loud, please? For the recording.'

Alanna chewed on her lip, her eyebrows rising and dipping like the muscles were malfunctioning.

Finally, she leaned in closer to the recording equipment and said, 'Yes.'

'Can you tell me what you discussed?' Sinead asked her.

'Just stuff.'

'Stuff? Like what?'

'I don't want to talk about it.'

Sinead nodded in sympathy. 'He said some pretty nasty things. Didn't he?'

Alanna looked down at her hands. Her fingers were wriggling together, intertwining, like worms at an orgy.

She nodded, then remembered the recording. 'Yes,' she said, leaning in again. 'But he was upset, that was all. He was stressed. He didn't mean any of it.'

'What was he stressed about?' Tyler asked.

Alanna looked at him like she'd forgotten he was there. She brightened a little when her gaze fell on him.

'He didn't say. But he wasn't himself, so there was definitely something. I had no idea what it was at the time, though.'

'At the time?' Sinead asked, seizing on those three words.

Alanna reluctantly tore her attention away from Tyler. 'Yeah. Dougie filled me in yesterday when I went round.'

'You were round at Dougie's yesterday?'

'We were the two closest people to Johnny,' she said, which drew some more muttering from Charlie in the corner. 'It makes sense that we support each other at a time like this.'

'And what did Dougie say?' Sinead urged. 'Why was Johnny upset?'

'Well, because of what Ray said.'

'Ray?' Tyler glanced down at his notes. 'Johnny's manager?'

'Yeah. Him. Sleazy wee bastard. I never trusted him. I mean, I haven't met him, but based on what Dougie told me, and the vibe I got from Johnny, I'm not a fan.' She gritted her teeth and thumped a fist on the table. 'I *hate* him.'

'And what did he say? Ray, I mean,' Sinead asked. 'What did he say that got Johnny so upset?'

'He told Johnny he was going to stab him in the back and take everything.'

Tyler and Sinead swapped confused looks.

'Ray told him this?' Sinead asked.

'Yep.'

'Ray told Johnny he was going to stab him in the back and take everything?'

Alanna sniffed. 'Johnny refused to believe it, of course. Said he was lying, but Ray insisted.'

Tyler looked at his notepad again, in case it miraculously offered some sort of explanation that cleared up what the woman was telling them.

'Hang on, so Ray told Johnny that he, Ray, was going to stab him in the back and take everything?'

It was Alanna's turn to look confused. 'What? No. Why would Ray say that? You wouldn't, would you? You'd keep that to yourself.'

'But… that's what you said,' Tyler told her.

'What? No, I didn't! Why would *I* have said that? It doesn't make any sense.' Alanna laughed and pulled a *what's he like?* face to Sinead. 'Of course Ray didn't say he was going to do those things.'

She leaned in closer to the tape again, making sure the next part came over loud and clear.

'He said that Dougie was.'

Chapter 35

Logan's clenched fist thudded against the front door of Dougie's barn conversion, shaking it in its frame. He stepped back and looked over the front of the building, but the windows were too high to show anything but glimpses of the ceiling above.

There were no lights on, but then it was still reasonably light out, despite the covering of cloud.

A key box was fixed to the wall by the door, but it didn't open when Logan tugged on the latch. Four dials at the top could be spun to different digits, but even if he knew the code, he couldn't legally enter the house.

'Think he's out or hiding?' Hamza asked.

'No idea,' Logan said. He nodded along the driveway to where an electric Ford Mustang sat in the shadow of a covered carport. 'Car's here, though.'

He tried knocking again, putting even more welly into it this time. The door was heavy, and the side of his hand ached when he'd finished hammering it.

Still nothing.

Jack wasn't entirely sure why he'd been so keen to come here and talk to Dougie. Officially, he'd wanted to ask him about the tissue on his armchair, but they could've asked Alanna Swain about that. Tyler and Sinead probably already had, in fact.

But there was *something* drawing him here. Something he couldn't quite put words to. Not yet.

It had been months since his detective instincts had been called into action, but he could feel them stirring now. Dougie knew something. He was sure of it.

'We got a number for him?' Logan asked, eyeing up the door like he was considering kicking it down.

'Think so, yeah,' Hamza told him. He checked the shared drive, then nodded. 'Got it. Want me to ring him?'

Logan nodded then stepped in closer to the door, ear to the wood, breath held.

Hamza stepped away to make the call, so the sound of his phone wouldn't mask the ringing of one inside.

Once he'd punched in the number and hit dial, he gave Logan a nod. Jack listened, then dropped into a squat and opened the letterbox.

'I can hear it,' he said. He scanned the room through the narrow slot. 'Can't see him, though.'

Logan put his mouth to the letterbox and called Dougie's name. He identified himself, then went back to peering in.

Hamza had ended the call, so the inside of the house was silent. Still.

'Bollocks. Don't think he's in,' Jack declared, getting to his feet. He looked up at the front of the house again, spun one of the wheels of the key box, then tugged on it again.

Still locked.

It was then that his gaze drifted back over to the carport. The car, a sporty red number, was tucked back beneath a canopy so low the DCI would struggle to stand fully upright under it. It encased the whole vehicle in shadow, turning the space behind the windscreen into a deep well of darkness.

It was thick. Black. The sort of darkness someone could get themselves lost in. Like a pit. Or a cave.

Or some other godforsaken hole in the earth.

'Sir.'

Hamza's voice surprised him, and Logan took a step back, like he'd been teetering on the edge of an abyss.

He turned to see Declan Sinclair walking along the path, slowing as he got closer to the house and the detectives standing outside it. He had a guitar in a bag on his back, and the paleness of his face made his red hair seem even more fiery.

'What's wrong? Is Dougie all right?' the boy asked.

'We're not sure. He's not answering,' Logan said. 'What are you doing here, son?'

Declan shrugged the shoulder with the guitar case on it. 'Got a lesson,' he said.

He looked past Logan to the front door. There was a pained expression on his face, like he was wrestling with a difficult decision.

'I, um, I know the code,' he ventured. 'I could get the key. If you want, I mean.'

Logan looked over at Hamza. They couldn't enter without a warrant, but if there was reason to believe Dougie could be injured or in danger, there was some leeway there.

And his phone was in there. That was weird, wasn't it?

Besides, if Dougie had given the boy the code, didn't that imply Declan would also have the authority to let them enter?

Not really, he knew. Not even close.

But fuck it.

'Aye, fire on, son,' Logan said.

He stepped aside to let Declan get to the keybox, and it was then that he heard it. A low whine. An electronic hum, like a UFO in a Fifties sci-fi movie.

There was a crunching of gravel. Fast. Urgent.

Getting louder.

The world gear-shifted into slow motion, as Logan experienced a moment of complete and total clarity. Instinct kicked in. He lunged, grabbing Declan, pulling them both out of the path of the Ford Mustang as it powered past them, the wind of it whipping at Logan's coat.

Hamza spat out a cry of fright, throwing himself clear as the car swerved to hit him. He stumbled and rolled clear, the car's tyres chewing a trench through the grass just inches from where he landed.

'You all right?' Logan barked.

'Think so, aye,' Hamza wheezed, hauling himself back to his feet.

Jack was already running. He stabbed a finger in Declan's direction. 'Watch him!'

The Mustang hung a left out of the driveway, tyres squealing, racing along the single-track road, away from the barely moving traffic on the right.

Logan ran, stumbling, onto the road, reaching for his phone, squinting at the number plate as the car sped off towards a long, swooping curve in the road.

He hissed in fright as a horn blared behind him, and spun to find a battered Peugeot 208 skidding to a stop behind him. Dave Davidson's head emerged through the driver-side window.

'Hop in!' the detective constable urged, and his whole face was a mask of excitement. 'It's been bloody *ages* since I got to do one of these!'

—

The longer Sinead and Tyler spent in Alanna Swain's company, the more concerned they became for her mental health.

And, ironically, the less capable they thought she was of murder.

Or, of murdering Johnny Freestone, at least. Everyone else might be fair game, but her love for him seemed genuine. And, more importantly, she seemed to have taken his complete dismissal and humiliation of her as some sort of joke.

'That's just how we were together,' she'd said, laughing and rolling her eyes. 'He wasn't *actually* being serious!'

She'd become quite annoyed when Charlie had tutted and muttered something at that, and though he'd offered to leave—pleaded, practically—she'd insisted she needed him there as her legal counsel.

All of them—Charlie, Tyler and Sinead—had reminded her again that he wasn't her legal counsel, that he couldn't offer any advice, and that he was only there for moral support, which he didn't seem to have much of a knack for.

She'd waved all this away like it was insignificant, asked Tyler again what he used to get his hair so smooth, and then launched into another story about Johnny without waiting for an answer.

She didn't kill him. She was adamant on that. She wouldn't. She couldn't. He was the love of her life. The one good thing in it, she'd said, which had depressed Sinead no end.

Her protestations themselves were almost convincing enough, but it was the alibi that clinched it.

'Thurso?' Sinead asked. 'You were in Thurso?'

'At a gig, yeah. With Coleen and a couple of the girls from work.'

'What gig?'

'You heard of Bobby Williams?'

Sinead and Tyler exchanged sideways looks.

'You mean Robbie Williams?' Sinead asked.

Alanna stifled a laugh. 'Oh. Yeah. Sure. *Robbie* Williams is going to come to Thurso. Ha. No. Don't think so.' She shook her head in amusement. 'He's a tribute act.'

'For Robbie Williams?' Tyler guessed.

'No, for Elvis.' Alanna tutted, like she was suddenly annoyed. 'Of course for Robbie Williams! Why the hell would he be called Bobby Williams if he wasn't doing Robbie Williams?'

She shook her head more sharply this time, sighed, but then brightened again. 'To be fair, he also does some Take That, and a bit of Westlife, if the vibe's right.' She tapped her thumbs together. 'And he gets his knob out.'

Across the table, Tyler almost choked. 'Jesus.'

'You'd like him,' Alanna told Sinead, with a twinkle in her eye.

'I do like a bit of Robbie,' Sinead admitted.

'Aye, but not that bit!' Tyler objected. 'What's he getting his knob out for?'

'I don't know. It's just part of the act,' Alanna said. 'You don't hear anyone complaining, though! I mean, besides the bar staff. And the people with kids. But everyone else loves it. He's good.' She wrinkled her nose. 'I mean, he's not *great*, but he's all right. He's nearly seventy, so it's pretty impressive.'

'Seventy?' Tyler yelped. He rocked back in his chair, like this final revelation had almost knocked him flat on his back. 'He's a *seventy-year-old* Robbie Williams impersonator who gets his knob out?'

'No. He's *nearly* seventy,' Alanna corrected. 'He's like, I don't know'—she waved a hand again—'fifty-eight.'

'How's that nearly seventy?' Tyler asked, but Sinead'd had enough of this line of questioning, and silenced him with a look.

'When did you leave and get back?' she asked Alanna. 'For the gig, I mean.'

'Oof. Now you're asking.' Alanna jabbed a thumb back over her shoulder at her brother-in-law. 'Can he chime in here? Is that allowed?'

Sinead granted permission with a nod.

'They left about two on Friday afternoon. Got back after midnight,' Charlie said.

'That's a long gig,' Sinead pointed out.

'We did a bit of shopping and hit the pub first,' Alanna said. 'We had some food. Coleen was driving, so she wasn't drinking, of course, but the rest of us were throwing it back, so we were. You should've seen Sharon. From work. She was pissing in the street at one point! I mean, she didn't need to, the toilets were right there, but...' She smiled, wistfully. 'That's Sharon for you.'

'Aye. An arsehole,' Charlie commented, then he held up his hands and folded his arms to signal to the detectives that he was shutting up.

'And you can all vouch for each other's whereabouts that whole time?' Sinead asked.

'Yeah. Absolutely. We were together the whole time.'

Her face scrunched up and tears began to fall. It was instant, like some invisible switch had been flipped.

When she spoke, her voice was a series of tight, garbled sobs.

'And when we were all out enjoying ourselves, someone was murdering my poor Johnny!'

She slammed a hand on the table so hard that Tyler almost jumped out of his seat. Some other button had been pressed, turning her grief into an explosive discharge of pure rage.

It narrowed her eyes to slits and twisted her features into an ugly mask of fury.

'You'd better find them soon,' she hissed. 'Because if you don't find them, then I will.'

The hand on the table became a claw, then a fist.

'And God help the evil son-of-a-bitch when I do!'

Chapter 36

'Jesus fuck!'

Logan gripped everything. Tensed everything. He'd never been a religious man, but he whispered a prayer as he braced himself for the inevitable impact and fireball he saw looming in his immediate future.

'Chill, we're good,' Dave said from the driver's seat, giving the Davemobile another kick of acceleration with the hand controls.

Jack's left foot instinctively slammed against the floor, where he hoped against hope that a brake pedal might be.

No such luck.

There was a towel on the seat beneath him. As they'd screeched off in pursuit of the fleeing Ford Mustang, Dave had hurriedly explained that it was to cover one of the many damp patches caused by Tyler's vomiting incident.

That also explained the forest of Magic Trees hanging all around the car, which did little to mask the pungent pukey smell.

Logan hadn't been a fan of the towel when he'd first sat down. Now, though, as the Peugeot flew over the potholes in the single-track road, he had a feeling he might end up grateful for it when he inevitably soiled himself.

The Mustang's head start had been swallowed up in no time, but when the driver clocked Dave's car in the rear-view mirror, they'd floored the accelerator, and the powerful electric motor had lurched it away.

It had given Logan enough time to get the number plate—even though his hands had been over his eyes at one point—and call it in to base.

For all the good it would do. There was no saying the Uniforms back at the cave were cleared for high-speed pursuit. Even if they were, it would take them far too long to get out of the car park.

Dave was qualified, or had been at one point, at least. Of course, that only applied if he was driving an official police vehicle with the lights flashing and sirens on, not when he was hammering down a track in an adapted Peugeot 207 thick with the smell of day-old vomit.

A turn appeared in the road ahead, a sharp left that came at them out of nowhere, like a wildly thrown punch.

Logan hissed through his teeth, pressed one hand against the ceiling and gripped the seat with the other until his knuckles turned translucent.

'*Fuck, fuck, fuck!*'

The car tilted, swerved, shuddered, screamed. There was a jarring thump beneath Logan, as if the wheels on his side had touched down again, and then the car was picking up speed, racing ahead into a chicane that crossed over a stone bridge then rose up towards the top of a steep hill.

'I see him!' Dave cried, jamming the hand controls down.

The Peugeot's engine howled in protest. Logan knew exactly how it felt.

At the top of the hill, a flash of red metal crested the peak, then vanished again, disappearing out of sight.

He was a good twenty seconds ahead, even with Dave pulling out all the stops. He had to be doing eighty. More, maybe.

This was too risky. Someone was going to get hurt.

'Slow down,' Logan instructed.

Dave shifted the wheel left and right, steering the car through the chicane. There were barely six inches to spare on either side as he powered across the bridge, eyes locked on the top of the hill.

'I can get him,' he insisted.

Logan wanted to. Badly. The bastard had tried to run him down, after all.

But this was madness.

This was suicide.

'He's too far ahead. It's too dangerous,' Logan said. 'Slow down.'

Dave tutted, but he adjusted the hand controls and the Davemobile's speed dropped from 'ludicrously fast' to just 'fast'.

It took them almost half a minute to reach the top of the hill. As soon as they did, Logan's foot went for the invisible pedals again. A delivery van bore down on them, the driver's eyes wide with fright as he kicked hard on the brakes.

Both the van and the Peugeot screamed at each other as they skidded to a stop, nose to nose, just a few feet apart, smoke rising from the heat of their tyres.

'Holy shit,' Dave said. He turned to Logan, and he was grinning. He was actually grinning! 'That was a close one, eh?'

Logan exhaled, ridding himself of some of the tension that had turned his body completely rigid for the past few seconds.

Beyond the van, far in the distance, the Mustang's tail lights winked out of sight, like a thief vanishing into the night.

–

Logan tumbled out of the car at Dougie Cairns's house and stood bent double for a few moments with his hands on his thighs, and his heart simultaneously in both his stomach and his mouth.

The drizzle had thickened into a mist that clung to everything, beading on the Peugeot's windscreen, and dulling the world to a smear of grey.

Logan barely noticed. Instead, he mumbled a series of expletives that would've made Bob Hoon blush, then straightened, exhaling sharply through his nose to rid himself of the lingering traces of Tyler-vomit.

Behind him, Dave held onto the Peugeot's roof rail as he dragged his wheelchair out of the backseat, then dropped into it and heaved himself along the gravel driveway.

'Don't you even fucking talk to me,' Logan said, holding a hand up.

This earned a cackle from Dave, but he had the good sense not to say anything.

'Take it you lost him, sir?' Hamza asked, walking over to join them.

Declan was sitting on Dougie's front step, his guitar case propped up against the door, shielded from the drizzly rain.

'Not for want of trying,' Logan said, shooting Dave a look that, by rights, should have killed him dead. 'I called it in. Hopefully, we'll pick him up. Assuming he hasn't already crashed.'

Logan looked past the DS to the house, and to Declan sitting on the step.

'He all right?'

'Seems to be, yeah,' Hamza confirmed. 'Bit shaken. Wanted to go home, but I thought it best to keep him here for now.'

'You get that door code from him?'

Hamza shook his head. 'I wasn't sure if we were going to go in. Without a warrant, I mean.'

'After that performance?' Logan said, tilting his head to indicate the now-empty carport. 'Too bloody right we're going in. Declan!'

The lad leaped to his feet, running a hand back through his long ginger curls like he was trying to make himself presentable.

He looked scared. But then, who could blame him?

'A-aye?' he stammered. 'I mean, yes? Sorry. Uh-huh?'

'Get us that key, will you, son?' He marched towards the boy, and the door behind him. 'And let's see if we can figure out why Dougie was in such a rush to get out of here.'

–

Logan was the only one to enter the house. If anyone was going to get a bollocking or lose their job over this, it would be him and him alone.

Hamza stood on the doorstep, watching, while Dave and Declan both hung back, peering in through the gaps.

The phone that Jack had heard ringing was on the coffee table, face up, the screen dark. He tapped it with a knuckle of a gloved hand, and saw Hamza's missed call on the display. It was otherwise locked, though, its contents a mystery.

The rest of this room looked much like it had the last time Logan was here. Same decor, same furniture, but the air was tainted by the smell of alcohol now. Or possibly cheap perfume.

He called out Dougie's name, then a more general greeting to anyone else who might be in there with him.

Nobody answered. The house was deathly silent. It was a silken, textured sort of silence, rich in its emptiness, and Logan had no doubt that he was alone.

'See anything?' Hamza asked from the doorway.

'Not yet, no.'

Logan looked around, flexing his fingers. The rubber creaked as it stretched.

He checked around the living area, peeked into an empty waste paper basket, and came to the conclusion that there wasn't a lot here to find.

The kitchen, up the far end of the open-plan space, was a similar story. There was one dirty mug in the sink. One teaspoon on the counter next to a little saucer with four or five teabags heaped on it, all at various stages of drying out.

The topmost teabag was still wet. When he touched it, he could feel the slightest suggestion of warmth through his glove.

There was a half-bottle of whisky on the draining board. Whyte & Mackay. His old brand.

One of them, anyway.

One of the many.

There were no glasses that he could see, just the bottle itself. He gave it a shake. There were dregs at the bottom. Barely enough for a single shot.

The shake woke the smell, though. It was revolting and enticing in roughly equal measures. Jack held the bottle steady, right below his nose, like he was testing himself.

Finally, he returned it to the draining board and hurried back to the safety of the living area, not daring to look back.

'Anything?' Hamza asked again.

'No.'

'I can come in and help.'

Logan raised a hand, like he was directing traffic. 'Stay where you are. We're not all getting into the shit for this.'

His eyes were drawn back to the kitchen. To the draining board. To the bottle standing atop it. They lingered there for a while. Too long.

He forced himself to look away, and this time his gaze settled on the door with the foam insulation tucked right at the back of the room. The recording studio.

'Wait there,' Jack reiterated, then he stalked towards the door, ignoring the kitchen, and the draining board, and the bottle.

The door was heavy, like the wood was laced with concrete and steel. It glided open at his first nudge, moving silently on well-oiled hinges to reveal a room divided in two by a wall of glass.

On the other side of the glass, through a door, there was a free-standing microphone and a drum kit. The floor was a tangle of audio cables that ran to various other mics positioned around the room and suspended from the ceiling.

The side of the room that Logan was in was the business end. Mixing desks and control decks stood butted against the glass, a swivel chair was positioned so anyone sitting there would be within reaching distance of the hundreds of buttons, dials, levers and switches.

It made Jack think of Mr Sulu's seat aboard the Starship Enterprise. Push the wrong button, he reckoned, and the whole house would hit warp speed.

There was another mug here, this time with the congealing remains of chicken noodle soup lurking at the bottom. A laptop stood beside it, teetering half on and half off the only empty area of desk space in the room.

It was plugged into the deck beside it with two different types of cable, but the screen was dark.

Logan tapped a gloved finger on the trackpad and the laptop gurgled out a series of low grinding noises before the screen lit up.

He wasn't sure what he'd expected to find there. Some incomprehensible audio waveforms, maybe, or a list of connected audio equipment and their various control options.

Instead, he found a Word document.

A letter.

By the time you read this, it began.

'Aw,' Logan groaned, as he bent to better take in the rest. 'Shite.'

'No, I'm not prepared to appear on your programme. No, and nor are any of my officers.'

DCI McCulloch held up a finger to Tyler and Sinead, indicating that they should wait, then pointed to the phone he had to his ear, in case they somehow thought he was holding half a conversation with himself.

'I don't care if it *is* Kirsty Wark. I don't even know who that is,' he continued, then he scowled, the facial expression transferring into his voice. 'No, I don't want her career retrospective. My point is, I don't care. There will be a press conference in due course. Good day.'

Tyler and Sinead could still hear the other person talking when McCulloch took the phone from his ear and thumbed the button to end the call.

For a moment, he sagged, like the conversation had robbed him of his strength. Or maybe it was the dozen others before that one.

Either way, Tyler almost felt sorry for him.

Although *almost* was doing a lot of the heavy lifting in that sentence.

Down on the floor, Taggart had tucked himself in under the table the DCI was sitting at. He lay on his back, paws in the air, like he was waiting on belly rubs.

In all likelihood, he'd be waiting a very long time.

'Was that true, sir?' Tyler asked.

McCulloch raised his eyes. It took effort. 'Was what true?'

'Do you really not know who Kirsty Wark is?'

'I was a press liaison officer, Detective Constable. Of course I know who Kirsty Wark is. They don't need to know that, though.'

He pulled himself together and straightened in his seat. His phone rang, but other than a sharp, spiteful glance, he ignored it.

'What's happening? Why are you here? I suppose it's too much to hope that Alanna Swain has confessed?'

'Afraid not, sir,' Sinead replied. 'She's got an alibi.'

McCulloch ran a hand down his face. 'Oh. Great.'

'We need to look into it, but it seems pretty solid,' Sinead continued. 'We got a few bits and pieces of information from her, but nothing earth-shattering. We just wanted to check it's OK to send her home for now?'

McCulloch looked pained at the thought of losing another suspect. Even the ringing phone going silent didn't improve his mood.

'You sure about the alibi?'

'Confident, sir. Not sure. Her brother-in-law backed her up, though.'

'Well, of course he'd support her,' McCulloch reasoned.

'I wouldn't be so sure,' Tyler said. 'He doesn't seem to be her biggest fan.'

'We've got numbers for three other people who can verify her whereabouts,' Sinead said. 'And we can probably confirm with the venue she was at in Thurso, too.'

McCulloch nodded sullenly, then waved a hand. 'Send her away, then. But tell her to stay local. Let's not completely write her off yet.'

The phone screen lit up on the desk beside him. The ringing followed a moment later.

McCulloch almost stabbed at the icon to decline the call, then stopped himself.

'It's DCI Logan,' he announced, picking up the mobile. 'Get rid of her, then go give that old couple parked out front a knock. Elsie was it? I want to know what all those calls were about.'

'You want us to bring her in?' Tyler asked.

'I don't care. Talk to her there, talk to her here, use your initiative, Detective Constable. I'm sure you can borrow some from somewhere, if it comes to it.'

He pointed to the door they'd entered through, ushering them out, then brought his phone to his ear.

'Jack. If you don't have some good news to give me, then hang up and call me back when you do.'

Logan stood in the recording studio, his phone to his ear, the laptop still open in front of him.

'Depends on your definition of *good news*,' he told the other DCI. 'I've got a confession.'

He could practically hear McCulloch sitting upright at the other end of the line. 'A confession? Well, yes, that counts!'

'Aye, but there's more. It's not just a confession,' Logan continued. He scanned the typed text again. 'It's a suicide note.'

'Who? Where? Dougie Cairns?'

'Aye. He came flying at us in his car and sped off. We gave chase as best we could, but it was too dangerous. If I'd known about this note, though...'

He ran a hand down his face. Another decision he'd made. Another mistake?

Another man dead?

'I put a shout out, but I need you to do a signal boost. Get whatever help we can from Uniform. It's a big area, so if we can get a chopper in, let's push for that. Mitchell can escalate.'

'Yes, yes, of course,' McCulloch said. It sounded dismissive. 'What does it say? The note?'

Logan bent forward and squinted, reading the first few lines aloud.

'By the time you read this, I will be dead. I can't live with myself for what I did. Johnny was not a particularly good man, but he didn't deserve to die like that. He didn't deserve what I did to him. He was my cousin, and I killed him, and I can't go on living with the guilt of that.'

McCulloch sounded positively perky when he cut in. 'Well, that's all rather cut and dried, isn't it? I'd say we have our killer!'

'What?'

The voice came from over on Logan's left. Declan stood there, eyes wide, face flushed red as Hamza came hurrying across the open-plan space behind him.

'Sorry! He snuck in when I wasn't looking!'

Declan's lips parted, but no sound came out. He took a step closer, his hands becoming fists.

'What's that?' he managed, pointing to the screen.

'I'll call you back,' Logan said into the phone, then he returned it to his pocket. 'Easy, son. You're all right.'

'What *is* that? What were you saying just then?'

Logan looked past the lad to Hamza, who grimaced in apology and reached for Declan's arm.

'Let's just go back outside and—'

Declan hauled himself free, and the momentum carried him a few more paces into the room. He stared at the laptop, transfixed by it, but keeping his distance, like it was a bomb on the brink of detonation.

'What were you saying?' Declan asked Logan, his voice dropping into a whisper. 'Is that...? Did he write that? Did Dougie write that stuff?'

'It looks like it, son,' Logan said, but the boy was already shaking his head.

'No, that's not— Why? Why would he do that? Why would he?' Tears skiffed down the lad's freckled cheeks. 'Why would he do it?'

'Come on, Declan,' Hamza said. He took him by the arm again, and this time the teenager didn't resist. 'Come on outside.'

Declan kept staring at the screen of the laptop as he was gently led away. He was halfway across the open-plan space—halfway back to the front door—when he broke, sobbing and coughing, like he was about to throw up.

'Why would he do that?'

'Poor bastard,' Logan muttered. Then, he took a photo of the confession on his phone, sent it over to the group inbox, and headed outside to start making calls.

Chapter 38

There was some muttering and thumping inside the box van after Tyler knocked on the door. When Elsie finally opened it, she looked windswept and out of breath, and Tyler felt a prickle of embarrassment creeping up his face as he imagined what the couple might have been up to.

'Yes?' the older woman asked, her chest heaving.

Her husband, Reg, appeared behind her and placed an arm on the doorframe, as if blocking the entrance.

'Everything all right?' he asked. He, too, was slightly breathless and red in the face.

'Uh, yes. Hello,' Sinead said. Clearly, she'd been thrown by the couple's appearance, too. She produced her ID and held it out to them. 'DC Sinead Bell. You've met my colleague, DC Neish already. We were hoping we could ask you a few questions.'

'What, more questions?' Elsie asked, her voice pitchy with exasperation. 'Haven't you asked enough?'

'It's about the phone calls, Mrs Kellerman,' Sinead said. 'The calls you made to the deceased.'

She could have used Johnny's name, of course, but *the deceased* landed with much more impact.

'The *numerous* calls you made. We can discuss it here, or we can do it more officially. We're happy either way, aren't we, DC Neish?'

'Happy as Larry,' Tyler confirmed. 'We're easy-osey. No skin off our nose. It's not a problem for us, either way.'

He stopped then, partly because he'd run out of alternative ways of saying the same thing, but mostly because Sinead had placed her heel on his toe and pressed down quite firmly.

'Will it take long?' Reg asked.

'Well, that depends.'

'On what?' Elsie asked.

Sinead smiled up at her. 'On how quickly you answer.'

Reg looked down at his wife, but she kept her gaze fixed on Sinead. Finally, with a muttered warning to 'stand back', she deployed the folding steps and retreated into the mobile home.

'After you,' Tyler said, letting his wife take the lead.

She reached the top step just as he stepped onto the bottom. Even combined, their weight didn't rock the vehicle half as much as Logan's had.

It still tipped slightly, though, and there was a *thud* from a tall cupboard on the opposite wall. Reg darted over to it, slamming the door closed just as it started to swing open.

Elsie clapped her hands. The sound was sharp and sudden, and apparently for no other reason than to draw the detectives' attention away from her husband and the cupboard.

'So! Phone calls. Yes. I did make a few,' she said. 'I suppose it must look a bit suspicious, but—'

'What's in the cupboard?' Tyler asked.

Elsie's mouth snapped shut. She glowered at Reg, who remained rooted to the spot, still holding the door closed.

'Nothing,' Reg said.

'Right.' Tyler very deliberately looked to where Reg's hand was pressed against the wood. 'It's just, it seems like there is.'

'Are we not allowed to have things in our cupboard?' Elsie demanded. 'Is storage space a crime, all of a sudden?'

Sinead smiled at her. 'No. Course not.' She gestured to the two-seater couch. 'Maybe you could both just sit down so we can get through this as quickly as possible? I'm sure we can get it all cleared up.'

Elsie eyed her warily, chewing on her bottom lip.

'Fine,' she mumbled, crossing to the settee and sitting. She patted the empty space beside her like she was summoning a dog. 'Reg. Come.'

Reg didn't move. His eyes were still locked with Tyler's, his hand still on the door. He pressed it firmly, making sure it was closed, then scurried over to join his wife when she called for him a second time.

Sinead glanced at the cupboard as she passed it en route to the couch. She stood over the couple, up close, looking almost straight down. The sofa was on the same side of the living space as the front door.

The same side as Tyler was still standing on.

Sinead launched into her questions, but Reg was only half-listening. He kept stealing glances at Tyler, each one more furtive than the last.

Tyler smiled at him like he knew a secret.

He shuffled back a pace then, until he was backed up almost all the way to the mobile home's front door. He felt the weight of the vehicle shifting. Just a little. Just a fraction.

Not enough.

He waited until Sinead looked over at him. A message flitted silently through the air between them. She took a step forward, even closer to the couple on the couch, crossing the van's invisible equator.

At the same time, Tyler jumped. It wasn't a big jump, and there was no big thud of him landing. He just sprang up a few inches, landed on pointed toes, and then let his weight follow through on his heels.

Across the van, the cupboard door clicked and began to swing open. Reg tried to leap up from the sofa, but the cushions were too soft, and his bones were too creaky, and he could only watch in mute horror as the door opened all the way, and an object around three feet long toppled out.

It hit the floor with a thud. And with a twang.

'Holy shit!' Tyler cried. He didn't know what he'd been expecting to fall out, but this was a surprise.

'It's not what it looks like!' Reg cried.

He finally made it to his feet, but Sinead blocked him before he could get any further.

Down on the floor, the grey daylight bounced off the blood-red wood of an electric guitar.

Chapter 39

By the time Logan set eyes on the guitar, it had been photographed, dusted, and bagged. It sat now on the table in the village hall, the glossy red body dulled by a thin plastic sheet. Even through the bag, it was unmistakable.

It was Old Bessie. He was sure of it.

'And they had this in the van?'

'They did, boss, aye,' Tyler confirmed. 'Tried to hide it from us in a cupboard. But, well, I did this pretty clever thing where...' He realised Logan wasn't paying much attention, and shrugged. 'Doesn't matter. It was pretty impressive, though, if I say so myself.'

'Where are they now?'

'They're in separate rooms next door, boss. Sinead's watching over them. Their solicitor's on the way up.'

'There were still a couple of SOCOs knocking around, finishing up,' McCulloch said, appearing at Logan's side. 'We had them do their stuff in the van, then bag it up for us. You will note...'

He leaned in and pointed through the plastic. There was a dent in the guitar's body. The red paint was darker in spots around it.

It took Logan a few seconds to realise it wasn't paint he was seeing at all.

'God. Right. So...?'

'They reckon it's the murder weapon, boss,' Tyler said, stealing McCulloch's thunder.

'Clobbered to death by his own guitar,' Logan muttered.

'Maybe that's how he'd want to go, boss.'

Both DCIs turned to look at the detective constable. Tyler smiled sheepishly.

'But probably not.'

'Did they say anything about why they had it?' Jack asked.

'No, they went pretty tight-lipped, boss. Said they're not talking to us until their lawyer gets here.'

'The rooms they're in, are they lockable?'

'Maybe, boss. Not sure. But even if they are, I'm not sure it'll hold them. Elsie's the chairperson of the village hall committee. She'll know this place like the back of her hand. No saying we'll be able to hold her.'

'She's an elderly woman, son, no' the fucking Predator,' Logan pointed out. 'If we tell her to stay put, I'm pretty sure she'll do just that.'

He reached out for the guitar, like something was compelling him to touch it. His fingertips brushed against the plastic, making it crackle, then he about-turned and approached the whiteboards.

'Hamza's down at Dougie Cairns's place waiting for Uniform to secure the place. Palmer's on his way up with a full team to give it a going-over. Dave is running that lad, Declan, back home. God help the boy.' He shrugged off his coat and dumped it on the closest chair. 'Any sign of Dougie's car yet?'

'Nothing,' McCulloch replied. 'I checked between calls from the *Daily Record* and the *Daily Mail*. We'll be notified as soon as it's flagged.'

Logan nodded, but he wasn't going to hold his breath. In the central belt, there were ANPR cameras that would pick up the number plate and ping the vehicle's location. Up here, though, even regular speed cameras were thin on the ground, much less anything more advanced.

There were countless narrow roads and tracks winding like a nervous system through the wilds of the northern Highlands. Hundreds of miles, through open moorland and dense, dark forests. If they were going to find Dougie's car in all that, they'd have to get lucky.

And it had been a long time since Logan had considered himself that.

The helicopter would help, but it would be a while before it was approved, let alone got airborne. Even then, with all that area to cover, a needle in a haystack would be a walk in the park by comparison.

'How long until the lawyer gets here?' he asked.

'About another hour and a half, boss.'

'Right, fine. Lock them in, then get Sinead through here,' Logan instructed.

He put his hands on his hips, contemplating the boards and everything written there. The case felt like it was twisting in on itself, pieces moving in ways that didn't quite fit. He exhaled hard through his nose, then turned back to the others.

'And let's see if we can't figure out between us just what the fuck is going on.'

After getting a tea and a coffee for Elsie and Reg, letting them use the toilet, and then locking them back in their separate rooms, everyone assembled in the improvised Incident Room.

Uniform had arrived in the meantime to secure Dougie Cairns's place, and Hamza arrived back at the village hall just as the kettle was reboiling, with Dave a couple of minutes behind.

Between them, they rattled off a full recap of the situation as they saw it.

Logan spoke about how he, Declan and Hamza had almost been mowed down by Dougie Cairns's car, and though he skirted over most of the details of the subsequent chase, he could see Tyler turning green just at the thought of it.

He talked about the suicide note, and the confession contained within it, reading the whole thing out loud in the hushed silence of the hall.

He mentioned the whisky on the kitchen worktop with only the dregs remaining at the bottom.

'He must've tanned that quick,' Hamza remarked. 'He wasn't that long away from here.'

'Aye, well,' Logan said, not looking up from his phone screen. 'You'd be surprised how quickly some people can knock it back.'

'Good driver for a guy who's necked that much whisky,' Dave said. 'Some of them roads are pretty hairy.'

'Aye, tell me about it,' Logan said, grimacing at the memory.

Dave had a point, though. Dougie had been driving recklessly, yes, but he'd also been driving pretty well. Not *well* by any Highway Code definition, but he'd seemed in control of the motor, at least.

'Not bad at typing, either,' Sinead said. She was reading over the suicide note in the photo Logan had sent to the inbox. 'I don't think a drunk guy wrote this. Not half a bottle of whisky drunk, anyway.'

Again, Logan was forced to agree. The note didn't contain the mistyped ravings of a drunk. It was well written and properly structured. No typos, as far as he had noticed.

'He could've drunk it last night,' Jack reasoned. 'Or poured it down the sink. It was sat on the draining board. Either way, it implies some… difficulty with the stuff. Some stressor causing him to either knock it back or pour it away. We should check if he has any history of alcohol abuse.'

His tongue flitted across his lips, like he was tasting something on them.

'I know his cousin did. He was in and out of rehab. Maybe Dougie followed suit.'

'I'll get on that,' Dave said, making a note. He'd left his pad somewhere, so he scribbled it on the back of his hand, earning himself a flaring of the nostrils and rolling of the eyes from DCI McCulloch.

'Still no sign of the car, sir,' Hamza said, checking through the notifications on his laptop screen. 'Chopper's in the air, though.'

'Good,' Logan said.

'One thing I think might be important, sir,' the DS continued. 'After you left, Declan mentioned that there was some recording equipment missing from Dougie's studio.'

'We know about that, don't we?' Sinead asked. 'Johnny took it.'

'No, this is studio stuff, apparently. Hard drives. Couple of laptops. Declan said it should all be in a rack. But, well, it wasn't.'

Logan rubbed at his chin, fingernail picking at the raised edge of a spot he found beneath the stubble.

'Did he say when he'd last seen it?'

'Not specifically, no. He just said it was always there. There were a few cables in the rack, like stuff had been unplugged.'

'Could have been something on there he didn't want us to hear,' Tyler suggested. 'You know, like, incriminating stuff.'

'He left a full written confession,' Logan pointed out.

Tyler opened his mouth and raised a finger like he was going to offer a clever rejoinder to this point, but he couldn't think of one, so he didn't bother.

Logan took the lid of a pen and wrote the information on one of the whiteboards. From the way Sinead bristled, he'd picked the wrong spot on the wrong one, and she'd have to redo it later to match the rest of her system.

With that done, Hamza—aided and interrupted by McCulloch— quickly ran through the main bullet points of their interview with

Dougie earlier in the day. He confirmed that Johnny's cousin was unable to provide an alibi for the night Johnny died, which lent weight to the confession.

'Why'd we let him go?' Tyler asked.

Hamza looked to McCulloch for that, but the DCI didn't even acknowledge that he'd heard the question.

'We, eh, we thought we could bring him back in later,' Hamza said. It wasn't really an answer, but then he didn't have one to give. He cleared his throat. 'It was, uh… It was decided that, given his disability, getting down there into the cave to kill Johnny, then back up, would be difficult.'

'Not impossible, though,' Tyler said. 'I mean, he popped down the next morning, didn't he? When Elsie and Reg phoned him. He had no problem nipping up and down then.'

'No.' Hamza cleared his throat again. 'No, he managed that fine.'

'I know what you're all thinking.'

All eyes turned to DCI McCulloch. He stood at the back of the group with his hands folded behind him, like an army sergeant major inspecting the troops.

'If I'd kept him here, this could all be over,' McCulloch continued. His voice was flat. Level. No hint of emotion in it. 'Mr Cairns's life would not currently be in danger. We might even have an arrest. If only I'd kept him'—he pointed to the floor—'here.'

He looked around at them, one by one, meeting their eyes. He lingered on Jack's, then finally settled on DC Neish.

'That's what you're implying. Correct?'

Tyler hesitated, then nodded. 'It did cross my mind, sir, aye.'

McCulloch inhaled sharply. He straightened so much that he almost looked like a pencil. Tyler braced himself for a bollocking.

It never came.

'Good. Well done on speaking your mind, Detective Constable. Credit to you for that.' There was just the slightest suggestion of a smile on McCulloch's face, but it vanished again as quickly as it had appeared. 'But here's the bare-arsed fact of the matter. In this job, we make decisions. All of us. Some of those are easy. Many—most—are not. All of them are important. Some of them can even be life or death.'

He raised a skeletal finger and pointed around at them all. They all shifted uncomfortably, like a light was being shone on them, exposing their darkest secrets.

'Every one of us in this room has made a bad call. We've rushed in somewhere we shouldn't. We've asked the wrong questions. We've accused the wrong man,' McCulloch continued. 'And people have been hurt by that. Suspects. Victims. Colleagues. Ourselves. Because we have made mistakes.'

Tyler opened his mouth to reply, but McCulloch silenced him with a raised hand and a hiss of air through his teeth—the sort of sound normally reserved for scaring off stray cats.

'So, we do our best not to make those mistakes again. We do. And yet, we will. All of us. Daily. We will try to always do the right thing—the best thing—and we will fail. Not every time. God willing, not even most of the time. But we will make the wrong call. And people will suffer. And that's our cross to bear, because that's the job we chose to do.'

He ran his hands down the side of his face, as if straightening his sideburns. When he spoke again, his voice was softer. Almost human, in fact.

'So, yes. I made the call to let Dougie Cairns go. Was it the wrong decision? Maybe. Did I know that at the time? No. So, if you're going to judge me on anything, judge me on that.'

The lines on his face hardened again. The voice, too.

'But be sure to take a look in the mirror before you do.'

There was silence, then. A raw, uncomfortable quiet as everyone processed the speech.

He wasn't wrong, of course. Everyone on the team had made bad judgement calls at one point or another. Given the chance, there were things they would all go back and do differently.

Some more than others.

'Thanks for that, Evan,' Logan said. He held the man's eye for a moment, then nodded, just briefly. Just once.

Then, he turned to the board, clapped his hands, and startled everyone back to attention.

'Now, tell me all about what happened with Mr and Mrs Kellerman and that guitar,' he said. 'Before I march in there and go through them like a dose of the bloody runs.'

Chapter 40

Logan had expected the Kellermans' solicitor to be of an older generation. He'd pictured a grey suit and an even greyer combover. A fastidious, deliberate man, who would give McCulloch a run for his money on doing things by the book.

The grinning hotshot in the blue tweed was not what he'd expected at all. He knew immediately that he'd have preferred the imagined version.

'Hey. Hi. Rohan Mehta,' he said, thrusting out a hand to shake, while extending a business card with the other.

Logan took the card first, glanced at it, then accepted the greeting. 'DCI Jack Logan.'

'Nice!' the solicitor said, though it wasn't clear what in particular he approved of. 'So, you're the man in charge of this case, yeah?'

Logan started to confirm this, then pulled back. 'No. That would be DCI McCulloch. But I'll be conducting the interview with your clients.'

'OK. OK. Cool. Cool.'

Rohan clicked his fingers, then slapped an open hand against the side of a clenched fist. He swung a leg as he looked around the foyer of the village hall, like he was sizing the place up for a renovation project.

'Could be a good Airbnb this,' he remarked. 'We've got a department that deals with property stuff. They'd love it.'

Logan had no idea how to respond to that, so he didn't bother his arse to.

'Right! Anyway. So, yeah. Rohan Mehta. Officially, since I'm on duty, *Mr Mehta*. Or, so you might think, but I've got more of a chill vibe about it all than that, so Rohan's fine. Ro, even, if you prefer.'

'I don't,' Logan informed him.

The solicitor's smile took a dent, but rallied quickly. 'They call me *Sharky* back at the office. Know why?'

'Because they don't like you?' Jack guessed.

'Ha! No. What? No. It's because I'm a shark in the courtroom. And in interviews, I should warn you.' He pointed to a door. 'Shall we?'

Logan's eyes followed his finger, then he shrugged. 'You can if you want,' he said. 'But that's where they keep the paper towels.' He gestured in the opposite direction. 'So, you might want to come this way, instead.'

–

Judging by her 'Who in God's name is this?' remark when Logan and Hamza entered with Rohan Mehta, Elsie had never met her solicitor before.

It didn't seem to phase Rohan, who introduced himself, passed her another card, and pointed to the bit under his name that said 'Junior Partner'.

'Where's Callum? Callum Maclean. He's our lawyer,' Elsie said, after peering at the card for a good thirty seconds. 'I wanted Callum.'

'He can't come,' Rohan told her.

'Oh, for goodness' sake! Why not?'

'He's dead,' the solicitor explained.

'Dead?! How? When?'

'Heart attack. Massive one,' Rohan said. He sucked in his cheeks and shook his head at the tragedy of it all. 'About eight years ago. Feels like only yesterday, though.'

He placed his briefcase on the table and took a seat.

'Never met him myself, of course. Before my time. But I hear he was very good. Good news for you, though.' He winked, made a clicking sound, and pointed at himself with both thumbs. 'I'm just as good. Better, some might say, but I wouldn't like to comment. I was top of my class at Napier University. In Edinburgh. Ever been?'

Elsie shuffled her chair a little further away so he could fully appreciate the scowl on her face. 'To Napier University?'

'To Edinburgh?'

'What do you…?' Elsie looked despairingly up at the detectives, then back to Rohan. 'Of course I've been to bloody Edinburgh!'

'Good. It's nice,' Rohan said.

He opened his briefcase, revealing nothing but an A4 notepad and a Nintendo Switch. The pad was placed on the table, then the solicitor indicated the woman beside him with a pointed finger.

'We would like some time to confer before the interview begins.'

'Christ, no. We really would not,' Elsie said.

She reached over the manager's desk, plucked a pen from the little stationery holder next to the computer monitor, and handed it to Rohan, who had been patting the pockets of his blue tweed suit with increasing desperation.

She eyeballed Logan, and indicated the seat across from her, like she was the one conducting the interview. 'Let's just hurry up and get this over with.'

The recording was started. The formalities were taken care of. Elsie was informed that she wasn't yet under arrest, but given the discovery of the guitar, and their attempts to hide it, charges were looming in her immediate future.

It was in her best interests, then, to be helpful. If she talked, if she told them everything, then the detectives and the procurator fiscal would look far more kindly upon her.

She didn't react to any of it, beyond a tap-tapping of a fingernail on the desk that grew gradually faster, the taps coming closer and closer together.

As soon as Logan finished his spiel, before he'd even asked his first question, Elsie started to talk.

'We didn't kill him. Obviously, we didn't kill him. We just found him, that's all. Completely by chance. We thought he'd fallen. We didn't realise it was anything more sinister. Of course we didn't! How could we?'

The guitar was the elephant in the room, of course. Logan skirted around it for now.

'We were looking through Johnny's phone records,' he said. Across the desk, Elsie tried very hard to keep her expression steady. 'Anything you'd like to tell us?'

'I'm sure you have something you want to tell me.'

'Do you know how many times you called the victim in the week before his death, Elsie?'

She sniffed. Shrugged. 'A lot.'

'Aye. It was that, all right. DS Khaled?'

'A hundred and three times, sir.'

'*A hundred and three times*,' Logan stressed, staring at the woman.

'Wow, that's a lot,' Rohan whispered below his breath.

'I expected it to be more,' Elsie said, with a note of defiance. 'He refused to answer most of the time, so I kept calling. I can be very persistent when I want to be.'

'You can say that again,' Logan agreed. 'You don't think it's a bit on the excessive side?'

'I wanted to talk to him. So, I kept trying. Like I said, I am nothing if not persistent, particularly when it's an important matter, like this.'

'What was it, exactly? What did you want to talk to him for?'

'Well, about his new music. About the'—she wrinkled her nose in distaste—'comeback tour he had planned to kick off here. You know what he told me a couple of months back? When he first came? You know what he said?'

Logan shook his head. Elsie's voice became shriller.

'He said he was going to put Durness on the map. *On the map!* Can you believe that? We're already on the bloody map! We're too much on the map. We want off the map, if anything!'

She clenched her jaw and shook her head, swallowing back her rising anger. '*On the map!* The bloody cheek of him.'

'So you were calling to—'

'I was calling to get him to reconsider. To think of the locals. We can't be doing with yet more bloody tourists up here. They're a blight already!'

She folded her arms tightly across her stomach. Her legs were crossed, and one foot swung up and down beneath the table, tapping on thin air.

'This used to be a lovely place to live. Friendly. Quiet. Yes, it's miles from anywhere, but that was the point! And he wanted to bring *more* people here? I told him, he could bloody well think again!'

'You must've been angry at him,' Logan said.

'Furious. Utterly furious. But—and I know where this is going—I didn't kill him. Of course I didn't, don't be ridiculous.'

'So, you just happened to walk a little further into the cave that day, and randomly chanced upon his body?'

'Yes! Exactly! I know it's inconvenient for you, but that's the size of it,' Elsie shot back. 'Why would I even want to kill him? Hmm? You think people aren't going to come for that? Morbid people? Warped people? You think they aren't going to come to leer over the site where a pop star was murdered?'

'Rock star,' Logan corrected on autopilot.

'Oh, pop, rock, bloody… boogie-woogie, it's all the same these days. Just noise.'

She leaned forward so sharply that Rohan drew back in fright, dragging his pen across the page of his pad and leaving a line through the paragraph of notes he'd just scribbled down.

'Let's be honest here, Johnny Freestone—Johnny Cairns, to give him his real name—was a washed-up nobody. Yes, I was worried his new songs and his tour might have an impact. But his death? I'm *sure* that will. A much bigger one, too.'

She sat back, breathing deeply, wrestling her temper back under control.

'Whoever killed him, they certainly didn't do it for the sake of the community,' she said. 'Because his death is only going to make things significantly worse for all of us.'

Logan considered this. She was right, of course. There was every chance that any comeback tour or new album that Johnny had planned would die on its arse like his previous efforts.

A celebrity murder in a picturesque location, though? The TikTokers, YouTubers, and all that lot would be swarming the place in no time.

'Why did you have his guitar?' Logan asked.

'Sorry, I'm catching up. Who had whose guitar?' Rohan asked.

'Your clients. Mr and Mrs Kellerman. They were in the possession of what is not only a guitar believed to belong to the victim, but also what we suspect to be the murder weapon.'

'What?' The colour drained out of Elsie's face at that. 'The murder… We didn't know. We had no idea, we thought he'd fallen, we didn't know!'

Neither Logan nor Hamza spoke. They sat there, watching her, letting the silence grow until it filled the room.

'It was Reg's idea,' she finally said, lowering her voice like she was scared her husband might hear her from the room next door. 'He saw it there, he thought it might be valuable.'

'So you stole it?' Logan pressed.

'What? No!' Elsie screeched. 'How dare...? Stole it? No. He was...
I mean, it was clear that he was... He wasn't exactly going to need it,
was he?'

'I ran your plate earlier,' Logan told her. 'I noticed your tyres were a
bit flat. Sure enough, the van's out of MOT. Has been for a good eight
months. That's why it's parked out there, isn't it? Off the main road.
You can't afford to get it fixed. Can you?'

'The parts are expensive. They don't do them any more,' Elsie said.
'They have to be imported, or specially made, or... God. I don't know.
But they cost a fortune.'

She rubbed the back of one hand with the fingers of the other,
scratching at the skin.

'We shouldn't have done it.'

'You disturbed a crime scene.'

'We thought he'd fallen!'

'You perverted the course of justice.'

'Hang on!' Rohan raised a hand and bobbed his head from left to
right, like he was physically inserting himself into the conversation.
'No.'

Logan scowled at him. 'Sorry?'

'It'd only be perverting the course of justice if they were aware a
crime had been committed, and they were trying to hide that fact,'
the solicitor said. He spoke slowly, like he was explaining a complex
concept to a toddler. 'If they weren't aware of a crime, you couldn't
pursue them for perverting the course of justice.'

'Yes! Thank you!' Elsie said.

'Just theft,' Rohan added, helpfully. Or unhelpfully, depending on
whose side you were on.

Logan shrugged. 'Right, well, we'll start with theft, then, and see
about building a case for the other stuff.' He fixed the woman with
one of his more intimidating glares. 'You took a murder weapon from
a crime scene, Elsie, knowingly or not. You stole a very valuable item,
with the intention of reselling it.'

'It was Reg's idea!' she cried, no longer concerned about her
husband overhearing. 'He brought it back up here before we called
Dougie. He stashed it away. I tried to tell him not to, but—'

'Bollocks you did!' The voice came from through the wall. Even muffled, Reg's anger was apparent. 'You suggested it, you lying old bastard! "Let's grab that guitar and flog it", you said.'

'Oh, shut up, Reggie!' Elsie screamed.

Hamza started to interject, but Logan nudged him under the table, silencing him.

'She's talking shite! Don't listen to her! She's the one who got me to swipe the poor bastard's guitar!' Reg bellowed.

His next outburst shook the wall so much that a pin popped out of a corkboard, sending the whole thing sliding to the floor.

'And all his recording equipment, too!'

Chapter 41

'Did you miss me that much, Jack, that you had to bring me back?'

Logan grimaced when he heard the voice. He only had himself to blame, too. One encounter with Geoff Palmer in a week was unlucky. Two? That was downright careless.

'You find it?' Logan asked, cleaving a trench straight through the Scene of Crime man's bullshit.

'Maybe,' Palmer teased. He winked, and then produced a plastic evidence bag from behind his back. 'Is this, pray tell, what you were searching for, good si—?'

Logan snatched it from him with a grunted, 'Aye, looks like it.'

He held up the bag and studied the contents. Some sort of portable recording device with two microphones built in at the top, an assortment of buttons around a screen on the front, and eight separate ports for other mics to be plugged into.

'It was under the cushions in the couch,' Palmer said. 'There's storage under there. Quite a clever wee set-up, if space is a premium. I could do something like that in my flat to keep the comedy awards!'

This was enough to get Logan's attention. 'Comedy awards? What do you mean? Have you won comedy awards?'

'Well, no. Not yet,' Palmer said. 'But give it time, Jack. Give it time!'

Logan sighed with relief. For a moment, the world had turned upside down. The thought—the very idea—that Geoff Palmer could've won a prize for his comedy had almost bowled Logan over. Had he been a religious man, it would all have been thrown into question.

Thankfully, it was all in the bastard's head.

'Anyway, there were a couple of microphones in there, too. We're bagging them up. Plenty of prints, but I'm guessing that's going to be—'

He turned, made a pistol with a finger and thumb, and fired off two imaginary shots at the elderly couple being loaded into separate police cars.

'Ptchow-chow. That pair. But we'll run it all through and see what we've got. We'll take the guitar *doon the road, too*,' he said, inexplicably putting on a high-pitched voice for that last part. 'And I'll get the report back to you ASAP.'

He turned to head for his van, but winked up at Logan.

'Seriously, though, Jack. If you wanted to hang out, you should've just said so! We can do coffee again, if you want?'

Logan shook his head. 'No.'

'Tea?' Palmer suggested.

'No.'

Palmer's mouth formed a few different shapes, as his brain rattled through a few other possible suggestions.

'Couch to Five K?'

That one caught Logan off guard. 'What?'

'The running thing. You know, breaks you into jogging.'

'I know what it is, Geoff, I just...' Logan shook his head again. 'Doesn't matter. No. You're fine. Good luck, though.' He held up the bag. 'Cheers for this.'

And then, before Palmer could suggest a picnic in the park, a trip to see a West End show, or whatever the hell else he might suggest, Logan turned and went striding over to where Hamza was overseeing the handover of Elsie and Reg Kellerman.

The different cars had been a must. Even if the detectives hadn't wanted to keep them apart, it was in the couple's best interests to remain separated, lest one of them strangled the other. They were both in enough trouble without that on their plate.

The solicitor, Rohan, had mumped and moaned a bit about having driven all this way only to have to drive back again, but he'd been given short shrift by the detectives, and so had eventually shut up.

He was sitting behind the wheel of an eight-year-old Ford Focus, waiting for the police vehicles to pull away. The Focus was a bit battered looking, like it had fallen off the end of the assembly line and bounced across the factory floor.

There was a green strip across the top of the windscreen, with the names 'Rohan' and 'Chelsea' printed on it in white.

'*Sharky* my arse,' Logan muttered, as the solicitor gave him a smile and a wave.

'Come on, hurry up!' Elsie's voice was a sharp bark from the back of the car she'd been loaded into. 'I'm not having that bastard getting away ahead of us. *He* can follow *me!*'

A Uniformed constable closed the door on her, turned wearily to the detectives, and raised a thumb to signal he was ready, if not particularly enthusiastic, for the three-hour journey ahead.

'Good luck, son,' Logan told him. 'You can always stick on the sirens to drown her out, if it gets too much.'

The constable smiled. 'I'll keep that in mind, sir.'

Once both Kellermans were rumbling off down the driveway with their solicitor following behind, Logan and Hamza turned back to the couple's converted box van. SOCOs in white paper suits were filing in and out with cameras and equipment, giving the place a full going-over in case there was any forensic evidence lurking in the fabrics or the corners.

Palmer was nowhere to be seen. Probably skiving back in his van. Logan and Hamza took the opportunity to head back into the village hall without him spotting them and inviting himself along.

They met Sinead in the hallway. She'd been headed out to get them, and almost ran straight into Logan in her rush.

He could tell by her face that something had happened. Something had changed.

'What is it?' he asked.

'We got a call, sir. Dougie Cairns's car's been found.'

Logan tensed. Something about her tone. About her demeanour.

'And?'

'And it's not good, sir,' she told him. 'It's not good at all.'

–

Logan stood alone in the bracken and heather, his coat pulled tight against the evening chill. A stone's throw away, spotlights and headlights fought back against the approaching dusk.

Other lights, blue and orange, spiralled and flashed. Firefighters, paramedics and Uniformed police officers formed cliques by their vehicles, while their more senior representatives huddled with a couple of recovery drivers trying to figure out next steps.

The car had been spotted by a woman walking her dog along the edge of the loch. She'd seen the tail lights glowing beneath the dark surface of the water, thirty feet below the ledge she'd been strolling along.

Logan looked back at his car parked in one of the laybys at the edge of the single-track road. When one of the flashing lights caught the back window, he could see Taggart with his nose pressed up against the glass, desperate to be allowed out to run around.

It couldn't happen here, though. Not now.

The sound of approaching footsteps made Jack turn back. DCI McCulloch was striding towards him, his skinny legs taking long, bounding strides along the roadside's edge.

'Any news?' Jack asked.

McCulloch stopped beside him. It was abrupt, sudden, and Logan was once again reminded of those stop-motion skeletons.

'We're going to need divers and a crane,' McCulloch said. 'It's hard to be sure, but it looks like he's in there. Behind the wheel.'

Logan ran a hand down his face. 'Shite.'

'Hmm. Yes. Not ideal,' McCulloch said.

He was staring in the direction of the submerged car, and all the activity going on around it. As he watched, he emitted a series of low hums and groaning noises. They were quiet, tucked in below his breath, and Logan wondered if he was even aware he was making them.

'You shouldn't blame yourself, Evan.'

'What?' McCulloch roused from the trance he'd been slipping into. 'Oh. No. I don't blame myself. I made a call. No point dwelling on it. This is going to be an all-nighter, though.' He raised his wrist and checked his watch. 'We should get down the road. We can wrap all this up in the morning.'

'Wrap it up?' Logan asked.

McCulloch regarded him strangely. 'Well, yes. We have a confession, and it's looking like we have the confessor, too. The Kellermans are a sideshow. We can hand them over to CID to deal with. No point us getting bogged down with that.'

'Well, aye, but—'

McCulloch put a hand on his shoulder and squeezed it.

'I'm SIO, Jack,' he said. 'And I'm not looking to take any advice on this decision.'

He removed his hand just before Logan removed it for him, and shoved them both into the pockets of his waterproof jacket.

'Go home, Jack. Tell the team they can head off, too. We're done here,' McCulloch said.

Then, with a single sharp jerk of his head, he turned and went striding off to direct the first responders, leaving Logan alone with his thoughts.

And his doubts.

Chapter 42

Logan opened his front door and was met by the sound of gunfire. This, in recent months, was not unusual.

'Robocop again?' he asked the girl lounging on the couch.

Although, it was debatable if the position she was in qualified as lounging, or if it belonged in some higher category of relaxation.

She appeared to have melted onto the couch, with both legs draped over the arms so they were almost touching the floor, and her shoulder sliding off the cushion so her head was tilting upside down.

The movie was playing, and her head was pointed towards it, but she was also looking at her phone that she held directly in her line of sight. She swiped up at the screen, scrolling through endless videos, while occasionally shifting her focus to the events on the television.

'It's a classic,' she replied.

Taggart ran over, jumped up on the empty space beside her head, and licked her face. She made kissing sounds for about five seconds, then they both got bored of it and the dog lay down, curling himself up between the back cushion and the crook of her neck.

Olivia Maximuke was, for the next few months, Logan and Shona's foster child. After that, she turned sixteen, and they could technically throw her out on her arse.

They wouldn't, of course. Shona wouldn't allow it, and even Logan—though he'd had his differences with the girl over the years—would've felt bad about it.

And there was a very real possibility that she'd sneak back in and murder them in their sleep.

Jack checked the time. It was almost two in the morning. He tried to raise this point with Olivia by asking if she knew what time it was, but she'd just told him as if he'd been asking a real question.

'Shona away?'

'Yeah, she had to go up to the thing. The dead guy thing. You hear about it?'

'Aye, I was there,' Jack confirmed.

Olivia shifted focus so she was looking directly at him. 'Did you kill him? Not again, Jack. This is becoming a habit.'

'Hilarious,' Logan said. His expression disagreed. 'You had anything to eat?'

Taggart's ears pricked up at that. His deep brown eyes locked onto Logan, like he was willing himself into any future eating arrangements.

'I had chips at Ben's cafe.'

'When? That shut ages ago.'

Olivia shrugged. 'After school. Harris was working.' She lowered her phone—or raised it, technically, since she was the wrong way up—and flashed a look of indignation up at the DCI. 'Can you believe I had to pay for them?'

'Yes. That's generally how businesses operate,' Jack said. He took off his coat. 'You want something now?'

'It's two in the morning,' she pointed out.

Logan stepped out into the hallway just long enough to hang up his coat. When he returned, he was already rolling up his shirt sleeves.

'I know,' he said. 'But that's not what I asked.'

–

Olivia studied Logan across the compact kitchen table as he tried to stab a chunk of microwave chicken curry with his fork. The piece he was trying to impale on the prongs was particularly rubbery, though, and was putting up a damn good fight.

Down on the floor, Taggart sat waiting patiently, having devoured all his own food in around three seconds flat.

'What's different?' Olivia asked, before shoving a forkful of basmati rice in her mouth.

Logan looked up at her, then back down to his plate. 'I don't know. It's a korma, I think. Not a lot of taste to it.'

She shook her head. 'Not about the curry. About you,' she said, spraying grains of rice back onto her warm plastic tray. 'Something's changed.'

Logan shrugged and shook his head, pulling a face that said he had no idea what she was talking about.

'You've been grumpy as shit this last while.'

'I'm always grumpy,' Logan said. 'It's my personal brand.'

Olivia shook her head, took a big swig of Pepsi Max, and then burped. 'No. You're always surly. *That's* your personal brand.'

'And that's different, is it?'

'Oh, completely. You can be surly and happy. You can't be grumpy and happy. Grumpy's an emotional state. Surly's a state of mind. Totally different thing.'

Logan finally managed to prong the chicken. He shoved it in his mouth, and got two chews in before deciding it hadn't been worth the bother.

'That's philosophical stuff,' he told her.

'I'm smarter than I look.'

Logan swallowed, forcing down the chicken chunk. 'Tell me about it.'

Olivia's eyes narrowed. 'Is that a compliment or an insult?' she asked.

Logan loaded a fork with rice, raised it to his mouth, then reconsidered and dropped it back into the tray.

'Not sure,' he admitted.

Olivia smirked. Apparently, she was pleased with that answer.

'Shona's glad you went back to work.'

'I didn't go back to work,' Logan countered. 'I went to assist—no, *advise* the people I used to work with.'

Olivia tutted. 'Same thing. She's happy, anyway. I think she was worried you were going to get all depressed and just sit around the house all day in your dressing gown.'

'I doubt she was worried about that.'

Olivia slurped noisily from her Pepsi can. 'She was. Because that's what you have been doing.'

Logan shifted uncomfortably in his chair. The groan it made echoed his feelings on this conversation.

'I haven't been sitting around *all day*.'

'Were you drinking?' Olivia asked.

Logan laughed. Logan recoiled. 'What? No!' He clasped his hands together, suddenly aware of the way he was fiddling with his fingers.

Olivia ran her tongue around inside her mouth, clearing out a few stray grains of rice that had become stuck between her gums and her teeth. Her gaze remained locked on the man across the table.

'A couple of months back, just after everything happened. You know, you getting suspended, all that stuff coming out about the guy you said you killed, that freak in the cave—'

'I remember what happened,' said Logan, who had no desire to go over it all again.

'Right. Fair enough. So, Shona found a quarter bottle of whisky. The one with the mad chicken on it, or whatever it is.'

Logan's reply was a wary monotone. 'It's a grouse.'

'*Whatever it is,*' Olivia reiterated, stressing this wasn't the important part. 'It was in the bin, not the glass recycling box. She only found it because she was looking for something she thought she'd chucked out by mistake. Dunno what. Doesn't matter.'

A prickly heat crept up Logan's chest and onto his neck. 'Oh aye?'

'Yep. It was tucked in under a black bag. Like it had been hidden. She freaked out,' Olivia said. 'Like properly went into a panic. Crying, and everything.'

She let that linger for a moment as she took another drink.

'I told her it was mine,' she said, once she'd let out another gassy belch. 'I said I'd nicked it. I thought she'd be angry, but she just hugged me for ages, then told me not to do it again.'

Logan was suddenly aware that one of his legs was bouncing up and down beneath the table. It shook the floor. Shook the kitchen. Shook the whole damn house, and the world beyond it.

'Right,' was all he could say. All he could think.

'It wasn't mine, though,' Olivia said. There was no triumph in it. No *gotcha*. Just a flat, dead-eyed look that made her seem far older than her years. 'I don't know how it got there, but I didn't want Shona to be upset.'

Her chair gave a creak as she leaned in closer.

'You're not going to make her upset. Are you, Jack?'

The heat that Logan had felt rushing up his neck was replaced, all at once, by a sudden chill. The girl across the table was no longer just Olivia Maximuke. She was her father, Bosco, with all his ruthlessness and guile.

Logan swallowed. 'No,' he said. And he meant it. He really did.

Buying the alcohol had been a mistake. A moment of weakness at his lowest point. He'd only done it the once, that was all.

Maybe twice.

Olivia's face lit up like a dial had been twisted all the way to eleven. 'Good! Because I would really hate to see her upset.'

She got up from the table, tipped the remains of her curry into Taggart's bowl, then dumped the plastic tray into the sink and ran the cold tap to swirl away the last traces of sauce.

'Something's definitely different,' she said, looking him up and down while she waited for the water to do its job.

She snapped off the tap, shook the tray dry, then put it in the recycling bin.

'I think all this murder stuff is good for you. I think that's why you and Shona get along.'

She patted him on the shoulder on her way out the door. Her eyes were already going to the phone in her hand, her brief stop here in the real world now apparently over.

'You're both right miserable bastards when you haven't got a dead body to poke at.'

Chapter 43

Logan and McCulloch sat in silence, Jack slouching, McCulloch sitting straight up as if he was attached to some sort of spinal board. Logan's coat was unbuttoned, and sagged around him like a collapsed tent.

Beyond the briefest of greetings, neither man had spoken while they waited for Detective Superintendent Mitchell to finish reading through McCulloch's report.

She was in no rush. If anything, Logan reckoned she was deliberately taking her time so they'd have to wait longer. It was a power play, and fair enough—rank had its privileges, after all—but that didn't make it any less petty. Or annoying.

Jack had no idea what time McCulloch had finally got to sleep, but he seemed none the worse for wear. Logan himself had tossed and turned for hours, nodded off just before six, and then was woken by Shona returning half an hour later and collapsing, face-down, onto the bed.

He'd made her tea and either breakfast or supper, depending on which side you were approaching it from, then left her to sleep. Olivia was already up and about, and though Logan was highly suspicious of her offer to take Taggart on his morning walk, he didn't have the energy to say no.

He had gone for a shower, contemplated shaving, but decided that would be a step too far. Instead, he'd looked out the window to make sure that Olivia was nowhere around, kneeled down by the cupboard under the sink, and fished around at the back of the metal basin until he'd found the quarter bottle of whisky he'd stashed up there.

He'd shoved it in one of his coat pockets just as the girl and the dog returned, Taggart leaping and bounding around excitedly like he hadn't seen Jack in weeks.

That had been two hours ago. It felt like one hundred and nineteen of the subsequent minutes had been spent waiting for Mitchell to read this bloody report.

'Right,' she finally declared, setting the printout down. She interlocked her fingers and looked from McCulloch to Logan and back again. 'That all seems fairly straightforward.'

McCulloch nodded his agreement. 'The confession helped, of course. But really, it was fairly evident that Dougie Cairns was behind it.'

'How?' Logan asked.

McCulloch answered the question, but kept looking directly at Mitchell throughout.

'There was clearly bad blood there. There had been for some time. Dougie thought that Johnny was having a change of heart with his proclamation that family was the most important thing, but then, when he once again failed to follow through on that, Dougie snapped. It's there in his confession.'

Logan disputed that. 'It doesn't say half of that stuff.'

'It does if you read between the lines,' McCulloch said.

'Anyone could have typed that,' Logan pointed out. 'I don't like it. It's too neat.'

'No,' McCulloch said, finally turning to him. 'It's just neat enough. And anyway, you say that word—neat—like it's a bad thing. It isn't. Police work should be neat. It's about following processes and procedures, narrowing down suspects, until we have our culprit.'

Logan wasn't having it. 'It doesn't feel right. Something's off.'

'Yes, well, investigations don't run on feelings, Jack.'

'Mine do,' Logan said.

McCulloch's nostrils flared. 'Fair enough. But this one isn't yours, is it?' He began to count on his fingers. 'We have the body. We have the murder weapon. We have a confession in writing.'

'From a man who conveniently can't be interviewed,' Logan interjected.

'Nevertheless, it's a confession, written on his computer.'

'Exactly! Anyone could've typed that bloody suicide note!'

'He drove his car at you, Jack!' McCulloch shot back, raising his voice for possibly the first time since Logan had met him. 'He tried to run you down. That lad and DS Khaled, too. Then, he sped away and drove off a sheer drop into a loch. What's your gut saying on that? Does that sound like an innocent man?'

He cupped a hand behind his ear and pretended to listen to Logan's stomach.

'No, funnily enough, it's not got a lot to say on that.'

Logan briefly pictured himself throttling the other DCI. He'd thought they'd got past all this antagonistic chest-beating bullshit in Durness, but apparently not.

McCulloch turned to Mitchell, who remained motionless across the desk.

'It'll be ready for the procurator fiscal this afternoon, once we get preliminaries back from Scene of Crime and Pathology. They have the car and the body now. I don't expect there to be any surprises. The full report will be ready to submit once I have their data.'

'Very good. Thank you, Evan,' Mitchell said.

'Unbelievable.' Logan shook his head. 'This isn't done. I'd stake my job on it.'

'You don't have a job, Jack,' McCulloch reminded him. 'You were there to help, and you did, but now that's done. It's over.'

Logan shoved his hands into his pockets to stop himself acting on his throttling urge. The knuckles of his right hand rapped against the glass of the bottle he'd stowed there earlier.

He didn't know whether he wanted to drink it or smash it. He'd likely hate himself for it, either way.

'He's right, Jack,' Mitchell said. 'This is DCI McCulloch's investigation.'

'Oh, I know. He's reminded me of that enough times.'

'Would you like to step in?' Mitchell asked.

McCulloch, who had already been sitting bolt upright, somehow managed to straighten even further.

'Wait, what?'

'It's yours if you want it, Jack. If you believe there's more to this. If you think you're the man to handle it, it's yours.'

'Now hold on a minute...' McCulloch began, but a sharp look from the detective superintendent robbed him of any notion to continue.

'You think you can do better, DCI Logan? You believe there's more to uncover? Then, by all means, go ahead. It's your decision.'

She placed McCulloch's report in front of him. He stared vacantly down at it, like he wasn't quite sure what he was looking at.

'My decision?' he mumbled, and the words almost choked him.

The room grew warmer, the air thicker. The pressure of it pushed in on him, squeezing him from all sides. Like he was back there, back *then*, deep underground, with the weight of the world pressing down on him.

His fingers toyed with the smooth glass of the bottle in his pocket. Over the ridges. Over the curves.

His decision?

His decisions had cost lives.

Too many to count over the years. Far too many.

'I'm not… I'm not saying that,' he muttered, nudging the paperwork back in the detective superintendent's direction. 'I just think—'

'Fine. In that case, good work, DCI McCulloch,' Mitchell said, picking up the report. 'Get the preliminaries in, add the findings to this, and all being well, we'll have it wrapped up by close of play.'

'Ma'am,' McCulloch said. He moved with a smooth, mechanical grace, his bent knees and hips straightening him up into a standing position. 'I'll get on it right away.'

He shot Logan the most fleeting of looks, dipped his head in acknowledgement, then left the office like he was in a hurry.

It took Logan longer to get to his feet, and he lingered by the detective superintendent's desk rather than go rushing out the door.

'Was there something else you wanted, Jack?' Mitchell was eventually forced to ask.

'No,' Logan told her, but he still made no move to leave. Instead, he looked over at the half-open door, checking McCulloch wasn't still lingering there. 'I hear they're looking for his replacement down in the Borders.'

'So I'm told,' Mitchell confirmed. 'Why, you fancy it? They're a decent team, I hear. Very'—she glazed over for a second, like she was rifling through some inner thesaurus, searching for the right word—'methodical.'

Logan snorted out something that wasn't quite a laugh, but was somewhere in that neck of the woods. 'Thanks for the offer,' he told her, making to leave. 'But they don't sound like my cup of tea at all.'

He stopped at the door. Looked down, then looked back.

'Close of play today?' he asked.

Mitchell didn't look up from the notes she already had her nose in.

'Close of play today,' she confirmed.

When she did look up, a few moments later, Logan was gone.

Chapter 44

'Right.' Ben Forde nodded to the man sitting at the corner table, typing away on a tiny laptop. He was bald on top, but with a ring of straggly grey hair that hung down from the back and sides like a dirty net curtain. 'That's him.'

Rodney Nisbet, former bandmate of Johnny Freestone turned landscape gardening magnate, picked up his espresso, blew on it, then took a sip that barely wetted his lips.

'I had to promise him a free coffee,' Ben said, lowering his voice. 'Don't tell Moira, for Christ's sake, or she'll have my goolies for garters.'

'Is it no' usually "guts for garters"?' Logan asked.

'Aye,' Ben said darkly. 'Usually.'

Logan ordered a cup of tea, paid for it and the espresso, then went to join Rodney at his table.

'Are you the guy I'm waiting for?' Nisbet asked, barely glancing up from his laptop screen. He continued to type while talking, as if his fingers operated on a separate relay to the rest of him.

'Aye. Jack Logan.'

'Rodney. Rod. Rod Nisbet.'

'Oh, I know,' Logan said, pulling out the chair across from him. 'I was a big fan.'

Rod's fingers continued to tip-tap across the keys. 'Right. Of Johnny's.'

'Of all of you,' Logan corrected. 'The whole band. I mean, aye, Johnny was always up front, but your bass? That intro to "Flash in the Pan"? That's what hooked me in.'

The typing slowed, then stopped. Rodney took another minuscule sip of coffee, then shook his head.

'Bollocks.'

Logan laughed. 'I mean it. *Bom-bom-ba-bombom-bom.*' He tapped two fingers in time with the beat. 'I still get goosebumps when I hear that.'

'I wrote that,' Rodney said. He closed over the lid of his laptop. 'Pretty much wrote that whole song, actually. Not that you'd know from the royalties.'

'It's a classic. You should be proud,' Logan told him.

'I'd rather be rich,' Rodney countered, but then he smiled and extended a hand for Jack to shake. 'Didn't get your name. I know you said it, but I wasn't really listening.'

'Jack. Jack Logan.'

'Jack,' Rodney said, like he was locking it into his memory banks. 'You're a detective, I hear.'

'Aye. No. I mean… It's complicated,' Logan said.

Rodney looked confused by this, but didn't remark on it. 'You wanted to talk to me about Johnny?'

Logan confirmed that part, at least, was accurate. He filled the former bass player in on what he could about the investigation. When he mentioned that Dougie was in the frame for the murder, Rodney laughed until it turned into a fit of sharp, raspy coughing.

'Wee Dougie? A killer? You're barking up the wrong tree there, I'm afraid,' he said, once he'd got his breath back. 'After all the shite we put him through, if he was going to snap and kill someone, he'd have done it years ago. No, it's not him. What's he saying on it?'

'He left a confession,' Logan said.

The laughter died on his lips. For a moment, it was like all the air had been sucked out of the room. 'Left?' he asked, his voice quieter now. 'What do you mean *left*?'

'I'm afraid I can't go into any more detail at the moment.'

'Aw, fuck. God. Jesus Christ almighty.' Rod sat so far back in his chair it was like he was trying to realign his spine. 'Not wee Dougie.'

He was a big man, who had once walked among gods, but the crack in his voice and the blurring of his eyes were all too human.

'Right, well, I'm not… I don't know what you want from me,' he said, picking up his laptop and stuffing it in his bag. 'Sounds like you've got it all figured out.'

'I'd just like to ask you a few questions, Rod.'

'Why? I don't give a shit about Johnny being dead. Good enough for the bastard. So, what's the point? I mean, Jesus, you don't even know if you're a detective,' Rodney snapped. 'Are you in charge of the case? Are you investigating it?'

Logan clenched his jaw. Shook his head. 'No.'

'Then why the fuck would I waste my time talking to you?'

He knocked back the rest of his espresso, tried very hard not to grimace at the bitterness of it, then started for the door.

'Because I don't think he did it,' Logan called after him. 'I think someone wants us to believe he did, but I don't think Dougie murdered Johnny. I don't think he did anything.'

Rodney stopped, but didn't turn back. Logan took this as his cue to continue.

'They're going to say that Dougie's a murderer who took the coward's way out rather than facing up to justice,' he said. 'And I don't believe one word of that is true.'

Jack rose to his feet. He glanced across the cafe, to where Ben had been polishing the same mug for the past five minutes, trying very hard not to look like he was listening in.

'I'm not asking you to help me find Johnny's killer,' Logan said, turning his attention back to the bassist. 'I'm asking you to help me clear Dougie's name.'

Rodney did turn then, though it was slow and reluctant. He shrugged his bag down off his shoulder, and dumped it on the floor beside the table.

'Right, then,' he said. 'In that case, I'm going to need another coffee.'

–

Detective Constable Dave Davidson was waiting at the door of the mortuary when Shona shuffled up, yawning so widely her head looked like an egg from the *Alien* movies, getting ready to spit out a facehugger.

She blinked several times when she saw him, then stuffed the heels of her hands into her eyes and rubbed them, as if he might be some sort of hallucination brought on by lack of sleep.

She had managed an hour and a half in bed before McCulloch had rung her up to insist that she crack on with the post-mortem. She'd informed him where he could shove the post-mortem, but had then felt bad enough about it that she'd called back a few minutes later to say she was on the way.

She'd half-expected to find him waiting for her, tapping his watch, demanding she get a shifty on. What she had not been expecting, particularly after his last performance, was Dave.

'All right?' he asked.

'I'm all right. You all right?'

'I'm all right,' Dave confirmed.

'Did McCulloch send you? Are you here to keep an eye on me?' the pathologist demanded.

'God, no. He doesn't trust me to do anything,' Dave replied. He took a breath and gestured to the door beside them. 'I just thought, after how things went last time, I should have another crack at it.'

'What, and try not to pass out this time?' Shona asked. It was meant to be funny, but even to her ears, it sounded mean. 'Sorry, that was a joke. I think. Not a very good one. I'll be honest, I haven't slept much.'

She yawned again, making a sound like a wounded bear.

'No? You hide it really well,' Dave said, and Shona just nodded, completely missing the sarcasm. 'I could go and get coffee while you set up,' the detective constable suggested. 'Strong, right? Loads of sugars?'

'Yes!' Shona clicked her fingers and pointed at him. 'That,' she said, with as much enthusiasm as she could muster on ninety minutes of sleep. 'Let's do that.'

-

'Ray Simpson? God. I should've known that parasitic sack of shite would have been poking around.'

It was fair to say that Rodney Nisbet was not a fan of Johnny Freestone's manager. Had the phrase 'parasitic sack of shite' not been enough of a clue, the look of disgust on his face would've hinted strongly towards it.

And the outburst that followed would really have sealed the deal.

Ray Simpson, Rodney told Logan, had been the driving force behind the doomed comeback tour in 2013 that had resulted in two arrests, a nervous breakdown and another stint in rehab for Johnny.

Rodney himself had been on the receiving end of a kicking from an angry husband who'd found out what Johnny had been up to with his wife after one of the gigs.

Ray had made sure that security around Johnny himself was rock solid, and so the wronged husband had taken his frustration and anger out on the next best thing—Johnny's bandmates and crew.

'Morris, one of the roadies—he used to tour with us back in the day, too—got his nose and jaw broken,' Rodney recounted. 'I had a black eye and a couple of cracked ribs, which was getting off pretty lightly.'

He slurped on his coffee. Logan wasn't sure if it was the bitterness of the taste or the memory that made the bass player's face screw up.

'And all because Johnny loves to have his way with married women. Well, any woman, really. He's not fussy.'

He fell silent for a moment, and though he didn't say as much, Logan could tell he'd realised he needed to start shifting references to his old bandmate into the past tense.

'He ever mention an Alanna Swain?' Logan asked.

Rodney shook his head. 'Not to me. But then, we weren't friends in recent years. We weren't ever friends, I don't think. Not really. I'm not sure he was capable.'

Logan was starting to see a pattern. Dougie had said something very similar about Johnny's ability to care for anything or anyone other than himself.

It was true what they said—you should never meet your heroes. Even the dead ones.

'Johnny was going to fire Ray,' Logan said. 'So Dougie told us, anyway.'

Rodney's coffee cup *clinked* as he set it back in the saucer. 'Well, there you go, then. There's your answer.'

Logan raised an eyebrow, encouraging him to continue.

'Johnny was Ray's only income, as far as I know. His sole client. Nobody else took him on. Or, if they did, they didn't stick around long. Like I say, parasitic sack of shit. Everyone knew it. Everyone could see through him. If Johnny was canning him, he'd have nothing.'

'How's that different with Johnny being dead?' Logan asked.

Rodney frowned, like this should be obvious. 'Well, if Johnny dies while he's still got a say in the rights to his back catalogue, Ray can use that to his advantage. He'll find ways to latch on, drain every last drop he can get, milk it for all its worth.'

'So, being Johnny's manager gives him rights to all that? Even with Johnny out of the picture?'

Rodney shrugged. 'Depends on the contract. But he came on at a low point in Johnny's career. One of the many. And Johnny was a singer, not a businessman. I'd imagine the deal is weighted pretty heavily in Ray's favour.'

Logan sat back, eyes darting left and right, processing all this. If Rodney was right, Johnny's death was the difference between Ray losing his stake in the Freestone legacy and hanging onto it for all it was worth.

Rodney had said that a share in the songwriting credits would have made him rich. What would sole management of them do for Ray Simpson?

And how far would he be willing to go to protect that?

'Ray's been trying to sign a local lad up there. Think Dougie was standing in the way of that.'

'Good for Dougie, then. He knows what the bastard's like,' Rodney said. 'Got a following, has he? The lad?'

'Hmm? Oh. No. Don't think so. Just starting out.'

'Fuck. Ray must be getting desperate. Usually, he waits until they've done all the legwork, then jumps in just before they hit the big time. He must've seen something in the boy that put dollar signs in his eyes.'

He drained the last of his coffee, checked his watch, then started to stand.

'Sorry, I need to get going. Got a thing at my granddaughter's school this afternoon.'

He fished a business card from his pocket. It was a bit dog-eared, and stained at the edges with soil marks. 'If I can help in any other way, give me a call.'

'Thanks,' Logan said, pocketing the card. 'You've been very helpful.'

'I doubt that,' Rodney said. He shook Logan's hand. 'If you want to repay me, though, you can do me a favour.'

'Aye?'

'If you see that kid that Ray's been sniffing around. You tell him to run, and to not look back.'

Logan promised to pass the message on, then sat sipping on his tea until Rodney had left the cafe.

'Well?' he asked.

Behind the counter, Ben slung his dishcloth over his shoulder and frowned. 'Well, what?'

Logan turned in his seat. 'Don't try and pretend you weren't listening to every bloody word,' he said. 'You nearly polished the arse right out of that mug.'

'I resent that!' Ben said. He looked into the mug, just to be on the safe side, then placed it upside down on the shelf behind him. 'Though, I may have picked up a bit of it here and there. By accident, no' on purpose.'

'Course not,' Logan said. He got up, gathered up his mug and Rodney's cup and saucer, then brought them up to the counter. 'And?'

Ben smirked and held his hands out to his sides. 'I'm just a humble...' He frowned. 'Coffee man. What do you call them again? There's a name. It's not... It's not bastards, but it's like it.'

'Baristas.'

Ben clapped his hands. 'Yes! That's the boy! I'm just a humble barista, Jack. What would I know about—'

Logan started to turn away. Ben practically pounced on his back.

'I don't think your case is closed, by the sounds of it!' he ejected. 'I'd say that Ray fella's worth looking into.'

Logan returned to the counter, and nodded at his old DI. 'Aye. I mean, Johnny's not exactly been a money-spinner for a while now, but even without the new stuff he was recording—'

'There's always a big splash when a famous person snuffs it,' Ben said, finishing the thought for him. 'Albums brought out again. Fan campaigns. Memorial stuff.'

'Johnny's *death* could be a money-maker,' Logan reasoned. 'But, if he'd been sacked—'

'He wouldn't have got another penny!' Ben concluded. He slapped a hand down on the counter. 'We should talk to Mitchell.'

'We?' Logan asked.

He watched Ben's confusion turn to realisation. The older man laughed. The lines of his face crinkled in all the appropriate places, but his eyes didn't fully get in on the act.

'Och, you know what I mean!' he said. He took his dishcloth from his shoulder and flapped it in Logan's direction, like he was shooing a fly. 'Go. Get a move on before McCulloch closes this case off.'

Logan looked over at the door, but didn't move towards it. The weight of the whisky in his pocket weighed him down. Held him back.

'I don't know if I can take it on,' he said. The words were low. Muttered. Not necessarily for anyone's benefit but his own. 'I don't even know if I want to.'

Ben smiled at his old friend. This time, his whole face committed to it. 'I'm not sure it matters what you want, Jack. All that matters is who you are.'

Logan took a breath before replying. 'And who's that?'

'Just a man doing his best to do the right thing,' Ben told him. 'And what more can anyone ask of you than that?'

–

Dave Davidson had come to the conclusion that post-mortems weren't really his thing.

The smell bothered him. That was high on the list of *cons* he'd started making in his head the moment he'd rolled on through to the mortuary.

Being within spitting distance of a greying, slightly bloated dead body was on the list, too. That was also pretty high. So were the sounds of blades slicing through flesh, and bone being rended in two.

Fortunately, he hadn't got to those parts yet. The body of Dougie Cairns was still intact. Even his artificial leg was still attached.

Judging by the array of sharp, pointy things that Shona had set out on her little trolley next to the table, though, he wasn't going to remain that way for long.

'You all right?' the pathologist asked him.

He smiled, but his mouth was hidden behind the mask he'd been instructed to wear, so he made an *OK* sign with a finger and thumb.

When Shona reached for her scalpel, though, he started to have some doubts.

Why was he here? Nobody had asked him to come in and do this. This was self-inflicted. He could've been sat in the Incident Room. Or the staff canteen. Or anywhere where there wasn't a human corpse lying naked in front of him.

But, oh no, he'd been determined to prove himself. Determined not to be the guy who had fainted at his first post-mortem.

What was wrong with fainting, anyway? Consciousness could be vastly overrated sometimes.

Times like now, for example.

The scalpel caught the light. He stared at it, grimaced, then lowered his gaze.

It was then, while his mind was desperately trying to come up with an excuse to leave, that he saw it.

Something out of place.

Something that didn't make sense.

'Wait!' he was relieved to be able to say. He pointed at the thing he'd seen. At the thing that could change everything. 'Is it just me, or is something very wrong there?'

Chapter 45

DC Neish leaned over and tapped DS Khaled on the plastic band of the bulky headphones he was wearing. Hamza jumped in fright, whipping the headphones off and ejecting a 'Shit!' that resonated around the Burnett Road Incident Room.

Tyler grinned at him. 'Sorry, mate. I was trying to get your attention for ages.'

Hamza pointed to the empty space in front of his desk. 'Couldn't you just have stood there and waved like a normal person, instead of sneaking up and making me shite myself?'

The outburst upgraded Tyler's grin to a burst of laughter.

'Fair point, aye.'

'Sinead not in yet?' Hamza asked.

'Nah. She's taking a bit of flexi-time. Morning off. Spending it with the kids.'

'You not fancy that?'

Tyler laughed. 'What, *my* kids? No chance. Have you met them?'

Hamza chuckled at that. 'Fair point.'

Tyler nodded to the headphones. 'What you listening to?'

Hamza turned back to his desk. 'The recordings from the equipment the Kellermans nicked.'

'Johnny's stuff?' Tyler asked, pulling out the chair next to Hamza. 'Anything interesting?'

'It's just him playing the guitar, mostly. Just guitar stuff.'

'Let's have a listen,' Tyler said, holding a hand out and pinching his fingers together, like a crab pincering the air.

Hamza handed him the headphones, waited until he'd put them on, then held down a key on his laptop, before tapping the spacebar.

Tyler almost leaped out of his seat, ripping off the headphones as the full-volume screeching nearly blew out his eardrums.

'Jesus!'

'Sorry.' Hamza smirked and dialled the volume back down again. 'That was petty.'

'What?' Tyler asked. He pointed to his ear, his face contorting into an exaggerated scowl. 'Can't hear you, mate. I've suffered a workplace accident due to the negligence of a senior officer.'

Hamza laughed, gave him the middle finger, then hit the spacebar again. Tyler looked along the desk at him, enjoying this moment.

He'd miss these moments. It would be a shame when it all had to change.

Tentatively, he pulled the headphones on again, then sat staring blankly into space as he listened to the now significantly quieter sound playing through them.

'It's a guitar,' he said, speaking too loudly.

'I know. That's what I said.'

'What?' Tyler all but shouted.

Hamza rolled his eyes and gave him a thumbs up.

The guitar was electric. There had been a small portable amplifier found with all the other stuff in the Kellermans' secret stash, and Tyler couldn't tell if the crackly sound quality was due to that, or the recording equipment.

The actual performance was impressive. Tyler didn't know much about playing the guitar beyond how to strum the C and A chords, but Johnny clearly knew his stuff. There were a lot of fast and high notes, some longer wobbly ones, and some more muted *bawom-wom* type stuff that didn't sound half bad.

Again, he really didn't know much about playing the guitar.

The echo of the cave added another layer to it all, elevating it from *very good guitar playing* to something almost ethereal and otherworldly.

'It's all right, isn't it?' Tyler practically roared.

Hamza rolled himself back a few inches in his seat to avoid the hearing damage and the flying spit, and nodded his agreement.

And then, Tyler cocked his head, eyes darting left, right, up, down, like he was searching for something.

Hamza knew what had happened. He could see the flat audio waveform on his laptop screen.

'It's stopped,' Tyler said, his voice returning to a more normal level. 'Is that it? It just ended.'

'That's it,' Hamza confirmed. 'That's all there is.'

Tyler removed the headphones and set them on the DS's desk. He worked his jaw up and down, like he was trying to make his ears pop, then leaned back and twisted in his office chair.

'That's all that's on there?'

'Seems to be, aye.' Hamza indicated half a dozen audio files on his screen. 'It's mostly just a lot of guitar playing. Can't say I recognise any of the tunes.'

'The boss'll know,' Tyler said. Then, for the avoidance of confusion, he added, 'Logan, I mean. Mad that he was a fan, eh? If you told me he'd never listened to any music in his whole life, I'd have believed that.'

'There's one other thing,' Hamza said.

He pulled out the headphones' cable, dialled the volume up a few notches, and then double-clicked on one of the files.

'More guitar?' Tyler said, after the first few bars had come blasting out.

Hamza put a finger to his lips, then pointed to the laptop.

Tyler leaned in closer, ears pricking up. There were more wobbly notes. More high, fast, short ones.

They were followed by that rock and roll strum that signalled the end of a song. Tyler didn't know the name of the chord, but it was always there at the end of any guitar track played live—a swing of the arm, a big, emphatic strum of the strings, and then a plectrum raised to the Heavens like an offering to God.

It was the opposite of the sound that signalled the start of every Scottish folk tune. That one was a sort of collective sigh from all the instruments involved, like they were all bracing themselves for the next few minutes of frantic drumming and fiddling, and whatever the fuck an accordion player did.

Bellowing, maybe?

Tyler knew even less about playing the accordion than he did about the guitar, so he couldn't say for sure.

He looked at Hamza, and was about to ask him if he'd missed something, when he heard it. A voice. Male. Older. The accent was Scottish, but with a mix of other places in there, too. Johnny hadn't quite gone full *John Barrowman* with the American accent, but he had been headed in that direction.

'Check this.'

That was all he said. Two words, muttered almost absent-mindedly, and then he launched into another screeching guitar solo.

The audio track ended then, mid-twang. The waveform on the screen looped back to the start, and Hamza tapped the spacebar before it could start again.

'I cut that bit out from a longer track and boosted the gain a bit. It's the only time he speaks. That's the only voice on there.'

'Right.' Tyler nodded knowingly, then shrugged. 'What does that mean?'

'I have no idea,' Hamza admitted. 'He could've been talking to himself, but... I don't know. "Check this." Would you say that to yourself? You'd say that to someone else, wouldn't you?'

Tyler nodded, but he didn't seem particularly sold on the idea. 'I mean, if that's all that's said in the whole thing, he could just be talking to himself. I do it all the time.'

Hamza didn't react to that, since it wasn't in the least bit surprising.

'Still. He could be talking to someone,' Hamza said. 'It's possible, at least. Which means someone could have been down there with him.'

'Aye, could be,' Tyler said, drifting off a little.

He drummed his fingers on the desk and looked over at the door to the Incident Room. The police station, as ever, was a hive of activity. Any minute, McCulloch or someone else would come marching in.

It was now or never.

'Listen, mate,' he began, leaning in. 'I've been thinking. About this DI job. You should totally go for it.'

Hamza grimaced. 'Oh. That. I don't know...'

'What are you talking about? You should. You'd be great. You're a shoo-in for it. And, like I said, we might get Heather Filson, if you don't. Can you imagine? Her and McCulloch? It'd be like Hitler and'—Tyler's grasp of the hierarchy of the National Socialist German Workers' Party failed him then—'woman Hitler.'

'She's not that bad,' Hamza replied, though it didn't sound convincing. 'Anyway, you already told me I should go for it.'

'I know, but I didn't mean it then,' Tyler admitted. 'But now I do. You deserve it, mate. You should absolutely go for it.'

Hamza hesitated before replying. 'It could make things tricky,' he said. 'For you and Sinead.'

'If I get promoted to DS, you mean?'

'If *she* gets promoted to DS,' Hamza corrected, and both men smiled.

'Whatever. We'll work around it. We'll be fine. Don't let us hold you back.' He punched the detective sergeant lightly on the arm. 'All right?'

'All right.' Hamza rubbed his arm. 'But that assault totally cancels out your unfortunate workplace accident with them headphones.'

'No chance,' Tyler said. He got to his feet, flicked Hamza on the ear, then darted past him. '*That* one does, though.'

A shadow passed across the frosted glass of the Incident Room door. It was large. Familiar.

'I think that's the boss,' Tyler whispered.

Hamza stood up, joining him. 'Why's he not coming in?'

'Dunno.'

Both detectives stood watching. The shape on the other side of the door shifted slightly, as if moving its weight from foot to foot.

'Should we say something?' Hamza asked, then he recoiled when Tyler bellowed right next to his ear.

'Haw! That you, boss?'

The figure straightened until the shadow took up the whole of the window.

A handful of seconds later, the door swung inwards. Logan remained out in the corridor, like he couldn't quite bring himself to step into the room.

'McCulloch here?' he asked.

'No' unless he's hiding, boss,' Tyler said, indicating the largely empty Incident Room. 'Want me to give him a call?'

Logan shook his head. 'No,' he said. He took his hand from the door, and it started to swing closed again. 'I think I know where to find him.'

Chapter 46

'We can't close the case,' Logan announced, barging into Detective Superintendent Mitchell's office without bothering to knock.

DCI McCulloch sat across from her, legs folded, a cup of tea held balanced on one knee.

'It's already in progress, Jack,' McCulloch said. 'I've spoken to the procurator fiscal this morning.'

'Well, you'll have to *un*progress it, then,' Logan said. 'I don't think Dougie did it.'

'And yet, he confessed,' McCulloch said. He sighed and looked across the desk at Mitchell. There was something pitying about it. 'We've spoken about this, Jack. We went through it.'

'I just need one more day,' Logan said. 'I'll go back up there myself, ask a few questions, see what—'

'How many times?' McCulloch asked. It was a rhetorical question, whispered below his breath, and accompanied by a massaging of his temples. 'It's not complicated, Jack. I'm SIO. I make the calls.'

He set his tea on the desk and stood up, eye to eye with Logan. Nose to nose. He was one of the very few people who could achieve that, and one of the even fewer who would dare.

'Unless you want to fight me for it?' he asked. He searched Logan's face, a smile tugging at the corner of his mouth. 'Oh. Maybe he does. Maybe he thinks he can do better.'

'I just want a day,' Logan said. 'That's all.'

'No,' McCulloch said, that smirk still stuck in place. 'I forbid it.'

Logan almost laughed at that. At the sheer bloody nerve of the bastard.

'Listen, Evan, that sort of attitude might work when you're back in the Borders dealing with stolen motors and burglaries, but we're talking about murder here. The stakes are too high for us to rush this.'

McCulloch rolled his head back, like the conversation was exhausting him. He exhaled sharply, then met Logan's gaze again.

'You know what the most addictive drug in the world is, Jack? It's not heroin. It's not cocaine. Not alcohol.'

Logan could've sworn McCulloch put emphasis on that last one, like he knew something.

He dismissed it as paranoia.

'No, it's none of those. The most potent, addictive drug in the world is nostalgia, Jack. The longing for things to go back to the way they were. A refusal to accept that the world has moved on and the gnawing fear that maybe it has done so without you.'

He rocked back on his heels, proud of himself for sharing this nugget of wisdom.

'Now, you were a fan of Johnny Freestone back in the day, so I get the obsession. I do.'

'It's not a bloody obsession!' Logan protested. 'It's due diligence. It's doing the job properly. Ray Simpson, the manager, we need to talk to—'

'We have a confession, Jack.'

'He stood to benefit more than anyone from Johnny's death,' Logan continued. He'd given up on McCulloch, and directed this at the seated Detective Superintendent Mitchell. 'I want to talk to him, see what he has to say.'

'It's irrelevant!' McCulloch said, raising his voice like he was seeing off a group of unruly teenagers. 'Dougie confessed, tried to run you down, then took his own life. What's so hard to understand about that?'

There was a knock at the still-open door. A clearing of the throat.

All three occupants of the office turned to find Dave Davidson sitting in his wheelchair out in the corridor.

'Sorry, don't mean to interrupt,' he said.

'And yet, here you are,' McCulloch said.

For a second, Dave seemed to shrink down into himself.

Only for a second, though. Less, maybe, than that.

'Aye, well, it's important,' he said. 'I just came from Dougie Cairns's post-mortem. Didn't go so great last time, so I thought I'd have another crack at it.'

McCulloch sucked in his bottom lip, then spat it out again. 'And this is relevant how?'

'I'm getting to it,' Dave told him. 'Shona had the body laid out on the table, and I spotted something. Something that didn't seem right.'

'Go on,' Logan urged.

'It was his leg. The artificial one,' Dave said. He tapped his knee. 'Wasn't on right. The fastener wasn't attached properly.'

'Well, it obviously got dislodged with the impact,' McCulloch said. He looked down at Mitchell, like he was expecting her to back him up, but she was staring at Dave.

'No, that's the thing,' Dave said. 'It was still attached, just not properly. It was on wrong, fastened around the front of his stump instead of the back. Saying it happened in the impact is like saying you could fall over and your shoes would end up on the wrong feet. It can't happen.'

'So, what are you saying, Detective Constable?' Mitchell asked.

Logan had already figured it out and answered for him. 'Someone else put his leg on for him. Someone who didn't know what they were doing.'

'Bingo!' Dave said.

'He could have just put it on in a hurry,' McCulloch said, though it sounded like even he thought that was a stretch.

'It'd have fallen off as soon as he put any weight on it, so he wouldn't have got very far,' Dave said.

Logan spun around to face Mitchell. He leaned down, fingers splayed on the desk.

'I want it,' he said. 'This case. I want it. I want back in.'

McCulloch didn't say a word. The whole room seemed to hold its breath as Mitchell sat back in her chair, fingers interlocked across her stomach.

'You do, do you?'

'It's all wrong. Dougie didn't do it. I know he didn't.'

'You *think* he didn't,' Mitchell countered. 'That's not the same.'

'Then, let me go up there and prove it. A day. That's all it'll take. Just me.'

Seasons came and went while Mitchell silently studied him. So it felt from his side of the desk, at least.

'Let me get this clear,' she finally said. 'You are requesting to return from your leave of absence and to just step right back into your previous role as leader of Northern MIT?'

Logan didn't give himself a chance to reconsider.

'Aye. That's right,' he said. 'That's what I'm requesting.'

Mitchell's face remained motionless. 'And is that what you *want*?'

This time, Jack did hesitate.

He'd had a lot of time to think about decisions of late. How they could change the course of a life.

Or end it prematurely.

This decision was a biggie. Monumental. It was one of the hardest he'd ever had to make.

It was also the easiest.

'I do,' he confirmed.

McCulloch opened his mouth, presumably to object, but Mitchell held a finger up, silencing him. Logan took immense pleasure in the strangled choking sound the other DCI made.

'One day. That's all you've got,' she told Jack. 'Put this to bed properly, and the job's yours.'

–

Logan stood in the Incident Room, his back to the bare Big Board. Hamza, Tyler and Dave all sat there, poised and expectant, waiting for some big speech. Some big comeback announcement.

But Jack wasn't ready for that. Not yet. He wasn't about to swoop in and save them from the menace of DCI McCulloch. That wasn't what this was about.

'I need your help,' he told them.

They all sat up straighter. Leaned forward. Pledged their allegiance without a word.

'McCulloch reckons Dougie Cairns killed his cousin, Johnny, then topped himself by driving into a loch,' Logan continued. 'But I disagree.'

'Go on yersel', boss!' Tyler cheered, then he quietly cleared his throat. 'Sorry, got a bit carried away with myself there.'

'I'm going to head north again,' Logan said. 'I'll have phone signal for some of it, so you can catch me up on the way with any new developments we've had.'

'We'll come with you, sir,' Hamza said, but Logan rejected the offer with a shake of his head.

'I want you three here, digging. Dave's already played a blinder at the PM, but Shona should have more for us soon, and Palmer will have his report for us, too. In the meantime, I want you to get me anything and everything you can on Ray Simpson.'

'Johnny's manager?' Hamza asked.

'Aye,' Logan confirmed. 'Him.'

He rattled through everything that Rodney had told him in the cafe, about what the future could have held for Ray after Johnny had fired him, and how that contrasted with the potential goldmine he was sitting on now.

'Dougie would've been next of kin. Whatever rights Johnny had to his music would've gone to him,' Hamza reasoned. 'He could've made it hard for Ray to get access to any of the royalties.'

'I want to know everything about the bastard,' Logan said. 'Criminal record, financial status, his bloody shoe size, if you think it's relevant. Check in with some of the forces south of the border, see if they have anything on him. He's from Essex, I think, so start there. Dig around.'

He checked his watch and picked up his coat from where he'd slung it over the back of his seat. The whisky bottle clunked as it swung against the chair's hard plastic back, but the pocket acted as padding, preventing it from breaking.

'I'm going to go swing by the hospital and see Shona, then get on the road. I want a full report by the time I'm crossing the Kessock Bridge.'

He whistled as he went striding towards the door. From under the table came a gangly explosion of legs and fur.

'See that?' Logan said, drawing everyone else's attention to the dog. 'That's the sort of obedience you should all be bloody aiming for!'

–

Shona was still deep in the guts of the post-mortem—literally—when Logan nudged open the door.

She stopped, and though she instinctively smiled at him behind her mask, it died away when she saw the look on his face.

A few moments later, she joined him in the office, having rid herself of her blood-stained PPE.

'Hey. You all right?' she asked. 'Dave get you?'

'He did, aye,' Logan confirmed. He indicated the mortuary with a nod. 'How's it going?'

'Well, I don't really want to spoil the report for you, but since you asked—big twist—he didn't drown. Lungs are clear.'

Logan's lack of reaction came as no great surprise.

'But you already guessed that, didn't you?'

'I had my suspicions. What was it? Knock to the front of the head?'

Shona laughed. 'Impressive. Yeah. How did you know? Did you see?'

'No. Makes sense, though,' Logan said. He shrugged. 'Could feasibly have happened when the car went into the water. Or, I mean, feasible if you don't know what you're doing.'

'Someone killed him,' Shona said. 'Do you know who?'

'I've got a pretty good idea,' Logan told her. 'I'm heading up the road to try and end this.'

He looked down at his feet, then up at the ceiling. Anywhere but in her eyes.

'That's, eh, that's not why I'm here, though.' His jaw clenched. 'There's something I need to...'

The words wouldn't come, even though he tried to force them out of his mouth. To drag them, kicking and screaming.

Instead, he reached into his pocket, clamped his hand around the cool glass, and then placed the half-bottle of whisky on Shona's desk.

She stared at it for a long, long time. Her eyes were wide. Her head shook, just a little, just for a second, like she was denying the reality of what he'd placed before her.

'There was an empty bottle a few months back. In the bin,' Logan said. He still wasn't looking at her. He couldn't. 'It, eh, it wasn't Olivia. It was me. I put it there.'

Slowly, like a great weight was pulling against them, Shona raised her eyes to look at him. Logan forced himself to meet her gaze. He owed her that much. And so much more.

'You were drinking again?'

'No,' he told her. 'Nearly, though. I came close. Too close. I poured it down the sink and hid the bottle. That one was hidden in the house.' He swallowed. His throat felt rough, like sandpaper. 'But I didn't touch it. I know that'll be hard for you to believe, but—'

She stepped in, slipping her arms around him, pressing her head to his chest.

'Thank you,' she whispered.

'What for?'

'For telling me.'

She stepped back and slapped him hard on the arm.

'Ow! For fuck's sake! That hurt!'

'Good! It was meant to!' Shona cried. 'That's for not telling me sooner! Do you know, I told Olivia she couldn't play her Playstation for a week after she told me that bottle was hers?'

Logan winced. 'Eh, no. I didn't.' A thought occurred to him. 'Wait a minute, she's not got a Playstation.'

Shona crossed her arms, a little self-consciously. 'No, I know. But I had to say something.' She looked up at him. 'And I knew it wasn't hers.'

Logan didn't know what to say to that, so he kept his mouth shut.

'I also knew you poured it down the sink.'

'How?' he asked.

'Well, because the sink stunk of cheap whisky for about three days afterwards.'

'Here, it's no' that bloody cheap,' Jack protested.

The pathologist laughed at that, then she picked up the half-bottle from the counter, unscrewed the cap, and poured the whole lot into the wash basin over by the mortuary door.

'Why didn't you say anything?' Jack asked. 'If you knew?'

It took her a while to answer that.

'I thought about it. I nearly did. But, I know what you're like. So I just kept an eye on you. Kept checking in to make sure you were OK, and waited. Because I knew you'd tell me yourself, when you were ready.'

She tossed the empty bottle into the waste paper basket.

'And I was righ—'

The bottle smashing took some of the shine of her speech. She recoiled in shock as the glass exploded out through the wide mesh of the bin, scattering across the floor all around it.

'Ooh, shit,' she proclaimed. She put her hands on her hips, clenched fists pressed against her sides. 'Probably shouldn't have chucked that, should I?'

'Probably not,' Logan agreed.

'It just felt right in the moment. Know what I mean? Like, it was dead cool.'

'It looked pretty cool, right enough. I mean, until it shattered and you shat yourself. Up to that point, though, it was positively cinematic.'

'That's what I was aiming for,' Shona said.

They shared a smile. Any tension had been broken at the same time as the bottle.

Logan moved to help her tidy up, but she shooed him away. 'Don't worry, I'll get it,' she said. She looked him up and down, like she was memorising him as he was right now in this moment. 'Time for your comeback tour.'

Chapter 47

The drive to Durness was a journey of enlightenment. Though the phone signal was patchy, Logan spent a lot of the trip listening to updates that came funnelled through DS Khaled.

Hamza told him about the audio recordings from the cave, and a lot of technical gubbins about the extended period of silence at the end of the one that had been cut off.

Logan wasn't sure he followed the more technical details, but he got the gist of it, and instructed the sergeant to send him a simplified breakdown via email.

From there it was recaps of the reports from Shona and Palmer. Shona's hadn't told them much more than they already knew, but Palmer, for once, had played a blinder.

If Logan had any doubt when he left Inverness about why he was driving up here, Palmer's discoveries had put those to bed.

Just over three hours after he left the Burnett Road station, and following some judicious use of his lights and sirens to force his way through the queueing traffic, Logan stood on the back step of the Sinclairs' house, and announced his arrival with a thumping fist.

The kitchen door opened to reveal a confused-looking Coleen. She stood staring at Logan, brow furrowed, before eventually scraping together a few words of greeting.

'Oh. Hello. It's you,' she said. 'I thought you'd all gone?'

'We did. I'm back,' Jack told her. 'I'm told Ray Simpson's here to talk to Declan.'

Coleen's confusion deepened. 'How did you know that?'

'A woman in a hot tub told me. You mind if I come in? It's in your son's best interests.'

Coleen glanced back over her shoulder into the kitchen, then stepped aside. 'They're through in the family room. I'll show you.'

She led him through the house. He heard Ray Simpson's voice as soon as they left the kitchen.

'We'll do tours. Smaller stuff to start with, but the building up. You heard of *Britain's Got Talent*?'

'Yeah.' That was Declan's voice. 'Course. Why?'

'I can get you on that. National stage. Simon Cowell. Alesha Dixon. That creepy looking kids' author.'

'I don't think he does it any more,' Declan said.

'Whoever. Doesn't matter. I can get you on there. And that's just for starters. The world'll be your oyster, Declan. Trust me.'

Logan pulled ahead of Coleen and shoved the door to the family room wide open. Declan was sitting on a small sofa, a stack of paperwork in his lap. Ray had been pacing back and forth, but stopped and turned when Logan came striding in.

It was the room that he'd seen through the window two nights ago. He'd spotted an electric guitar mounted on the wall then, but there were actually three of them. A couple of shelves held framed photographs of Declan performing through the ages—a Fisher Price guitar when he was two or three, a Guitar Hero video game controller when he was eight or nine.

From there, all the photographs had him clutching real guitars, with varying levels of confidence. In the most recent one, he had one foot up on an amp, his back arched as he hammered the strings along the narrower frets, his red hair blowing out behind him like a burst of flame from a jet engine.

'Trust you?' Logan said, turning the full weight of his attention on Ray. 'I don't think that would be in Declan's best interests, do you?'

Ray looked momentarily terrified by the sudden appearance of the detective, but he hurriedly plastered on a smile to try to disguise his fear.

'I absolutely think it would be in his best interests. That's all I want. What's best for him, and his career.' Ray pointed to the contract in Declan's lap. 'Sign that, and I'll take care of everything.'

'You'll *take* everything, you mean,' Logan countered. 'Don't sign it, son. Dougie was dead set against it.'

'Very true!' Ray said, his smile widening. 'But do you really think we should be taking his word for anything? Given what he did? Sign it, Declan. I'll make you a star.'

'What did he do, exactly?' Logan asked.

Ray snorted. 'God. Do I need to explain your job to you? Everyone knows. Everyone's talking about it. He killed Johnny, didn't he? Then, he took the coward's way out so he wouldn't have to face justice for it.'

Logan narrowed his eyes, studying him like he was an insect.

'That a fact?'

Ray searched in his pockets, took out his wallet and car keys, and set them on the coffee table while he continued to pat himself down.

Logan's gaze fell on the keys, and the Mercedes emblem emblazoned on the keyring.

The car was on finance. That was one of the things that Hamza had dug up. Payments were three months overdue. Repossession was just around the corner.

Ray Simpson was broke. Desperate. Ruthless, too, if any of his past business dealings were anything to go by.

'Here. Use this,' Ray said, when his search turned up a shiny gold fountain pen. He handed it to Declan, who stared blankly at it, like he didn't understand what it was. 'And you can keep it. That's eighteen carat gold plated. That's as good as cash in the bank, that.'

Coleen, who had been hovering just inside the door at Logan's back, stepped in. 'Maybe we should wait until your dad gets home. Have him look it over.'

'I'll be gone by then. Sorry,' Ray said. 'Busy man. Things to do. If Declan doesn't want to be a star, there's plenty out there who do.'

'Oh, Jesus Christ, enough with the shite, Ray,' Logan said. 'You've never made anyone a star in your life. You've latched onto people you thought were going places, or who you thought you could milk a load of cash out of.'

'Well, that's bullshit,' Ray said. He cranked his smile up another notch or two. It looked unnatural now, bordering on the monstrous. 'Kylie Minogue? Elton John? Heard of them?'

'Aye. Don't forget David Beckham, The Queen and that arsehole off *The Office*.' It was Logan's turn to snort. It was a targeted, derisory thing. 'You ran a lookalike agency, Ray. No' a very good one, going by the photos I was sent. I mean, I'm no expert, but I'm fairly sure Jack Nicholson isnae black.'

Ray made a series of aborted attempts at replying to that. They emerged as sounds and half-syllables, as he struggled to formulate a coherent response.

While he stammered away, Logan took in the rest of the room. On the wall across from Declan's photos, in pride of place between two guitars, was a signed poster of Johnny Freestone.

He was in his prime in the picture, performing at Wembley Stadium or somewhere similar, clad in leather and denim, his face red, sweaty, and screwed up, like he was in pain, or maybe enduring some sort of life-changing religious experience.

His guitar was pointed to the sky. His sticking-plastered fingers flew across the frets so fast they were a blur, a smudge across the camera's lens.

This was the Johnny Freestone of Logan's childhood. This was the god he remembered, not the deeply flawed, much-reviled man he'd come to know in the past few days. It was the same pose, the same poster, as the one on his childhood bedroom wall.

Maybe McCulloch had been right. Nostalgia really was a potent thing. Just looking at that poster made Jack's heart beat faster.

Made the hair on the back of his neck stand on end.

Made him uneasy. Deeply, painfully uneasy.

There was something about the poster. Something his subconscious had identified, but which he hadn't caught up with yet.

'Declan, just sign the contract, OK? This guy doesn't know what he's talking about,' Ray said, rounding on the boy.

'Dougie did, though. Dougie knew what you were,' Logan said. He dragged his eyes away from the poster. 'Is that why you killed him?'

Ray huffed out a half-laugh. 'You what?'

'Or was it because he'd get control of Johnny's rights and was going to shut you out?' Logan asked.

His eyes twitched, trying to look at the poster again. Trying to figure it out.

The floorboard beside him creaked. Coleen.

Coleen.

'What's he talking about?' Declan asked.

'Nothing. He's off his head. Ignore him,' Ray snapped.

'That equipment that was taken from Dougie's studio. It wasn't in his car,' Logan continued. 'But, you know what was?' He took out his phone. 'Here. I had our forensics team send me a photo.'

He tapped at the screen a few times, getting into his email.

The poster of Johnny nagged at him on his right. Coleen shifted her weight from foot to foot on his opposite side.

And beyond that...

He found the photograph and held it up. It showed a single silver charm. An acoustic guitar.

Ray instinctively reached for his bracelet and slid it up his wrist, under his jacket.

'Bit late for that, I'm afraid,' Logan told him. 'There was blood in there, too. Hair that matches Dougie's. You shoved him in there, didn't you, Ray? You were the one driving his car. He was already dead, stuffed in the boot.'

'Oh, God,' Coleen whispered, which drew the ire of the manager.

'Don't fucking listen to this! He's lost his mind! This isn't true!'

'You found a quiet spot, stuck him in the driver's seat, then rolled the car down a slope into the loch,' Logan continued.

'Lies. Absolute bullshit.'

'Do you know something interesting about water, Ray?'

The poster fought for Jack's attention again. He ignored it as best he could.

'On its own, it won't wash away fingerprints. Not without a bit of effort, anyway. A wee wipe. Some soap. But fresh water from a loch? That won't necessarily do the job. Especially when the print's on a metal surface, like the back of a car, for example.'

'That— No— I—'

Ray was a skipping CD now. A scratched record.

'And, of course, your prints were on file down south, after all those assault charges you faced. And the burglaries, of course.' Logan shoved his hands deep in the pockets of his coat and rocked back on his heels. 'My team's very busy finding out all there is to know about you, Ray.'

Ray laughed. It was high-pitched and riddled with desperation. 'It's not true,' he told Declan. 'Don't listen to him.'

'You wanted the new tracks that Johnny had recorded. That's why you took the equipment from the studio,' Logan said. 'I want to look in your car.'

'Oh yeah? Well, tough shit!' Ray spat. 'You need a warrant. Don't you? You do! You need a warrant!'

'I've got one coming,' Logan said. 'So, no point delaying things.'

'Bollocks you do!' Ray made a grab for his keys, but Declan got to them first. He ran, barging between his mum and Jack, racing out the door and skidding into the hallway.

'Declan!' Coleen cried, hurrying after him.

Ray moved to follow, but Logan blocked his way.

'Move! Move!' He clenched his fists and stepped back, like he was preparing to throw a punch.

Logan really hoped he would.

Instead, he crumpled to the floor, his legs giving way from under him, both hands now clutching at his chest as he gasped for air.

'Heart attack! Heart attack!' he wheezed.

'Like I said, we've done our homework on you, Ray. The fake cardiac arrest thing might've worked the first few times.' Logan looked back at the poster of Johnny on the wall. 'But we're no' as gullible up here as they are down south.'

Ray spat out a response to that, but Logan didn't hear it. There was a sudden ringing in his ears. A lead weight in his gut.

He'd thought it had been nostalgia that had made the image of Johnny with his guitar seem so achingly familiar.

But, it wasn't that.

'Oh, God,' Jack whispered.

Suddenly, it all made sense.

'Are you even fucking listening to me?' Ray screeched, his heart attack apparently forgotten.

'No. Not really,' Logan told him. He looked down at the manager, still sprawled on the floor. Outside, a flashing blue light came spiralling into the campsite car park. 'Ray Simpson. I'm arresting you for the murder of Dougie Cairns.'

He bent, and hoisted Ray back to his feet. As he did, he looked at the poster again, at the guitars, at the shelves that lined the wall.

'Jesus,' he whispered, as he pulled Ray's wrists together at his back.

The manager followed the detective's gaze. There was amusement in his sneer when he met Logan's eye.

'Yeah,' he remarked. 'That's pretty much what I said.'

Chapter 48

Declan and Coleen were standing at the back of the Mercedes when Logan led the manager outside. The boy was turned away, head bent as he leaned on his mother's shoulder, his whole body heaving with big, breathless sobs.

'Get this bastard out of my sight,' Logan said, shoving Ray into the custody of a couple of Uniformed constables who were still pulling on their hats. 'And there's a woman in a hot tub up there somewhere. Take her in, too. Accessory to murder.'

He didn't wait for a response, and instead joined the Sinclairs at the back of Ray's car. Just as Logan had expected, a stash of hard drives and a couple of laptops sat in cardboard boxes in the boot.

There was no saying what all would be on there. Johnny's new music, maybe. Despite the cameras outside Dougie's house, there had been no sign of any footage when they'd searched the house. Maybe that was on there, too, showing Ray approaching Dougie's place.

Another nail in the bastard's coffin, if so.

Scene of Crime would need to come up and log it all, but Logan had seen enough for now. He pulled the boot shut, and the slamming of it was like a starting pistol that launched Declan into an anger-fuelled sprint.

'You killed him! You killed Dougie!' he roared, throwing himself at Ray.

'Oof, steady!'

The manager scuttled back as best he could with the constable holding his arm, while the other Uniform stepped in front of the lad, blocking him and holding him back.

'Declan, don't!' Coleen cried, hurrying to catch him. She was crying now, too, hot, bitter tears streaming down her face.

She caught him and pulled him back. He collapsed into her arms again, his face buried in against her neck as she gently smoothed his hair.

'He killed him, Mum. He killed Dougie, because of me. It's my fault!'

Logan clocked the look on Ray's face. Until now, he'd seen him as a bumbling, spineless charlatan. Now, though, in those eyes, he saw him for what he really was.

A vicious, cold-hearted killer.

The manager started to say something, but Logan loomed over him, raising his voice to drown him out.

'Get him in the car, Constable. And if he says a word, you have my full permission to take your baton to the back of his head,' Logan said. 'In fact, no. You don't have my permission. It's a direct order.'

'Uh, right you are, sir.'

He leaned in closer to the officer who had blocked Declan's attack, and lowered his voice so neither the lad nor his mother would hear.

'Let your man there take Simpson on his own. You wait here. Call in another car,' he ordered, then he spun on his heel while the Uniforms bundled Ray into the back of the vehicle. Coleen had taken Declan by the hand and was leading him up the back step into the kitchen.

Logan followed them without waiting to be invited. He found them over by the sink. Coleen had pulled a square of kitchen towel from the roll, and was wiping her son's face and making soft cooing noises like he was a toddler with a grazed knee.

Declan stood there taking it, shoulders slumped and back curved.

'You all right, son?' Logan asked, once the clean-up operation was completed.

Declan nodded, but couldn't yet bring himself to speak. The muscles in his throat and jaw contracted and relaxed as he fought back against another burst of emotion.

'I get it. I do,' Jack told him. 'We're going to make sure he goes down for what he did. You have my word on that.'

Once again, all Declan could do was nod. He wiped his eyes on his sleeve and lurched from foot to foot, visibly uncomfortable.

'I need a wee chat with your mum,' Logan said.

Coleen didn't look back at him. She just stopped—stopped moving, stopped breathing, stopped everything—like time had frozen around her.

Declan frowned, not understanding. He looked at her, but she must've given some signal, invisible from Logan's angle, that it was fine. Whatever it was, it did the trick. He looked relieved as he took a can of Irn-Bru from the fridge, and went scurrying out of the kitchen.

It was only once the door had closed that Coleen returned to life. She picked up the kettle, flipped open the lid, and sloshed in some cold water.

'Tea?' she asked, still not looking at him.

'No, I'm fine,' Logan told her.

He waited until she'd placed the kettle back on the base and flicked the switch.

It was the least he could do. A moment's grace before he ruined her life.

'Does he know?'

Coleen caught the edge of the worktop. Gripped it. Held it. Leaned there, staring out through the window at the campsite beyond.

She still hadn't looked at him, but he could see her face reflected in the glass. See the pain and the torment etched in every line.

'I don't know what you mean,' she said.

Logan ran a hand down his face. He'd been hoping not to have to go through it all. He'd have liked to have saved her from that.

'Johnny didn't sleep with your sister that night back in Glasgow, did he?'

Coleen wiped her tears with the sodden paper she'd used to dry her son's.

'I wouldn't know.'

Her voice was fragile. Delicate. Like it might shatter at any moment.

She drew in a long, shaky breath.

'No,' she admitted.

Logan nodded, his suspicions confirmed. Freestone's bandmate, Rodney, had said it himself—Johnny had a particular soft spot for married women.

It had been eighteen years since that gig in Glasgow.

Seventeen and nine-ish months since Declan had been born.

The resemblance was there, when you looked for it. Maybe not enough to notice it in the day-to-day, but that poster? That photograph of Declan playing on stage? It was impossible not to see it.

'Does Declan know?' Logan asked again.

This time, Coleen didn't bother with the pretence.

'No,' she said. 'He has no idea.'

'And your husband? Charlie?'

'No.'

'You sure?'

Coleen turned to face him, but kept holding onto the edge of the worktop like it was some sort of safety device, tethering her in place.

'He doesn't know,' she insisted.

The kettle came to the boil, but she'd lost interest now. She aimed herself at the kitchen table, let go of the counter, and stumbled over to a chair.

Logan pulled out the chair across from her, and they both sat facing one another across the divide.

'So, who else knows?' Jack asked.

'Nobody. Nobody knows. Just me and him.'

'Well, Ray figured it out,' Logan told her. 'That's why he was so keen to sign Declan up. The son of Johnny Freestone? Right after Johnny's death? That's a marketing hook, if ever I heard one.'

Coleen flinched like she'd been slapped. 'My son isn't a *marketing hook!*'

'Not to me. Not to you,' Logan said. 'But to someone like Ray? That's exactly what he is. How did Ray find out?'

'I don't know. I didn't know he had!' replied Coleen.

The words were sharp. Piercing. She recoiled at the sound of them, and shot a glance at the door, like she was terrified she might find her son there, listening in.

'Johnny phoned me a week or so ago,' she continued, much quieter now. 'It was the first I'd heard from him in years. Since...' She shifted in her chair. 'Since that night. He told me he knew. He told me he was going to tell Declan. Tell him everything!'

'That must have been terrifying for you.'

'Of course. I couldn't breathe when he said it. It was like... everything, this secret I've been holding onto, it was going to come out, and it was going to ruin everything. I asked him not to say anything. I pleaded with him, begged him.'

'And? Did he?'

'No. I mean, I don't think so. Declan's never mentioned it, thank God. He loves his dad. It would break his heart. It would destroy him.'

'I have a daughter,' Logan said out of the blue.

Coleen was taken aback by it, and could only shrug in confusion. Or maybe indifference.

'I wasn't always the best father in the world. But there's nothing I wouldn't do to protect her. I would walk through fire if it meant keeping her from getting hurt.'

He smiled, not unkindly, while he let that thought settle in.

'You were away the night that Johnny died. Right? In Thurso?'

Across the table, Coleen nodded slowly, as if sensing some kind of trap. 'That's right.'

'And you've got witnesses who'll back that up?'

Another nod, even more careful this time. 'Yes. A few. I didn't kill him, if that's what you think!'

'You were terrified of what might happen to your family,' Logan said. 'To your son.'

'I didn't kill Johnny!' Coleen hissed.

'But his death certainly benefitted you. Cleaned things up nicely.'

She started to protest her innocence again, but Logan blindsided her.

'What was your husband up to that night?'

'Nothing!' Coleen yelped the word out, then dropped her voice back into a whisper. 'He was here. Doing the nightly checks.'

'No. Declan did those,' Logan said. 'We've seen the footage and spoken to a few guests who were here that night. They confirmed that they saw Declan throughout the evening, and that he checked in on them around half-nine.'

He sat back, watching her expression very closely.

'One of them had been here a week. Said that Charlie had done it every other night. But not then. Not that night. Why is that?'

'I... I don't know.'

'You must have some idea.'

'I don't. I'm not... I can't speak for him. You'd have to ask him yourself.'

'Don't worry, I intend to.'

'Ask me what?'

Charlie stood by the back door, his hands dirty, his grubby grey T-shirt marked with dark patches of sweat.

He stepped inside, looking from his wife to the detective, searching their faces, trying to figure out what the hell was going on.

'Well?' he demanded. He closed the door behind him with a firm, definite *click*, and focused his full attention on the detective. 'What was it, exactly, that you wanted to ask?'

Chapter 49

Charlie sat where his wife had been sitting, just a few moments before. He'd refused at first, bristled with rage as he'd insisted he was fine standing. Insisted that Logan should hurry the fuck up and explain what he was doing here, and what he wanted to ask.

Jack hadn't risen to any of it. He'd waited, saying nothing, while Coleen worked to calm her husband. She was at near breaking point herself, though, and her tearful, trembling attempts to placate Charlie just seemed to make him worse.

Eventually, Logan had suggested that she go check on Declan. Charlie had agreed that this was a good idea and, when his wife left the room, a lot of his anger went with her.

Once it was gone, Logan wondered if it had even been anger to begin with. Nervous energy, maybe. A panic he was barely able to keep a lid on.

When he lowered himself onto the chair across from the detective, though, he seemed strangely poised, every movement deliberate and carefully considered.

Logan chose his words with a similar level of consideration.

'We've arrested Ray Simpson for the murder of Dougie Cairns.' he said.

It was a swing out of nowhere, spoken with the sole aim of surprising Charlie, and putting him on the back foot.

'Oh. Right,' was all Charlie had to say on the matter.

'Ray wanted to sign Declan. Dougie wasn't having it,' Logan explained. 'I mean, there was more to it than that, but that was part of it.'

'Right,' Charlie said again.

'Do you have any idea why Ray would want to sign Declan?'

Charlie sniffed, holding eye contact. 'Because he's talented.'

'I'm sure he is, aye,' Logan said. He glanced at the kitchen door. 'Seems like a nice lad.'

'He is. He's one of a kind.' Charlie took a breath and swallowed, building up to something. 'What about Johnny?'

Logan, like the man across from him, remained perfectly still. 'What about him?'

'Did Ray kill him, too?'

The question hung there in the silence of the kitchen, suspended between the ticks of the grandfather clock.

'No,' Logan said.

The lines of Charlie's face shifted then, just a fraction, like something had tightened beneath his skin.

'Do you know who did?'

More silence. Taught. Tense.

Tick. Tick. Tick.

'I think so.'

Charlie's expression shifted again, almost imperceptibly.

'And?'

Logan looked away for a moment, either getting all his words in the right order, or bracing himself for what was to come.

'It only clicked into place when I got here,' he said. 'Part of me... Part of me wishes it hadn't. It would've been nice if it had been Ray. Nice and tidy. But then, these things rarely are.'

He took a breath. Took a moment.

Prepared himself for the pain in the other man's eyes.

But then, if he was right on this, Charlie was already well aware.

'Did you know?' he asked. 'About Coleen and Johnny?'

This time, Charlie's expression didn't change. His eyes blurred, though, tears welling above the bottom lid.

'About Declan?'

Charlie's tongue moved around inside his mouth, like it was tying up the word, trying to restrain them.

It failed.

'I've known since he was ten.'

Logan didn't know whether to be pleased or devastated.

'How did you find out?'

Charlie gently cleared his throat. It sounded tight. Hoarse.

'We, um, we'd been trying for another baby. For years, without any luck. So, I got to wondering, and I, eh, I went and got myself tested.' He tried to smile, to laugh it all off, but his tears skiffed down his cheeks. 'Turns out, I can't have kids. I just… I can't have them. So, I knew that Declan—'

His voice cracked. He looked down, hiding his tears and his shame.

'You knew he couldn't be yours.'

Charlie just nodded, head still lowered, eyes on the table where he'd sat with his family for breakfasts and dinners. For Christmases, birthdays, and all the days in between.

'I never said a word. I never told Coleen I knew.' He forced himself to look up, and that not-quite anger was back on his face again as he thumped a hand against his chest. 'Because that would mean admitting that Declan wasn't mine. And he is. He's my son, my boy! I'm his dad, nobody else!'

Logan didn't argue with that. If his theory was right, then Charlie's dedication to his son would never be in doubt.

'Remind me again where you were on the night Johnny died.'

Charlie said nothing.

'Because we checked with some of the guests. They said that you usually came round to do the evening checks. Make sure everyone was all right. But that night you didn't. Declan did. We've got video, in fact, taken from the camera out front. It shows one person. Just one.'

Logan shrugged. It was a relaxed, casual gesture that belied his watchful gaze.

'If it hadn't been for the guests' statements, I could've believed it was you out there. Big jacket. Hat on, head down. I could've absolutely believed it was you, but it was Declan who showed face.'

Charlie didn't flinch at that. It took effort, though.

'So, if Declan was out there that night, where were you?' Logan pressed. 'Why break the usual routine?'

'It's not a set routine. We take turn about,' Charlie said. It sounded weak. He was clutching at straws.

'Right. And that night was Declan. That still doesn't tell me where you were.'

'Am I under arrest here?' Charlie demanded.

Logan gave a shake of his head. 'Not currently.'

'Right, then I think you should leave.' The legs of Charlie's chair scraped on the floor as he stood. 'I want you to get out. I want you out of my house.'

Logan didn't move. He just sat there, holding Charlie's gaze across the table.

Holding all the cards.

'It was the alcohol in Johnny's system that threw me at first.'

Charlie blinked. Swallowed. He sat down again, or maybe his legs just refused to hold him up.

'All that booze in his bloodstream, and in his stomach. He had to have drunk it recently. And yet, there was no trace. No cans, no bottles. Nothing.' Logan raised his eyebrows and shrugged, like he was perplexed by the mystery of it all. 'We asked the Kellermans—the ones who found him—if they'd seen anything. But, nope. Not a sausage. *Weird that*, I thought. Where could it have gone?'

He scratched at his chin, like he was still puzzling it out.

'Only thing that made sense was that someone took them. And the only way *that* makes sense, is if they were worried something about them might be incriminating. Fingerprints, maybe. DNA.

'Or maybe they didn't want anyone to see how many there were, and realise that Johnny hadn't been drinking down there alone.'

Charlie buried his face in his hands before Logan could say anything more. He sat like that, hunched over, for several seconds. When he lifted his head, Jack expected to see tears. Instead, there was only a look of grim determination.

'I met him outside the shop,' he said in a low, solemn monotone. 'Bumped into him, I mean. I didn't plan to.'

Charlie's chest rose and then fell again, like he was struggling to get enough air into lungs.

'He, eh, he said there was something he needed to talk to me about. Something important. And... I knew. I knew what it was. I knew that he'd figured it out.'

The tears started to come then, but he screwed his face up, fighting them back.

'That night in Glasgow. The night they...' He grimaced at the thought of it. 'It was two weeks before our wedding. Me and Coleen's. And he knew that. The bastard knew that! Alanna had mouthed off about it in the bar that night while she was trying to get him to notice her. He knew she was engaged. He *knew*!'

'I'm sorry,' Logan said. And he truly was. 'What did you say to him? At the shop?'

Charlie looked up at the ceiling as if in search of something divine. Forgiveness, maybe. Or inspiration.

'I told him I wasn't interested, and he said that I would be. Said that if I didn't want to hear what he had to say, maybe Declan would.'

Charlie rubbed a hand across the surface of the kitchen table, feeling every bump and scratch, and all the grooves worn by the passage of time.

'So, I agreed. He was going down to the cave. Some guitar thing he was doing, I don't know. He said we could talk there. It was later on, so there generally aren't a lot of tourists kicking about at that time. And I... went.'

There was a questioning tone to the last word, like he couldn't quite believe it himself. 'I went with him. I asked him what he wanted to say, but he told me not to be in so much of a rush. We had a few drinks. He played his guitar. And then he told me that he knew. About Declan. He knew who he was.'

He balled his fingers into fists, the nails pressed into his palms. He braced himself and took a few quick breaths, like he was pregnant and facing a painful contraction.

'He said he was going to tell him. He was going to take my boy away. And so... I...'

He closed his eyes. Steadied himself.

'Hit him. I hit him with his guitar. Twice, on the head. I hit him, he fell. I knew he was dead. Don't ask me how, I just knew. So, I dropped the guitar. I wasn't sure which bottles were mine, so I took them all. I took them, and I ran.'

His face was pale now. Grey, almost. He looked exhausted by his admission. But he'd come too far to stop now.

'I killed him. I killed Johnny Freestone to protect my family. To protect my boy. And I'd do it again, too. There's nothing I wouldn't do to keep Declan safe.'

That was it. The confession.

Though not the one the man thought he was making.

'That's what I'm worried about,' Logan said.

On the other side of the table, Charlie's face became deathly still. 'What do you mean?'

'The day he died, Johnny told Dougie that he'd come to some big realisation about how important family was. Said he was going to explain what he meant that night. Dougie thought he meant him, but he didn't. He meant Declan,' Logan said.

Charlie's shoulder twitched in a shrug. 'So?'

'So, it sounded to me like he'd planned to say something that evening. Before he randomly bumped into you outside the shop. I think he was planning to tell Declan.'

'Well then, it's lucky I met him,' Charlie replied, after a pause.

'Not for him, it wasn't,' Logan shot back.

Charlie said nothing to that.

'I was thinking back to when I first got here. The village hall. You remember? A few of you were gathered for the meeting. You were there. Coleen. Declan, too,' Logan continued. 'And I remember thinking at the time, he looked rough. Declan. The way he was holding his head. The red rings around his eyes. Some people would put that down to grief. Shock. That sort of thing. But me? Well, let's just say I've got a lot of first-hand experience of what a hangover looks like.'

'I don't know what you're talking about,' Charlie said, blurting the words out.

'How's your audio editing experience?'

Charlie scowled. 'What?'

'Are you familiar with the— Hang on.' He took his phone from his pocket, and squinted at the screen as he read the contents of Hamza's email. 'The Sennheiser T870 portable recorder?'

There was no response from the other side of the table this time. Logan pressed on regardless.

'Complicated bit of kit by the looks of it. Digital audio recorder, built-in microphones. Fancy stuff. Not cheap.'

'What are you talking about?'

'Do you know how to scrub audio from a recorded track on the machine? Aye, not delete the track, just wipe a section of it? It's possible, but I'm told it's tricky. You need to really know what you're doing. Can you do that, Charlie?'

Logan waited for an answer, knowing that one wouldn't come.

'Because I think that whoever killed Johnny knew how to do that. I think whoever killed Johnny knew that deleting the track would still leave a copy of it on the internal storage. That's a thing it does, apparently. A safety feature, so you don't accidentally lose a recording by hitting the wrong button.

'Wiping the audio from the file though? That's different. Once that's gone, it's gone for good. But, like I say, Charlie, it's a complicated business.'

Logan gave the other man another opportunity to respond. Charlie didn't take it. He just sat there, stoic. Staring.

'The easiest thing, of course, would be to just take it and chuck it. Smash it to bits, or whatever. That's what I'd do.' Jack shrugged. 'But then, I'm not a nice kid who cares about the person the equipment belongs to.'

'This is bullshit!'

'It wasn't you down in that cave with Johnny. Was it, Charlie?'

'I already told you—'

'You told me you'd do anything to protect your son,' Logan said, cutting him off. 'And I get that. I do. I get that, and I respect it. But don't do this. Not this.'

'I killed him.'

'I don't think you did.'

Charlie leaned forward, flecks of foam hissing through his teeth as he stabbed a finger against the tabletop.

'Declan was here all night! People saw him!'

'You were here, Charlie. That's you on the video. Declan did the door to door wearing your jacket, long after Johnny was dead, cementing the idea in people's heads that they'd seen him earlier. But it was you on the video. Wasn't it? You were here, not Declan.'

Charlie stared at him. There was pure rage in that look. Raw, naked hatred.

'You said you've got a daughter.'

'I do.'

'And that you'd do anything for her.'

'I would,' Logan admitted.

'Then you get it. I'm giving you my full confession here,' Charlie said. 'I can tell you exactly how I killed Johnny and when. I've got motive. I had the opportunity. I know every detail of what happened that night, and I will own up to every last bit of it.'

'Charlie—'

'Whatever you believe happened, I'm telling you it didn't. All right? I will stand up there in front of a jury, and I will swear on everything I hold dear that I murdered Johnny Freestone. Me. No one else. And whatever the consequences of that are, then I'll take them. Happily. I'll do life. I'll take the fucking death penalty, if it means keeping my son safe.'

He placed both hands on the table between them, side by side, the purple-blue veins of his wrists pointed upwards.

There was a calmness to him now. His decision had been made, and he was fine with that.

'So, I think you'd better arrest me,' he declared. 'And don't look so miserable. You did it, Chief Inspector. You caught the bad guy.'

Chapter 50

'Dad?'

Declan ran around from the side of the house, full tilt, having seen what was happening through the window of the family room.

Until then, Charlie hadn't resisted the firm hand of the Uniformed constable on his arm, guiding him out of the house, steering him towards the waiting police car. Until then, he'd gone quietly.

He resisted now, though, one foot inside the vehicle, his hands cuffed at his back.

'Declan, go inside, son,' he warned. 'It's fine, we'll talk later.'

'No, but Dad. *Dad!*'

Charlie managed a smile for his boy. 'It's OK, Dec,' he soothed. 'It's OK.'

Logan stood back, knowing everything—or most of it, anyway—but saying nothing. He watched as Charlie gave one last nod to his son, locked eyes with Coleen, who'd come rushing out of the house on the boy's heels, then relented to the constable's demands and got in the car.

'No, Dad! Dad, please, don't!'

He ran to the car and tried to pull on the handle, but the constable blocked him, and his mum grabbed his arm.

'Declan, stop!' she pleaded. 'It's OK. We'll fix this. He'll be back soon.'

Inside the car, Charlie bowed until his forehead was pressed against the glass. Even from where Logan stood, he could see the tears that soaked his face, and hear the crack in his voice.

'I love you, son. My boy.'

At that, Declan's face crumpled. He tried to speak, but the words got stuck in his throat. His mum tried to hug him. He pulled away, twisted his fingers through his long red hair, and squirmed on the spot as the car with his dad in the back pulled away from the car park, leaving them there in the gathering gloom.

'Declan, come on inside,' Coleen pleaded.

He shook his head. Desperately. Frantically. All snot and tears.

'No. No, this is your fault,' he sobbed. He wrenched himself away from her with such force that she staggered back, thrown off balance. When he spoke again, it was a shout. A scream. 'This is all your fault!'

He looked from his mum to Logan, to the house, to the sky. He flexed his fingers, shifted his weight. Babbled a few words, too garbled and choked to make out.

And then, like he'd been fired from a gun, he ran.

'Declan, don't! Please! Come back!'

Coleen moved to follow, but Logan shrugged his coat off and thrust it into her arms.

'Wait here,' he instructed. 'We'll get him.'

She looked him up and down, correctly surmising that, regardless of his unusually large stride length, he had little to no chance of catching up to her son, who was already a hundred yards away, tearing along the track towards the main road.

'How? How the hell are *you* going to catch him?'

Logan opened the back door of his car. A tangle of legs, ears and big floppy tongue, tumbled out then shot off in pursuit.

'I said "we",' Logan reminded her, then he groaned, gritted his teeth, and lumbered off to follow the dog.

He'd barely hit fifty yards before he felt the stitch jabbing into his side, and the fires sparking up in his lungs. He'd been too sedentary for too long.

Or maybe he was just too damn old to go chasing down teenagers.

'And to think,' he wheezed, as he struggled on up the track. 'This wasn't even meant to be my bloody case.'

-

'You looking for a kid and your dog?'

Logan had lost the ability to speak. Even if he'd been able to get his lungs to work, his throat was too raw from the stomach acid he'd brought up and swallowed down at least twice on the mad dash from the house.

The constable who he'd saddled with Taggart just a couple of days ago, now stood as the sole guardian of Smoo Cave, angrily gesturing at tourists to turn their cars around and fuck off. And, ideally, to keep fucking off until such times as they were no longer his problem.

Logan put his hands on his lower back, his face contorting in pain as he nodded. He managed an 'Aye', but it came out as a rasping gasp, inaudible over the sound of blasting horns and angry shouts.

The constable gestured down the slope behind him with a thumb. 'They went that way,' he said.

Logan looked past him, down the hill, to the dark gaping maw of the cave.

'Shite,' he panted, breaking into another artless shamble. 'Should've bloody guessed.'

He slowed when he reached the bottom of the hill, staying just on the right side of the shadow line that marked where the surface of the world ended, and its dark underbelly began.

The air rising from inside was fetid. Sour. His heart, which had already been racing from the effort of the run, thrummed into top gear. He smelled blood, and gunpowder, and death. He heard screaming from deep down, from months past.

Every instinct told him to turn around. To flee, run, get clear, get away.

From somewhere in the bowels of the earth came the sound of a dog barking.

Logan made a decision, for better or worse.

'Bugger it,' he muttered.

And he headed on downwards into the dark.

Chapter 51

Declan wasn't hard to find. The annoying, yappy wee dog that had followed him into the cave soon gave the game away.

Logan tracked him to the same chamber where Johnny's body had been discovered. He was sitting on the edge of the drop, feet dangling into the chasm of black below.

The only light was from his phone torch, which shone upwards from the ground beneath him, painting shadows across his face, and over the stalactites that hung from the glossy, damp ceiling.

Logan swept his own torchlight across the ground in front of him, carefully picking his way along, trying not to think about the weight of the earth pressing down on him from above.

Trying, but failing.

If he never set foot in another cave again, it would be too bloody soon.

'You all right, son?' he asked. He was still a little breathless, but the cave amplified his voice, turning it into the boom of some vengeful God.

The volume of it immediately made Taggart stop barking. He lay down on the ground, nose tucked between his front paws, like he was about to get into trouble.

Declan, meanwhile, turned so sharply he almost tumbled over the edge of the drop. Only a quick grab of a ridge in the rock saved him from plunging out of sight.

'It's OK, Declan. Relax,' Logan urged. 'You're fine.'

The drop wasn't huge, but it wasn't tiny, either. If Declan slipped off, he could break his legs. If he was determined, he could do much worse.

And Logan was more determined than ever not to lose anyone else to a damned hole in the ground.

'Stay back!' Declan warned. He'd been crying. Still was, in fact.

Logan held his hands up, indicating that he had no intention of rushing in. He looked around until he found a boulder to sit on. The muscles in his legs responded gratefully when he took the weight off them.

'You OK?' he asked.

Declan laughed at that. It was a strained squeak of a thing, too quiet for an echo to bother with.

'What do you think?'

Logan reached down and patted Taggart, who had come trotting over to join him.

'God. There's a question,' he said. The dog panted happily as Jack scratched between his ears. 'I never really got on with my old man. That's an understatement, actually. I barely knew him. Bit of a waste of space, from what I could gather, though. He had no interest in me or my brother.'

Declan was looking down into the darkness just beyond his feet. He was listening, though, Jack could tell from the angle of his head, and the way his eyes darted around, processing it all.

'My stepdad was better. I mean, still not perfect,' Logan said. 'But then, nobody is. We all make mistakes. God knows, I have.' He glanced up at the shadowy ceiling of the cave. 'I'm doing my best to face up to them, though. I think that's important. I think, at the end of the day, it's all we can really do.'

Declan didn't say anything. Not at first. Not for a while.

And then...

'What if they're too big, though? What if you can't?'

'Now there's another good question,' Logan said. 'It would be the easiest thing in the world for me to say that they can never be too big. That you can always face up to them. But, well, I'm not going to sit here and fill you with shite. I've run away from plenty of mistakes. Buried my head in the sand. Or in a bottle. There were secrets I would've taken to my grave if I hadn't been forced to own up to them. Secrets—mistakes I'd made—that I thought would be the end of me.'

He shrugged and ran his hand down Taggart's back.

'I thought I'd lose everyone. I nearly did. But it wasn't the mistakes I'd made that pushed them away, it was me hiding them from them. Or me trying to hold onto them. Or... God. I don't know. Whatever,

I didn't lose them. The people who cared for me, they stuck with me. Despite what I'd done, despite the mistakes I'd made—the huge mistakes—they stuck by me. The people that care about us'll do that.'

Declan rubbed at his eyes. His voice, when he spoke, had a tremble to it.

'Is my dad going to go to jail?'

Logan didn't sugarcoat it. That wouldn't have been fair to the boy.

'Aye. He confessed to murdering Johnny. Told me how he'd done it. Told me why. Made very clear that he'll stand up in court and plead guilty to killing him in cold blood.'

Declan choked on a sob and looked down. At his feet. At the fall. At the pit of black beneath him.

'He made it very clear that he's prepared to do life for this. And, honestly, Declan? There's a part of me that's inclined to let him.'

Jack shifted around on the rock, switching arse cheeks before either could go numb.

'See, someone reminded me recently that this job is all about making decisions. You make the wrong call, and it can cost someone their life. That's obvious, really. But the difficult thing—the thing that I really struggle with—is that sometimes the right decision can be just as devastating. That's the bit that's hardest to live with.'

He stood up, shaking the blood back into his legs.

'My old man wouldn't give me the time of day. Yours is willing to give you his whole life. That's how much he loves you, son.'

He looked back over his shoulder at the passageway leading up to the surface. The urge to run had left him. Down here wasn't a place of horrors. No more than up there was, anyway. The nightmares were everywhere, if you looked for them.

'Whatever happens next, I just thought you should know that,' he said.

He whistled through his teeth and Taggart pounced up, ready to move. The light from his torch swept across the ground, pointing the way to the way out.

'Wait,' Declan cried.

He rubbed at his eyes with the heels of his hands, sniffed a few times, then got to his feet.

Logan almost stopped him, almost begged him not to say a word.

But he couldn't, of course. All he could do now was listen.

Declan swallowed hard, straightened his shoulders, and looked the detective in the eye.

And his voice, when he spoke, left an echo that still reverberated long after.

'There's something I need to tell you.'

–

Charlie was with the custody sergeant, being checked in, when Logan entered.

At first, his expression remained largely neutral, like he didn't even recognise the DCI. It was when Declan appeared behind him, though, that everything changed.

'No, no, no,' Charlie pleaded. He looked at Jack, betrayal flashing like lightning behind his eyes. 'No, please, no.'

Coleen appeared at her son's back and hovered there, at Logan's side, as Declan ran to his dad, already choking out an apology.

'You shouldn't be here, Declan. Coleen, take him away,' Charlie hissed, but he threw his arms around his son when he ran at him, hugging him, squeezing him, like he was the only thing holding him together. Like his arms alone could contain the inevitable explosion.

'He didn't do it,' Declan said, raising his head to address the custody sergeant directly. 'He didn't kill Johnny. I did. I did it.'

'No. No, that's not—' Charlie began to protest, but Declan put a hand on the back of his head and pulled it in against his shoulder. 'It's OK, Dad. It's OK. I have to say it. I have to tell them.'

Charlie's strength left him. He slid down to his knees, his son still holding him all the way to the floor. Coleen wept at Jack's side, then hurried to join her family. She huddled there on the floor beside them, arms around them both, holding them tight. Holding them together.

'If it's any consolation,' Logan told them. 'I really am sorry.'

Chapter 52

The next morning, Logan wasn't entirely surprised when he found DCI McCulloch sharing a cup of tea with Mitchell in her office.

He didn't bother to sit while he filled them in on everything that had happened the day before, and the details of Declan's confession.

Johnny had invited the boy along to the cave on the pretence of recording some audio together for the new album. Once there, he'd plied the teenager with drink, and then dropped the bombshell about his parentage.

Declan had not reacted well. He'd called Johnny a liar. Called him a lot worse, too, but Freestone had kept going, kept at him, telling him they'd go on tour together, make music, live the rock and roll lifestyle on the open road.

He'd laughed, Declan said, when the boy had pleaded with him not to say anything to Charlie. He couldn't stand the idea of his dad's heart being broken like that. Couldn't bear the thought of his family being torn apart.

Johnny had snapped at him then. 'I'm your fucking family!' he'd screamed. 'I'm your dad, not that sad, fat loser!'

And then...

And then...

Declan had been a little vague on exactly what had happened next. It wasn't that he was hiding anything, Logan thought, just that he couldn't fully recall.

He remembered picking up the guitar.

He remembered the rage.

And he remembered the sight of Johnny lying down there at the bottom of that pit, the blood pooling around his head.

He'd dropped the guitar and started to run. It was only when he was halfway back to the surface that he remembered the audio equipment had been recording the entire conversation.

He also knew enough about how the hardware worked to be able to remove all traces of it.

He'd raced all the way home, and met his dad on the way back from his nightly tour of the campsite. Charlie had realised immediately that something was seriously wrong, and had managed to wangle half of the truth from him.

Declan had told his dad what he'd done, but had lied about the why of it. He'd claimed that Johnny had attacked him, and he'd defended himself.

Charlie, however, knew the truth.

He got Declan cleaned up and calmed down, and sent him knocking on the doors of the pods to establish his alibi. Then, he'd headed down to the cave, to clear away any evidence that might point to his son's involvement.

'He took away the alcohol,' McCulloch reasoned.

'Aye, and wiped the prints off everything he could find,' Logan confirmed.

'And he's confessed?' Mitchell asked. 'The boy, I mean.'

Logan nodded, though there was some reluctance to it. 'Aye. He's given a full statement. He's explained everything. Well, as much as he understood it himself. He's just a kid. Just a good guy who made a really bad choice.'

'Yes, well, we've all been there,' Mitchell said. 'I'm sure circumstances will be taken into account.'

'I hope so,' Logan replied. 'I really do.'

'Well!' McCulloch slapped a hand on his thigh, then got to his feet. He was smiling. It was a big beamer of a thing, like he was exceptionally pleased about something. 'Looks like my work here is done.'

'*Your* work?' Logan couldn't believe what he was hearing. 'You had Dougie down as the killer. Ray Simpson would've walked away scot-free if we'd left it up to you!' He turned to Mitchell. 'He's in custody, too, by the way. He killed Dougie and tried to make it look like a suicide.'

'Well, of course he did!' McCulloch said. 'You said it yourself—anyone can type a bloody suicide note.'

The ropes of Logan's neck muscles twisted his head back and forth, from McCulloch to Mitchell and back again. He felt like he was missing something.

It was only when he noted the smirk on the detective superintendent's usually stony face that it clicked.

'You were never going to be moving up here, were you?'

'Oh, God, no!' McCulloch said. 'I mean, it's nice, don't get me wrong. You know, barring the weather. But move? Up here? Full-time? Perish the thought.'

'But they're advertising for your job down in the Borders. Aren't they?'

'I bloody hope so.' McCulloch loosened his tie. It was a small gesture, but it made him look a touch more human. 'I'm retiring, Jack. Not before time, either. I've had quite my fill of killers, thank you very much. This time next month, I'll be lying on my back in Portugal, baking by the pool.'

Logan had nothing to say to that. Nothing that wouldn't see him facing an official reprimand, at least.

McCulloch seemed far more relaxed than he had at any point in the past few days. It made sense, of course. His final mission had been accomplished. He had nothing left to prove.

Logan rounded on Mitchell instead. She sat behind her desk, fingers clasped, that smile still hovering on her lips.

'I take it this was your idea?'

'Oh, yes. Absolutely,' she confirmed without hesitation. 'I knew you needed a push. So, I pushed. And it worked.'

'Who says it worked? I don't know if I'm coming back yet.'

'Come on now, Jack. We both know that's not true,' she told him.

Logan met the smiling McCulloch's eye, then turned his attention back to the detective superintendent and stabbed a finger in her direction.

'You're a sly bastard.'

Mitchell's smirk faded. A silence fell over the room.

'I'm sorry?' she said, touching her ear and pushing it forward. 'What was that?'

Logan sighed. He'd walked into that one.

'You're a sly bastard, *ma'am*,' he said.

'Better,' Mitchell told him. She waved him away with the back of her hand. 'Now, I'm sure you've got plenty of work to be getting on with. Don't let me keep you.'

Jack straightened. Nodded. Slipped right back into old habits.

'Right you are, ma'am,' he said, and every word was carefully injected with a dose of sarcasm. 'Whatever you say.'

He turned to leave, before a thought occurred to him.

'Oh, and I want Hamza in the DI job.'

'Done,' Mitchell agreed.

Logan tried very hard to hide his surprise at that. He'd expected some resistance.

Might as well push his luck.

'And if Sinead or Tyler go for DS, the other one's staying on the team, too.'

Mitchell winced at that. 'Them upstairs won't like that. They'll want them separated.'

'Aye, well,' Jack said. 'They'll have to go through me first.'

—

Logan stood in the corridor, on the wrong side of the doors, listening to the sounds of the Incident Room.

A phone rang. A computer chimed. A ball bounced on the carpet tiles, then four stubby legs went chasing after it. Tyler wondered out loud who'd invented bread. And how. And when.

He'd kept wondering, too, until Sinead had patiently suggested he go Google it, preferably in a different room.

Another phone rang. Dave answered. He spoke too quietly for Logan to hear, but then raised his voice as he called across to DS Khaled.

'Here. Hamza. It's someone about some old case. They want to speak to whoever's in charge. Should I go try and dig up McCulloch?'

Logan knew this was it. This was his moment. Now or never.

He closed his eyes, took a breath, then threw open the doors like a sheriff bursting in on the Last Chance Saloon.

'Here,' he said, crossing to Dave's desk. 'Give it to me.'

The others watched him, slack-jawed and wide-eyed as he took the phone.

'Detective Chief Inspector Jack Logan,' he said. 'What do you want?'

He listened for ten, maybe fifteen seconds, then interrupted the caller.

'Right. So it can wait, then. Give us a ring back in forty-five minutes.' He pointed around the room to where the other detectives' jackets hung on the backs of their chairs. 'We're heading out for break-fast.'

The voice on the other end of the line said something. Jack checked his watch and tutted. 'Right. Well, we're heading out for *brunch* then. No need to be an arsehole about it.'

He handed the phone back to Dave, who looked at it like it was some otherworldly object, before returning it to the cradle.

'Right. We're off to Ben's place. My shout,' Jack said. 'But I'm warning you now, don't get used to it.'

Hamza, Tyler and Sinead got to their feet. Dave joined them in grabbing for their coats.

'Cheers, sir!' Hamza said.

'Nice one,' Sinead added.

'Bagsy not having a cappuccino,' Dave chimed in.

They all exchanged slightly cagey looks, like they weren't sure how to tackle the elephant in the room.

Tyler, however, had no such reservations.

'So, is that it then, boss?' he asked. 'Is that you back?'

Logan looked around at them. His team. His friends.

His responsibility.

Some decisions in this job were hard. Some would eat you up, if you let them.

But this?

This one was easy.

'Too fucking right I am, son,' Jack said. He pulled up the collar of his coat, and shoved his hands down deep into the empty pockets. 'Now, let's get a shifty on before Ben goes bankrupt.'

He opened the door, and with Taggart scampering along beside him, he led them out into the windy, rainswept summer of the Scottish Highlands.